Retribution

I0673982

Regina Smeltzer

Retribution

Contact Information: titleadmin@pelicanbookgroup.com

Cover Art by *Nicola Martinez*

Harbourlight Books, a division of Pelican Ventures, LLC
www.pelicanbookgroup.com PO Box 1738 *Aztec, NM * 87410

Harbourlight Books sail and mast logo is a trademark of Pelican Ventures, LLC

Publishing History
First Harbourlight Edition, 2016
Paperback Edition ISBN 978-1-61116-517-3
Electronic Edition ISBN 978-1-61116-516-6
Published in the United States of America

Dedication

To my husband, Paul. The best parts of me are because of you.

Also Available from Regina Smeltzer

Deadly Decision

1

"You got any matches on you?" The boy, not more than sixteen, snickered over his words. He had a crowd of followers: boys dressed in jeans with waists cinched around their thighs and girls wearing shirts that looked as if they had shrunk in the dryer. The teens rallied around the outspoken leader like groupies to a rock-star.

Lillian did her best to ignore the barb even though the pain of his words took her breath away. She had been taking a chance going to town alone, but she only needed to make a couple of stops. Her mother's worried face flashed in front of her. Only one hour out of the house on her own. She used to be a trial attorney, free to do her own thing. But that freedom had disappeared two years ago, along with the rest of her life.

Across the street, Cynthia, who had served as her maid of honor five years ago, walked arm-in-arm with her new husband. Feeling a sudden rush of bravery, Lillian crossed the street. "Cynthia, it's nice to see you. I heard you got married…"

The woman clutched her leather purse to her chest as her face paled beneath layers of well-applied makeup. "Lillian, it's been a long time." The sleeve of the man's black cashmere coat bunched beneath her grip. "Sorry we can't stop and chat, but we're already late…" Cynthia glanced around, apparently trying to decide where she was supposed to be. The couple walked on; their pace doubled. As she reached the corner, Cynthia turned her apprehensive face toward Lillian.

Wishing she had not tried to resurrect a friendship, to break the ice on a pond that should never have frozen, she stiffened her back and entered the pharmacy. Vitamins for her eyes. That's what the optometrist had recommended.

A middle-aged woman rounded the stack of first aid supplies. "Can I help—" She stopped and stared, her eyes narrowing. "What do you want?"

Not rude exactly, but far from jovial. Hadn't she represented this woman's family member once? A cousin or something? The vitamins were quickly rung up, bagged, and thrust toward her. No "good bye." No "what else can I do for you?" Just steel-cold eyes that chilled her blood.

Anger built as she headed back to her car. After the fire, no one had listened to her side of the story, preferring instead to fabricate their own. Clenching her jaw until it ached she pointed the car toward her parents' home—her home for the past two years.

The ad for a job in South Carolina had come as a surprise. Even more surprising was her acceptance if she wanted it. She tromped on the gas, decision made. She would escape Cleveland and create a new life for herself.

~*~

Heavy velvet curtains covered the den windows and hid Cleveland's October chill. The air, scrubbed clean twice every hour, thanks to the ventilation system that guaranteed removal of ninety-nine percent of the disease-causing viruses, smelled like fake pine. Thick beige carpet muffled Lillian's footsteps as she entered the room.

Engrossed in their routine after-dinner activities, both her mother and father were oblivious to her presence. The tranquil family scene tugged at her heart, but she was about to destroy it as she wrapped icy hands around her arms. "I have accepted the position at Francis Marion University. I leave tomorrow."

The silence pounded against her ears even as the tension in the room blistered her face. She swallowed against the thickness in her throat. What could she say that would sway her parents from the verdict they had already chosen?

Ralph Goodson neatly folded the newspaper, pursing his lips to form a hard line across his face. A line-backer in college, Ralph Goodson had maintained his athletic physique through long hours of personal training. Graying only around the temples, he still turned the ladies' eyes.

Even though they had been over this before, she knew he would bring it up again, perhaps hoping she would change the story about how a faculty position became available in the middle of a semester, and why she needed to leave home.

Attorney Goodson stared at Lillian with his intimidating trial-glare for several seconds before rising from the leather recliner. Perhaps out of habit, perhaps buying time to compose his deposition, he hesitated long enough to pick a speck of invisible lint from his jacket before walking to the fire place.

As she waited, her heart pounded against her ribs

more violently than at any trial she had led. Hours spent researching her adversary had allowed her to arrive in court, prepared to battle wits with the opponent, and she had been successful.

But this man used to bounce her on his knee, share pretend tea parties, and even play dress-up on occasion. Together they had buried Goldie the goldfish. As his reputation as a top-rate trial attorney grew, Ralph Goodson's time at home had diminished. Now she hardly knew the man who leaned against the white brick with one arm draped across the polished walnut mantle.

"We knew you were considering the job," her father said, running a long finger across the wood. His stare threatened to burn a hole through her retina. "Considering is fine. Consider all you want, but accepting is another matter altogether. You should have consulted me."

Anger shot from her heart. "This is one of the reasons I need to leave! You control everything I do."

"Sweetheart—"

"No, don't start, Mom. You know I'm right. I can't leave the house without your approval. When I'm on the phone you hover just around the corner. You tell me when to go to bed and when to take a shower, as though I no longer have a mind of my own." She sounded more like an adolescent than a grown woman, and she hated the reversion.

Her father thrummed his fingers against the wood. "Have you discussed this with Dr. Widder?"

"Yes."

"And?"

Lillian matched her father's gaze; she had learned from the best. "He thinks it's too soon to go off on my own."

"You should listen to him. He *is* your psychiatrist."

Lillian's back stiffened as she tried to control the emotion that welled up. In the past two years, her feelings had coiled together in her gut like a nest of snakes, impossible to separate anger from fear or hate.

"Why won't you listen to the advice of your doctor?" Her father's dark eyes narrowed. "All of a sudden you think you know everything?"

"I've asked advice from the wisest of all. I've been talking to God about this move ever since the announcement came in the mail." She sighed, knowing her parents held little regard for the power of prayer.

Mr. Goodson rolled his eyes. "You know what I think about that. Why even bring it up? I regret the day you ever met that man—"

"That man has a name. It's Craig, and he was my husband." She spit the words toward him. "And yes, he shared Jesus. It was the best thing that ever happened to me." She took a deep breath and allowed the pressure to escape through her nose. "If you only understood the peace that God can bring–"

"Peace! I didn't see peace on your face a couple of years ago when we had to practically carry you home. Where was Jesus then? And for that matter, where has he been for the past two years?"

Mrs. Goodson shifted in her chair. Her artfully applied cheek color now appeared clown-like against her pallor. "What do you hope to do in South Carolina that you can't do here?" She placed her cup in its saucer. The cheerful ting of china against china sounded incongruent next to the pounding tension. "I just don't understand why you need to move so far away."

"I can't live the rest of my life inside this house." Lillian looked at her mother.

Designer clothes and sculpted hair battled against Lillian's soft curls and sweat shirt. Two years ago, her parents' home had felt like a womb, protecting and safe. Now the walls loomed over her like a prison, both of her parents acting as wardens.

The furnace turned on and its low rumble broke the hard silence. The curtains puffed away from the window as air blew from the vent. The artificial scent caused her stomach to churn.

"If you insist on going," her father said, "I'll go with you. Help you get settled."

"I should go, I'm her mother."

She sighed. "Neither of you are going. I am capable of doing this myself. I'm not a baby anymore. I'm adult, an attorney."

"You *were* an attorney," her mother mumbled, "and we still don't know who set the fire that—"

Lillian's mouth tightened. "According to most of Cleveland, I set that fire." It always came back to the fire.

Her mother studied her hands. "No one believes that, dear."

Unfortunately, many did. Lillian had no alibi for the time in question.

She squeezed her eyes against the scenes that rolled across her memory. Her heart thundered against her ribs, trying valiantly to seek escape from its confinement. She pushed both fists into her chest, wishing she could force her fingers through tissue and muscle and create an escape for her dead heart.

The movie was playing; she had to narrate for her

parents or be alone in the horror. "It was Sunday afternoon," her voice shook. "Craig begged me to stay home, but I wanted to go to the office and clear away the papers from the trial. I promised to be back in time to put Susan to bed." Tears streamed down her face. "She was only two. Two years old. She needed her mommy to be home, and I left her." The pounding heart became quivering gelatin. It swelled and filled her throat, choking her words. "The next time I saw her..."

"Lillian, stop!"

She turned to her father. "If you think you can fix this, you can't. My husband is dead, and my daughter is dead, and it's my fault."

"Lillian—"

Wild with grief, she faced her father. "You know it's true. The two of you have done everything in your power to keep your feelings from becoming public. It isn't good for your social status or your profession to have a daughter who was suspected—"

"Lillian, stop this nonsense!"

"Too many conversations have ended when I came into the room. You always ask me about my mood." She turned to her mother. "If no one believes I set the fire, then why did you stop going to the bridge club on Thursdays?"

Martha Goodson looked toward the curtains that now lay flat against the windows, centurions against the dark. "You know I don't like to leave you alone."

"You quit because you didn't like defending me every week against your so-called friends."

Her father's steel-gray eyes locked with hers. "It didn't help when you refused to tell the police where you were."

"So I was labeled a person-of-interest." Regret burned like acid. "I need you to believe me; I did not set that fire."

"Lillian, it will blow over given time. Think about what you are doing."

"I am thinking about it."

"You don't know anyone down south," her mother interjected. "What is this Francis Marion University? You've been educated to be more than a teacher. You won't fit in..."

Her father tapped his fingers on the mantle. "And you don't always choose the best friends."

"You mean Craig. Go ahead and say it!"

"You could have had any man you wanted." Her mom reshaped the nap of the carpet with her foot.

"I got the man I wanted, and now he's gone. And my job is gone. My friends avoid me; my family..." Tears flowed down her cheeks. Hands fisted at her sides.

"Honey, this is where you belong," her mother murmured. "You need our supervision for awhile yet. Let Dr. Widder spend more time with you."

She looked from one distressed face to the other. "I don't need professional counseling; I need a life." She stumbled from the room.

~*~

As he walked, his breath came in tight gasps, not from exertion but fear. Why did he continue to allow the memory to control his steps? No one forced this torture on him; no one even knew of his weekly tour into the nether regions of evil. But until retribution had been served, the compulsion to relive what amounted to the end of his life continued, as though it were a movie that automatically rewound at will. He walked through the familiar neighborhood, crossing one quiet street, then the next, not stopping to look both ways, not caring. As his destination neared, the taste of bile filled his mouth.

Evening dusk dropped its blanket of gray. Shadows elongated into reaching arms, and the dark edges of buildings shielded their menace. He jumped when a low branch brushed his face. The empty lot was still four houses away when the nightmare started.

The roar of the fire blanketed the sound of sirens. He ran closer and boiling waves of heat and smoke rolled over him, burning his lungs, stealing his air. With his heart racing, he searched his yard, then the yards of neighboring houses. Where was she? No! She couldn't be inside! Blackness enveloped his mind. As always, he found himself standing in the empty weed-infested lot. As the evening air chilled his skin, he shoved fists into his eyes, hoping to block what came next.

The spasms of reality hit, folding him over against the pain. He tightened his jaw, determined not to give in to the hopelessness that bent him like iron in the fire. The moment passed and the present returned. It always did.

He had watched the city crew a month later, after all the legal issues of her death had been properly handled, as they shoveled the charred remains of his home into trucks and hauled his memories to the dump. Now he clung to his anger because it was all he had. Anger at a world that had given him nothing.

The last vestige of gray transitioned into the blackness of night. Moonlight cast a ghostly sheen over the vacant lot. Leaves shivered above him. Light spilled from windows of the adjacent houses. Sounds: voices, television, the clank of dishes. The essence of normal life seeped from the dwellings and taunted him like the beckoning finger of a vixen woman. Even the weeds came alive as they shifted in the breeze, the mocking silver ghosts of hopes stolen.

So many nightmares. But the end neared. Vengeance would soon be accomplished and then, at last, his life could be reborn. An eye for an eye. A life for a life.

Roger Jenkins headed back to his empty house, confident in the knowledge that Lillian Hunter would soon be on her way. Her death would be his balm.

2

Tremulous breaths hung frozen around Lillian's head as she placed her suitcase in the trunk of the car. She turned on the headlights and swords of light penetrated the darkness that lay thick right before dawn. Driving around the circular drive, she allowed herself one last look at the well-manicured lawn and two-story brick house. Tears skated down icy cheeks as she moved toward the unknown.

Two faces peered out of an upstairs window. A silent hand lifted to the retreating taillights. She sighed, knowing she wasn't meant to witness the farewell; her father had told her they would not see her off.

The past had not been all bad, had it? Recent years colored the good, shading the weeks and months more darkly than perhaps memory alone would have done. In their own way, her parents did love her. But since she had become a Christian, a gap had grown. She and Craig had prayed for them so many times during their five years of marriage. Now her prayers were uttered alone. Was it possible to love someone and not like them at the same time? She swallowed against the fullness that threatened to block her throat.

Accelerating onto the highway, the dream of a new life loomed large. She had left her parents' home before, and memories wafted into her consciousness: her own two-story wood-framed house, a husband who adored her, their child. For a second she felt a glimmer of hope, but then with determination she tightened her jaw and shoved her foot harder on the gas pedal. Loneliness would be her retribution. Alone for the remainder of her life, the spinster lady living at the end of the street, the one all the neighborhood kids said hid a dark secret. Only for her, it would be true.

Why did one fail to appreciate what they had until it was gone? She would give anything for the chance to spend one more restless night beside her snoring husband, to feel his steady hands on her body, to have his kisses tell her all was good. Or to wrap her arms around her fussing toddler, feel her baby-softness and smell the scent of her newly bathed skin. To walk hand-in-hand with her at the mall, her sweet curls bobbling as she did her best to act grown-up. And the delightful messes at the table. Tears misted her eyes.

"God, I am so sorry. I am so sorry!" The words reverberated from windshield to roof to floor but the heaviness in her heart remained. Had her sorrow penetrated no further than the fabric and metal above her head? *God, did you hear me?*

She ached for the comfort and wisdom of Craig. He always knew what to say, how to handle every situation. More than that, he knew God. He would know if this move south was the right thing, or if she was going off on an old-fashioned snipe hunt. But Craig lay beside their daughter in the Greenlawn Cemetery, their charred bodies long cold, their souls soaring with the God she fervently sought, but whose Presence remained elusive.

Something about the offer in South Carolina had nagged at her from the start, but she had brushed the feeling away in her eagerness to see the job as an answer to her prayer. The fact that Francis Marion University had not yet posted the position made her squirm, but hey, God could do anything, couldn't He?

She exhaled deeply, trying to rid herself of the doubt. This had to be God's plan. If not, she was headed toward chaos. Craig always told her to trust, but she didn't know if this move was jumping or trusting.

Outside the left-hand window, a line of red seeped across the horizon: the birth of a new day.

But to Lillian it looked as if God Himself had lighted the world on fire.

~*~

A clicking sound aroused Roger from his fitful sleep, and he lay in bed, mentally alert but immobile. He scanned the dark room, but nothing moved. When the air conditioning unit clicked off he relaxed, realizing what had awakened him. He rolled over, looked at the clock and a smile creased his face. Five in the morning.

Most likely Lillian had started her journey or was saying a last good-bye. She had no idea how final those moments would be.

Too wired to go back to sleep, he headed to the kitchen. Coffee, that's what he needed. The gurgling of water in the coffeemaker blended with the metallic tick of the clock hanging on the opposite wall. Each tick marked one second. How many seconds must be endured before his adversary arrived?

Wandering the house, room by room, he thought of Ted and Trina. Lucky for him, they owned a bed and breakfast where Lillian could stay. He smirked in satisfaction.

Ted and Trina were nice people, and the next week would bring nothing but trouble for them. An unexpected surge of guilt grabbed his stomach and shoved it into his lungs. *It's not like I had a choice.* He slammed his cup onto the counter, brown liquid flying over his hand, speckling the beige laminate. *The McIverson Bed and Breakfast was the only place available. I had to send her there.*

Internal rationalization waged war with the white flag of truth. When he had shown up at church with the goal of meeting the couple, Trina had immediately invited him to the house for lunch. And now he was using them. But he had used people before. If Ted and Trina knew the story behind the woman soon to become their guest, they would welcome the chance to help him to correct a wrong.

He opened the living room blinds. A line of red seeped into the horizon: the birth of a new day. But to him it looked as if God Himself had lighted the world on fire.

~*~

As Lillian drove, the flames on the horizon faded to orange and yellow, giving birth to daylight and renewal. The sky continued to lighten, and the few clouds that dotted the endless blue looked like cotton candy, spun and light. Clear weather had been promised. How ironic. Sunshine on the day she entered the hurricane of change.

But Jesus rebuked the waves. Why did scripture keep coming to mind? Jesus might have rebuked the storm for the disciples, but she still grasped any piece of reality that would keep her afloat. Was she clinging to nothing more stable than a wish?

Mindless miles of highway rolled beneath her. Strangers in cars and semis, all moving toward destinations of their own. Her future lay at the end of one of the roads. God had to be the instigator. He promised good would come from bad, if she would just trust Him. OK, she trusted and the job ad had arrived. She wanted to do some good with what was left of her shambled life. Last night she had felt so confident, but now, in the isolation of her car, doubt crept in.

She remembered her first day at Ohio State University. Her parents had carried her suitcases, her computer, boxes of necessities she never used. They even helped make her bed. And then there was nothing more that needed to be done. As her mom and dad had walked across the parking lot, her fingernails dug into the plastic chair in front of the window, tears running down her face. The *new* had looked like a scary monster under the bed, but it had worked out. It would work out again.

Now, breathing out the tension, she eased her death-grip on the steering wheel. College had been one of the best times of her life. This change could be too.

The vibration of tires on pavement lulled her into a state of automation. She shifted from lane to lane as needed, exited when appropriate, slowed and accelerated, all without conscious thought. Traffic-weary air filtered through the freshener clipped to the vent, leaving behind the scent of vanilla. Which caused cancer sooner, air pollution or air jells that masked the toxins? What did it matter, anyway?

Ohio passed in a blur. At the Ohio River, she

breathed deeply in and out, visualizing herself exhaling her fears, allowing her internal darkness to swirl from her nose like sulfur from a caldron. She cracked the car window to allow the imagined foul stench to escape, and along with it the vanilla sent from the deodorizer that most likely had planted seeds of cancer in her lungs. She smiled at her own fantasy. Her face felt strange. When had she smiled last? She couldn't remember, but it felt good and she chuckled, hoping her demon had really been sucked out the window.

West Virginia arrived, draped in yellow and red splashes of autumn color: God's latest fashions modeled by the trees. Gas for the car and a quick lunch. Sitting alone at a picnic table beside the combination gas station/markette, spearing day-old lettuce, she closed her eyes. The air remained cool but the sun warmed her face. She lowered her shoulders and sat quietly, content to just be. Sounds penetrated but didn't disturb. Voices, indistinct, but there. Birds. And somewhere close by, running water.

Mixed with the scent of gasoline were hints of pine, real this time, and the smell of dried leaves. She smiled, remembering the maple leaves she and her sister used to rake only to jump into the pile, sending their hard work flying across the grass. The tree had been removed, deemed too messy. She missed the tree.

Another hunk of lettuce found its way into her mouth. A leaf drifted into her lap, and she worked to smooth its curling edges, feeling the veins that had provided life until the leaf had separated from the body.

That was how she felt: severed from her life, cut from her family, now drifting alone. A tear formed in the corner of her eye. *Stop it!* She might be alone, but life bubbled within her. Even though the mantle of guilt had become a constant second skin, she *would* survive.

~*~

Roger knew he should have gone to church this one last time. Especially today. But the goal for his religious affiliation had already been met, and he wasn't accustomed to actions without a purpose. He and God stood on opposite sides of glory. There was no illusion on his part for which side he would end up on.

A hot shower should ease some of the tightness in his back and neck. He closed the bedroom door and engaged the deadbolt. In the bathroom, the click of a second lock assured his privacy. Even though steam coated the glass shower doors, the deadbolts allowed him to enjoy the shower without worry over unexpected guests. He should know. The pounding water had masked his approach on at least two occasions. It wouldn't happen to him.

When the shower turned cold, he buffed himself dry, wrapped a towel around his waist, and trimmed his short beard. He unbolted the bathroom door, muscles tense until he examined the bedroom door. Finding it closed and locked, he entered the room and dressed for the day. Strapping his watch onto his wrist, he glanced at the time and frowned. Tapping on the crystal, noting the second hand moved as usual, he still matched the time to his bedside clock. The shower should have taken more than 20 minutes. It was going to be a long day.

Too early to eat lunch, but if he walked to one of the local diners, maybe *Joe's*, since it was the furthest away; it would kill at least two hours. He chuckled over his choice of verbs, his own private joke. Besides, he could use the exercise. His dead end job robbed him of his coveted gym time, but soon keeping in shape would be a choice and not a requirement.

As he locked the door to the house, a sense of isolation gripped him. He should be surrounded by his wife and daughter. But here he was, alone. *Stop it!* He might be alone, but life bubbled within him. Even though the mantle of guilt had become a constant second skin, he *would* survive.

~*~

Seeing the "Welcome to Virginia" sign on the side of the road, Lillian felt as if she had finally entered the south. Towering pines lined the highway, so different from the maples in Cleveland. She flexed tight fingers one hand at a time, feeling the burn as she bent each muscle. Had her decision to make the fourteen-hour drive in one day been a mistake? No one watched for her at the end of the road. The light salad eaten at the gas station sat heavy in her stomach.

Glad when a roadside rest appeared, she pulled off. Half a dozen cars, mostly SUVs, had claimed the spots closest to the restroom. She pulled her stiff body from the seat, and stretched; her back cracked with each movement.

The restroom stood on top of a small knoll, and people walked up and down the cement path, their purposeful strides reminding her of ants going to and from the nest. Surrounding the walkway, yellow and pink mums still bloomed in beds mulched with pine needles. Empty picnic tables stood off in the distance, perhaps intentionally placed away from the smells and contamination of the main attraction.

A man dressed in blue workman's overalls emptied the metal trash receptacle just outside the double, glass doors, placed the full bag into his two-wheeled cart, and replaced the bag with a clean one.

She smiled at him as she passed.

He tipped a finger to his eyebrow. "Ma'am."

A giggle bubbled up her throat. *Ma'am?* After using the facilities, she hummed as she slipped coins into a vending machine secured behind metal bars. *Why didn't I pack snacks? We always used to pack snacks, Craig and I...*

Her newfound levity evaporated as quickly as it had come. The bleakness of reality felt heavier after experiencing freedom, if only for a few minutes. She walked back to the car, her head down. Was discouragement always to ride in the passenger seat of her life?

She punched the locks on her doors, started the engine, and lowered each window just an inch. As she pulled the candy bar from the wrapper, chocolate clung to her fingertips. She gasped as horror filled her. Her fingers, they were charred and black. Just like Craig. Just like Susan. Gasping, she threw the candy and it stuck to the passenger window, looking like an appendage severed from its burnt body. Gagging, she bolted from the car.

Hanging over the bathroom sink, the terror faded into the vortex of the swirling water. What in the world had happened? She had never reacted like that before. Suddenly she felt as heavy as the boulder sitting outside the door, as though gravity itself tugged at her, trying to pull her into the bowels of the earth. Could her dad be right? Fingers of doubt tickled along the edges of her mind. Maybe leaving home wasn't the answer. She stood and patted cool water on her face as red-rimmed eyes stared back at her from the mirror. The room spun and she grabbed the sink. In a blur, she heard a voice.

"Can I help you? Are you sick?"

She slumped forward and felt hands grab her before she lost consciousness.

~*~

"Try to breathe slowly. I'm a registered nurse."

Lillian felt a hand at her wrist. Coldness seeped through the back of her jeans and shirt, but she lacked the energy to do anything about it. She opened her eyes and a middle-aged woman smiled; soft wrinkles formed around her mouth.

"Who's with you? I can get them."

Lillian felt numb. Where was she? The ceiling was made of exposed wood. The skylights were dirty. She would have to clean them. Someone had spray painted "Missy loves David." The rest area. That's why the skylight hadn't been cleaned. Who cared in a rest area? She tried to focus on the face peering over her.

"What car are you driving? I can get your companion."

"I'm alone." She licked her dry lips, the words tasting bitter, as she struggled to sit up.

"Do you need me to call an ambulance?"

Her head spun and she placed a hand on the floor. "I'll be all right. I think I drove too long without a break."

"Did you have lunch?"

"A salad."

"Maybe your blood sugar dropped. Let me get you a candy bar."

"No, please..." She shifted to her knees and then stood. The room swayed, but soon steadied. "I feel better." She forced a smile.

The woman continued to stare at her with concern. "Let me help you to your car, at least."

"I think I'll get a can of pop and sit outside on the bench for awhile. Really, I'm fine."

The woman took her arm. "Do you want to get your soda before you sit down?"

Parked cars lined the lower sidewalk, hers among them. Her heart lurched as she saw a man opening her car door. No, she had parked further down, but in her fright, she had not locked her car. How long had she been gone? Most likely, someone had helped himself to her purse by now. "I...uh..."

"What kind of pop do you like?"

"Anything. I don't really care, but you don't have to do this. I have money..."

"And it's in the car. I can see it on your face. Not a problem."

After purchasing a can of lemon-lime soda, the two women settled on a bench. Lillian lifted her face to the sun, the warmth penetrating her skin and giving renewed energy.

A middle-aged couple passed, holding hands and smiling as though life were the best.

An ache crept into her heart. It should have been like that for her.

The air smelled clean in spite of the traffic in the

parking area. A large lady, her flowered caftan fluttering around her, tugged on the leash of a small white dog, trying to pull him up the sidewalk. The dog won, and the lady retreated down the sidewalk.

After a few sips of pop, Lillian's stomach relaxed and strength flowed back into her muscles. Even so, she felt reluctant to leave the relative security of her spot on the bench.

"So tell me about yourself," the woman said.

How could she summarize her life to include all the good, all the drama, all the unknown? Since childhood, she had been told not to talk to strangers. As an attorney, she had learned the hazards of taking others at their word without proof. She glanced at the woman beside her. About her size but with graying hair cut short. She seemed to radiate strength and caring as her soft blue eyes focused on Lillian, curious but not invasive.

Lillian took a deep breath. "Well, I was a spoiled rich girl who married an amazing middle-class man and together we had a fantastic little girl. Then two years ago they died, and I am heading to South Carolina to try to put my life back together."

"Oh, my dear child!" The woman wrapped her arms around Lillian and pulled her close.

Lillian stiffened, but then, as though touched by the sun itself, she melted into the woman's embrace. It felt so good to be cared for, to have someone feel compassion for her.

The woman placed her hands on Lillian's shoulders. "You have suffered so much. And yet, here you are, going on with your life."

"I don't have a choice."

The woman patted Lillian's folded hands.

"Indeed, you do. I have seen people give up under less bitter circumstances." She smiled softly. "God has an amazing plan for you."

Not wanting to offend the woman, Lillian took a slow sip of her soda.

"You see that camper down there?" The lady pointed toward the truck parking area.

"The blue one?"

The lady laughed. "Oh, not that one. The gray one beside it."

The gray camper had been around a few years. Not shiny like the blue one, the gray body had dulled and the decals were mostly worn away.

"That camper is my life right now. My husband has Alzheimer's; his memory is still intact but slipping. We bought this camper many years ago, always intending to travel the states, but never got around to it. Now we're doing it." She glanced at the camper, then back to Lillian. "You know, I didn't plan to stop here. Mother Nature had not called, if you know what I mean. But Harry and I have this little game going. We want to visit a rest area in every state. So I pulled in, saw you washing your hands, and I knew you needed help."

Lillian listened to the gentle flow of the woman's words, soothing and earnest. The stranger would have been a great counselor.

"Do you believe in God?" the woman asked.

"Yes."

"Then you know this meeting was no accident. I don't know what your future will bring, but God knows, and He knew you needed a kind word right now, at this rest area." The woman squeezed Lillian's hand and stood. "I had better get back to Harry before he comes looking for me or wanders off, which he does sometimes." She paused and looked long into Lillian's face. "God be with you, dear one."

Lillian watched until the woman and her camper disappeared around the building toward the highway. She tossed the empty pop can into the metal container and walked toward her car, searching her mind for the lady's name. Had she ever told her? The woman had not even asked for hers.

Her feet quickened as she approached the unlocked car. Surely, her purse would be gone. And what if someone took the car keys just to be hateful? Squinting in the bright light, there didn't appear to be anyone in the car. The doors were all closed, even though she couldn't remember closing hers.

Cautiously, she moved forward and glanced into the driver's window. Her purse, which she had left on the passenger seat, was gone. Choking back tears and words of self-recrimination, she jerked open the car door. A folded strip of paper lay on the driver's seat. She picked up the paper, a grocery store tape, and read the note scratched on the back:

"I saw you run from your car. I put your purse under the seat, and cleaned up the chocolate bar. The car keys are under the seat, too. I hated to leave them there, but felt out-of-sight was better than in the ignition. I hope you are all right." There was no signature.

She stared at the paper. Who would do something that kind? She retrieved her purse and digging inside, found her wallet, credit cards and money. With surprise, she leaned back against the seat of the car. The day had started as a challenge and she had asked for God's protection. He had provided a lady with no name and someone willing to clean and protect her car. Amazing.

She picked up the insulated cup that sat in the holder below the dash, a gift from her sister Beth. Bits of sand and tiny sea shells swirled in mock-ocean water. She would miss Beth, but her sister, in her residency in medical school, seldom had time to come home.

On impulse, she dug in her purse and pulled out her cell phone. Beth's number came up. It always did. She seldom called anyone else. The phone made jingling sounds as the number was automatically dialed.

"Dr. Goodson."

"Beth, it's Lillian."

"Lilly! I didn't bother to check caller ID. How are you?"

"Do you have time to talk? I figured you would be on duty, but..."

"Hey, you're my sister. Barring a cardiac arrest or severed artery, I can take a few minutes' break. Are you alone?"

"I'm sitting at a roadside rest in Virginia."

A sigh sounded thorough the receiver. "So you left?"

"I had to."

"I know." Silence filled the line for a few seconds. "Will you be all right? You know you can always come and stay with me in Chicago."

"And do what? I love you for the offer, but I need to work. Sitting around all day is driving me crazy. Besides, I would never see you. Residents keep awful hours."

"Tell me about it."

"Bets, you won't believe what just happened." She shared the two strange encounters.

"Wow. I don't know what to say."

"You don't need to say anything, just know God is taking care of me."

"Well, just be careful, OK?"

"You sound as if you don't agree with my move. Do you know something I don't?"

"No, really, I'm on your side, sis. Listen, I'm trying to get off for Thanksgiving."

"I'll come home, too! We can stay up all night and talk, just like we used to."

Laughter filled the phone. "You steal Dad's flashlight and I'll get the snacks."

"I miss you, Beth." The ache of loneliness tugged at her heart. Tears filled her eyes.

"I miss you too. And Lillian, I worry about you."

"Beth, I told you—"

"I know what you told me, and I believe you, but let me worry if I want to. You're my sister, what else can I do?"

"You can pray for me."

"Did I tell you I've been attending the chaplain's services on Sunday when I have time? He's made me think, Lilly."

Lillian smiled. "Put that on our agenda for Thanksgiving. I want to hear all about it."

Muffled voices filtered through the phone. "Sis, I've got to go, but I love you."

"I love you too." Lillian pushed end and wiped tears from her eyes.

How easy it would be to just stay here, to fall asleep in the Virginia rest area. For a precious period of time, all would be as it had been. Before the trial that distracted her from what was important. Before the fire. Sighing, she turned on the ignition.

The sun accomplished its journey across the sky. North Carolina rolled on forever. Jives, the Australian voice on the GPS, kept her moving, one route to the next, one gas station to the next, all looking the same. Fast food for supper, a burger this time, washed down with a chocolate milkshake. She imagined her mother's scowling face as the contraband food entered her body. She smiled and savored the fat and calories even more.

~*~

The sun arched across the sky. Roger had been tense all day and was ready for the action to start. Sitting with nothing to do while she drove from Cleveland to Darlington was harder than a day at his deadbeat job. He hated his job, hated this town, hated his life. For the past two years, he had been on stage with no intermission. The play needed to end.

He glanced at his wrist and sighed. How many times had he looked at his watch? If he had one wish, it would be for time to fly. Just for today. But then, no one had ever offered to grant him a wish. No, Roger Jenkins had to fight and scrap for everything he ever had, and today would be no different.

Soon he would be able to head to Ted and Trina's. Nothing unusual about that. Many nights he, and sometimes the annoying Paul Studler, would settle on the front porch. Trina almost always provided cookies, and Trina's dad, Bill, would entertain them with stories from his childhood. Who knew life had changed so much? Black-and-white TV and home-delivered milk and bread?

Should he try to eat something before he headed out? He opened the refrigerator door, and smelled the milk. Still good, and enough left in the jug for a bowl of cereal. He reached for a bowl in the cupboard beside the refrigerator, red plastic, on sale at the thrift store at the time he had bought the house. Service for one. The raisin bran box felt light as he lifted it from the shelf. Only crushed sediment remained in the bottom of the plastic liner.

He threw the bowl into the sink where it cracked into pieces. He pulled a tight hand down his face, nostrils flaring as he gripped the side of the sink. Most of his life he had been able to control his temper, but lately, it was getting harder. He closed his eyes and tried to slow his breathing. Better get control and not let this rage come spilling out around Lillian. She had to trust him. That was part of his game.

Scanning the kitchen, he found a package of cookies stashed on top of the microwave. Sitting at the table, for all appearances a respectable gentleman ready for a Sunday snack, he munched on the chocolate cookies. The empty cupboards didn't bother him; he didn't plan on living there much longer. There was one good thing about living alone. No one cared what he ate. He savored the fat and calories even more.

~*~

An hour into South Carolina, as dusk settled in, Jives announced the anticipated exit from the interstate. At the traffic light, Lillian hyper-extended her aching back. Since Virginia, the trip had gone smoothly. Not far now. She opened the rear windows wider and warm air brushed against her skin. It had been cold at home.

She bristled with tension. She was about to start her new life. Was she ready? Anticipation of a new, quiet existence calmed her. No one knew her in Darlington, and she would keep to herself as much as possible. Craig used to say that people can only be happy when they live within God's will. She squeezed the steering wheel. Well, this move had better be in God's will because there it was, the sign for Darlington. Just five more miles.

Restaurants and hotels lined the state route. The smell of steak made her mouth water, but no time to stop now. A farmer's market and a technical college both flanked the right side of the street. On the left were fields with bits of cotton clinging to stubble.

The road narrowed to two lanes. Smaller businesses, a hair salon, the front window of a house with a poster offering alterations, refrigerators lining the walk of a used furniture store. Nothing like Cleveland with its many lanes of traffic and high-rise buildings.

Finally, Darlington city limits. She sighed, anticipating the journey's end. What if the bed and breakfast turned out to be a one-star dive? Bedbugs and dirty sheets? She blew a stray curl off her face, frustrated that she had not thought to do a web-search in spite of the great flyer. But as tired as she was, she could survive anything for a night.

The thought of destiny's end, perhaps a soak in a tub of hot water and a good night's sleep in clean sheets and no bugs sent tingles of anticipation through her. This was Darlington. No cameras flashing. No TV crews. No hostile stares. No sirens. No one asking her for matches. A strange sensation filled her. Was it hope?

Pulsing blue lights reflected in the rearview mirror. She slowed to allow the vehicle to pass, but the cruiser pulled behind her. Fear coursed through her veins. Had fate followed her after all?

3

Roger sat stiffly on the front porch swing at the McIverson Bed and Breakfast and stared straight ahead, acutely aware of Bill, Trina's dad, who sat beside him. When he had arrived an hour ago, a neighbor had occupied one of the two wicker chairs across from the swing. He had thought about changing spaces when the neighbor left, but, for now, he remained in place.

As the sun fell behind the sheltering limbs, the air cooled, but not enough to warrant a jacket. The ceiling fan wobbled as it rotated, and the moving air passed over him in soft waves, just enough to keep persistent fall gnats from becoming a nuisance. Two years in the south, and he still couldn't get used to the warmer weather.

Bill towered over him by at least a foot, but then, Bill towered over almost everyone. It wasn't the man's height or bulk that made him cautious: the big man seemed to know more than he should.

Lillian could arrive any time now, and Roger's nerves were raw from being constrained within his forced good behavior. Hiding his tension from Bill ate at his energy. Roger hated Lillian. Although nothing would undo the past, some things, when the law proved to be inadequate, demanded a personal touch. Soon he could restart his life. Darlington, and even his partner, would become nightmares of the past, dreams he would never revisit.

Sitting on the edge of the second wicker chair, Ted puckered his brow and clenched his lips as he watched the approaching cars.

A little girl, perhaps three years old, stumbled on the uneven sidewalk. A man, presumably her father, grabbed her and picked her up. She wrapped slender arms around the man's neck and rested her head on his shoulder.

An ache tightened Roger's throat and he turned away from the scene of trust.

The rhythmic squeak of the porch swing, and its lulling, rocking motion, usually soothed him, but today it did little to loosen the balled muscles in his neck. Tilting his chin upward and rotating his head, he felt the ache, like a flame being held against a rope. He ran his hand down the short beard he had grown to cover what he considered his greatest physical flaw, a weak chin.

The sidewalk stood empty now, but in the yard, a pair of squirrels scampered up the old oak, their cheeks bulging with acorns. A siren sounded and his heart thumped wildly, even though the wailing remained muffled by dense air and distance.

He was too reactive and needed some activity to burn off the adrenalin that laced his blood, but a walk, which usually helped calm him, was out of the question. He might miss her arrival. A piece of loose skin dangled beside his right thumbnail and he pulled it off. Blood oozed out and he stared, watching it grow to a small bubble before he wiped it off with his other hand.

He rose from the swing and went upstairs to the

bathroom to wash his hands. Back on the swing, he turned to Bill. "Did you make it to the festival?"

Bill's size fourteen shoes maintained a steady rhythm as he pushed the porch swing back and forth. "I walked up for awhile," he mumbled, brushing his hand across the top of his head, the short salt-and-pepper stubble barely disturbed by the action. "Seemed wrong not to, but there wasn't much that interested me."

"You made quick work of those sweet potato fries," Ted said, his gaze darting from his father-in-law and back to the street.

Bill knew things about people, what they were feeling, if they were good or evil. Kind of like Santa Claus. More than once in the past hour, Roger had turned to find Bill staring at him. Did he suspect?

The minutes suspended, mocking, refusing to move on.

"So, Bill, anything new between you and Sandra that I should know about?" he asked.

The steady rocking stuttered. "I don't know what you mean."

"You and Sandra. You're a couple, aren't you?"

"I don't know where you got that idea."

Bill and Sandra were always together. And the way the big man looked at her, something zinged between them.

"I just thought—"

"Well, just quit thinking."

The disagreement fed Roger's tension. If there was one thing he did well, it was observe. Any other day and he might have challenged Bill, but not today. He couldn't risk an out-and-out argument and have to leave the house. Not with Lillian on her way.

Vibrations as Ted bounced his leg radiated across the porch floor. The iced tea on a stand at Ted's side rippled, as though a beast approached each time Ted's heel struck the floor.

Roger stared at the ripples; in a way, a beast was approaching.

Ted glanced at his watch. Again.

"She'll be here soon," Bill murmured.

"I know, I know." Ted pushed thin strands of blond hair off his forehead. "But Trina's so much better at this than I am. She usually greets new guests, not me. I just wish she were home."

Bill chuckled. "Can't expect her to miss her own baby shower."

"Trina's having a baby shower today?" Roger asked.

"You might know these things if you showed up at church now and then." Humor ringed Bill's eyes, but Roger knew the man was serious.

As Roger ran a hand across the dark hair on his chin, he knew to let Bill's second challenge also go unanswered. Going to church had been his way of meeting Ted and Trina, nothing more. Some may have regretted the trouble the young couple would soon experience because of their guest, but not him. Regret wasted energy and time, both commodities he held close to his chest. At least he had worked out the details to protect them. Killing the family would be wrong.

He mulled over his personal metamorphosis from a man who pleased into a man who killed. When had it happened? He didn't see himself as a bad person. There was no lust for blood. And this would be the last time. One more death. That's all he needed to be finished.

~*~

With the blue light reflecting in her rearview mirror, Lillian eyed the sandy soil beside the road, clenched her teeth, and pulled off. If the car sank to its rims, it wouldn't be her fault.

She lowered the window and waited for the smug grin of the small-town cop. *So this is my new home, population 6,500. Transported to the 21st century, complete with speed traps.*

"Ma'am, do you know how fast you were driving?"

She turned and stared, her eyes level with the officer's belt buckle. "About 45."

"The speed limit's 30."

"But the sign said…"

The officer bent over and quickly perused the interior of the car before resting his attention on Lillian's face. "The speed limit changed back down the road a ways, about half a mile. I followed you to see if you'd slow down, but you didn't."

Lillian melted at the sound of his southern drawl, and then chided herself for the stupidity of her emotion. "I missed the sign," she said, still trying to get a handle on her unexpected attraction. "I'm sorry."

The lanky officer returned to his cruiser, carrying Lillian's driver's license and car registration.

Through her rearview mirror, she watched the patrolman's long-legged stride. Definitely not what she had expected. And cute, too. Shame flamed her cheeks.

Thirteen hours on the road. I'm almost there. No wonder my mind is acting crazy. And now a traffic ticket.

She felt the hardness of the seat against the back of her head. *Is it too much to want a quiet life, maybe a house someday and—*

She sucked a lung-full of air as a large hand reached through the window.

"Sorry ma'am. I didn't mean to startle you."

Two deep breaths, and she grabbed the documents secured between the officer's gloved fingers.

"I have to give you a ticket, you know." His breath smelled like mint.

Passing cars slowed. Their occupants stared.

"You're from out of town."

She looked up at the officer, shielding her eyes against the pulsing light. "I'm from Ohio, Cleveland, actually."

He smiled, exposing white, slightly crooked teeth. "I've never been to Cleveland. Would like to get there someday and see the Rock and Roll Hall of Fame."

The throbbing lights. The stares. Memories of flashing cameras sent her back to Cleveland...back when...

She jumped as he spoke.

"Where you headed?"

"The McIverson Bed and Breakfast."

"Ted and Trina's place!" Lines crinkled the corners of his eyes. "You're gonna love it, but it won't be easy getting there today." He glanced toward town. "Hey, tell you what. I'm off duty in a few minutes anyway. What say I lead you there?"

"I have directions..."

"Not going to do you much good. It's the Sweet Potato Festival. The main streets into town are shut down. It's Ms. Lillian, right?" As he sprinted toward the cruiser he called over his shoulder, "Just pull out behind me and follow close."

She groaned. *Why God?*

~*~

The tension push from the inside of Roger's body, ready to explode from his skin, leaving him exposed and vulnerable. How much longer before she would arrive? He picked at the skin on his thumb again, pressing a finger against the raw flesh, relishing the burn, wishing it were more.

The pair of squirrels ran back across the grass and scampered up the tree. A jet, looking like a shining dart in the sky, left behind a signature trail of vapor. As a child, he used to lie on the grass and trace the streak with his finger, wondering where the plane was going, hoping one day to be on it. Eventually he had caught the flight, only to find out its destination was no better than where he had left.

"So what's this lady's name again?" Bill asked.

Ted remained focused on the street. "Lillian Hunter. She just got a faculty job at Francis Marion University."

"What's she like?" Roger hoped he sounded only mildly curious, as he would for any new guest, but he wanted to know Ted's impression of his nemesis.

"Trina's the one who booked her. I talked to her for the first time a couple of hours ago when she called to update me on her location."

A car approached.

A crackling and wheezing sound came from the wicker as Ted lifted from the chair.

The approaching car slowed and then passed the house as it moved up the street toward the square.

Roger let out his breath. "What's this Lillian Hunter like?" he repeated.

"She seems nice enough." Ted slumped back into the chair.

"Isn't she the one that's coming from Cleveland?" Bill asked. "I can't keep track of these people coming and going." The big man leaned over and placed his empty glass on the floor.

Roger grabbed the arm of the swing, the tipping motion reminding him of a Ferris wheel. He never liked Ferris wheels, not since his mom threatened to toss him off one if he didn't quit crying. He had been six at the time, and hadn't stepped foot on a Ferris wheel since.

Even after Bill sat back in the swing, Roger maintained his death-grip on the arm, tightness building in his chest. *Come on Lillian, come on.*

~*~

Flashing lights stabbed her eyes as the cruiser passed. The officer extended his arm out the driver's window motioning her to follow.

Wishing she were invisible, Lillian pulled onto the road. Squat houses and stores lined both sides of the street. They looked old, weathered by heat, history and time. Teen Mission. Nick's BBQ. A funeral home with a white limo parked alongside. Someone's flower garden still full of roses. A single railroad track, flanked on the left by a long, gray building with a picture of cotton painted white on the front.

Just before the orange barricades that blocked off rows of vendors, the patrol car turned right.

The two lanes of Broad Street were squeezed into

one, the space filled with crowds: walkers, adults pushing strollers, a toddler tethered to a leash as a plush dog face anchored the straps to the child's back. Middle aged people. Teens. The smell of grease and cotton candy. Voices. Laughter. All headed toward the square.

"Hey Paul!" A man waved toward the cruiser.

The officer waved back. Then the cruiser's siren burst out a short wail, scattering those milling in the middle of the street like birds from an approaching cat.

Slinking down in her seat, feeling like an oddity on display, she followed in the wake of the patrol car. After another block, the crowd thinned to couples and families, all walking on the edge of the road, heading toward town. Cars filled the front parking lots of the closed hardware and farm and feed store.

Another left turn onto Irby Street. Mature trees, single family houses, small front yards, and potential quietness. Spanish moss hung in thick clumps like gray lace draped across the arms of Victorian ladies. She lifted her face, welcoming the warm air, so unlike the biting chill of Cleveland. *Maybe this won't be so bad after all.*

Two more blocks and a right turn onto Cashua. The houses were large, ornate, and appeared well cared for. Sidewalks separated the yards from the road, some flanked by wrought-iron fences. Dark leaves of magnolia trees stood in contrast to the white and pink flowers adorning camellia bushes. At one house, yellow and orange mums in ceramic pots graced the steps leading to the front door.

Officer Paul pulled into the drive of a large brick house with a wide front porch. The pulsing lights from the cruiser cast a surreal glow, as though all was not exactly as seen.

The knot in the pit of Lillian's stomach tightened and she swallowed against the acid that rose in her throat.

Three men were on the porch, all staring at her. Coated in blue, they appeared bloodless and monster-like.

If I step out of the car, there will be no turning back. God, what should I do?

Suddenly she wanted nothing more than to be back in Cleveland.

4

Icy fingers skated up and down Roger's spine and he shivered with anticipation. Finally, the moment had come. When man manipulated what should be, life had a way of normalizing itself. Justice created by the social norms of a few eventually collapsed under the weight of the many. He was here to correct a failure, a hero of the common man.

Officer Studler jogged to the car and leaned into the window. When the man stood again, a wide grin spanned his face.

Roger gritted his teeth. No one had a bigger mouth than Paul Studler.

"Hey!" the officer shouted as he headed back toward his vehicle. "Brought y'all a guest." The man's slow southern drawl pulled at Roger's nerves.

Bill leaned across the wooden railing. "Why the escort?"

"Saved her from a traffic jam at the square. Sweet Potato Festival. Roads are closed." Officer Studler climbed back into the cruiser, turned off the lights, and drove the car behind the house where the drive ended at a small alley.

Standing by the swing, Roger wiped his palms on his pants.

Bill ambled to the porch stairs and stopped.

Ted continued out into the yard, his back stiff, arms rigid at his sides.

The car door opened.

Roger held his breath.

As though on cue, the sun, in a last show of power, streaked the graying horizon with orange and bathed the woman in gold.

Roger stared at the false goddess. Just as the sun would set, so would Lillian fade from existence. Would she remember him? He didn't think so, or he wouldn't be there. Two years ago he had stayed in the background, and with the beard...still, his heart raced. This would be the final test.

As Lillian and Ted approached the porch, the woman's steps slowed. Ted's words were swept away before they could reach his starving ears.

She was different somehow. Wrinkling his brow, forcing memories that he had thought he would never forget, he resurrected the Lillian of the past, the woman who had been able to hold groups captive by the power of her personality. This Lillian, the one standing in the yard, seemed faded by comparison, like a dowdy twin, edgy, unsure of herself.

His mind hardened.

Ted murmured and she shook her head.

Sandy red curls framed a pale, oval face. She was shorter than he remembered, and thinner. Gauntly thin. Time had diminished the woman who, two years ago, had set his fate.

Lillian preceded Ted up the porch steps. "This is my father-in-law, Bill Iver."

Lillian accepted Bill's outstretched hand, hers quickly becoming lost in the man's over-sized paw. "Mr. Iver." Her voice still held the familiar timbre, but it lacked the force of authority; the power had been stripped. The darling of the court would no longer influence the fate of others.

"Please, it's Bill. Not much formality around here."

Ted turned to introduce him.

Life narrowed, as though all of reality was being sent through a funnel, and only the critical essence slipped through the narrow hole at the end: he and Lillian. Nothing else existed. Not the sounds of traffic, the music from the square, the other men on the porch. All were all gone. Left were just he and the woman he had been taught to hate. An unquenchable fire blazed in his chest.

Over the past months, he had visualized this moment thousands of times: how it would feel to have her in front of him, to force her to meet his eyes. Dozens of lines had been practiced, and he had crafted her response to each. Imagination had strengthened him as he had waited.

Now, well-rehearsed words lay heavy, unsaid, as he stared into hazel eyes that shouted sadness more loudly than words ever could. But she didn't recognize him.

As the screen door screeched, Roger's private world vanished.

"I'll show you to your room," Ted said, standing in front of the open front door, "and when you're settled, feel free to join us on the porch...if you want to." He shifted from one foot to the other. "You don't have to, but if you want to."

Lillian glanced toward the drive. "What about my car?"

"I'll move it to the back for you." The floor creaked under Bill's weight.

Hesitating, Lillian finally dropped her keys in

Bill's outstretched hand.

"I'll haul your luggage to your room, too."

The first time Roger had been in the house was when Ted and Trina had invited him for lunch after church. At that time, the entry walls had been sixties orange. Scraps of plaster molding hung from the ceiling, more gone than present. Deep scrapes had created raw wounds in the hardwood floor. The house had felt old. Dying.

All things have a season. Wasn't that what Preacher Steve had said in one of the few sermons Roger had actually listened to? A time to live, a time to die? Over the past few months, the necrotic house had been reborn.

As soon as he entered the house, the hair on the back of his neck bristled. Glancing around, he spotted a vase of fresh red roses on the table in the center of the foyer, most likely Trina's touch. Childhood memories of sneaking through a gap in the backyard fence played with his mind. The fence had been covered with twining roses, and the gashes on his arms always gave away his forbidden escape.

"You look just as I imagined," Lillian said to Ted.

"Oh, really?" A tinge of heat colored the man's cheeks.

"When I heard you were a painter, I imagined you as tall and lanky."

"The starving artist concept?"

"Maybe." She turned away. "It's just what came to mind."

Ted cleared his throat. "Well...to the right and left are the parlors. Feel free to use either one whenever you want."

The room on the right held an overstuffed couch

and two chairs and, just inside the door, a worn leather recliner. A comfortable place for the family. On the left, period-style, high-backed chairs covered with turquoise fabric, and thin-legged end tables had been arranged to face the fireplace. Too museum-like for Roger's taste, but it seemed a lot of ladies preferred it.

After one more glance toward the road, Ted turned to Lillian. "Let me show you your room."

The entry was separated from the long hallway by leaded glass doors that were pushed back against the wall. Lacking access to direct light, the inner space felt cool. Lined in walnut paneling that gleamed from recent polishing, the long central hallway extended the remaining length of the house and ended at the kitchen door. The inner space felt almost like a medieval church with its diminished light, wide façade, and the sound of echoing footsteps. Two ceiling fans gently rotated overhead.

"This door goes to the dining room."

Light spilled into the hall from the opening on the right. In the center of the room stood the old table flanked by ten chairs. Ted pointed to a pair of corner hutches.

"My father-in-law discovered a cellar under the house. This china had been hidden there since the War Between the States. Trina and Sandra washed all of it and placed it into the cabinets. We use it for special occasions."

Was Lillian remembering her loss? Did Ted's tour bring back memories of her home? Although her expression never changed, he knew the self-control she once possessed. It would be well for him to not forget her strengths.

"It's a lovely room, and what a wonderful family

history."

Ted grinned. "Trina would love nothing better than to tell you about the house. Between her and Sandra—"

"Sandra? Does she work here at the Bed and Breakfast?"

"No, Sandra's a family friend. Another one of those stories Trina can share with you. In the meantime," Ted turned to the left and ran his hand along the turned railings and a handrail worn smooth from fifteen decades of use, "these are the stairs to the second floor. It's called a lady's staircase and Trina can fill you in on that too."

"From what I've seen so far, your home is beautiful. Your wife mentioned that the two of you did most of the restoration yourselves."

A door slammed followed by thumping footsteps. Bill's bulky form soon filled the kitchen door. "Ms. Hunter?"

Roger stiffened. He didn't like the look on Bill's face. Something was wrong.

"Is this all you have?" A black suitcase dangled from Bill's hand.

"That's it."

"Are you sure?"

Lillian's eyes narrowed. "Yes."

"OK." He stared at her for a second before heading to the second floor.

"We might as we follow," Ted said.

Roger forced slow breaths in and out of his lungs as he tagged along with them up the stairs. Had it been a mistake bringing Lillian here? What could Bill suspect from one piece of luggage? He loosened his clenched fists, needing to act the part of the family friend.

At the top of the stairs, Ted turned left and stopped at the first door to the left. "This is our premier room, according to Trina. It's big and faces the back yard." Ted turned to Lillian and whispered, "She just likes it the best."

The walls had been painted warm blue, and the original oak floor, sanded and waxed to a shine, had been partially covered by an old wool rug. To the left stood a refurbished metal bed, floral paintings mounted in distressed white frames hung on the wall above the headboard. On the opposite side of the room, an armoire, tall and stiff, looked like a sentry stationed to guard the sleeper.

Lillian stood just inside the door. "It looks very comfortable," she finally said.

Bill placed the suitcase on the tapestry strips of the luggage rack at the foot of the bed.

"When you're settled, feel free to join us on the porch if you want." Ted looked around the room. "Do you need anything else?"

"I'm fine, thank you."

Roger positioned himself to leave the room last. As he glanced back, Lillian stood with eyes clenched, rivulets of water running down her cheeks. He had never seen her cry before. Indeed, he hadn't been sure she was capable. Tears signified weakness, his mother had always said, and he had learned early on to never cry. Not even when hidden in bed feeling very alone. Seeing Lillian's tears, he knew that she was as damaged as he.

He quietly closed the door and tried to clear from his mind the flicker of confusion between sympathy and hate. She may have been a victim as much as he, but no matter, the quicker he finished what he had to do, the sooner life could start over.

The pounding that had been hammering his chest ever since Lillian's arrival gradually slowed. Power surged through him like a swirling phantom, starting in his gut and working outward, until the sensation filled him. He closed his eyes, enjoying the invincibility that always came before a battle.

~*~

So far, Lillian's glorious arrival had turned out as anticipated, with the exception of her diminished persona. It was more than her gaunt appearance; her whole aura had dimmed.

Roger had expected her to remain the same, unchanged by loss and rejection. Two years ago, when she had made him feel small, anyone who could penetrate his well-hewn defenses had to be made of iron. He had forgotten that iron rusted.

Entering the kitchen, he looked toward the tray of cookies and sniffed. "Oatmeal raisin?"

Ted shrugged, not bothering to glance up as he poured tea from the gallon jug into the plastic pitcher. "It's the only kind Trina bakes anymore. She can't get enough of them."

The kitchen door opened. "Suits me fine," Bill said as he grabbed a cookie from the plate. "She seem strange to you?"

"Trina?" A stack of napkins dangled from Ted's hand as he stared at his father-in-law.

"Ms. Hunter."

"No, why?"

"There's something about her that's off."

Why would Bill think Lillian strange? The big man hadn't known her when she had been the ice princess. True, Bill had a way of seeing through people, understanding the whole picture when everyone else was still trying to figure out the problem, but surely not even Bill could deduce who had brought Lillian to Darlington. "Off, like how?" Roger finally asked.

"Her suitcase, to start with."

"What's wrong with her suitcase?"

Black, small, but too big to use as a carry-on. Nothing special about it. Certainly nothing that raised an alarm in his mind.

"*One* suitcase." Bill wiped crumbs from his hands on his pants and glanced at Ted. "When was the last time someone checked in with one suitcase?"

"Maybe she likes to travel light." Ted moved the napkins from the left to the right of the tray, his mouth pursed in thought.

"She's moving here." Bill leaned against the counter. "She should have more than one suitcase." Bill reached for another cookie.

Ted pulled the tray away. "Save some for our guest."

"You get more like Trina every day," Bill mumbled as he snatched a cookie and shoved it into his mouth. "And what about this job?" Crumbs spewed and he grabbed a napkin. "Doesn't she need books and things?"

Roger glanced from man to man, following the conversation but hesitant to add to it. He had heard stories of Bill's spiritual gift: the man's ability to feel things that others couldn't. According to Trina, God had even sent Bill a vision.

Roger hesitated to disregard the man's abilities.

Regardless of where the knowledge came from, Bill knew things, and Roger's already thin nerves frayed even more.

"You're too used to Trina and all her plunder." Ted stood back and examined his work. "Most likely, Ms. Hunter has her things stored somewhere and she'll get them when she's ready. Or maybe she shipped them." Ted picked up the loaded tray and headed toward the hall. "You guys coming?"

Bill snickered. "You forgot your frilly apron, Ted."

Roger hesitated. Should he go home or wait to see if Lillian would appear on the porch? His muscles sagged as the familiar emptiness settled over him. He had not always worn the invisible black cloak. Oh, he had never been like Ted, favored by God Himself, but there had been a time when he had lived in the light. Now, forced into a life of someone else's creation, he slunk from one dark day to the next.

He knew exactly when he had changed from man to monster. The first time he had said yes, the dark beast had taken up residence in the deepest chambers of his heart. And whenever he had said yes after that, the beast had grown, and the light had faded, until he had lost control of his own destiny.

And now, another partnership. He hated this person more than he had ever hated anyone in his life. More than his mother and her string of boyfriends. More than the juvenile system that failed to protect him. More than a lot of things. And yet the partnership defined his life right now. Was the monster inside him a demon going along for the ride, or simply a figure of his own imagination? It didn't matter.

Lillian remained his only hope to forever be free from its grip.

5

Alone in the room, Lillian wiped her wet face with her hands. Although trained to cautiously make first impressions, several issues nagged at her exhausted brain.

Ted was a dear, and the bed and breakfast appeared to be more than adequate. But the other two men bothered her.

Too tired to think, she fell onto the bed. The soft spread nestled against her, and she closed her eyes, enjoying the comfort. As she relaxed, a smile creased her face.

The room smelled of sunshine. She tried to push the thought aside. After all, what does warmth and light and comfort smell like, anyway? Even though it would never stand up in court, she knew sunshine smelled just like this room. Her mind created scenes of living in the sunshine.

Perhaps moving would turn out to be the best thing. Leave behind the triggers of memories that haunted her. Not that Craig or Susan would ever be far from her mind, but she had to learn to live in a way that their lives were part of her, but didn't control her.

With renewed energy, she climbed from the bed. It took less than five minutes to unpack clothing and distribute the few possessions which included putting her Bible on the nightstand and her toothbrush in the bathroom. She picked up the Bible. The traditional black cover and gilded pages already showed signs of wear. Pressing the book to her heart, she closed her eyes. *Thank You, God. Thank You for this sanctuary and for what is to come.*

By pushing the empty suitcase under the bed, she planted her first roots in Darlington. No one but God could have brought her to this place. The doubt crept around her skull, but she refused it's admittance to her mind. Tired, but ready for her new life to begin, she changed out of her travel-weary clothes into a fresh pair of jeans and a sweater, washed her face, and headed back downstairs.

~*~

Gospel music from the square created eddies of sound within the silence that had settled on the porch. Nature seemed to be waiting, holding its breath, as night descended on the town.

Ted continued to scan the street, the weary sound of his sigh melting with the restless breath of the trees.

Roger and Ted were so different. He thought about his life, not so much the growing-up years, even though they had held their challenges, but more the adult years, the years after he had married Carla.

Ted would never have adjusted to Carla's family, but then, few men would. To be honest, in spite of the success, he felt little pride over his past. But all of the reasons for those decisions were gone, and with the elimination of Lillian, he would be free.

Perhaps it was the twilight that caused him to be melancholic as his mind continued to wander. What if fate had switched him and Ted at birth? Would Ted still be a man of faith, or would life have forged bitterness? Maybe in his next life he would be the good Christian man. He chuckled inwardly. Not much chance of that.

Ted poured a glass of iced tea and drained the contents, continually staring at the darkening street.

A car drove by, headlights on.

Silence continued.

He glanced at the front door. Would she come down, or was he waiting on the porch for nothing? A breeze, trapped in the branches, shifted the leaves on the oak tree. Their rustle sounded like the water in his shower. A single bee, late in heading home for the night and not deterred by the overhead fans, buzzed toward the cookies.

Ted absently swatted at the pest, and it flew off, perhaps hunting for an easier meal.

The music changed from Gospel to country.

"We need to watch her," Bill murmured.

"Who?" Ted asked, still focusing on the road.

"Ms. Hunter."

"Did I hear my name?"

By instinct, he balled his hands into fists as he reverted back to the basic stage of survival. His primal mind prodded him to leap from the swing and grip her throat. Not here. Not now. The air thickened and he glanced at Bill, but the big man was staring at Lillian.

If Bill noticed the change, he gave nothing away.

Ted pointed to the vacant wicker chair. "Do you want some sweet tea?"

"That would be nice, thank you."

"He has cookies, too," Bill stated. "Oatmeal raisin. That's all we get anymore."

Ted handed the plate of cookies to Lillian. "They're my wife's favorite right now.

The jeans and soft gray sweater complemented her coloring. Almost mesmerized, Roger reminded himself that her softness and vulnerability were illusions. Scenarios he had planned for the next few days spun through his head like a flip chart, each on its own page.

"So what brings you to Darlington?" Bill questioned.

Roger tensed. Could she share anything that would feed Bill's curiosity? "Give the lady some space."

"What?" Bill raised his eyebrows. "Ted and Trina came for a visit and never left. I'm here because of them. You came for a job. I just wondered what drew her here."

"A position became available at Frances Marion University," Lillian explained, "and I needed a place to stay until I decided where I wanted to live." She took a sip of tea. "A packet of marketing material about Darlington came in the mail, and it included a flyer advertising this bed and breakfast. It sounded homey and wasn't that far from the university." Sadness pulled at her face. "I guess I'm not ready to give up hearth and home for a sterile hotel."

"You got one of our flyers?" Ted's eyebrows lifted. "Who sent it?"

Roger ran his fingers down his beard. "I think the county sends them out now and then. I got one at the office. I'm surprised you didn't get one, Ted."

Bill's eyes narrowed as he turned to Roger. "So why did Miss Hunter get one?"

"The county buys mailing lists of professionals from the different states. Most likely all the lawyers in Ohio got one." He had happened on this information by accident when the county commissioners requested he solicit properties from absentee homeowners.

Bill's eyes seemed to penetrate through Roger's skull.

Roger breathed easier when the man turned to Lillian.

"So what did you do in Cleveland?"

"I was an attorney."

"So you're doing legal work for the university?"

"No, I thought I'd try my hand at academics." Her eyes remained fixed on Bill. "One of the faculty members resigned in the middle of the semester and Francis Marion needed someone to finish the courses and continue to teach political science."

Conversation died, and the night sounds, like white noise, lulled them into a relaxed stupor, or so it seemed.

Without an outlet for the adrenalin still zipping through his veins, Roger's attention bounced like a rubber ball out of control.

The squirrels were gone, probably in their nests for the night. Barely visible in the deepening dusk, an elderly couple, hand in hand, strolled down the sidewalk, their feet making soft patting sounds on the concrete.

The swing, dare he plant his feet and stop the nausea that was welling up inside him?

Two golf carts rolled by, carrying what looked like families, their voices and laughter cutting the silence as efficiently as the headlights split the darkness.

He rolled his shoulders, hoping to reduce the tension that had settled across his back. He needed to relax and trust his preparation, the long months of selecting and choosing and rejecting and molding, until all the pieces fit just like the thousand-piece jigsaw puzzles Trina always had in process at their Friday night get-togethers. What if he failed? His mouth tightened. Failure would mean death.

"I noticed when I drove through town that there are still roses blooming," Lillian murmured from across the porch, her image fuzzy in the fading light.

Ted chuckled. "That's part of the culture shock when you move from the north to the south. There's something growing year-round. Wait until you go to the grocery store; you'll really know you're in the south when you get to the meat section and see pig snouts and chicken feet."

A faint smile creased her face as she took another sip of tea.

"You see anything interesting on the way down?" Roger asked, trying to avoid any further discussion of her reason for coming south.

"That's a stupid question," Bill said.

"Just trying to lighten the mood."

"There's nothing wrong with the mood. What's up with you, anyway? You're as jittery as an old lady."

A red SUV pulled into the drive.

"Trina's home!" Ted jumped from his chair as the car disappeared behind the house. "Trina does a much better job of making guests feel at home."

"If I were any more comfortable," Lillian said, her head resting against the cushion, "I would fall asleep right here."

As footsteps approached from inside the house, Ted opened the front door.

"Why are you guys sitting in the dark?" The overhead light snapped on and Trina waddled onto the porch.

Lillian gasped. Her ivory face turning ashen as her

eyes widened.

He tightened his grip on the swing. Why had he not anticipated this? His partner should have known. Were months of work ruined?

"I'm sorry," Lillian mumbled as she made a wide circle around Trina and stumbled into the house. The sound of her footsteps ran up the stairs, followed by the bang of a door.

"I told you there was something strange about her," Bill mumbled, pushing the swing back and forth. "She has secrets, and they're weighing her down."

For the first time, Roger wondered what Lillian had been doing for the past two years while he had been busy planning her death. Was there more at stake than he knew?

He made his excuses and left. Things had suddenly become complicated.

~*~

Lillian's behavior hung heavy on Trina and Ted's minds, but they hadn't talked about it. Shocked glances passed between them had sufficed.

Even when the three of them had moved to the parlor, and the news on the television had dragged on, no one had mentioned their new guest and her unexpected behavior.

Looking back, Bill could see that the whole day felt strange, as though something was not quite in synch. When had it started? God had gifted him with the ability to pick out vibrations in the environment that others might miss, little nuances, perhaps changes in molecular chemistry of the air around him, who knew? Something had been different today, and most obvious had been Lillian, especially her behavior when Trina got home. Finally, he broached the subject. "So what are you going to do about her?" he asked, resting back on the leather recliner.

Trina sat in the middle of the floor encircled by gift bags decorated with bears and blocks, white boxes laying open, revealing green and yellow sleepers, blankets, and packs of diapers. She glanced at her father, and then returned to the task of feeling, sorting and re-sorting the piles.

"She seemed fine until she saw Trina." Ted's brows knit together. "Babe, have you ever met her before?"

"What?"

"Have you ever met Lillian before? She seemed surprised to see you."

"Not that I remember. I mean, in Ohio we only lived sixty miles apart, but she didn't look familiar to me."

Bill had hoped they might come to the same conclusion he had. "Maybe it wasn't your face that upset her."

"What else could it be? My big belly?" Trina chuckled and patted her round abdomen.

Bill shrugged his shoulders. "It seemed that way to me."

"What do you mean?" Ted asked. "Lillian's upset because Trina's pregnant?"

"Look, guys," Trina said as she grabbed the edge of the sofa and struggled to her feet, "I don't want to second-guess her behavior. She'll explain in the morning."

"You have to admit, it was strange," Bill said.

Ted turned to his father-in-law. "You don't think

she's dangerous, do you?"

"Enough, you guys! The poor thing had a long drive."

"I suppose Paul didn't help," Ted added.

"Did Paul stop by?"

Bill chuckled. "Better than that. He escorted her here, lights flashing, the whole works. Said she needed help to find the place because of the festival."

"Oh, no! What was he thinking?" Trina shook her head. "Poor Paul. I'm surprised he hasn't called to make sure she got into the house without his help."

"Speaking of phone calls, Bill, did your sister call?"

"Oh, Dad, I forgot. Today was your open house!"

Bill shifted in the recliner. He had hoped they would forget. "Betsy called. Four or five couples went through the place."

"That's good," Trina said.

Ted stared at his father-in-law. "You don't look too excited."

Trina lowered herself onto the couch beside Ted. "You know you don't have to sell the place."

"I can't live here and maintain an empty house in Ohio."

Trina pursed her mouth into a soft frown. "That's what I mean. I love having you here, but you don't have to stay if you'd rather go back home. This is my life, and Ted's life, but we understand it may not be yours."

He stared into Trina's huge eyes. The depth of love he found there had sustained him through so many bad days. And now, with his growing relationship with Ted, and a grandchild on the way, he had fewer bad days. "I can't think of anywhere I would rather be right now than here. Besides, who'll teach my grandson to play football?"

"What if it's a girl?" Trina asked. "Besides...I thought there might be another reason you were hanging around."

"I'm going to bed." He pushed himself out of the recliner.

"Come on Dad, I know you like Sandra. She's a great woman."

Trina deserved an answer; she was his daughter. Sighing deeply, he wished he could purge himself of all the confusion that rambled around in his mind as easily as he pushed out the air held within him. "Sandra's a great woman, one of the best I've had the privilege of knowing, next to your mother."

"But...?" Trina asked.

"I'm not ready to make another commitment. I'm not sure I ever will be." He walked from the room, his heavy footsteps echoing in the hall as he headed toward the stairs.

"Dad!"

He kept walking; the discussion was over but their words filtered to him.

"Let it go, Babe."

"But Ted..."

"Give him some space. He'll make the right decision in his own time."

There had been one offer on the house already, and he had turned it down. True, it had not been a great offer, but the mortgage had been paid off for years. The problem wasn't money, but sentiment. The house was all he had left of his life with Nancy. They had bought the house together. Raised Trina as a couple until Nancy died. So many memories. And his commitment to one woman. How could he explain to Trina that even after fifteen years the commitment to a dead wife remained strong?

But his future had to compete for synaptic brain time with a new threat: this strange woman, Lillian Hunter. He rubbed his arms, trying to scrape off some of the tension. As the evening had progressed, like an electrical charge before a storm, the tension had grown. What was God trying to tell him?

He passed the room assigned to Lillian and hesitated. Not a sound penetrated through the door. Should he knock and check on her? What had been written on her face when Trina appeared? Shock? Pain?

The thought drifted into his mind as gently as a mother's touch, but it left him rocking as though punched. Would they find Lillian Hunter dead in the morning?

Then he knew. That's what he had been feeling all day. Death.

6

After Lillian had escaped from the porch, she had waited, expecting Ted to pound on the door of Trina's favorite room and demand that she leave. No one had come, and as the darkness outside had deepened, she had heard footsteps enter the house.

Voices, mumbled and indistinct, had flowed under her door like wisps of smoke.

Numbness had covered her in its cocoon, and eventually sleep had overtaken her.

Now, early morning sun dappled patterns on the walls, leafy, lacy designs that shifted from stout to elongated with the bend of the limbs outside the window. She blinked in the brightness. The warmth of the rays battled with her mood.

God, why here? You know how far I've come to regain my life. I shared secrets with You that I keep locked in the darkest corner of my heart. My arms ache from emptiness. The pain feels like parts of me are being ripped off my body each time I see small children. Or pregnant women, their joy just beginning. You should have stopped me...

She rolled away from the window, and tears escaped through her clenched eyes. A guttural moan rose from her throat as she pushed her face into the bedding and wrapped the edges of the pillow around her head, muffling her pain from any listening ears.

With tears purged, she dragged unsteady hands

across her wet cheeks and reached blindly toward the nightstand. Breath caught in her throat as her fingertips touched wood. Launching upright in bed, she stared at the table with its small Big Ben clock and antique lamp. The Bible that she had laid there was gone.

The suitcase stood open against the wall and she collapsed back onto the bed, sighing in relief. Last night, in her anger, she had tossed all her possessions into the suitcase before throwing herself on the bed in tears.

The Bible found, but lacking the strength to cross the room to retrieve it, she rolled onto her back. Her eyes kept dropping closed. Perhaps it was the lack of sleep, or the long drive that made her unusually tired. Or the task that lay before her.

The homeowners deserved an explanation. Did she have the physical or emotional energy to share the truth with strangers? And what was the truth? Had God let her down? She had not doubted His love during the months of agony after Craig's and Susan's deaths, so why the prickling doubt now? Craig would tell her to trust, but it was so hard...

Eventually she had to go downstairs and confront the woman and her swollen belly. Dr. Widder had predicted correctly; her behavior in the past twenty-four hours had been erratic. First, the incident at the rest area, then her childish enjoyment over the handsome patrolman, and finally her reaction to the homeowner, pregnant and glowing.

She had to leave the McIverson Bed and Breakfast.

With dragging feet, she headed to the bathroom. As the water from the shower pulsed against her back, she again considered how to explain her actions. There was no excuse for her poor behavior except the truth, and she refused to dig that deeply into her shame with strangers.

Standing in front of the mirror, she examined her beige slacks and hunter-green silk blouse. Folds of fabric that her body once had filled sagged around her. As she patted the loose material, hoping to minimize the gaps, strawberry blonde curls, still damp from the shower, sprang around her face. She shoved part of the unruly hair behind her ear, knowing the effort was futile; the curls would eventually form childish ringlets around her face.

Now, she needed to settle the bill and put this behind her. She tossed her brush into the suitcase, closed the zipper, and grabbed her checkbook. Standing tall, she took one last look around the room that had been home for twelve hours. It would have been the perfect place to start a new life. *God, if You're still listening to me, help me through this day.*

Clenching her jaw, she descended the stairs.

Guided by voices, she stood at the kitchen door.

The morning sun streamed through the large window, filling the kitchen with light. To the left, Ted and Bill sat on opposite sides of an oak harvest table, while Trina worked across the kitchen at the counter, her back to the men. Plates were stacked in the middle of the table, glasses and juice on the near end, and a basket with silverware and napkins on the other. Bill and Ted clutched mugs in their hands.

The scent of eggs and sausage taunted Lillian's empty stomach.

"Dad, it's chicken salad today for your lunch," Trina said. "Hope that's OK."

"Sounds great, honey."

Digging for her determined spirit, that legendary streak of stubbornness that she could always count on during hard situations, Lillian found only an empty hole. Here she was, in the south, starting her new life, and already giving up after the first uncomfortable situation.

When Trina turned and locked gazes with her, she tightened her spine, ready for whatever came next. Would the woman offer a piece of her mind on a breakfast platter? Or maybe her style was more the famed southern hospitality, and she would stoically perform her duties as hostess.

Sweat dampened Lillian's underarms. *Be polite.*

Trina's face broke into a smile "Lillian, I didn't hear you come down. Come. Join us, unless you would rather eat in the dining room. Since you're alone, I thought maybe you would prefer company."

Definitely southern hospitality.

Ted pulled out the chair at the end of the table. His smile was welcoming, not like the daggers she had expected.

What kind of people let one insult them at night, and then shared their food the next morning? Maybe her hostess had mixed arsenic in the muffins...or some of those chocolate laxative wafers. She had heard of a person doctoring a birthday cake, and all the guests ended up with diarrhea.

Three pair of eyes stared at her.

"I'll just grab something in town."

"Nonsense." Trina put her hands on her hips. "You're paying for a bed *and* a breakfast, so have a seat." A huge grin followed the command.

Hesitantly, Lillian walked toward the chair Ted had pulled out. Even though all her instincts told her to leave, she sat. Whatever the agenda, at least she wasn't being greeted with the flat side of a frying pan. But anything with chocolate, no matter how good it looked, was off-limits.

Icy fingers went up her back as Bill sipped his coffee and stared at her. With his blank expression, it was impossible to read his thoughts. Was he preparing to drag her out of the room if she misbehaved?

Her throat tightened. This was a mistake.

"Did you sleep all right?" Trina wiped her hands on a towel. "I worried after you..."

Her chest heaved, almost filling out the silk blouse. The dreaded time had come. "I apologize—"

"It's all right," Trina replied, her eyes softening.

How dare she minimize my behavior? I know when I'm out of line. Is she trying to replace my parents as the boss of my life? When will people let me own my feelings? She gritted her teeth. "No, it isn't. I behaved poorly." She worked her fingers against the wood of the table, trying to keep her anger in check. "It won't happen again."

Trina's hand rested on her arm. The woman's touch felt soft and gentle, like Beth's. "I understand, and it *is* all right. Now, what would you like for breakfast?"

Ted cleared his throat. "I recommend the egg casserole."

Bill's eyes burned against her face. Even though Trina had said to forget the incident, Bill didn't seem as willing.

"What can I get you to drink?" Trina asked. "I have coffee ready, but if you prefer, I can make you hot chocolate."

"No chocolate!" The words spat out with more

force than she had intended. "Coffee is fine. Where are the cups?" she asked, rising from her chair. "I can help myself and save you a few steps." *And keep you from adding arsenic.*

Trina's face morphed into mock horror. "You're our guest! You can't work!"

"I don't like being waited on."

As Trina handed her a hot cup of coffee, Lillian forced herself to glance at the woman's belly—the bump that had sent her spinning out of control the night before. She swallowed hard. "When is your baby due?"

Trina patted her stomach. "Not for three more months. January 17th actually."

"My birthday," Bill mumbled, a hint of a smile cracking his taciturn expression.

"Do you know if it's a boy or girl?"

"Yes, it's a boy or a girl," Ted said, grinning.

"That's Ted's favorite reply when someone asks," Trina said. "We decided we didn't want to know until the birth."

"You two decided," Bill said. "No one asked my opinion."

"It's *our* baby, Dad," Trina placed a tile trivet decorated with a strutting rooster in the center of the table.

Bill stared at his coffee cup. "One day you may find that envelope missing."

Trina turned to Lillian. "Our doctor wrote the gender of the baby on a piece of paper and sealed it in an envelope in case we changed our minds. Ted taped it to the mirror in our bedroom."

"And now I have to stare at it every day." Bill drained his cup. "You could at least have hidden the thing."

"And just how many times in a day are you in my bedroom?" Trina scrunched her face in thought. "Hmm…none!"

Ted glanced at the timer on the stove. "I hope you're not in a hurry."

"I don't have to be at the university until 9:00."

Trina giggled. "I love the sound of your Ohio voice."

"I was just thinking the same about you." Lillian gazed at the pregnant woman who radiated warmth and acceptance. Under different circumstances, they could have been friends.

"We've only been in the south seven months, so we still sound northern," Trina continued, "but wait until you hear Sandra's accent! She's a native, and our landlady. We're renting the house and running the bed and breakfast. Actually, the house partially belongs to us, but it's a long story." Trina was definitely a morning person.

The timer buzzed.

Ted untangled his legs and grabbed the strawberry-patterned pot holders. "Mmm. Smells good."

Trina placed wrapped sandwiches into a brown paper bag and moved the bag to the end of the counter before sitting beside her husband. "I love starting our day together," she said, taking Ted's hand and reaching across the table for her father's. "These men are my whole life, and soon there will be the baby."

"Let's pray," Bill said.

Ted held out a hand to Lillian and Bill took the other. Not one to rely on emotions to get through a day, she wasn't sure what to do with this sudden immersion in warm-fuzzy. She had just met these people, and yet the goodwill they shared was feeding a hunger she didn't realize she had. A praying family. Just what she needed. Except...

Confusion swirled like a dust storm in her head. What was happening here? It went beyond forgiveness, but she couldn't define it. Trina and Ted seemed to care about her, and they didn't know her family lineage, her income, or her social position. She felt puny, having resented Trina for the blessing she carried in her womb. *God, please forgive me, but give me strength.*

"Lord, bless this food, and the day before us. Help us to use our talents to honor You...and be with our guest. In Jesus's name, amen."

Ted shoveled a hot bite of egg, potato, and sausage casserole into his mouth. "I love it when you fix this for breakfast."

"I know, but you had better learn to make it." She patted her protruding belly.

Bill, forking in mouthfuls of casserole, glanced at Trina. "I told you I'd take over kitchen duties for awhile after the baby's born."

"Actually I was joking; neither of you have to cook. Sandra's already offered to help out."

Who was this Sandra and why the covert looks? Maybe Bill disliked Sandra, too, or maybe he had an issue with women in general. Lillian sighed. It really didn't matter since this would be her last breakfast at the house.

"Sandra's going to be here a lot after the baby's born," Trina mumbled behind a mouthful of egg.

"She practically lives here now," Bill retorted.

"She does not," Trina said, laughing. "Besides, you

like it when she's here."

Bill carried his dishes to the sink. "I've got to get to work. Rowdy students wait for no man. Welcome, Ms. Hunter. Have a good first day of work."

"Dad teaches at the Darlington Career Center," Trina explained as Bill grabbed the bulging sack off the counter and headed out the back door.

"I need to get busy too." Ted kissed his wife on the cheek and cleared his part of the table. "I'll be in the workshop if you need me. And Miss Hunter, welcome to our Bed and Breakfast. I hope you'll be comfortable here."

"Actually, I—" The back door slammed a second time, cutting off her words. She stared at the closed door. "Do they always leave like that?"

"Umm." Trina wiped a piece of cheese from her lip. "Dad seemed to be in a bit of a hurry, but usually mornings move fast around here."

Lillian picked at her casserole, knowing she had to share her intent to leave, and yet, for some reason, not feeling ready to sever the unexpected welcome.

"Would you like some orange juice?"

"I'm fine, thank you."

"I hope you like the casserole." Trina eyed the half-eaten serving on Lillian's plate. "I can fix muffins if you prefer. There's still time before you have to leave. The men, they like a heartier breakfast, but I often make something different for our guests. And since you're our only guest right now..."

"I'm generally not much of a breakfast eater, but this casserole is wonderful." She placed another forkful into her mouth.

"So you start work today?" Trina shifted her body in the chair. "Too bad you couldn't have a day or two to get settled first."

"I really don't have much to settle, and I won't be—"

"Dad noticed."

The words hit Lillian like a fisted punch. Bill had been scrutinizing her, but what had he noticed? She tried to reconstruct their conversations, both last night and at the breakfast table. What had they talked about? The way he had looked at her when he thought she wasn't watching had made her nervous. But he had been pleasant enough.

She had made the right decision to move on.

"He was surprised that you only had one suitcase. Most of our guests come with enough stuff to last a year."

That was all? Her suitcase?

Trina placed her hands on the table and pushed off the chair. "Want more coffee?"

"No, thank you. But I need to tell you that—"

"Have we met before?" The young woman stood in the middle of the kitchen, coffee apparently forgotten.

"No, why?"

"I just thought, well, you know, you were surprised last night when you saw me, and I thought maybe…"

Trina didn't realize that it was her pregnancy, not the woman herself that had sent her running from the porch.

Taking a long slow breath, her jaw tightening, Lillian planned her words. "I really am sorry about last night. I know I shouldn't offer excuses, but it had been a very long day, then to be led into town with a police escort—"

"That Paul, always trying to help, and most of the time he makes things worse." Trina's face brightened as she sat in Ted's vacated chair. "He really is the nicest guy you'll ever meet, but he has this thing about men-folk being responsible for women-folk. Sometimes it drives me nuts."

As Trina talked, the fabric on the woman's shirt moved, and memories resurrected from a time when life had grown within her, too. And holding Susan for the first time with Craig snuggled close beside her. Baby baths and smoothing lotion on tender skin. Watching as Susan took her first steps, the first time she used the potty…a small casket beside a larger one.

The smell of smoke everywhere. Numbness. Meaningless platitudes from well-meaning friends. And before the pain could settle, the police investigation started. There had been no time to grieve.

She stared at the face across the table and felt an acceptance that had been missing in her life for two years. Before she could stop them, the words flowed. "I lost my child." Tears blurred her vision. "She was two years old."

Trina's eyes grew round as she clutched her hands to her chest. "That must have been awful. I can't even imagine."

Lillian felt Trina's hand clutch hers and she became rigid. Hesitantly, she wrapped her fingers around the other woman's, feeling strength bind them in a strange union.

"You don't need to say another word. It would be hard for me to look at a pregnant woman if I lost my unborn baby, but to lose a child…will you be OK staying here, or do you want me to help you find another place?" Trina's eyes became hazel pools of compassion.

This was her way out as well as the smart thing to do, not only because of the pregnancy, but also because of Bill's strange reaction to her. Trina had just provided the opportunity to gracefully escape.

But the words remained fixed in the back of her throat, caught on a tonsil she didn't even have. All she could do was focus on their hands clutched together across the table.

One summer before fourth grade, she and her best friend, Karen, had each picked off a scab and rubbed the open wounds together, proclaiming them blood sisters. The sisterhood had lasted all summer, but once school started, and they ended up in different classes, the pact was forgotten. Neither thought about the bond they had cemented that June.

Whatever was happening now felt similar and yet different. Certainly, the connection had not been there when Lillian had walked down the stairs an hour ago. Earlier she had prayed for God's strength for the day. Was God even still there for her? If so, why had He guided her to South Carolina to live with a pregnant woman? Could this be His way of helping her heal? Staying at the McIverson Bed and Breakfast had seemed a matter of convenience, but now she wasn't sure. But she knew what she needed to do. "I want to stay."

As soon as the words were spoken, thorns of doubt dug into her skin. She thought about Bill, and how he seemed to scrutinize her. What did she know about him, or this family? Maybe the room had been wearing its best garments, wooing her, waiting, needing her to stay for its own agenda. She tried to shake off the sense of "something else," but the feeling of oppression remained. It made no sense, but it chilled her none the less.

She had to rely on being within God's will, but was she?

7

"Dr. Hunter, we are so happy that you can join the faculty on such short notice."

Lillian accepted the outstretched hand of Dr. Gilbert Roman. "Unless it is protocol, please call me Lillian." The man towered over her like a rugged lumberjack, whiskers, red hair and all.

"Lillian, it is. You'll meet the rest of the team this afternoon at the faculty meeting, but how about I give you a tour of the building and show you your office? I know President Carter wants to meet with you this morning, and we won't want you to be late for that!"

"The university isn't very old," Lillian said, examining the carpeted hall and spacious classrooms, mostly filled with students.

"It was opened in the 1970s, and has grown tremendously since then. I think you will enjoy it here, if you like academics. Actually, this is one of the original buildings." His brow puckered. "I know Hazel..."

"She was the professor who died?"

"Actually, she was found dead by one of the students."

Her heart lurched in her chest. "That must have been awful for the student."

"It wasn't too easy for the staff either. But lest I become morbid, let me show you the faculty lounge where you can make coffee or eat lunch, whatever."

They toured all two levels and finally ended at what was to become her office. A placard with "Dr. Lillian Hunter" on the side of the door already identified the room as hers.

Dr. Roman opened the door and she grimaced as the smell of disinfectant burned her nose. Dr. Roman didn't seem to notice. One more thing to deal with, but the smell would lessen as soon as the room had a chance to air out. A long narrow window allowed in natural light. To the right sat a large desk with phone and computer, flanked by a filing cabinet. On the left wall, the floor-to-ceiling shelves were three quarters filled with books.

She ran her fingers along the spines.

"Hazel's family donated her books, so we left them here for you. If you decide you don't want them, they can be removed."

"Thank you. I'm sure they will be useful." She didn't bother to tell him she had come without a laptop, without a lecture note, and without a single book except her Bible.

After glancing at his watch, Dr. Roman moved toward the door. "I don't want to rush you, but here are the keys to the building and your office. Your appointment with Dr. Carter is in ten minutes. I'll walk you over."

After meeting with Dr. Carter, she was guided to Personnel. From there she found her way to the book store and the cafeteria. Students filled most of the tables in the three large dining rooms. After finding an empty seat, she picked at her chicken and something the server had called "greens." Students filtered in, some reading between bites, others catching up on last night's events. Had she ever been that young? That carefree? She glanced at her watch; she had just enough time to drop off her bookstore purchases before the faculty meeting at 1:00.

Outside, the quietness seemed profound after the clank of dishes and loud voices. Surrounded by shrubs, oak trees and loblolly pines and looking more park-like than a college campus, the path back to Founders Hall wound around quiet nooks, a few occupied by students deep in conversation, others talking on cell phones.

Small gray squirrels gathered acorns from the plethora that lay scattered among pine needles and leaves. The air smelled clean, fresh with hints of a floral scent.

Being outside was wonderful. Even though the start had been rough, an exciting thrill ran through Lillian. She could rise above the difficulties of staying in the home of a pregnant woman whose father hated her, the discovery that her predecessor had been murdered, and the stench of her office. Her smile broadened and her pulse quickened. She could do this.

At Founders Hall, she took the stairs to the second floor. A few students passed, carrying backpacks slung over shoulders, water bottles dangling from their hands. Pushing open the office door until it hit the back wall, she steeled herself for the sanitized smell. Swallowing against the gag, she unpacked the mug, zip drive, and a card she had purchased for Beth, each item gracing the barren desktop.

A soft knock sounded on the door. "Dr. Hunter?"

"Agnes Brown, isn't it? Please call me Lillian."

The middle aged woman fanned her hand in front of her face as she stepped into the small room. "Whew, it still stinks in here. I told them we should keep this door open, but too many gawkers forced Dr. Roman to order it shut."

"Too many gawkers?"

"You know how morbid some people can be. And not just the students. We had plenty of faculty and staff members wander by, too."

Her muscles stiffened, knowing she didn't want to know what the department secretary would tell her.

"It's not every day someone gets murdered on campus. Everyone wanted to see the room where it was done, you know, kind of like folks staring at a car accident, hoping to see the gory aftermath."

Air caught in Lillian's throat as she tightened her grip on the back of the desk.

"Found strangled right there at that very desk." Agnes pursed her lips and shook her head. "Dr. Roman sent me to tell you the faculty meeting will be in room 115. Welcome. And if you need anything, let me know."

Another death. And in the room she had inherited. Those had been Hazel's books. Her desk. Lillian jumped from the chair and staggered away from the desk. As she stared, a woman appeared in the chair, scribbling notes on paper. The gray bun secured on the back of her head matched the gray rim of the glasses perched on her nose. As quickly as the image had come, it melted away. Gasping, she backed out the door.

Her mind had been playing tricks on her, but even so, she couldn't stop trembling as she headed toward the staff meeting. No wonder the office reeked of disinfectant.

Something bumped her from behind, and she jumped.

"Sorry," a girl mumbled, as she continuing to plow down the hall.

In a blink, it all became clear. She existed within an earthly nightmare created for those who deserved to be in purgatory when they died, but by grace would land in heaven.

Her terror was just beginning.

8

Roger played solitaire on his cell phone as he sat parked across the street from Takis, the local 1950s restaurant. He had followed Lillian from Francis Marion to the restaurant, and he knew she would leave there and go directly to the bed and breakfast. Over the past three days, she had not deviated from this pattern. He scratched his chin, digging under whiskers for the errant itch. Soon he could introduce himself again and extend the hand of friendship. By the weekend she should be getting lonely, ready for companionship in the evenings.

A police cruiser drove by, the nerdy Paul Studler behind the wheel. What kind of a name was Studler anyway? His jaw tightened. He couldn't afford for Lillian to turn to someone else for friendship. His plan depended on her trusting him, being willing to be alone with him.

The door of the restaurant opened and his heart thumped as she appeared. Fed and ready to go home, he knew which way she would turn. As she pulled onto the street, he pulled out four cars behind, safely hidden, a lion stalking his prey.

She turned between a fast food restaurant on one corner and a laundromat the other.

Two cars behind, Roger caught a red light. Not a problem; he knew where she was going. Oh, to be so predictable. Most people deviated very little day-today from a set routine. Lillian conformed just as he had expected. Even from this distance, the odor of cooking burgers made his stomach rumble. During an active chase, he never ate, but mindless work made him hungry.

Breaks squealed. Tires bit into the pavement. Lillian's car slammed to a stop. She jumped out and ran toward the front of the car. Headlights glared against her slim body.

He hissed out his frustration, squeezed his car out of the traffic, parked on the sandy shoulder, and sprinted across the fast food parking lot.

A ragged man sat on the road, illuminated in the headlight's glare.

"Talk to me, please! Are you all right?" Lillian's voice held a ragged edge as she knelt beside the man. "I didn't hit you, did I?"

He touched her shoulder and she spun around, eyes wide. "He walked out right in front of me!"

The driver behind Lillian's car sauntered their way.

A teen dressed in baggy jeans and a Clemson sweatshirt waved a cell phone. "Do you want me to call an ambulance?" A skinny girl gripped his other arm.

Roger swallowed against the hard knot in his throat. He didn't need complications. He had worked too hard to cover all the possible scenarios. If Lillian made friends, he would know about them. He would know where she went, and who she was with. Her world had to be his world. But now this.

"Let me handle him," he said, squeezing her shoulder, hoping to end the drama before the *News and Press* showed up, or, more likely, the police. He groaned, realizing Paul Studler was on duty.

Weathered skin conformed to the man's bones, like shrink-wrap to yesterday's leftovers, his whiskers standing out from his drawn face. Dressed in pants that might have been blue and a nondescript sweatshirt beneath a sweater with the front pocket hanging loose, the man looked as if he needed a trip to the laundromat, body and all. The more-than-one-day stench clashed with the aroma of the burgers. Roger knew this kind; he dealt with them all the time at the County Housing Office. A free-loader. Probably looking to earn a fast buck.

"Hey, buddy." He forced himself to sound friendly. "We need you to move to the sidewalk."

The man struggled to his feet.

Lillian grabbed his arm. "We'll call an ambulance."

"No." The man pushed against Lillian's hand. "Not hurt. Not hurt."

The teen, still holding the phone, shrugged his shoulders. The girl whispered in his ear, and they moved on.

"He's all right." Roger brushed his hands together and turned to Lillian, but her attention remained fixed on the man.

"I didn't even see you until I was almost on top of you." Lillian tightened her grip. "You need to go to the hospital."

"No hospital." The man tried to pull away.

Knots of people gathered on the sidewalk, their forms blending together in the darkness. Faces peered out of the brightly lit windows of the fast food restaurant across the street. From within, the animated bodies of the two teens reflected their version of the accident.

Roger groaned, knowing how stories grew. "Look, Lillian, he's fine. He says you didn't hit him, and it was his fault."

Roger put his arm around her shaking shoulders and tried to pull her to the side. They were running out of time before Paul Studler showed up, or worse, the press with their flashy camera. Her picture would appear on the front cover of the paper. People look through strangers, but tend to notice a familiar face. He needed Lillian to remain overlooked.

"You need to get home," Roger said through clenched teeth, turning his face from the huddled groups on the sidewalk. "I'll drive your car and then run back for mine later."

She ignored him.

He glanced around, searching for cameras, listening for the sound of a siren, frustrated at any attention.

"Where were you going?" she asked.

Head slumped, the man shuffled back and forth. "Pearl Street."

Roger blew a breath between pursed lips. "There's a homeless shelter on Pearl Street. He'll be fine there." They needed to get away, leave the chaos behind.

Lillian bent and peered into the man's face. "I'll take you." She pulled the stranger toward the car.

The homeless shelter was not Roger's destination of choice, but anyplace was better than sticking around here. After another glance around, he jumped into the driver's seat of her car and gagged. The man's last place of residence must have been the city dump.

"The shelter is in the old post office," Roger said as Lillian sat opposite him in the front. "About a year ago, after a newspaper story came out about finding a homeless man frozen to death on the square, the local churches set aside their theological differences and convinced the mayor to rent them the space."

Lillian stared ahead, her right foot tapping the floor.

Roger barely had time to stop the car before she jumped out.

"I'll take him in. He should be watched tonight for any medical problems—"

"There's nothing wrong with him, Lillian."

Narrow slits peered back at him.

Alarm dribbled into his body, like an intravenous flow, one deadly drop at a time. When had her strength returned?

She turned to the man. "Do you have a headache?"

Frustrated over her unwarranted concern, irritated because she spurned his help, and concerned from the resurrection of her past personality, Roger slammed the door behind him, rounded the car and leaped the half dozen cement steps to the door.

Already across the room, Lillian and a middle-aged woman, most likely one of the church ladies doing her good deed for the month, stood in conversation.

Roger stayed in the shadow of the door, not wanting to draw attention to himself any more than necessary. The old post office had been vacant since before he had arrived in Darlington, and he had never been inside. The fifteen-foot ceilings still wore their painted tin tiles, and two pillars stood about twelve feet apart, half way from the door to the back wall. Six pendant lights, probably original to the building, provided dim light, perfect for his purposes. The scent of supper made his mouth water. Whatever they were serving didn't smell like bologna sandwiches.

Bright light spilled through a door on the back wall. Only a corner of the room was visible, but that was enough to reveal long rows of tables and several men with their heads bent over plates of food. Lined up as they were, the men looked alike: losers with nowhere to go, burdens on a social system that encouraged misuse.

Normally meticulous about her appearance, Lillian had dark stains on the knees of her slacks. As she waved goodbye to the woman and moved toward the door, her footsteps staggered and she swayed.

If Roger had not been watching her, she would have hit the ground. Instead, he grabbed her around the waist and she slumped against him. He felt her heart beating against his chest, and she felt more real to him than at any other time.

Lillian pulled away, and wiped a hand across her forehead. "Thank you. I...I guess almost hitting a man upset me more than I thought." Her hazel eyes didn't waiver from his own.

With his sworn enemy recently clutched in his arms, and now with her expressing appreciation, both feelings of glee and of self-hatred comingled in his mind. Roger shook his head, trying to sift out the ambiguity.

Back in the car, the smell of the drifter remained. Would the stench ever fade from the upholstery?

She leaned her head back against the seat. "You don't know how glad I was to see you." Her hands shook as she adjusted the seat belt. "I'm thankful you were close by."

He remained focused on the road, grateful to

escape with little attention, but acutely aware of the woman at his side. How much of a risk would it be to drive her somewhere quiet, and end it now? Roger could be in the Pacific Riviera this time tomorrow.

"You must have been going somewhere," Lillian said, "and I interrupted your plans."

"Actually, I was headed home, sitting at the traffic light when I heard the brakes. I didn't realize it was you until I reached your car."

"You jump to the rescue of everyone?"

He felt the warmth of her eyes studying his face. "It must have been fate. You needed help and I showed up."

"Isn't this where we should turn?" Lillian asked.

"I thought I would take you somewhere quiet and give you time to settle your nerves before going to the bed and breakfast."

"No, really, I appreciate your help and all, but I want to go home."

The sharpness of her voice reminded him that she would not succumb to his plans quietly. His shoulders slumped as he turned toward Cashua Street.

A halogen light illuminated the yard behind the bed and breakfast. A tan SUV sat where Lillian usually parked her car. Apparently, a new guest had arrived.

Roger pulled into a spot farther from the house and escorted a shaking and rumpled Lillian through the kitchen door.

"Hey, Roger…" Ted's eyes widened.

"She had a run in with—"

Trina entered the kitchen. "I thought I heard your voice, Roger." Her expression turned to concern as she spied Lillian. "You're as white as a ghost. Do you want to lie down?" She wrapped an arm around Lillian's shoulders and guided her toward the parlor.

When Ted started to follow, Roger tapped the man's arm. Now would be a good time to plant a seed of doubt about the infamous attorney. A blot on Lillian's integrity would be invaluable later. He smirked behind shielded eyes. This might work out better. "Some bum jumped out in front of her car on Broad Street." He turned on the kitchen faucet. Hot water ran over his hands.

"No wonder she looks as if she's in shock. Is the man all right?

"He's fine, just playing her for sympathy." He meticulously soaped his hands, rinsed and finally pulled off a paper towel.

"Did you call Paul?"

He sniffed and tossed the damp towel into the waste basket. "No need to involve the police. The man wasn't hurt, but he did a good acting job for Lillian's sake." He pulled his face into tight lines as he looked at Ted. "You saw her; she's really shook up."

The women's voices flowed softly from the den.

"Lillian seems to have gotten over her fear of your wife."

"She explained the next morning. She had a child who died. Seeing Trina pregnant, and after the long trip and being tired...I guess she overreacted."

"And you buy that story?"

Ted stared at him. "Why shouldn't I?"

He shrugged his shoulders. "It just hits me as strange. She overreacts to seeing Trina, and now she overreacts to this guy jumping out in front of her. Like Bill said, 'something ain't right.'" He forced a laugh. "I commend you, brother, for opening your home like this. I don't think I could sleep at night if strangers were sleeping under my roof, and my wife was pregnant and all. But then, that's the business you're in, isn't it?"

Ted's eyebrows knit together. "Do you really think she'd hurt Trina?"

"Who, Lillian? Heck no. Don't listen to me. It's been a tough day." Roger turned and let himself out the back door, struggling to keep the spring from his step. The unexpected event had only helped him meet his goal. He had been there when she needed him, and he mentally patted himself on the back.

Now the next step, getting her alone.

9

Roger wiped a smudge of toothpaste from the corner of his mouth. Self-satisfaction oozed from his pores as he peered in the bathroom mirror. He had hit a home run last night with Lillian. Fate had thrown the man in front of her car. And as an added benefit to a glorious night, Ted had doubt growing in his gut. There was no one Ted loved more than his wife. And Bill already had questions about Lillian. Life couldn't be better.

He straightened his tie and imagined Ted finding excuses to be in the house rather than out in his shop when Lillian was home. And if Ted looked hard enough, he would find something suspicious about her.

What had Lillian told them after he left? Gloating, he imagined praise and gratitude for his rescue. As the coffee slowly leak into the carafe, he envisioned shielded glances directed toward Lillian as the men, over the rims of their cups, tried to catch a glimpse of her murderous heart.

Glancing at the clock, he gulped the hot coffee and placed his cup in the dishwasher. Why not visit Ted and Trina before heading to work? He locked the door behind him.

The barb of guilt, still shiny in its newness, snagged his conscious. Clenching his jaw, he focused on the goal. Justice must be served, and sometimes the innocent had to play a role. Anger bubbled to the surface as he gripped the steering wheel, and he embraced the familiar feeling. No one deserved a second chance more than he. He dwelled on the anger, massaged it, and rolled it in his mind like putty to be shaped and formed at will. And as though having a will of its own, the anger seeped into his veins and coalesced in his heart, where it fed the darkness.

He parked his car along the curb a block from the bed and breakfast and watched until Lillian pulled out of the drive and headed toward Pocket Road, her chosen route to the university. He didn't want to see her; the information he sought was best coming from the couple themselves. Too bad Bill had already left for work.

As he walked through the back door, Trina entered the kitchen carrying an empty tray. "Hey, Roger."

Ted, mouth full, nodded a welcome.

"More guests?" Roger asked.

"Came yesterday. Nice couple from Texas." Trina placed the tray by the sink and lowered herself into a chair at the table.

The space seemed changed, different somehow.

Instantly on alert, he stiffened but quickly realized he had never been to the house in the morning. The early sun streamed by the red gingham curtains and highlighted the room. In the natural light, the fresh paint on the old cupboards gleamed. The original wood floor glowed with mellow age.

The tension drained from him, replaced with a homey sense of comfort. He could live in a room like this. He slammed his mind against the sentimentality. What was wrong with him lately?

"Want a banana muffin?" Trina asked. "Coffee's on the counter."

The muffins smelled good. Maybe that had been part of his gut reaction to the room. "I don't wake up to home bakes like this at my house," he said, settling at the table.

"Whose fault is that?" Trina asked. "The way I see it, you have two choices: get up earlier and do some cooking, or find yourself a wife."

"Or I could just stop here," He forced his best smile.

"So, that's why you stopped?" Ted asked. "You smelled muffins half way across town?"

"No, actually I came to check on Lillian." He looked around as though hunting for the woman. Voices filtered from the dining room and he stared that direction even though he knew she had eaten her breakfast at the family table, not with the guests.

"You just missed her," Ted stated. "She left for work about five minutes ago, but she seemed back to normal."

Trina handed Roger a muffin, and he chewed slowly. Ted got lucky with Trina; she could cook. He took a second bite. "She was still shaking when I dropped her off last night. In the car she kept saying how grateful she was…" He took an intentional sip of coffee.

"Poor thing, she's had a really bad start in the south," Trina said. "Did you know the professor she's replacing was murdered right in her office—the one Lillian has now?"

"Is that right?"

"She didn't know if she wanted to be in that office or ask for a different one, but she's so tough." Trina shook her head. "Really, she's amazing. She decided to keep the office and see how it goes."

"It's not like the body's still there," he said, remembering the slumped form draped over the desk.

Ted set down his cup. "Not too many people would want to have an office where someone had been murdered. I know I wouldn't."

From across the table, Trina frowned. "Roger, about last night. Paul said you should have called the police." She drained her juice.

His back stiffened. "How did Paul get involved?"

"He usually stops by after his evening shift."

His cup clunked as he placed it on the table. Two pairs of eyes stared at him.

"After you left," Trina said, "Lillian wanted to go back to the shelter and check on the man she hit, but thankfully Paul arrived and convinced her to let him go instead."

"She didn't hit the man." He clenched his teeth against his rising anger. "The man jumped out in front of her. The car never touched him, and he refused to go to the hospital."

"But Paul said you should have called."

His mind tried to process this unexpected information: Paul had been talking to Lillian. What were the potential ramifications? The muscles around his head tightened and he rubbed his forehead. "So Paul's been here almost every night?"

"It's kind of funny," Trina mumbled through a mouthful of muffin, "I think he's sweet on her. You know he rescued her when she arrived in town, so now he's got this idea he has to protect her."

"She doesn't need police protection."

"Have another muffin," Trina offered.

"No thanks." Roger pushed himself from the table. "I probably have people waiting at the office." He flexed his fingers against the anger that wanted to vent through his fists. In spite of Roger's efforts, Paul had still managed to worm his way into Lillian's life. But that didn't mean she wanted him there. After all, if Paul was assuming the role of protector, the Lillian-of-the-past would never allow that.

But what about this new Lillian? Last night, even though he had played a part in her rescue, had she really needed his help? And had she even appreciated him being there? He dug at an itch under his beard. Sure, she had thanked him, but what had he really done other than drive the car? She had made all the decisions.

Paul had become a threat to his plan. Did he need to deal with the threat, or could he use it to his advantage? This would take some thought, and right now his brain wasn't up to the task.

"I meant to ask you before and forgot," Trina said, her usual spark resurfacing. "You are planning on coming for supper tonight, aren't you?"

He wrinkled his brow, his mind still envisioning his hands wrapped around Paul's neck. "Our usual Friday night?" he finally mumbled.

"Sandra's coming. And Jimmy. I want them to meet Lillian."

Trina had invited Lillian? She never invited the bed and breakfast guests to the Friday night family time. He glanced at Ted, but the man stared at him with expressionless eyes. It seemed as though Trina and Lillian were becoming more than landlady and guest. Surely, Ted would kill that relationship.

"Sandra and Jimmy are coming?" Roger mumbled,

still trying to process the fact that Trina had invited Lillian.

"She said they would."

"You ever consider buying this place from Sandra? She could use the money to raise Jimmy. I heard her son didn't leave her much, once the bills were paid from the car accident."

Ted stared at him. "I never heard that. Who told you?"

He shrugged his shoulders. "I can't remember now. It's just one of those things that you hear and it sticks with you."

"So what about Friday night?" Trina asked.

Ted locked eyes with Roger. "Paul's coming."

"Great. Good. Count me in."

How can I keep Officer Studler from interfering with my plan? Maybe I need to move up my timetable.

~*~

At work, the hours dragged, and his foul mood bled over to his clients, resulting in heated arguments over nothing or, worse still, giving in to their meaningless requests.

The job had been one of desperation. He needed to relocate quickly, and the job at the Housing Authority had popped up on his web-search. Not a job of choice, but one of convenience. The work wasn't hard, but tedious.

The number of families who couldn't afford housing grew every year, while the number of landlords willing to rent their property to a government-subsidized program became disproportionately smaller. As a result, hours were spent trying to stretch resources that long ago stopped meeting the need.

People expected him to be some sort of magician, able to pull miracles out of a hat. He wasn't sure why he tried so hard; it wasn't like he really cared. Like church, its usefulness would soon be over.

Latoya entered his office. "Desmond Brown's here, askin' to see ya. I pulled his file." She handed Roger a thick manila folder.

Latoya was Roger's success story, if there was such a thing. She had been one of his first clients: homeless, two kids wrapped around her legs, and pregnant. He had found her an apartment and helped her get a job. Over the next eighteen months, she had earned her GED, and attended classes at Florence Darlington Technical College. When his receptionist quit six months ago, Latoya had applied. Devoted to the end, she would protect his back.

The willowy secretary's long nails were painted red today. Not bright cherry red, but a deep red, like blood. How did she react to the sight of blood? Was she a screamer, or a fainter, or did she grab a rag and start cleaning it up? He had a feeling she was well acquainted with grittier things.

"Sir?"

He pulled his attention from her nails to the folder dangling from her hand. Desmond Brown held the title of most detested client. "Tell him to come in."

Within seconds, the man, built like a bull and just as mean, barreled into the office. Steam almost billowed from the man's nose. Desmond thrust a paper across the desk, ignoring his extended hand.

A verbal fight was building and, as in the past, he regretted the paper-thin walls. Very little money had been spent modifying the historic house from an elegant home to an office complex. Each substantial wall torn down had been replaced by three flimsy ones. Even though fortunate to have his own suite, he shared one of the new walls with the City Planning Department. Of course, he had overheard several heated debates from their side of the wall, too.

"Have a seat, Desmond." Not removing his gaze from the man, he settled into his chair.

With large palms flat on the desk, Desmond leaned toward him. The man's breath reeked of stale beer and cigarettes. His black eyes became slits. Bulging arms flexed. The bull was preparing to charge. "How can you do this to me?" Desmond yelled. "You gonna put three kids out on the street, just like that?"

Although Desmond intended to intimidate, Roger also knew the underside of life: he had spent most of his years there. Leaning forward and placing his hands on the desk, he mirrored the man across from him. "Desmond, I sent you that certified letter because you are three months behind in your rent."

Desmond stood upright, his hands at his sides.

Roger did likewise.

"I told you I'm gettin' a new job soon. I'll be able to make it up."

"That's what you said last month."

"Well, that job fell through. He promised it to me, and then backed down. I can't control that. I've been lookin' for better work."

Still standing, Roger fingered the file Latoya had handed him. He knew what was inside.

So did the man on the other side of the desk.

Roger opened the folder and pretended to read. "You still have your job with Takis, right?"

"Yah, but I go home smellin' like stale food. The kids don't like it. They run to the back of the house."

"Cleaning tables is honest work."

"But I can do better. They have me workin' split shifts now."

"That's because you asked for more hours."

"Because you made me!" The man's glare drilled into his face. "So what you gonna do about this letter?"

Roger's open door provided a modicum of safety. Latoya could hear every word. So could the City Planning Department next door, most likely.

"Look, sit down and let's talk this through."

Desmond dropped into the chair opposite the desk, his dark scowl deepening.

"You make enough money at Takis to pay your rent." Roger spread out the budget sheet they had developed together. "You only have to pay 40% of the actual rent. The government pays the other 60%. Where's the money going?" He frowned at the big man.

"The government can pay it all." Desmond's shoulders slumped. "They're the reason a man can't get a decent job."

"But you have a job, Desmond."

"So you gonna put my old lady and my kids out on the street like all the others you shoved outta their houses?"

"You're doing it to yourself." Roger hissed through clenched teeth. Freeloaders. Bums. All standing with their hands out instead of doing an honest day's work. He knew how to take care of users unwilling to meet their obligations, but in Darlington, his options were limited to those socially acceptable. Desmond ranked among the worst of the abusers.

"What are you doing with the money you're supposed to send here? You signed a contract. You agreed—"

"You can't tell me what to do with my paycheck!"

"I can if you're not paying your rent!"

They stared at each other, blazing gray eyes meeting hateful black slits.

Desmond might believe cleaning tables was beneath him, but he had endured this job for the past two years. Even after the fire, he still had come to work. Men do that. At least Desmond had the decency to not bring his kids this time. Last month their pathetic faces had bought him another thirty days, but that trick wouldn't work again.

"You have a week to pay up before I evict you."

The wooden chair hammered against the wall as Desmond jumped to his feet. "Just try," he snarled. He turned to leave then stopped. "You know, there are more ways than one to get what I want."

"Are you threatening me?"

The man laughed and gooseflesh rose on Roger's arms.

"I see you hangin' around Takis when that woman is there eating." He leered at Roger. "Not enough of a man to come in and talk to her; you got to spy on her. It sure would be sad if something happened to that pretty face." His laugh followed him from the room.

No doubt, Desmond was capable of hurting, or even killing another human being. But would he? And how would that work into Roger's plan if Lillian were removed by someone other than him? *How long before someone puts a bullet through my chest?* This business with Lillian needed to be finished before someone like Desmond ended it for him. He clutched his head as a second hammer joined the first in his brain. Grimacing against the pain, Roger passed a disinfectant wipe across the surface of the desk in steady, even swipes.

"You all right?" Latoya asked from the doorway.

"Do me a favor, will you? Call Children's Services and let them know they'll have three kids needing foster placement in a week."

The phone jangled. He turned his back to the glare of the window. "Roger Jenkins."

"Meester Jenkins?"

His heart clenched. Why today? Why now? He would rather be dealing with a scum like Desmond than taking this call. "Hello, Mrs. Hernandez."

"I went to see the place you told me about. It is so small."

"It will only be temporary." He talked slow, enunciating each word, hating that he didn't have better options for Mrs. Hernandez. Then he remembered. Because of Desmond, there probably would be a vacancy. "There is another house that might be available next month."

"So we stay here for now."

"You can't stay there, Mary. We've talked about this. The inspector found lead paint on the window frames when he was there. By law, I can't allow small children to live in that house."

"But I keep it clean. I keep Mica in his playpen."

"You know what could happen to Mica if he eats lead. You don't want him to be retarded." They had talked about the risks of children in lead-tainted houses.

"We work so hard…"

"I know that."

"I send money home to my parents. They want to come here, you know. They can help me with the children. I can work more hours."

"Mary, your children cannot live in a house with lead paint."

The unfairness of life. His throat swelled with frustration. He needed to pound the desk until only splinters remained. Or punch Desmond in his smug jaw. Instead, he kicked the waste basket, sending it flying against the far wall, leaving bits of torn paper scattered across the thin carpet. After taking a deep breath, he swallowed a mouthful of stale coffee, regaining control before speaking to Mary again.

The sound of children filtered through the receiver, their Spanish voices mixed with the clatter of small feet.

"I called your homeowner," Roger finally said. "I asked him to pay for the lead abatement that would allow you to stay there. I told him how well you care for his house, what a good woman you are."

"And he said yes?"

The hope in her voice added to the spikes already in his head. "He said no."

"*Sì*. You have done your best."

"I'll arrange a moving van for you." He ended the call, knowing that because of the size of the family he could have made an exception, but no...the lead. The headache devoured his brain. He closed his eyes, seeking relief, but instead the limp body of his newborn daughter filled the anticipated blankness. A knife pierced his heart. He stumbled from the office. "I'm going home."

Latoya stared at his face. She knew. She had been in Darlington when it had happened.

~*~

Roger drove blindly, the pounding in his head keeping time with his pulse. Stumbling into the kitchen, he gulped two pain killers and collapsed on the living room couch, the pressure between his temples intense. How much more could he stand?

An hour later, with the worst of the pounding gone, he walked to the bedroom and closed the blinds. From the top shelf, he pulled down the fireproof box, lowered it to the bed, and inserted a key into the lock.

Most days his fingers wandered through the contents, randomly drifting from one item to the next: his marriage license, Elizabeth's birth certificate, the title to a non-existent house. He would linger over pictures of smiling faces, an envelope with a snip of auburn baby hair. And then he would come to the death certificates on the bottom of the box: three of them.

Ignoring the memories, he dug through the box, searching for the blue thumb drive, an ordinary object purchased at an office supply store that now earned placement among his treasures.

The sound of his fingers tapping against the desktop seemed loud as he waited for the computer to boot up. He logged in with an encrypted ID, pulled up the new data he had sent himself, and downloaded the contents to the thumb drive.

He stared at the list of sub-files. He had made them all, added content as needed. Choosing one, he opened it, typed for a couple of minutes, hit save, and logged out. The thumb drive was returned to the metal box, and then the box was locked and shoved deep onto the shelf.

~*~

By the time Roger arrived at Ted and Trina's, Paul's car was already in the drive. He had wanted to show up early and watch Lillian's face when Paul walked through the door, gauge her interest in the man, but no big deal. There would be opportunities to check out Lillian's feelings throughout the evening. After a cursory push to the front doorbell, Roger let himself into the foyer.

"Hey Roger, right on time," Bill said from the hall. "Put these on the table, will you?" He handed Roger a stack of dinner plates and lumbered back to the kitchen.

The smell of basil, oregano, and thyme permeated the air. And garlic. Always garlic. Roger whiffed appreciatively as his stomach growled in hunger. He had missed lunch. Again.

Laughter erupted from the kitchen. While Roger stood listening for Lillian's voice, Paul, his fist full of silverware, walked into the room with Lillian close behind, holding napkins.

Always attractive, but tonight there seemed to be a special glow about Lillian, as though a stage light had been assigned just for her. With eyes flashing and a smile that seemed to be ongoing, she didn't look like a helpless maiden in need of rescue.

Jimmy, Sandra's six-year-old grandson, ran through the door and slid to a stop on the wooden floor. "Miss Lillian, I have another one for you!" His blue eyes sparkled.

Lillian waved the napkins in the air. "No more!" she said, laughing. "My sides will split open if you tell me one more joke."

"After we eat?" he asked.

"After we eat."

"Hi, Roger." Lillian smiled and nodded toward the plates in his hand. "Looks like you have a job, too. Trina runs a tight kitchen."

Thankfully, she said nothing about the ruckus of the other night. Best to avoid the topic with Paul around. No sense angering the man in Lillian's presence.

Roger scowled, wondering whose side Lillian would take. He began placing the plates on the table.

Lillian followed with the napkin and Paul trailed her with silverware.

The thump, rustle, and chink as they worked reminded Roger of musical chairs. Who would end up without a seat? *It won't be me.*

"Watch out! Heavy load coming!" Sandra balanced a tray with glasses of ice water.

Paul rushed toward her. "Here, let me take that." He lifted the burden from her hands.

"Thanks, Paul. You're good to have around."

What a kiss-up. Roger took a deep breath; already his nerves felt as if they had been sprinkled with some of the red pepper flakes that he knew Trina would put in the pasta sauce.

Trina entered carrying a cloth-covered basket, and the aroma of baking bread mingled with Italian seasoning. "All right, guys, time to eat."

Roger frowned when Trina directed him to a seat across from Lillian, until Paul was given the spot beside him, with Bill next. Lillian sat between Jimmy and Sandra. Ted and Trina filled the ends of the table.

"Let's pray," Ted said, extending his hands to Bill and Sandra.

Roger hated that part of the Hancock tradition. He extended his hand, hoping Paul would ignore it, only to feel the pressure of the man's grip.

~*~

The taste of garlic mixed with oregano, basil, and a hint of thyme made Lillian's mouth water. Looking at the heads bent over food, listening to the clink of silverware on stoneware, she smiled. These were her friends.

Jimmy sat beside her slurping strings of spaghetti through his lips.

Sandra turned toward the boy, but Jimmy remained focused on his plate.

Lillian smiled, glad she could run interference for him.

"Do any of you know anything about the homeless shelter here in town?" Lillian asked.

Roger raised an eyebrow.

"What do you want to know?" Ted asked, licking sauce off his lips.

"Is it a good place? Is it well run? How is it staffed?"

"I used to go one day a week and help cook and serve supper until I got too big to fit behind the counter," Trina said with a laugh. "But the rest of the family still goes."

Jimmy tugged at Lillian's arm. "I help too."

"You thinking about volunteering, or are you just curious?" Sandra's strong southern drawl sounded right at home in the historic house. "We can use all the help we can get."

Trina giggled. "Remember that time mashed

potatoes was on the menu and the electric potato scraper broke? We had to peel 30 pounds of potatoes by hand."

"I remember," Ted interjected. "I thought my hands were going to fall off."

"Well, I got the blasted machine fixed," Bill said. "I'm not peeling any more bushels of potatoes. Reminds me of the Army."

"It wasn't bushels, Dad."

"Close to it."

"But the men really enjoyed the meal," Sandra added. "That's what's important, y'all."

"Do any of the local attorneys volunteer?" Lillian asked.

Roger's head turned toward her as if he stared, but when she looked at him, he was intent on twirling spaghetti in his fork.

"Not that I know of," Sandra said.

"What if I volunteered a few hours a week, maybe on the night you guys work? Do any of the men need legal counsel? I won't be able to serve as their attorney, but I can advise them on the law."

"I can't think of a greater need." Bill wiped his mouth with his napkin. "Some of the men are homeless because of the red tape they don't know how to navigate."

"Are you sure this is a good idea?" Roger bit into warm garlic bread.

"Why wouldn't it be?" Lillian challenged him.

"You're young. And pretty. All those men—"

"Oh, for heaven sakes, Roger," Sandra said. "What do you think those men will do to her?"

"I have to agree with Roger," Paul said. "We don't get that many calls at the station from the shelter, but the ones that do come are serious. Knifings, for instance." His eyes softened but maintained their seriousness as he looked at Lillian. "Some of the men have shady backgrounds. The city has a volunteer legal service for the low income. I think the office is actually located in your building, isn't it Roger?"

Roger nodded. "I'll be glad to connect you with them, Lillian."

"We can discuss this later." Sandra tipped her head toward a wide-eyed Jimmy.

"Anyone for seconds?" Trina passed the pasta bowl to Paul.

"I saw in the paper one of your houses burned down last night." Bill sopped up the last bit of sauce on his plate and popped the saturated bread into his mouth.

Lillian's throat tightened and she tried to close her ears against the conversation.

"What happened?"

"The fire marshal's reporting it as arson."

Lillian felt the color drain from her face.

"That big one on Miller Street?" Trina frowned. "Who would want to burn down that old house? I thought it was beautiful."

"The owner comes to mind first," Roger replied.

Lillian lowered her fork to her plate, her heart blocking her throat. "What happened to the family?"

"They moved out a couple of days ago."

"So the house was empty?" Trina asked. "Thank goodness for that."

"Excuse me," Lillian murmured as she slipped from the table.

Trina smiled as she passed. "Now you're taking up my habits!"

She ran up the stairs and closed the bathroom door behind her. Wobbly legs supported her as far as the edge of the tub, where she settled on the side and put her face in her hands. Craig and Susan's burned bodies filled her mind, the stench of their burned flesh still real. A sob shoved its way from her tight chest, releasing the emotional flood it had been blocking. When would the pain end? As the sound of fire crackled within her mind, she moaned and rocked back and forth against the pain. Her family. Her life. All gone.

A soft knock sounded at the door followed by Sandra's voice. "Lillian. Are you all right?"

She brushed the tears off her cheeks. "I'm fine. I'll be down in a minute."

After splashing cold water on her face, she ventured back down the stairs. She eased back into her chair and picked up her fork, but little food actually got to her mouth.

Conversation lagged. Faces held guarded expressions, as though an unwelcome guest sat in their presence. What had they been talking about while she had been gone? The fire? Most likely her, and the embarrassment made her want to retreat to the safety of her room.

"You all right, Lillian?" Bill asked.

"I'm fine."

"Just thought you looked a bit wane."

"Dad means tired," Trina said. "Dad, no one says wane anymore."

"It's a good word," Bill said, his lips rigid.

The monster in the room had its claws in more than her. She had never heard Trina correct her father before, at least not in public.

And Bill seemed to be on the verge of exploding.

"All right y'all, time to do dishes." As Sandra rose from her seat, she winked at Bill, and, as though on cue, everyone stood and carried a handful of dishes to the kitchen.

Soon the last plate was dried and the sink wiped clean.

Sandra draped the dishcloth across the sink. "Trina, let's go see that baby room you've been talking about."

The evening had started pleasantly, but for the second time Lillian found herself tense. First the fire, now the expectation that she accompany Trina and Sandra to the nursery. Hopefully, her well of tears had gone dry.

Sandra accompanied Trina up the stairs. As Lillian followed, her throat tightened and she fought tears that wanted to pocket in the corners of her eyes. Why had she not invited Sandra into the bathroom and cried on her motherly shoulder? Rigid independence had blocked her ability to accept Sandra's friendship. The aloneness that always pressed against her suddenly pushed until the weight felt as if her feet might sink right through the tread of the stairs.

Laugher broke through her thoughts as Jimmy bounded up the stairs, passing all of them in his rush to be first.

The revelation occurred so suddenly that she stumbled. A huge smile formed on her face, and a laugh erupted from within her.

"You OK back there, Lillian?" Sandra asked.

"Never better." She had been living a solitary life surrounded by stoic and serious people. She needed Jimmy's goofy jokes and Ted's loving glances at his wife, the unconditional friendship of Trina. The weight holding her down crumbled and the lightness left her feeling as if she could float up the stairs. God had not abandoned her. He had given her just what she needed. A cleansing breath poured from deep within. She sat in God's protective hand.

~*~

After the women headed upstairs, Ted wandered toward the parlor, and Bill went in search of the deck of cards.

Roger found himself alone in the kitchen with Paul.

"I need to talk to you about the other night." Paul's lips pressed together so hard they almost disappeared.

Blood rushed to Roger's head, suffusing his face in heat. He stiffened his back, ready for the fight. "What about it?"

"When someone is hit by a car, you need to call the police. We have to fill out a report. You know that."

Roger glared at Paul. So smug and self-assured, thinking he owned the world. The knot of hate that lived in his stomach swirled into his mouth. "No one was hit, so there was nothing to report." The words hissed from his mouth. "The man stumbled off the curb and Lillian stopped in front of him. I would think the police would have better things to do, like catching the person who burned down my house last night."

"So it's your house now?" Paul's eyes narrowed. "You make too much of yourself. We play as a team around here."

"A team? All your team does is set up speed

traps."

Paul's face reddened. "You know very well—"

"What's going on in here?" Bill stood in the doorway. "You boys better stop or take it outside. I don't want the women upset."

"Sorry, Bill," Roger looked at the floor. "I forgot myself for a minute."

"I'm out of here." Paul walked stiffly from the room.

"Aren't you staying to play cards?" Bill asked.

"Tell Trina thanks for supper," Paul said over his shoulder as the outside door closed behind him.

"What was that all about?" Bill asked.

He shrugged his shoulders. "Who knows? Paul's always been moody." It was all he could do to keep the snicker out of his voice.

~*~

Trina placed her cards on the table and yawned.

Roger knew the time to reveal his plan had come. His heart trilled within his chest. After two years, payment would be made. "It's late and I need to get home," he said. "Besides, no one can win with Lillian playing!"

"Hey, Ted won the first two games," Lillian quipped, a smile lighting her face. "Do you guys do this every Friday?"

"Most weeks," Ted said.

Trina grabbed Ted's arm and pulled herself up. "You're welcome to join us. Even after you move."

Lillian laughed. "Are you trying to get rid of me?"

"Never!"

The evening had brought out the best in Lillian.

She recovered her pleasant mood soon after the card game started, and Jimmy had helped to keep her entertained until Sandra took him home. Lillian, looking like someone without a care in the world or a sin to atone for, stretched her arms above her head. "This has been nice. I can't remember the last time I had so much fun."

Her façade of innocence sickened Roger, but he could play that game too. While others had focused on the cards, he had stacked one scenario on top of another until he had come up with the best course of action. He only needed a reason to bring it up it, and Lillian had just given him the opening. "The fun doesn't have to end," he stated, maintaining eye contact. "How about going jogging with me tomorrow morning?"

"You're a runner?"

Ted's gaze was on him.

"I'm not sure I would call myself a runner, but I like to put in a few miles every now and then. I thought you might like to see Williamson Park. It's a great place to get some exercise, if you avoid the tree roots." Roger gave her his little boy, friendly puppy smile.

"Sure. What time?"

"How about eight? Is that too early?" The earlier the better for his purposes. Most Saturdays, people didn't start showing up at the park until after lunch.

"Eight's fine."

"Oh, I almost forgot." He furrowed his brow. "I have to make a quick stop in the office first. Can I meet you there instead?"

"Sure, no problem. The parking lot is off Spring Street, isn't it?"

"That's the place. Or I can come by and pick you up, but meeting you would save some time. We want to get our run in before the crowds start showing up."

"I'll just meet you there." Lillian smothered a yawn behind her hand.

"It looks like Trina's not the only one tired." He turned and waved a hand as he headed toward the door. "Thanks for the supper and the company." *And enjoy your last night in a bed, Lillian.*

The click of the deadbolt sounded behind Roger. Retribution would not happen at the bed and breakfast; he could spare his friends that much.

The evening had ended more perfectly than if he had planned it. Paul running off and Lillian accepting his invitation. A smile creased his face as he bounced toward the car. And it had been a good touch on his part to throw in the "I have to go to work first" line. That would be his alibi.

Tomorrow promised to be both an end and a beginning.

~*~

Lillian gathered the popcorn bowls from the table. Green plastic, cheap, most likely purchased from the thrift store, but they had provided more fun than she had had any time in recent memory. She ran her finger along the bottom of her bowl and placed the greasy tips in her mouth. Salt. That brought to mind a sermon she had heard on friendship being the salt of life.

As she carried the bowls toward the kitchen, she contemplated the possibility of friendship. Friendship was beyond what she hoped for, and she had been content moving to Darlington to live a solitary life. But then something happened. It felt as though she had known Trina for years. And then Ted and Paul and Roger. Dare she call them friends?

"You look deep in thought," Trina said as she sidled past Lillian in the kitchen doorway. "Anything I can help you with?" She dumped the paper plates into the waste basket.

"Sorry. I guess I was lost in my own world for a minute."

"I would be in a daze too if I had two eligible bachelors dangling on my every word." Trina grinned, walked to the table, and indicated the seat next to her.

Should this conversation happen? She knew where sweet Trina's thoughts were headed, but Darlington was to be her retribution, not a place to kindle romance. The scent of popcorn still clung to the air and with it thoughts of the evening: the laughter, the times when she had felt accepted, almost part of the family.

The wooden chair slid over the waxed floor with a soft scrape as she pulled it from the under the table. The overhead light brightened the room.

Comfort. That was the word she had been searching for, the emotion she had been experiencing. When had this house become a safe haven for her? Was it possible that those living in it were part of her safety? She shook her head at the odd thought. Safety from what? She had left the danger in Cleveland.

Rather than being able to see through the kitchen window, a reflection off the glass shone back at her, hiding what lay beyond. Her gut twisted. God had led her to Darlington, but she still *knew* danger waited for her just beyond that black window; something hidden beneath a light-filled image. She shivered and tried to shake off the strange premonition.

Trina bounced in her seat, eyes sparkling. Her eagerness to share girl talk raked against Lillian's somber mood.

"You've only been here a week, and already Roger is swooning over you. I have never seen him act like this with anyone. And Paul." Trina chuckled, her eyes crinkling around the edges. "He gets chased all the time by the women. You know how it is, man in a uniform. But he's never given any of them a second look until you came along. He's smitten all right."

Lillian stared at Trina, remembering her accelerated heartbeat when Paul had stopped her coming into Darlington, and the emotion had nothing to do with the ticket. And Roger. Dark, handsome Roger. She couldn't go there.

"You've got a battle going on for your heart."

"Who has a heart?" Ted asked as he entered the kitchen.

Trina used her hands to shoo her husband away. "Girl talk. Go to bed. I'll be up shortly."

Ted raised his eyebrow. "I thought you were tired."

"Go to bed," Trina said, her voice stern but her eyes laughing.

When Ted's footsteps sounded on the steps, Trina turned back to Lillian. "So which one is it going to be?"

The eagerness on Trina's face made her regret not being able to share the joy. There would be no relationship with either man. Trina's conversation was as if two high school friends were discussing which of the hunks they hoped would ask them to the prom. But this was real life. The prom had ended and her carriage had turned back into a pumpkin. She tried to get up from the table, to end the nonsense of the conversation, but the warmth of the kitchen seeped into her bones, and Trina's voice became a soothing lotion rubbed into her long-neglected skin. "I really don't...."

"Well, each one will try their best to win your heart." Trina put her elbows on the table and rested her chin in her hands. "So what are your first impressions of Roger?"

"He's nice enough." The typical tall, dark, and handsome, but with a secret pain kept close to his chest. "We're going jogging in the morning."

"What about Paul?"

Before she could stop it, a grin spread. "He makes me laugh. But I'm not ready for a serious relationship. It's too soon."

Trina squeezed her hand. "When you're ready, there are two men waiting."

Hope filled the hollow in Lillian's heart. "You're so good for me, Trina."

"You belong here, I know it. God has something in mind."

As she followed Trina up the stairs, she contemplated whether God could have romance as part of His plan. Just one week ago, she had not even hoped for friendship. God had provided so much more than she had expected. Why not a second chance at love? A shiver of excitement crept over her.

Too many changes too fast. And tomorrow, a date with Roger. Was it really a date? No, they were meeting to go running together, just as friends did.

But as unexplained jitters became her bed partner, she flipped on the lamp and grabbed her Bible. Was this another premonition?

10

Blood coated his hands. Blood from the others; justified, each one. He fingered the garrote in his pocket. They were old friends, but it had been a long time since he had needed it. Baggy running shorts, not his usual choice but perfect for today, hid the bulge. Fingers caressed the smooth wood and followed the curl of the thin wire as he stood at the edge of the parking lot waiting for his last assignment.

How many times had he needed this silent weapon? Six? Seven? Instructed in its use by his father-in-law, the older man had also dictated its use.

After the first time, the nightmares started, but the financial compensation helped make up for the loss of sleep. By the fourth assignment, the victims no longer resurrected in his dreams.

The knowledge that his indebtedness to his partner was about to end bubbled like a cool fountain at the end of a long, forced hike. But mingled with this excitement. The acknowledgment that his freedom depended on today's success created a negative tension that battled against the premature euphoria.

Three cars hummed by the park but none stopped. No one would be able to describe the man hunched over in the picnic area if, indeed, anyone had even seen him. He rubbed his hands back and forth across the skin on his legs.

Lillian pulled her vehicle into the empty parking

lot.

He took a deep swig of water to moisten his dry mouth and walked to the parking area. He smiled as she exited her car.

Dressed in smart-looking gray running shorts and a matching knit top trimmed in lavender, and paired with top-of-the-line running shoes, she could have been posing for a fashion magazine rather than running a race for her life.

He, however, had dressed for obscurity, having learned the art of blending in, of being invisible while in plain sight. Black nylon shorts and a purple Darlington High School t-shirt made him look like a hundred other runners in the area.

He had never failed to complete an assignment, not once, and today would not destroy this record.

~*~

"Where's your car?" Lillian asked. The morning sun felt warm on her face, so unlike cold Ohio. A run in the open air seemed like heaven after months of being stuck inside.

"I don't live far, so I left it at home. After the office, I changed and jogged here. Ready for some exercise?"

"As ready as I'll ever be." The jitters she had felt last night returned and she shrugged them off.

Roger's muscles bulged from beneath the sleeves of the cotton shirt as he tossed an empty water bottle into the trash.

With his protection, no one could be safer than she. Besides, what could happen in a quaint little place like Darlington?

He stood waiting under a shelter a few yards from

the parking lot. A map of the trails was tacked in place on a bulletin board. From the parking area, two mulch-covered paths led into the tree-shrouded park. Roger pointed to the right-hand arrow. "Let's start here. We can jog to the farther side of the park and then wind back on this left-hand trail." He traced the route on the map. "Did you bring water with you?"

"I left it in the car. I usually don't run with anything except my cell phone for emergencies." She bent over and stretched her hamstrings. "Lately, I've spent most of my time running on a treadmill. It feels good to be outside again." Yes, it felt good to be away from the staring eyes and threat of someone hurling a rock at her every time she left the house. The pine-scented air also held a hint of something floral, even in October. Again, her nerves sent shivers up her spine and she tried to ignore them. Old habits must be unlearned; she was safe here. No need for this level of self-preservation. She smiled at Roger. "Ready?"

He took the lead, his feet making soft muffled thuds on the mulch, barely disturbing the sounds of birds and the hum or bugs around them.

She followed closely behind him.

"Let me know if I'm setting a good pace for you." He glanced back. "I can speed up or slow down."

"So far this is great."

As they rounded the corner, the road disappeared.

Surrounded by nature grown wild, she began to relax, and she allowed her long stride to move her forward.

The morning sun filtered through the limbs, creating patches of light and dark. A squirrel skittered up a tree, its nails biting into the bark as it reached the first branch and then darted along a limb that grew increasingly narrower. It jumped onto the next limb, its body flying as it arched across space. Somehow, the creature knew not to creep along the floor of the swamp where certain death lurked.

Trina had told her that snakes, foxes, and the occasional alligator all lived under the protection of the twisting undergrowth. The paths provided safety, but if she strayed from the path...

A hollow echo replaced their soft plodding footfalls as they ran across the wooden planks of the first bridge. Then back to mulch. The two-mile marker showed on the right.

"Why don't you lead for awhile?" Roger asked as he moved to the side of the trail. "You set the pace you want."

She jogged toward him, feeling like a child at an amusement park. "This is an amazing place. I had no idea all of this was back here. From the road it looks so small." She chuckled as she passed him, wondering what he had in that pocket that caused him to keep checking to make sure it was still there. Bulky enough to bulge beneath his shorts, it had to be uncomfortable. That's why she always ran as unencumbered as possible.

Loblolly pine, hickory, cedar and oak trees fought for space as they towered toward the sky. Knees from Cyprus filled the wet areas. Dozens of varieties of ferns spread their fans in a kaleidoscope of green, completely hiding the floor of the swamp. The occasional spider web connected one fern to another, its massive span trapping small insects and bits of forest litter.

"Does anyone ever get off these paths?" she called over her shoulder. "Trina said there are snakes."

"Snakes and a lot of other things better left alone. Smart people stay on the paths."

The smell of damp loam and stagnant water mingled with the scent of her sweat.

Feet pounded.

They were alone.

Tightness gripped her throat as though her inner sense had detected a hidden danger. Listening for sounds from the underbrush, she heard nothing but the rustle of leaves and her own panting breath, but her nerves continued to ping in response to an unseen adversary. Her jitters had to be from the unfamiliarity of freedom. It had been a long time since she had been able to run in a public place and not fear at least public taunting. She pushed the pace slightly, hoping to leave her concerns behind.

~*~

"I hope you will have a pleasant stay, Mr. and Mrs. Dillon." Trina placed a tray with coffee and warm muffins on the porch table. "I usually serve guests iced tea and cookies, but it's so early in the morning, I'm glad I thought to ask you about coffee." She poured two steaming cup. "Don't feel as if you have to sit outside if you're cold. You're welcome to use any of the downstairs rooms."

Mr. Dillon grinned. "What, you don't think love can keep us warm?" He pulled his wife closer to him on the swing. "By the way, thank you for allowing our early arrival. We're celebrating our forty-fifth next week, so we wanted to get away for a few days."

"Forty-five years. That seems like a long time to me." Did she even know anyone who had been married that long? Not from lack of love, but both her mother and Sandra's husband were dead. Maybe she and Ted would be able to reach that milestone, but it seemed a long way off.

"It will go faster than you think," said Mrs. Dillon, petite and smartly dressed in mauve slacks and a matching sweater. "I couldn't help notice you are expecting."

"Kind of hard to miss." Trina patted her expanding belly. "I'm due January seventeenth, but I hear first babies are often late."

Mrs. Dillon's smile warmed her face, soft wrinkles flowing from her eyes and accenting her lips. "Take care of yourself, honey."

The front door swung open. "I've taken your luggage up to your room," Ted said. "Anything else I can do for you folks?"

Trina looked at her husband and blinked. His face still wore a smile, but his eyebrows were pulled together in a tight knot above his nose. What had happened in the past ten minutes to make him so tense? She bunched her hands at her sides, anxious to leave her new guests and get Ted alone.

"The two of you have been more than gracious," Mr. Dillon said.

"Well, if you need anything, we're around." Trina pushed Ted back into the house.

After pulling him to the kitchen and then glancing back toward the porch, she looked up into his face. "What's wrong?"

"I have that feeling again." Ted shook his head. "It just came over me, all of a sudden when I was carrying the Dillons' suitcases upstairs."

"God's telling you to pray? Do you think it has

anything to do with the Dillons?"

"I don't know." He looked deeply into Trina's troubled eyes. "I know you need me to help you right now. New guests and all…it's just that…the urgency is so strong." Ted glanced toward the parlor, his favorite place to pray, and then back to Trina.

This was one of the reasons she loved him: his deep faith in God, and his special gift of prayer. She didn't understand it, but she didn't need to. "Go, pray. The Dillons shouldn't need much until tomorrow morning, and I can always get Dad to help if something comes up."

Ted's prayer vigils could last five minutes or five hours. Again he glanced toward the parlor, anxious to meet with God.

"Go, I'll be fine."

Ted started down the hall and then turned. "Where is your dad, anyway?"

"He's at Sandra's helping her plant fall flowers."

Trina doubted Ted heard her as his lanky legs had already taken him around the corner to the family parlor. She tiptoed in his direction and found him on his knees in front of the couch. Over the course of his intercession, he may move from the couch to the chair, or even prostrate himself on the floor, stand with his arms raised, or fold himself into a ball. Love for her husband filled her, and she brushed away the tears as she pulled the parlor doors closed.

~*~

From his position behind her, Roger watched Lillian run.

Damp tendrils of sandy-colored hair clung to her

neck while ringlets danced with each measured footfall. So much like Medusa, with her head of writhing snakes.

With each measured step, the bottom-dwelling monster that lived within him awakened. Lillian shrank to nothing more than prey, the source of his hunt. Any hint of humanity, any indication of remorse for his behavior disappeared. Shadows deepened. Nefarious spectators only he could detect hid in preparation for the show.

Roger batted against the gnats. Even the breeze held its breath against what was to come. Time was running out. His heart pounded. His anticipation grew.

They reached the last raised wooden bridge before circling back toward the front of the park.

"Aahh, muscle cramp," he muttered loudly.

Lillian turned. "Are you all right?"

"Just need a breather for a minute and the cramp'll pass." He stopped and massaged his leg, while concentrating on his breathing, centered his focus on the task ahead.

Lillian placed her hands on her knees. "I am totally winded anyway."

Do it now. Hit while her strength has been used for the run.

He took a slow, deep breath. Had he missed any detail? No one had seen him as he had waited. The call from his cell phone to the bed and breakfast would help to establish his alibi. He would claim no knowledge of Lillian's whereabouts. The police would find her car, but not her body. Anything dumped in the thick undergrowth would remain hidden until the January frost, assuming there would be a winter frost. And by then the body would be decomposed, most likely her bones carted off by wandering creatures.

Lillian leaned against the wooden railing, her face lifted to the sun, neck extended, eyes closed. A faint smile shaped her lips.

With muscles as taut as the garrote held between his hands, he strained to discern any approaching footsteps.

The chorus of swamp bugs sang encouragement. Trickling water played back-up to their song.

His beating heart lent the solidifying percussion. The symphony of death. He positioned himself directly behind her and stretched the garrote, feeling the vibrating twang of the wire penetrate through the wooden handles. The taste of blood filled his mouth.

~*~

Fear crashed into Bill like storm waves pounding over the sand. His breath came in small gasps as the spade fell between his knees. He pressed his hands to his chest. The terror left as quickly as it had come, leaving him momentarily disoriented. As thought returned, he jumped from the ground, his heart racing as he scanned the yard.

Next door, the golden retriever, heavy with her pregnancy, barked from the back porch.

A car whined in the distance and he stiffened. Looking for a weapon, he grabbed the hoe, clutching the handle tightly in his hand. A white truck passed, its driver male. The beat of the radio's bass vibrated against Bill's skin.

He scanned the area again, trying to quell the unease that clung to his back. She had to be here. One minute he had been happily planting pansies and marigolds. The next minute, fear had overwhelmed him, and a name had sounded in his head over and over: *Lillian.*

Since her arrival, he had been aware of a sense of danger cloaking her. Some days, the presence wafted like a scent on the wind and then disappears into nothingness. Other times, the vibrations of fear thrummed the very air around her. But he had never been overcome with visceral sickness like this. Something was different.

Then it hit him like a hammer to the chest. Trina!

Heart pounding, eyes bulging, he raced to the back door. "Sandra, I've got to go home." The words felt thick and heavy as he pushed them out. "I'll explain later."

"Bill, what—"

Loose gravel shot from beneath his tires as he pulled onto the quiet city street.

The mile between the two houses felt like ten, his throat tight with fear. He had to get home.

Ted had planned to paint in the workshop out back all day, some urgent project that needed to be finished.

Trina would be in the house alone.

Alone with Lillian. Alone with danger.

His tires spun as he turned off the street and into the drive.

Lillian's parking spot stood empty. The tightness gripping Bill's chest increased. Had Lillian persuaded Trina to leave with her? Was he too late?

Running to Ted's workshop, he tugged at the knob with sweaty hands. "Ted!" He pounded on the wood, and pulled the handle again, getting no response.

Pain radiated from his chest into his throat. He

stumbled toward the house, through the kitchen door and out into the hall, panting for breath as he ran. Urgency increased. He had to find Lillian and stop her.

Trina stood just outside the parlor, Ted at her side.

Bill's large arms swallowed the slight form of his daughter while he examined his son-in-law.

The younger man's face had lost much of its color, and his eyes were pinched, as though in pain. The palms of Ted's hands looked red. Knees exposed below khaki shorts bore the indents of carpet. Ted had been praying.

His eyes widened. God had sent an alert to both of them.

Trina's muffled laugh came from beneath his arms as she struggled to free herself. "Dad, hello to you, too."

"Where's Lillian?" He glanced from one parlor to the next.

"Dad, calm down. I don't want to scare our guests."

"What's wrong?" Ted stared into Bill's face.

"Lillian." Breaths wheezed from Bill's mouth. "Where is she?"

"She's out with Roger." Confusion ringed Trina's eyes.

"No, she's not," Ted said. "Roger called. He had an emergency at work and had to cancel. He couldn't get her on her cell, so he tried here, but she had already left."

Nostrils flaring, still panting for breath, Bill ran a hand across the top of his head. "You treat her like family instead of the paying customer she really is. She comes and goes as she likes, and now you've become her social secretary."

"Dad? You've never talked like this about Lillian before. What's wrong?"

He looked down at his daughter, thankful that she was safe, but feeling no release from the tension. Pacing the hall, looking in each room even though he knew the spaces stood empty, the urgency increased, as though he was encased in a straightjacket with no way to get out of it. He needed to act, but didn't know what to do, and the quandary left him feeling helpless. "She's up to something, and I think it's happening right now. Someone's in danger because of her."

"I've been praying for that person." Ted said.

Trina put her hands on her hips. "Lillian would never hurt anyone."

His eyes flashed with anger as he turned to his daughter. He loved her with all his heart, but he had sheltered her too much. Right now, her naivety could mean someone's death. "What do you know about her? She came with one suitcase, has bought very little since she's been here, keeps mostly to herself…like a woman poised to run." Acid squirted double-time into his stomach. "We should call Paul." With hands feeling like blocks of stone, Bill struggled to pull the cell phone out of his pocket. "I should have thought of that sooner."

"And tell him what?" Ted asked. "Your fear and my need to pray are somehow connected. But since we don't know where Lillian is, and we really don't have anything solid to tell Paul, it would be useless to call him. What could he do?"

Bill threw up his arms. "But we can't just stand here and let *whatever* happen."

"We can pray," Ted said. "God knows where Lillian is, and He knows what's on her heart."

~*~

Roger inhaled slowly and deeply, filling his lungs with moist air. He planted his feet and pulled the garrote tightly between his hands. One more steadying breath and he would slip the wire over her head. The shadows watched, ready to feed on the tension, preparing to grow larger as the victim struggled, until their very presence filled the space. Thick, dark air. Separate, and yet part of him.

Lillian shivered. "This Bible verse just came to me." She continued to lean against the wooden railing, peering straight ahead into the undergrowth. "We did a study about angels at my church. I didn't realize I had memorized this verse from Psalms 91. If you make God your dwelling place, then He will send angels to protect you and no harm will come to you, or something like that. Strange that I should think of that now."

Children's voices. A dog. An adult calling to them.

The blackness slunk to the trees, retreating to the background. Waiting. Always waiting. Always there. Ready to consume.

A small boy, perhaps six, rounded the edge of the path, followed by a tiny girl a couple of years younger. A woman struggled to contain the excitement of the small Jack Russell terrier that strained against the leash.

Anger hissed from his nose as he coiled the garrote and slid it into his pocket.

"I told you I would beat you to the bridge!" the boy shouted, placing one sneaker-clad foot on the wooden slats.

"That's 'cause you're older," the girl yelled back, stopping on the mulch path and planting both hands on her small hips. "Just wait. Mommy says I will be as tall as you someday."

"Then I'll be taller!" The boy raced across the bridge, followed by his sister.

Take them all! Voices shrieked in Roger's head, the words like tongues stroking the neurons of his mind. *Take them all!*

His hands became hard weapons at his side. First Lillian, because she was the strongest. Then the children, because the mother would not leave them. Last, the other woman. It would be risky, but possible.

A surge of energy rocketed through him as the blackness danced.

~*~

Bill rose from his knees and eased his stiffened body to the recliner.

Trina had tiptoed from the room earlier, but Ted still remained on his knees by the couch, his face etched in concentration.

The sense of urgency continued to press against Bill, like hot August air right before a thunderstorm. His thick tongue did little to moisten his dry lips. Spiritually drained, he stared at Ted, willing the man's prayers to reach the ear of God.

Unexpected waves of fear rolled through the room with such force the very air seemed to distort in its advance. Blackness settled over them, different from the shadows that flitted comfortably against floor and walls with the shifting limbs outside.

Choking bile rose in his throat as recognition

dawned. He had seen this blackness before. Trembling with fear but feeling empowered, he knew what needed to be done. "You are not wanted here," Bill shouted.

Ted rolled into a ball on his side and groaned.

Ice filled the room. Blackness coalesced and advanced toward him in undulating swirls. *Oh, God, oh, God.* "This home and those who live here belong to God. In the name of Jesus, I demand that you leave."

Icy hands gripped his throat, closing his airway. Thrashing in the seat but unable to loosen the grip of something he could not feel, his oxygen starved body began to fade.

"Jesus," Ted murmured from the floor.

Air rushed into Bill's hungering lungs.

Ted unwound his limbs and sat up. With a dazed expression, he searched the room before settling his gaze on his father-in-law. "Wow."

"Yeah. Wow."

~*~

Roger gasped as icy fingers encased him, each pointed digit digging into his flesh. Trying to pry them off would do no good. Something had angered his spectral audience and now he suffered their punishment. What had he done wrong? Gradually the fingers melted away. As he leaned exhausted against the railing, he lifted his face to the swamp, ready for the angry blackness and the mind-numbing headache that would follow.

Soft shadows twined among the trees.

The blackness had deserted him.

He sucked in air, their abandonment left him

feeling powerless. What force would cause his blackness to retreat? As the mother approached the bridge, he wondered if he still had the strength to finish his task. Stiffening his jaw, he had to try.

"Sorry," the young woman said as she reached the bridge. "They seem to be in a snappy mood today." She looked in the direction taken by the two children.

Regaining his courage, he drifted toward Lillian, casually, never taking his gaze off the new woman until he felt the heat of Lillian's body close beside his.

"We were on our way to Pet Smart when the idea to stop at the park just popped into my mind." She gave a sideways grin.

He threw his weight against Lillian and reached for her throat.

The dog's shrill bark hurt his ears. The noise would draw the attention of anyone close by. As he thrust a foot toward the offending beast, his other foot slipped.

Voices swirled but Roger couldn't separate one from the other as he stared overhead at the arching branches.

Lillian's hand grabbed his arm. "Are you all right?" she asked.

The dog sat on its haunches and stared at him.

Wide eyed, the children clutched their mother.

The woman's voice penetrated his fog. "Should I call the squad?" she asked.

He grimaced against the painful light that filtered through the trees. With Lillian supporting his shoulders, he struggled to stand. "I'm all right." How could he explain his behavior? He glanced at Lillian, expecting to see fear etched into face, or at least confusion.

Her smile held concern as she looked up at him, her arm still wrapped around his torso.

"Are you sure you're all right?" the lady asked. "I really am sorry. Pepper never lunges at anyone like that. I don't know what got into her."

"I think you slipped on some of these leaves." Lillian pushed dry piles with the toe of her shoe and then grinned. "Your foot just missed hitting that poor dog as you went down."

Nothing sounded better than a hot soak in his tub and some time alone think. Too many strange things had happened, and they pulled against his need for consistency and control.

"If you're sure you're all right?" The woman glanced toward the entrance to the park.

"I'm fine. None of this was your fault, I should have been more careful." He wiped his face with the back of his hand, pulling his fingers down over his beard. Not once had he bungled an attack before today. This should have been easy, even considering the last minute change in plans.

Releasing a sigh, the woman turned to the boy and girl. "Come on you two, we need to get back to the car."

He felt their darkness, hidden but close by. They were not gone after all, but still there, lingering deeper in the thicket. He vomited into the growth beside the bridge, the exact spot where Lillian's body should have now rested.

11

Murmuring conversation drifted from the dining room as Trina returned to the kitchen, her tray empty. "And how are the Dillons this morning?" Lillian asked.

"They're the nicest couple." Trina placed the tray on the counter and filled a glass with juice before joining Lillian at the table.

Lillian drained the last of the coffee from her mug, contentment mingling with the caffeine. A long sleep and bacon for breakfast; what more could she want? "You say that about all the guests."

"I can't help it if only wonderful people come here." Trina's mouth curved into a crooked smile. "But you're the best of all. Sorry you had to eat alone."

"I could have gone to the dining room."

Trina's eyes widened. "You know you can, any time you want."

"Seriously, Trina, why would I do that?"

"So you're not bothered by my..." Trina placed her hand on her swollen abdomen.

"Of course not. In fact, you were just what I needed. God must have known that."

Trina's expression turned serious. "And what about work? I mean, having someone die in your office has to be hard."

"I have to admit being shocked. You should have seen the poor secretary's face when she realized I didn't know." Lillian chuckled. "But the smell of fresh paint and new carpet has chased away any hypothetical ghosts that may have been thinking of taking up residence. My first week at Francis Marion students kept wandering by my door and staring inside, but when no lingering vibes bounced between the walls, they stopped coming. Most days I forget the history of the room."

Trina took a sip of juice and closed her eyes. "You ever feel so happy that you wait for the bubble to break?" She looked at Lillian. "You know, no one deserves to be as happy as I am, so my joy must be wrong somehow?"

Lillian stood and squeezed Trina's shoulders. "No one deserves happiness more than you, little mama." After putting her breakfast dishes in the sink, she grabbed her purse off the counter and removed her keys. "Have a good day."

The morning sun felt warm against the chill in the air.

Lillian breathed in deeply.

The roses beside the house, still in bloom, cast a heady scent. Yes, life was good.

Her blue car sat in its usual spot, between Ted's red SUV and Bill's white sedan, but now both cars were gone. She smiled as she noticed the disturbed gravel. Ted must have had trouble loading something. *Hope one of his paintings didn't get damaged.* She smoothed the piles back into place with her foot.

As she opened the car door, the smell affronted her. Gas vapors. The floor of the car looked normal, and outside the gas tank cover remained closed. No oily patches coated the rocks. She got in the car and opened the windows. Putting the car in reverse, she looked behind and noticed them: three gas cans on the floor in the back. Her mind whirled.

Bill or Ted could have placed them there.

Someone was playing a joke on her.

The new guests had mistaken her car for their black sedan parked across the drive.

Frustrated, she shook her head. None of her explanations made sense. Someone had intentionally placed the cans in her locked car, knowing she would find them. Breaths came in tight threads as she gripped the steering wheel.

Had her history in Cleveland followed her? This could implicate her to the house fires here in Darlington. Breakfast worked its way up her throat. Who knew her past? Frantic, she searched her brain for conversations about the fire. There had been none—not about the fire in Cleveland, anyway.

She backed out of the drive and started her usual route to Francis Marion University, but she couldn't go there. Not today. Not now.

~*~

Roger eyed the fire chief sitting across from his desk. By now, he anticipated the chief's questions before the man asked them.

"This is the fourth house in four weeks that has burned to the ground. All of them yours." The chief stared at Roger.

Frustration twanged his nerves. These meetings were a waste of time; there was nothing he felt compelled to share with the chief. "I still don't have any more answers than before."

Latoya placed a mug in front of each man. She glanced toward Roger and raised her penciled eyebrows slightly before leaving the room.

The fire chief lifted his cup. Faint wisps of steam rose in front of his face and then disappeared. Unlike the vapor, he knew the fire chief wasn't leaving any time soon.

"The house was empty just like the other three," Roger said, settling back into his chair. "The renters moved out the day before the fire. The home owner's name is..." he glanced at the sheet of paper on his desk, "Nick Bloom, and he lives in Scranton, Pennsylvania. We've been renting his house as part of the government subsidy program ever since I took over the job. We had it five years before that, I think." He glanced at the chief. "I can look it up if you want."

"How does your arsonist know what houses are empty?"

Roger grimaced. "He's not my arsonist, and it wouldn't be hard." The scent of smoke mingled with coffee. Everything the chief owned probably reeked, including the man himself. Dark moons lay heavy under the man's eyes. He probably needed something stronger than coffee. Roger did.

"You make anyone angry lately?" The chief sipped his coffee.

The loud slurp reminded Roger of days past when he, too, would have been that uncouth.

"Not especially." Roger sighed. Hundreds of people had wandered in and out of the office over the past two years. How many had left upset? Too many, but most of them didn't have the initiative, or the follow-through, to burn down four houses. No need to mention Devon right now. It still rankled him that Devon had been able to spot him so easily outside Takis.

"How about disgruntled employees?"

"Definitely not."

Latoya poked her head in the office door. "You have an urgent phone call, Mr. Jenkins."

"I told you to hold all my calls."

"She says it's urgent. Her name's Lillian."

Eyebrows raised, Roger struggled to suppress his excitement. He smothered a tight-lipped smile. He had felt their vaporous presence all morning hovering in the back of the room, and now they settled around him, as eager as he.

The phone burned beneath his hand. He had not been alone with Lillian since they had gone jogging in Williamson Park almost four weeks ago. The Friday night dinners at Ted and Trina's gave him the opportunity to watch her, and he still followed her home from work a couple nights a week. He avoided Takis as she had taken to eating supper on weeknights with Ted and Trina. Shrugging an apology to the chief, he picked up the receiver. "Roger Jenkins speaking."

"Roger, I need to see you."

He swiveled his chair away from the chief. "You sound upset."

"Something awful…I don't know what to do."

"Hold on a minute." Roger put his hand over the receiver. "I really need to deal with this…"

The chief stared darkly at Roger before he shrugged his shoulders. "If anything helpful comes up, give me a call."

Alone in the room, he lifted the receiver to his ear. "Where are you?"

"Outside your office, in my car."

He glanced at his watch; it was barely after eight in the morning. The chief had been his first appointment. "Shouldn't you be at work?"

"I couldn't go. Please..."

"Stay in your car. I'm on my way out."

Retribution pushed its way to the surface. This time he wouldn't fail.

~*~

The fumes in the car thickened as Lillian waited for Roger.

The grocery store across the street already had a dozen cars. Maybe shoppers were after the advertised daily special of Boston butt, planning to smoke the fatty meat over the weekend.

She thrummed her fingers on the steering wheel. What was taking Roger so long? She coughed and wondered if he would find her dead of asphyxiation. Dare she roll down the window just enough to allow some fresh air to enter? No, Roger had told her to lock the doors. He must have had a reason.

Had she done the right thing to call him? She fumbled for her cell phone. Maybe she should call Paul, or even go back in the house and question Trina. As she choked on the fumes, she remembered why she had made her decision. Roger represented her only safe option. Besides, he had helped her once before.

Roger ran out the door and motioned for her to move to the passenger side of the car. She struggled from one seat to the other, unable to make her legs bend and flex, her motions stiff from tension. With tight lips, she turned to Roger as he settled behind the wheel.

He looked at her, opened his mouth as though preparing to speak, and then stopped. "I smell gas."

"We need to talk," she said, "but not here."

Not here, where everyone could see. Even this early in the morning people dotted the sidewalk, single walkers most likely headed to work. No one looked her way, but even so, she felt their shielded glances, just as in Cleveland, as though expecting guilt to be written on her forehead.

"Let's go to Williamson Park." Roger turned the ignition. "How about we roll down the windows?"

"Thanks for coming." She rested her head against the back of the seat, allowing the fresh air to blow over her. Curls fluttered against her face, and she let them fly where they chose. The weight pressing on her since the discovery of the gas cans decreased, shared, as it seemed, by another.

Roger's lips formed a thin line across his face and he gripped the wheel with both hands.

Thankful that he didn't try to pull her into discussion while in the car, she allowed herself a reprieve from fear. This could all be her imagination, after all, and Roger would see her as a flighty female, perhaps trying to get his attention. But then a whiff of gas reached her nose. None of this came from her imagination. She only hoped Roger would have an answer she had not thought of.

In the early morning, the parking lot at Williamson Park stood empty.

Falling leaves added to the soft mulch, muffling their footsteps as they walked down a path.

Roger took her hand in his, and warmth of his fingers entwining hers provided a sense of comfort. If life could stay just like this—peaceful and gentle.

They walked in silence until Roger indicated a cement bench and lead her to it, still cradling her ice-cold hand. Once seated he turned to her. "What happened that has you so upset?"

Her free hand trembled as she swept tangled curls off her forehead. "I might be making too much of this, but I don't know...I can't think." Now that she had to explain, it sounded so ridiculous, and yet the terror clung to her with its long teeth.

"Talk to me, Lillian."

She took in as much of the pine-scented air as her lungs would allow, and exhaled slowly, reliving the past hour. "I found three gas cans on the floor in the back of my car."

"Gas cans? That's what has you so worked up?" Laughter lines ringed his eyes even as his mouth remained grim.

"Yes, I'm 'worked up.'" She pulled her hand from his, angry that he didn't see the gravity of the situation. She thought he would understand. She had put herself at risk by trusting him, and for what? So he could find mock her distress? "Don't you see? I didn't put them there!"

"So how did they end up in your car?"

"I don't know." She tightened her shoulders and turned away from him. Her mind was a whirl of frustrating thoughts and at the core was his lack of understanding. "Let's just go." She stood to leave and he pulled her gently back to the bench.

"Come on, Lillian. You're not telling me something. I can't help you unless you're honest with me." He put his hands on her shoulders and she allowed him to turn her stiff body towards him. "You can trust me. You know that, or you wouldn't have called me."

Could she trust him? She felt the heat from his

hands through her thin jacket.

His eyes focused on her face, the mirth gone. "Tell me why you're so upset. It's just three gas cans."

The soft intensity of his expression melted her anger. "I think someone is trying to blame me for the house fires."

"Here in Darlington?"

"Yes."

"Why would you want to burn down houses in Darlington?"

"Why else would someone put those cans in my car?"

Skin puckered as he pulled his eyebrows together, his mouth forming a pensive line across his face. "You're sure Ted or Bill didn't ask you to get gas for them, and put the cans in the car for you?"

She had already asked herself these same questions. It made sense that Roger would follow her reasoning, but her ragged nerves had moved beyond needing sense, and hoped for something more than logic and reasoning. "I would remember that. Besides, they would put them in the trunk. I was meant to find them."

"What about at work yesterday? Did you leave your car unlocked? Maybe someone put the cans in your car by mistake."

"The cans weren't in my back seat last night. I would have smelled the gas. Someone put them there during the night, I'm sure of it." She shoved a sandy curl behind her ear. "I always keep my car locked. Someone had to work to get into it."

"Maybe it isn't about you, but convenience. Your car was there, this unknown person needed to get rid of cans..."

Exasperation filled her expression. "You know that isn't true."

"So why would someone want to plant gas cans in your car?"

She looked away.

In the distance car tires hummed on the blacktop.

Gnats swarmed around her, and she was grateful when a gust of wind pushed the slight bodies away from her face. What should she tell him? The thing she wanted most—to be able to leave the past behind—lay exposed in the back of her car. No one knew about the fire in Cleveland. No one knew her history, and she ached to keep it that way, to never expose herself to judgmental doubt again.

He couldn't help her unless he knew the whole story, but still...

Finally she spoke. "I know how close you are to Ted and Trina. They probably told you I was married once."

"They might have mentioned it."

"Then they probably told you that my husband and daughter are dead." The words sounded cold and clinical to her ears, not at all like the pain of reality. How could she begin to describe the torment of their deaths, or the emptiness they had left behind? "They were killed in a house fire; one that I was accused of setting." The words left her mouth by necessity.

Craig and Susan would have loved Williamson Park. Craig would be on his mountain bike with Susan buckled in the child-carrier behind him, the cute princess helmet snug on her head. She would turn and wave...

"You don't need to talk about it if you don't want to."

Pain from the past ate away at her soul one bite at a time. She couldn't go through it again. Staring at nothing, focusing ahead but seeing only gray, she continued. "When I left Cleveland, there were still people who thought I was guilty of setting my own house on fire. Apparently one of them has followed me here." Fear caught as she thought of the ramifications. "Roger, I could go to jail!"

His words were no more than a murmur across her ears. "I won't let anyone hurt you."

He wrapped his arms around her and the protective shield she had maintained for the past two years shattered. In spite of her stiff resolve, she fell into his chest sobbing, her tears wetting his shoulder as she released her fears one drop at a time. The relief of having someone understand overwhelmed her. In Cleveland, there had been no ally to stand with her. Now she had Roger.

Leaving his shoulder but reluctant to move too far from his warmth, she dragged her hand across wet cheeks. "I was never brought to trial, but people still believed I was guilty. I could see it in their faces, the way they stared at me on the streets. Friends who never got around to calling, even my boss...they all had doubts. They thought I got off because of my family's reputation. I had no choice but to leave Cleveland and try to start over."

"We need to call the police." He reached for the phone in his pocket.

"No!" Fear tightened her throat. She grabbed his arm, her nails bit into his flesh as she tried to restrain him.

"Lillian, someone put those containers in your car. The police need to know."

"If the police find out about my past, they'll be compelled to investigate me for the fires here. The public's demanding answers, and it's easier to blame an out-of-towner than one of their own. I can't go through the suspicions again."

"What about Paul? He really vented some heat on me when I didn't report the non-accident with the bum."

"His name is Joseph Callahan and he's not a bum." She wiped her nose with a tissue.

"All right, he's not a bum. But my point remains. We could tell Paul."

"And he'll be required to file a report. I can't take that risk." Her brain felt like gelatin, all quivery and unsettled. "I can't think right now." She put her head between her hands. "Maybe I'll feel differently later, but please, Roger, I don't want anyone else to know."

He pulled a hand down his short beard. "What about Ted and Trina, or Bill? I don't think there's a bigger guy in Darlington than Bill."

"Can't we wait?" She knew her eyes held a pleading look, like the one Susan used when she wanted ice cream, but she didn't care. "What if I'm getting worked up over nothing?" Had she been wrong to tell him? Was her judgment so far off that she could no longer trust her own counsel? She forced a smile. "I feel better already just telling someone. Thanks for listening."

"First thing we need to do is get those gas cans out of your car. Come on." Roger pulled her up. "Let's get to work."

The situation had moved from her control to his and she wasn't sure if she felt relief or fear.

~*~

As Roger drove down the cul-de-sac of his street Lillian remained quiet, seemingly deep in thought. He was taking a risk bringing her here, but sometimes fate created opportunities that human intervention could not. This might be one of those times. The adrenalin rush began. His muscles twitched, begging for action. His heart beat harder to supply the oxygen needed. "So what do you think?" He asked as he pulled into his drive and noticed her stare. "Care to share your thoughts on my domain?"

"I had envisioned you somewhere grander. Not that this isn't a nice little house, but you carry yourself differently, like a man used to wealth."

One point for Lillian. She had noticed his breeding.

"The basic two bedrooms and two baths, kitchen and living room. Disappointed?"

"Not at all. It's a cute house. I can see myself living in a place like this," she murmured. "You keep a nice lawn. No flowers, though."

"I'm not much into flowers." Trying to hide his eagerness, he opened her car door. It had never been in the plan to bring her to the house, but several times in the past, when a plan had gone bad, he had improvised with success. The thought of having his obligation met lightened his step. The neighbors were working people, and no one should be home, but he glanced up the street anyway as he guided her toward the house.

"This is nice, Roger." The muscles in her face seemed to relax as she entered the sparse kitchen.

"Sit down while I get rid of those gas cans. The

bathroom is down this way, first door on the left." He pointed to the hall leading off the kitchen before leading her to the living room on the right. He would deal with her car later; maybe take it back to the park like the original plan.

"I should help you."

"No need. I can do this. Make yourself at home, and I'll be right back."

As Lillian sank onto the couch, he headed toward the door, and then stopped. Had he shut down his computer? Sometimes he forgot, especially if he was running late. And this morning he knew the fire chief would be waiting in his office. He couldn't risk her wandering around, spotting the computer, and deciding to get online. Not that she could find his files, or even be able to open them if she did happen onto them, but the nagging doubt felt like a drip that wouldn't stop.

He detoured down the hall to his bedroom. The computer screen showed black, but the green light blinked. The system was on, but had reverted to sleep mode. He flushed the toilet in the adjoining bathroom and turned on the water in the sink, hoping to mask the sound of the computer shutting down. Pulling open the long center drawer of the desk, he tapped a finger against the map he had placed there. Once the computer screen darkened, he turned off the water and headed back up the hall.

Lillian sat with her head resting on the back of the couch.

After checking again for anyone lingering in the neighborhood, he slipped the three gas cans into the storage room attached to the side of his house. He locked the shed door behind him, headed to the kitchen, and washed his hands. "All done," he announced as he rounded the corner to the living room.

Lillian, with feet still planted on the floor, was fast asleep, her head resting on the side cushions.

From panic to peaceful within a couple of hours, while his anxiety remained part of him, each negative episode layering one on top of the other. What would it feel like to be at peace? He didn't even know, it had been so long. Anger bubbled through his gut like putrid fumes as he watched her even breaths. He clenched his hands. Maybe this *was* fate's way of repaying him for thwarting his agenda at the park. He moved toward her sleeping form, the beige carpet absorbing his footsteps.

Her dark eyelashes fluttered against her cheeks.

He stood rigid until her even breathing resumed.

The voice pounded in his head. *"Do it. Do it. Do it."*

Last night's phone call from his contact had reminded him of his commitment. Finish what he had agreed to do. Roger had tried to explain the reason for the delay, but the response remained the same. Get the job done.

No one knew Lillian was at his house. No one knew she had called him. Latoya knew, but Latoya would never tell. And the fire chief, well, he could be a problem, but what did the man really know? Emergencies happened every day at the office. Did Roger tell him it was a personal emergency? He stroked his beard, trying to remember.

She really was beautiful, her sandy-red hair fanning out against the brown upholstery. Black lashes hiding hazel eyes that could pull a man into their depths, or freeze him with a sudden icy stare. Roger knew her better than anyone else. He knew that her attractive looks hid a soul intent on her own gain, selfish and spoiled.

Cautiously lowering himself to the edge of the couch, he paused.

Still she slept.

Her throat lay before him, pale and thin.

Do it. Do it. Finally give her what she has coming. Pay her for what she did. She is evil, evil, evil…

A deep moan escaped his lips as he reached for her throat.

12

Three days had passed since Lillian had discovered her past had followed her to Darlington. Three days since she had awakened to find Roger leaning over her on the couch. Startled, she had jerked away from him, and then laughed as his expression of guilt and surprise. Later she had wondered about his reaction. Had he intended to kiss her?

As she pulled her car into the bed and breakfast, her jaw tightened. What had possessed her to trust him with her fate? She knew nothing about the man, and had reacted impulsively on some unfathomable gut instinct. That's one of the things Dr. Widder had warned her about: her latent impulsiveness. Her embarrassment over sharing her personal life increased her anxiety. And the kiss. It fell way beyond her level of comfort. But she had needed ally, and Roger had promised not to share.

Equally important, what had he done with the gas cans? They hadn't had a chance to talk since leaving his house on Tuesday.

Regardless, she had given him her trust, and her culpability curdled in her stomach. For the past three days, she had constantly looked over her shoulder, hunting for any familiar face. The stress of the unexpected had left her drained and tense. Who could have followed her here, and why? Surely, anger alone would not cause someone to go to such lengths unless personally affected. And no one had been impacted by the fire more than she. The hot and hungry flames had eaten her entire world.

She turned off the car and rotated tight shoulders. Could she beg off tonight's routine dinner, and plead a headache? Or should she simply turn around and head back to campus? The heavy workload wouldn't be a total lie. But the truth remained—she dreaded seeing Roger again. Their relationship had changed, but she wasn't sure in what way.

Gravel crunched beneath tires as she sat in indecision. Car lights shone into her window. Too late to escape now.

"Hey there," Paul called across the darkening space. He lifted a hand in salute. A bag dangled from his fist.

"Paul. Good to see you again." She checked the car door to verify it had locked.

"Brought Trina a surprise." Paul's conspiratorial expression forced a smile on her face. "One of the guys at the office has family in Ohio. You know that specialty soda Trina's always talking about? Well, I had him grab her some when he went back home last week. I've been saving it for tonight." He held up the brown bag, his fist clutching the paper around the bottle's neck.

She did remember Trina mentioning it, and cringed for not having thought to have some shipped.

Leave it to Paul to grab onto the small things, always making people feel special.

She kicked loose gravel with the toe of her shoe as they walked toward the back entrance.

The warmth of the kitchen felt good after the cool night air, and the odor of Italian tomato sauce permeated the air.

Taking a deep breath, Lillian wished for the hundredth time she was part of this family—as an equal and not one stained by her past.

"Hey, Lillian. Paul. Just in time to set the table." Trina looked so cute, her apron standing like a ball around her belly, spatters of red across her mid-section. With the back of a hand, she wiped strands of brown hair off her face. "Is it hot in here, or is it just me?"

"It's just you—and the baby you're heaving around," said Sandra. She pushed Trina into a kitchen chair. "Here, take a break. Reinforcements have arrived."

Trina settled into the chair at the side of the table. "What you got there, Paul?"

Paul leaned and kissed her cheek. "I brought a gift to my best girl." An impish grin filled his face. "Hope you don't mind, Ted."

"Have to see what you brought first, bro."

For a second Lillian felt the grip of jealousy at their camaraderie.

"Ohhh…" Trina pulled the two-liter bottle from its bag. "Sandra, can I have a glass?" She struggled to remove the twist-top.

"Now you've crossed the line," Ted said to Paul. "Her favorite drink."

"You'll have to use a mug," Sandra said as she dropped ice into a ceramic cup. "We plan to use all the good glasses for supper."

"No problem!"

Ted laughed. "You had better give it to her or she'll start drinking from the bottle."

Trina placed her nose just inches above the open

bottle and sniffed. She held out her arms and Paul leaned down for her hug. "Thank you."

Jimmy examined the bottle. "Can I have some? Is it good?"

"Well, I like it." Trina held up her mug. "Here, take a sip and see what you think."

Jimmy peered into the cup and back at Trina, his eyebrows creased. "I don't know..."

"Come on, it's pop," Bill said. "Kids like pop."

"It's soda, Jimmy," Sandra said. "Pop is the same thing as soda."

The boy took a small sip. "Yuck. You can have the rest, Miss Trina."

Trina took the mug from the grimacing boy. "Gladly. You just don't know what's good."

"Can I have some sweet tea?"

"At supper. Here, have some water." Sandra filled a plastic cup and handed it to the boy.

As life swirled around her, Lillian's muscles relaxed. The depression that had settled over her for the past few days melted away in the heat and familial setting. "Let me change my clothes and I'll be down to help." In the upper hall, she smiled as she passed a young couple walking hand-in-hand toward the stairs. "Have a good evening."

The young woman, looking to be no more than early twenties, snuggled into the side of the equally youthful man. "We're headed to dinner and then the movies." The woman gazed at the sparkling diamond on her left hand as she twisted the accompanying band with her finger.

Lillian sighed. Newlyweds most likely, but the thought did not bring the anticipated pain that it once had. In her room she chose a pair of thin-leg jeans and a pale-orange knit top, not so orange as to clash with her hair, but a nice warm orange that made her feel happy.

Back in the kitchen, Jimmy approached her with a wide grin. "Miss Lillian, what do you call a fake noodle?"

She loved the sparkle that this young guy exuded. So much tragedy had followed him, and yet he could smile. "I don't know," she replied. "What do you call a fake noodle?"

"An impasta!" He slapped his leg and laughed. "Get it? An impasta!"

"I get it, you funny guy." Lillian turned to Sandra. "What do you need me to do?"

Jimmy tugged at her arm. "Here's another one. What do you call an alligator in a vest?"

"Jimmy, enough for now," Sandra said. "Go find something to do."

"I don't have anything to do."

Lillian smiled, remembering being told the same thing from her mother a million times when she got in the way. "Let me see," she said. "An alligator in a suit?"

"No," Jimmy said, still laughing. "Not in a suit, in a vest."

"Oh, in a vest." She screwed her face in thought. "How about a handsome gator?"

Jimmy cackled. "No, an investigator!"

No one could be around Jimmy for long and stay morose.

"Jimmy, come help me set the table before your grandma feeds you to one of those alligators." Bill ruffled the boy's hair, and then reached for the white ceramic plates off the top shelf. "Can someone get the napkins and silverware?"

Paul grabbed the basket of silverware from the kitchen table and Lillian took the napkins. Napkin duty seemed to fall to her. Headlights reflected in the window and her breath caught in her throat.

Roger had arrived.

A rush of cool air followed Roger through the door. She tried to avoid looking at him, but she felt his magnetic gaze pull her, as though she were a helpless sliver of metal. He had the looks: dark hair that waved just enough to give it interest, dark eyes that seemed to penetrate to her heart. As she wondered what he looked like without his goatee, she swallowed the bitter lump that rose in her throat.

He knew her dark secret.

"Hey Jimmy," she said, anxious to shift his attention from her, "tell Mr. Roger those jokes you told me."

Jimmy glanced at Roger then at Sandra.

"Go ahead," she said with a sigh.

"So Mr. Roger, what do you call a fake noodle?"

"How about a noodle made out of plastic?"

Soon the table was set and trays of steaming lasagna and bowls of salad were carried to the table.

Sandra arrived last holding a basket of garlic bread.

The tone at the supper table remained light. No one mentioned the house fires, and there were no accusing glances directed her way.

But then, she had not expected the enemy to be here. Even so, she had trouble shaking the tightness she felt since Roger's arrival. He had stared at her several times during supper, and she had quickly glanced down at her plate to avoid meeting his glance.

After helping to clear the supper table, Roger caught her in the hall. "You don't seem yourself," he whispered, glancing toward the kitchen where laughing voices mingled with the clatter of dishes. "You haven't had any more problems, have you?"

"I'm not sleeping well." Her eyes misted. Why the tears, she wondered as she brushed the wetness away with her fingertips.

Roger gave her shoulder a squeeze.

Warmth flowed from her shoulder to her arms, and through her body. She hesitated to move, reluctant to break the sensation of protection. She resented him, and yet she longed for what he had to offer.

Footsteps echoed in the hall and Paul paused, a dish towel dangling from each hand. He stared from her to Roger and back again before he turned and retraced his steps.

She stared after Paul, her stomach clenching into a heavy mass. "I feel guilty about not telling him. He's been so sweet since I moved here. Maybe he could help?"

"Listen Lillian," Roger whispered, "you need to avoid Paul if you don't want your secret to come out. You said that yourself. Don't let his smooth looks fool you. He is a cop, and until we know what's going on, just stay away from him. It would launch his career if he broke this arson case, and he plans to do that, even if it means making assumptions he shouldn't make. You know how that happens..." His insinuations clashed against the laughing voices that came from the kitchen.

"I guess you're right." She continued to stare down the hall. "What did you do with the gas cans?"

"I got rid of them. Don't worry about it." He

tucked a finger under her chin. "Things will settle down, you wait and see."

She looked up into his face, seeing only his lips, moist and full. The sudden urge to place hers on his, to experience the taste of a man again made her heart pound. Her eyes sought his, and she stared at him with longing.

He moved toward her.

"Hey, you two, there you are." Trina's bulging belly preceding her up the hall, followed by Ted and Paul. "Way to get out of dishes."

Lillian felt the burn on her face, and quickly pulled away from Roger. "Sorry Trina, I—"

"Lillian, I'm just kidding. Come on, let's go sit down." Trina headed to the parlor, her body shifting with each step.

The light in the kitchen clicked off.

Bill emerged from the darkened doorway and stopped at the stairs. "I've had enough fun for one night. Besides, a new episode of my favorite television show is calling my name."

"Night, Bill," Roger said. Roger reached for her hand and she pulled away, but not before Paul noticed and scowled.

Her heart tightened. There was no reason she should care, but she did. Paul's opinion seemed important somehow.

"I'm heading home," Paul said.

"No, it's early yet." Trina's lips turned down. "You don't have to go, do you?"

His departure was her fault. There had always been a level of animosity between Roger and Paul, and it must seem to him that she was developing an interest in Roger, while her relationship with him remained superficial. It had to be that way; he was a police officer.

"You had a big day or something, Paul?" Ted asked. "You're usually the life of the party. You got a better offer somewhere?"

Paul planted a gentle kiss on Trina's cheek. "Thanks for the great supper, mama." He softly patted her belly and strode out the kitchen door.

"Well," Trina said, "what was all that about?"

"Come on," Ted murmured, "we have a game of cards to play."

At first, she thought she imagined it. Her muscles tightened as she inhaled deeply. Smoke! "The house is on fire!"

"I started a fire," Ted said.

She stumbled backward, filled with horror, ready to flee.

"In the fireplace, Lillian." Roger grabbed her arm. "Ted started a fire in the fireplace."

As she looked with panic-filled eyes from one to the other, Roger pulled her toward the front door, but pointed into the parlor. "The fireplace, Lillian. Look at the fireplace. Ted built a fire for us *in the fireplace*."

The flames leapt between logs, snapping and snarling as they tangled together. A lifetime ago she had enjoyed the sensuous movement of the flames as they danced around each other much like lovers, the smell of campfires, the memory of being snuggled warm beneath a blanket while sitting on a lawn chair. Craig would hold a stick over the fire, a hotdog sizzling at the end. The joy was forever gone.

The house wasn't burning. Ted wasn't an arsonist. Fire wasn't the enemy.

Her legs wobbled. How could she have made such

a stupid mistake? "I think I'll follow Bill's example and turn in early." Silence followed her as she left the room and lifted one foot in front of the other on the stairs, convincing herself not to run.

~*~

Lillian sat propped against the headboard of her bed, a stack of student papers spread around her. She scanned one and let it drop, and picked up another. With a huff, she tossed the second paper back on the bed, unable to concentrate, but too full of pent-up energy to sleep.

She had overreacted to the fire; the smell of smoke had caught her off-guard. If only she had known Ted had started a fire she could have been prepared.

The party had broken up after she went upstairs.

It always came back to the fire.

She had expected the relocation to allow her to start over. Why did she think her past wouldn't follow her? Thoughts drifted though her head, one after another. Paul, then Roger, then the fires: four of them now. But whoever had planted the gas cans in her car must have decided to leave her alone.

Marking pen forgotten beside her, she sank back onto the pillows. Fire had always fascinated her. Dr. Widder talked about fire repeatedly with her once her parents had shared her history with him. Could she be a pyromaniac? He had wanted to know.

A soft knock sounded on the door and she lifted her head in surprise. No one ever bothered her in her room, and as far as she knew, everyone had retired early. "Come in."

The door opened a few inches and Trina's face

peered through. "Am I disturbing you?"

"I'm supposed to be grading papers, but instead I'm letting my mind run in circles."

Trina entered the room and closed the door behind her. Dressed in a soft maternity t-shirt and a pair of Ted's boxer shorts, she settled on the bed beside her. "Are you all right?"

"Do I look sick?"

Trina smiled. "Not sick, but unhappy. And worried." She stared at her. "I thought you'd be in your pajamas by now."

She nodded toward the papers scattered on the bed. "Jumped right into grading instead."

"Do you want to talk about what's robbing you of your happiness?"

Did she want to talk? She returned Trina's gaze. Other than her sister, Beth, and her husband, Craig, she had never had an adult friend she felt comfortable talking to. Someone had once said that everyone needs a "Jesus with skin on." She didn't know who had said that, but found truth in it. She talked to God daily, but sometimes she ached for a live person to be in front of her. Like Trina.

Trina would understand. Her pregnant friend. God-sent just for her.

Roger knew, and soon he would tell her secret.

She felt the stress pulling him apart each time they were together and she regretted making him an accomplice in her fate.

Trina didn't need to know about the cans hidden in her car, but as Lillian glanced at her wide open eyes she knew she wanted to talk.

"I told you that my husband and child died. I didn't tell you how." She focused on the wardrobe across the room. "Our house caught on fire while they slept. They never got out."

Trina gasped and she felt the soft grip of the woman's hand on her arm. She dare not look into her face for fear of crumbling into tears.

"Lillian, how awful. No wonder you freaked out when you smelled the smoke from Ted's fire."

"I wasn't home. I was supposed to be, but I fell asleep in my office downtown. The fire marshal investigated and said the cause was arson, and I became the primary suspect." Gathering her courage, she turned toward Trina.

Would her friend's face be etched with horror? Would she pull her hand away slowly, so as not to seem obvious?

Tears ran down Trina's ivory cheeks. She slid across the bed and wrapped her arms around Lillian, pulling her close. Together they clung to each other and cried. When the tears ended, they dried their faces.

"I was afraid you would hate me," Lillian said.

Trina's reddened eyes widened. "Hate you? How could I ever hate you? How did you endure it?"

How had she endured? "I've lived with my parents for the past two years. I was never brought to trial, but there are still those in Cleveland who think I'm guilty."

"Then they don't know you very well, Lillian Hunter. How could they think such a thing?"

"I helped set my friend's bedroom on fire when I was about nine. Somehow the label of pyromaniac stuck."

Trina's jaw fell.

"In third grade I had a best friend named Karen. We found a book of matches on the playground from

Emilio's Italian Grill." Lillian grimaced. "I remember that because Emilio's was the place my dad took the family for special occasions. Karen and I lit a couple of the matches and watched the flames until they burned our fingers. I'm surprised we didn't burn the school down with our fascination.

"We took our treasure into Karen's bedroom. When Karen's mom yelled up the stairs to tell us she was going to the grocery store but would only be gone fifteen minutes, we saw an opportunity. We weren't careless, and we really believed the tin pie-pan would contain the flame." The memory returned fresh, even though she had not thought of that long-ago day in years. Her heart ached for the loss of her childish innocence. No longer could she blame mistakes on her youth, or lack of experience.

Sighing, she returned to her story. "Karen and I had been writing secrets on pieces of paper, and then taking turns burning them on the pie plate. One of us started giggling, I can't remember which of us, and we both ended up rolling on the floor. The pie pan tipped over, and the carpet ignited. It was just a tiny spot, and for a few seconds we stared at it in surprise. Then the stack of papers beside it began to burn.

"We beat at the flames but the fire spread faster than we could put it out." Her muscles tightened as she remembered the terror they had felt. She looked at Trina's staring face. "If Karen's mother hadn't arrived home, the entire house could have burned down." She repeated her grimace. "And that is how I became known as an arsonist."

Trina's expression was part horror, part shock. "I don't know what to say."

"You don't need to say anything. Sorry I upset

everyone. I guess that's why I feel so anxious about the house fires here in Darlington."

"At least no one here's blaming you for them!"

Someone was, perhaps no one from Darlington, but still the goal remained to lay blame at her feet, perhaps retribution for escaping judgment in Cleveland.

"Can I ask you something?" Trina asked.

Lillian stretched out on the bed and propped her head in her hand. "What do you want to know?"

A blush crept across Trina's face. "Did I interrupt something between you and Roger this evening?"

The change in conversation felt jarring, but when the new topic settled into her brain, redness covered her cheeks. She laughed. "We sound like a couple of girls at a sleepover." She didn't know if Trina wanted to avoid the topic of the fires and her role in the death of her family, or if she simply moved on in her own flight-of-thought way.

Trina bounced on the bed. "So, did I interrupt something?"

Lillian sat up and crossed her legs. "Yes."

"And?"

"And nothing. That's it." She looked at Trina's pouting face and laughed. Maybe Trina had the right idea. Put the past behind and move on. Since she had already trusted Trina with so much, she might as well take the leap. "All right, here goes. I am attracted to Roger, but something feels forced about our relationship. I hate to admit it, but when you walked in I had wanted him to kiss me, and I think the feeling was mutual."

"Ooh, Lillian! And I interrupted it. Sorry. There's no sense denying that he's a nice-looking man."

"I know…"

"But…"

"But why do I miss Paul when I'm with Roger? He's stopped dropping by every night so now I only see him on Friday nights and sometimes at church." His soft blond hair and huge grin floated through her mind. "He's so easy to be with."

"They both like you."

"I didn't come to Darlington for a relationship." Her eyes misted over, the joy of girl talk snatched away with the reality of life. "When Craig and Susan died, I told God I would spend the rest of my life alone as a punishment for not being home."

"Lillian, that's not what God wants. You didn't set the fire, so why are you holding yourself responsible?"

"I should have been there. I would have smelled the smoke and gotten them out safely."

"Most likely you would've died with them. God has something planned for you. He isn't ready to give you your reward."

Death as a reward? She had never thought of death that way, but more as something to be avoided. She pulled Trina close and hugged her. "You are such a blessing to me."

"If you're all right, I'm headed to bed."

"Have a good rest. You deserve it."

The room felt cold and empty after Trina left. Sleep eluded Lillian. She grabbed her jacket from the back of the chair and headed downstairs. Darlington was safe after dark. Maybe the night air would help settle the thoughts filling her head.

Her mood felt euphoric after the cleansing conversation with Trina. She had been in Darlington for six weeks now, and she felt more alive than she had in the past two years.

~*~

Roger headed to his bedroom, closed the curtains and reached for the box on the top shelf. Mindlessly he opened the lid and grabbed the thumb drive. Within minutes, the computer came to life. A message from his contact popped up, and anger surged through him. How many times did he have to tell her not to send him messages? Just let someone get hold of his computer, and it wouldn't take much to trace her. If she wanted to be careless and implicate herself when he was the one taking all the risks, then he should let her. He skimmed the message, already knowing what it would say.

With the thumb drive shoved into the port, the data began to load. He punched in the contact's phone number on the pre-paid cell phone. Her smooth greeting accosted his ears. "You sent me another e-mail," he said. "I've been too careful for you to be sloppy on your end."

"Careful? That's what you call it?"

"And what would you call it?" It was easy for her to judge when her hands remained clean. Maybe he had been too noble to take all the risk.

"I call it scared." The woman's words stung. "Or lazy. Maybe you never meant what you said in the first place; all words and no backbone."

Heat flamed his face. No one doubted his courage. He had learned to fight in third grade, a necessary survival technique for the frequent changes in schools. In each new location, he had worked to develop the reputation of being the toughest kid on the playground. He had backbone. "I have proven…"

"I know what you did. You don't need to remind me. But do *I* need to remind *you* of the real Lillian Hunter?"

"I know who she is." Then the near-kiss played in his mind. Did he really know which Lillian was real? Maybe the Lillian he had planned to kill was already dead, or perhaps she had never existed at all except in the imaginations of himself and his partner.

The tinkle of ice, and a throaty swallow filtered through the phone. He could almost smell his partner's breath. He knew exactly what room she was in, where she was sitting.

Her mood softened. "I know this is hard. Imagine how it is for me. I have to sit here, waiting, not doing anything. I need her to pay—"

When had the woman's voice turned cold? Initially she had lit the fire that moved him forward, provided the fuel to propel his actions. Her words had solidified his determination to act. Now he stood with the phone held away from his ear, wanting the call to end.

Reassurances given, he shut down the call and returned his attention to the computer. The download completed, he accessed a file and made notes. Next, he pulled out the map from inside the desk, marked changes, and carefully closed out the software.

Harboring too much suppressed tension to sleep, he slipped on a light jacket and locked the house behind him.

With no destination in mind, he wandered much like a dog followed its nose, going from spot to spot based on the step before. Feet mindlessly guided the body while the cool air soothed the mind. Control began to seep back into his muscles.

Even though it was not quite midnight on a Friday night, a few houses already stood dark, those who lived within them tucked safely in their beds. At other houses, the blue glow of the television reflected against the windows. Most likely, the occupants were watching the nightly news. Nothing that interested him. He had never participated in politics. He didn't imagine he would be around long enough to worry about things like social security and Medicare.

A car passed. From the dark silhouette, he couldn't tell if it was a man or woman, but the person was alone. Like him. He felt hollow and empty, more vulnerable than he had been in a long time.

The phone conversation haunted him. He should have taken care of Lillian a long time ago. That was the original plan: within a couple of weeks. It had been a month and a half since Lillian Hunter moved to Darlington, and she was still alive.

13

Roger wandered for over an hour, moving from one neighborhood to the next, like a man with nowhere to go.

A door burst open and light spilled onto the porch. Two men swayed down the steps, laughing and slapping each other on the back as they reached the sidewalk.

Roger stayed behind them until the next block, when he turned, leaving them to their own destruction. His mind whirled as he walked, trying to process his unexpected attraction to the woman he had learned to hate. There was something about her that he seemed unable to escape. What power did she hold, or was she playing a game with his mind?

And her attraction to him seemed equally real. The fear on her face when she talked about finding the gas cans wasn't staged for his benefit. And she had turned to him for help. That had to prove something. And then tonight.

What would it have been like to kiss her? His heart thumped in his chest. He was falling in love with the woman he had vowed to kill, and the realization caused a flicker of joy and then bitter pain.

The sound of his footsteps awakened a dog from his slumber, and the beast shared a half-hearted bark before settling back against the foundation of the house. Except for the rowdy party a few streets back, he could almost believe he was the sole survivor of the end of the world the pastor was so fond of talking about. Sleep had settled over Darlington.

The black sky shimmered just above the trees to the right, and soon an orange glow broke the darkness. The brightness increased into a mass of light that domed a section of the night sky.

Sirens pierced the silence.

Blood rushed through his veins. He began to run.

A fire engine roared past, then another.

Rounding the corner, he stopped. A low groan escaped his lips. Flames roared and wood cracked as the fire destroyed another house. Even from half a block away, the heat assaulted his face. His mind slipped into memories of two other fires. He squeezed his eyes shut, forcing the visions aside. He had to stay in the moment.

Voices layered on top of each other, commands shouted, hoses shot streams of water that hissed as they joined with the blaze.

His shoulders slumped as he watched the licking greedy tongues ingest wood and mortar. He should make his presence known as the proxy homeowner. A loud crack disturbed his thoughts, followed by sprays of orange and red sparks.

Voices shouted. Yellow-garbed firefighters stumbling backward, hindered by heavy gear. Arches of water sizzled, their sound almost lost in the roar of the fire.

The house was dying.

People dressed in nightclothes gathered on the lawns, holding their arms around themselves as if protecting all they loved. An older woman with bare feet, a housecoat tied at her waist, ran to a firefighter and pulled on his arm. A bald and shirtless man ran after her and tried to pull her away. As they struggled, she continued to point toward the adjacent house.

Roger could see her mouth move, and could imagine her screams, but the snarl of the fire drowned her voice.

Soon firefighters shot water at both neighboring structures. Save the other houses; let this one go.

He knew their thoughts. As he stood alone on the sidewalk, too far from the action for anyone to want to join him, he noticed another solitary person huddled within distant shadows.

As though knowing it had been spotted, the figure melted into the blackness.

His back stiffened. He knew this person, but it was impossible.

14

The old post office smelled of dirty bodies and pot roast.

The pinging sound of rain hitting windows mingling with the shuffle of feet, the guttural words of thanks, and the plop of food on paper plates. About fifteen men had shown up at the shelter for dinner and a place to sleep.

Continued showers were expected throughout the night.

Roger thought the rain would bring in more men, but it hadn't. Apparently, if one was homeless, one didn't get weather forecasts, but surely even the dregs of society had enough sense to come inside.

He blamed Lillian for his presence at the shelter, for forcing him into dishing out mashed potatoes to men he did his best to avoid. Eager to please, he had agreed to help, knowing it would also give him the opportunity to watch her.

And then there was the complication of Paul Studler. The man could show up anytime.

After her first experience volunteering, Roger had hoped she would give it up, but no, she had gone the second week. Now the third.

He felt compelled to tag along. Regardless of his growing attachment, he had a commitment to keep. He looked around the large room and imagined the dozen or so smaller spaces that stood in dark isolation throughout the building. What a perfect place, if he could just find the right time.

The men would never miss her when she was gone.

As a man slid his tray along the rail, Roger dropped a scoop of mashed potatoes onto the plate. The man mumbled something that resembled thank you and moved on. Another man followed. Then another. Roger didn't think his stomach would ever accept mashed potatoes again. The very thought of eating anything right now made him gag.

Taking advantage of the lull in the demand for potatoes, he glanced around, searching for Lillian. He spotted her among the tables, her voice carrying through the clatter. "Coffee or iced tea?" She smiled at each man, as though he were the only person in the room. Why did she work so hard at making these men feel special? He would have thought it all an act except for their conversation the night before; that's when he knew he had to come. How could an attorney be so blind to the dangers of what she was doing?

"It's the family's night," she had said as they sat close together on his sofa. "You're part of the family. Come and help."

He stiffened against the softness of her eyes. "How do you know any of the men want to talk to you about legal issues?"

She had laughed. "They don't. Not yet. You should've seen them the first night I helped out. They wouldn't even look at me. Sandra told me that homeless people don't usually trust strangers, especially someone who doesn't have the southern lingo down yet. I just wandered around, doing what I could to help. The second night was better. And this will be the third night. As they say, the third time's the charm."

"There are other things you can do if you're bored, Lillian."

"I'm not bored, and this *is* what I want to do."

Later that night, she had gone back to the bed and breakfast with his promise to come.

And now, movement at the shelter door caught his attention. He hissed under his breath. He should have expected the man, but so much had happened since the accident that he had moved the man to the back of his mind.

Now there he stood, the derelict Lillian had almost hit, still slumped, still staring at the floor, water dripped off of him like a soaked dog while rivulets formed around his feet. Struggling out of his coat, the man placed the wet garment over an empty chair and shuffled toward the food line.

"Good evening, Joe," Sandra said. "Good night to be inside."

Joe lifted his head long enough to give her an awkward smile.

"It's pot roast tonight, your favorite. I've been holdin' back this piece just for you." She placed a generous helping of beef on his plate, followed by a spoonful of green beans. Sandra had said the same thing to every man who had come through the line, greeting most of them by name.

Roger plopped potatoes onto the man's plate, and spooned gravy over the top.

As Joe lifted his head and grunted thank you, a spark of light pulsed through his dull eyes before he moved on.

The guy unnerved Roger. And why the look? It

was all he could do to not jerk the bum aside and ask for an explanation. But location was everything, and he had the good sense not to confront the man in his own environment.

"Joe! I'm glad to see you," Lillian said.

The man gave her a look of...what? Friendship? Appreciation?

The familiarity of the exchange sent flames of anger through Roger.

As Lillian poured Joe's beverage, a new line of men had formed, ready for their handout. He slapped potatoes onto plates.

Joe sat across the room, staring at him, a look of concentration furrowing the vagrant's brow.

As the men finished eating, each deposited his paper plate, empty cup and plastic silverware into the trash bin. They stacked their trays on the table next to the far wall.

Roger had no idea who washed them, but it wouldn't be him.

Sandra scraped the remaining meat into a corner of her stainless steel container. "Looks like our job's over for the night." She turned off the burners under each of the serving trays. "Will y'all carry your containers to the sink for me?"

At the sink, Roger handed his heavy container, remnants of mashed potatoes still clinging to the sides, to Bill.

"So how'd your first night go?" Bill asked as he placed the empty server into the deep sink. He pulled out a cloth that hung from his pocket and mopped the beads of sweat lining his face.

"OK, I guess."

The steam from the kitchen coated the high

windows, shielding the room from the night. The scent of supper clung to the air, and cheerful chatter mingled with the clunk and splash of large pots in the metal sinks.

Half a dozen workers, many of them teens, busied themselves putting away supplies, mopping floors and carrying out trash. They seemed to be working like a seasoned team, even though many were first-timers, like him.

He stared at their faces: intent looks of concentration, smiles, some chatting as they went about their assigned tasks. No one seemed to resent being there, serving bums. Shrugging his shoulders, he wondered if he would ever understand the mentality of the working class.

Bill looked his way. "Ted and I have dish duty tonight. Jimmy likes to wipe off the tables. I guess you're done unless you want to help dry."

"Jimmy has to finish his homework first," Sandra said as she lowered her handful of ladles into the soapy water. "If not, he'll never get it done. I can't believe how much homework second graders have nowadays." She wet a dishcloth at the sink and laid it on the counter.

In the back of the room, a thump sounded as Jimmy closed his school book. He slid off the stool, grabbed the dishcloth, and rushed past Roger, almost making it through the kitchen door before Sandra grabbed his arm.

"Hold on there. Let me check those math problems first."

Sandra, with Jimmy in tow, headed toward the discarded homework.

Bill added detergent to one sink, and bleach to a

second of the three-sectioned unit.

"Where's Lillian?" Roger asked. Once she had finished, maybe she had slipped out to spend time with Trina, who stayed at home on family work nights.

She's in the infirmary," Ted replied as he grabbed a white cotton dishtowel off the stack by the sink. "Middle of the hall on the left."

Roger gritted his teeth. First a food kitchen and now an infirmary.

She wasn't a doctor, and she certainly didn't need to be holding the germy hands of sleazy old men. Some things never changed. She had been out of control in Cleveland, and now, here she was again, taking things to extremes.

The hall felt cold. Half a dozen suspended lights provided light, but not the brilliance of the kitchen. He squinted as his eyes adjusted to the change. The smell of roast beef mingled with the scent of body odor and antiseptic, and he grimaced as he tried to control his breathing.

Men lined the wall in front of an opened door where light spilled into the hall, some of them standing, while others slouched against the green glazed tile.

His hard shoes clicked on the marble floor and he wished he had taken the time to change from his suit into blue jeans and sport shoes. Next time. But no, there wouldn't be a "next time."

None of the men glanced his way as he passed. Reaching the room, anger suffused his face. "What in the world?"

~*~

Lillian examined his skin, so cracked and calloused. She looked up at Joseph and smiled. "Go ahead and put your feet in the water." She squeezed soapy liquid from the cloth over his toes as he slowly immersed them under the sudsy foam.

While other men remained in line to see Margaret, the nurse practitioner, Joseph was the last for Lillian. Both last week and today, he had waited until she had cared for the others. It allowed her to spend extra time with him. "Let your feet soak awhile. I'll be back."

The room, intended as a storage area, held a chair against the left wall for those receiving Lillian's ministrations, while across from her the nurse practitioner had positioned a cot, a small wooden table with two chairs, and a metal rolling supply cabinet, the gray paint scratched and aged. A small dorm-sized refrigerator sat in the corner. Various plastic bins held used towels and medical supplies inside red plastic bags twisted closed in preparation for disposal. The room lacked windows, but the incandescent light melted harsh shadows to puddles of slush.

Lillian sat in one of the vacant chairs, giving Joseph's feet time to absorb the benefit of the warm water.

Margaret, the nurse practitioner, handed a paper cup to the man standing beside her. "You know the routine," she said, smiling. "I need a urine specimen. Put the cup on the shelf over there when you're done." The man ambled from the room and the nurse practitioner slumped into the empty chair beside Lillian.

"Hey there," Margaret said as she wiped the back of her hand across her forehead. "Busy night."

"It has been busy, but that's good, isn't it? That

means the men trust us."

Margaret chuckled. "It is a mixed blessing, for sure." She got up and pulled a bottle of water from the small refrigerator. "Want some?"

"No thanks. I still have to finish my last person."

"Ah, Mr. Callahan." The metal chair squeaked as she sat. "Seems he appears every night you're here. You must have made quite an impression on him."

Wincing, Lillian looked toward the man.

His head rested against the tile wall, his mouth gaped open slightly.

"I made an impact on him all right. I almost ran over him."

"I heard about that."

Lillian's eyes widened. "How did you...?"

Margaret chuckled. "Gossip spreads like thin molasses in small towns." She took a sip from her water bottle. "Speaking of gossip, I hear you bought all those." She tipped her head toward a laundry basket full of clean cotton socks.

Lillian blushed. "Yes, well...when I asked you what I could do to help, and you mentioned foot care, I noticed that most of the men didn't have clean socks to put on when I was done. Something simple I can do."

Margaret raised an eyebrow. "Not everyone can lower themselves to wash the smelly, calloused feet of homeless men."

Lillian glanced back at Joseph, his head still resting against the wall. "These men have touched my heart." It was true; she never felt more alive or needed than on her weekly night at the shelter. And it wasn't just Joe, even though she had to admit he was her favorite. All of the men touched a place in her that had been buried a long time—perhaps all her life. "I had better get back to Joe before his footbath turns to ice." She stopped to pick up a pair of clean socks, a bottle of foot lotion and powder.

"Joseph." Lillian touched his shoulder and his eyes opened.

She knelt on the floor and submerged her hands into the water. Gently she massaged one foot, focusing on the toes and the heel.

"He is not good." Joseph stared at Lillian. "Not like you."

"Who's not good?" she asked lazily, still cocooned in her personal thoughts.

"The man who was with you. He is here tonight."

"Oh, you mean Roger." She chuckled. "It's nice to know you like me better than him. Thank you."

Joe shook his head. "You should not be with him."

His black eyes blazed with intensity and she stopped. "Are you trying to tell me something?"

"He is not a good man."

What could Joe have against Roger? Surely he was confusing one man for another. After all, he lived on the street; ophthalmological appointments probably were not high on his list.

She smiled at Joe, trying to send reassurance. "Roger is a good man. He works with the homeless and poor people every day. He helps find them places to live."

"He is angry."

"Joseph, it's sweet of you to be concerned, but Roger is very kind to me." She searched his eyes, wondering what caused such depth of emotion. "I promise, though, I'll be careful." She returned to her work, running her fingers between each toe of the second foot, just as Margaret had taught her. She lifted his feet out of the water and wrapped them in a clean towel. He didn't speak as she exchanged the soapy water for fresh.

After rinsing his feet and examining each one for cracks or red areas, she rubbed them with a good foot lotion and applied powder before rolling on the first of the new socks.

A voice cracked the companionable silence. "What in the world?"

Lillian turned. "Hi, Roger."

"What are you doing?" Roger's voice reminded Lillian of her father.

Joe's muscles tightened against her hands.

"Helping with some much needed foot care," she said, forcing a smile as she slipped the second sock over Joseph's left foot, trying to calm the anger that rose in her throat. "Nurse Margaret suggested it."

"If there's a nurse here, she should be doing that, not you." Roger sent a glaring look toward Margaret, who remained busy taking the blood pressure of one of the men.

Lillian's throat burned.

Joe stared at the floor, and she could only imagine his pain. Another rejection, one more example of being demeaned, and by a man who made his living helping the poor.

She had thought if Roger actually spent time at the shelter, he would see that the men appreciated the help. And he had willingly come. She turned back to Joseph.

"I came to see if you were ready to go home. I thought maybe we could grab a cup of coffee somewhere."

Joseph jerked under Lillian's touch. A silent

challenge seeped from his eyes as he stared at her.

"I'm not quite done."

"The nurse can finish."

"But this is *my* job." She put a reassuring hand on Joseph's foot. "I won't be long."

Roger glanced at his watch. "Forget it. Some other time when you aren't so busy with your *job*."

As his footsteps echoed up the hall, she tried to suppress the tears that threatened to fill her eyes. "I am so sorry," she mumbled. "I am so sorry."

Joseph slipped his feet into his worn shoes. He looked long at Lillian before silently walking out of the room.

~*~

As Lillian cleaned her work area, Margaret finished the last patient. Once finished, Margaret grabbed two bottles of water and motioned for Lillian to sit. "He isn't our usual volunteer," she said. "Friend of yours, I assume?"

"Yes, he's a friend," Lillian mumbled, her brows drawn together. "Tonight was his first time to volunteer. He helped serve supper."

Roger continually confused her. One minute he seemed kind and caring, but then she would catch an expression that hinted at a storm building deep inside him. She shook her head, pushing aside the internal conflict that brewed in her head, and turned to Margaret. "So you work in Darlington?"

"No, I'm a nurse practitioner at McLeod Regional Medical Center. I work with cancer patients there." She sipped her water. "Volunteering here a couple of times a week helps keep me grounded. I check blood pressures, help with medication issues, and provide minor first aid. Things like that."

Lillian rubbed her lower back, trying to remove the ache from her muscles. "How do you manage such long days? No family at home missing you?" She wasn't sure why she asked the question, but she felt a kinship with this woman, as though somehow connected intrinsically. When a hint of sadness formed around Margaret's eyes, she regretted her forwardness. "I'm sorry. It isn't like me to pry."

"It's just Jack and me."

Lillian raised her eyebrows. "So there is a significant other."

"Jack is my cat," Margaret said. "I had a child once, but now there's just Jack to fuss over."

Lillian's gut ached. "I'm so sorry, Margaret. I had no idea. I didn't mean to bring back painful memories." She thought of her own loss, the sleepless nights and the days that had been darker than Hades itself.

Margaret smiled. "Thinking of my daughter doesn't cause me pain; it brings me joy. She's the reason I became a nurse."

The sound of footsteps shuffled down the hall and past the door. The men were settling in for the night, staking their claim to cots and lockers.

Margaret stared at her water bottle. "I got pregnant in college." She looked up and smiled, sharing a rueful expression. "I was attending the University of South Carolina—go Gamecocks!" She pumped a fist into the air. "When I told my boyfriend, he bailed on me. I dropped out of college for the year, intending to go back and finish my degree in business once the baby was born."

"How did your family react to all of that?"

"That actually wasn't a problem. My parents died while I was in high school. We had no close relatives, so I lived with foster families until I turned eighteen, and then I was on my own."

Lillian thought of her own family, and the disagreements she had with her mother. Now the arguments seemed petty when compared to Margaret's life. Even with the conflicts, her parents would be there for her.

"I was excited about having a baby. It meant someone who would belong to me." Margaret took a sip of water. "Shannon seemed fine at birth, but when I got her home, she fussed for hours at a time, and I couldn't get her to eat. At about six weeks, she started with projectile vomiting." Wistfulness mirrored in her eyes. "That little thing could send formula all way across the room." She chuckled. "We had the nastiest windows."

"And that was a good thing?"

"No, it was a bad thing, but hey, how many babies do you know who can shoot vomit six feet?"

Lillian smiled, but her heart ached for Margaret.

"Shannon lost weight, and the doctor put her in the hospital. I was a new mom, on my own, and scared to death. Thank goodness for my pediatrician. He explained that Shannon's behavior was not my fault, and he would run some tests and try to figure out what was going on. Her first seizure happened the next day; I was so glad she was in the hospital. I screamed for help and the staff came running. An MRI showed she had a smooth brain."

"A smooth brain?"

"You know how brains are all wavy and full of

ridges?"

"Yes."

"Well, the surface of Shannon's brain was smooth. The doctor called it lissencephaly." Margaret smiled as Lillian furrowed her brow. "I had never heard of it either; it's a rare genetic disease. Shannon lived to be two, but she spent most of her life in the hospital. During those long days and sleepless nights, one thing kept me going: the love of the nurses. They gave my Shannon such wonderful care, and their concern included me. They were there for us during her illness and even after. I never would have gotten through those tough months without their help."

Tears ran down Lillian's face. As she clutched the water bottle to her chest, she wasn't sure if her grief was for Margaret, Shannon, or for her own loss. Margaret had a toughness she didn't possess, and she wanted that strength, needed that determination to heal.

"I wanted my life to make a difference, like the nurses had made for Shannon and me, so after Shannon's death I went back to school and became an RN. And then a nurse practitioner. I decided to work with terminally ill children and their families because I have been where they are."

"How you can emotionally handle that? Doesn't it remind you every day of your loss?" She thought of how she had reacted to Trina's pregnancy and the anger that consumed her each time she saw children.

"My *loss*?" Margaret stared at Lillian. "God gave me a gift when He gave me Shannon for those two short years. And He uses all things for His good, if we allow Him to. By sharing Shannon with me, He prepared me to do the work I'm doing. I honor

Shannon's life and God's goodness every time I show up for work. Do I go home sometimes and cry my eyes out? Sure. But not often, and I may have cried even without having loved Shannon."

Lillian stared at her hands gripped tightly in her lap. "I had a child once, too." The words were barely a whisper. "And a husband. They died in a horrible accident. I should have been with them, but I wasn't."

"Lillian, I'm so sorry. If you had been with them, would you have died too?"

"Maybe."

Margaret slid her chair around the table, the scrapping of metal legs on cement echoing in the silent room. As she wrapped her arms around Lillian's shoulders, tears welled up in the corners of Lillian's eyes.

"You have to let the guilt go," Margaret murmured. "If God had wanted you to be with them, He would have made sure you were there. Apparently He has other plans for your life."

Margaret's breath against her face felt like angel wings. Someone had told her early in her grieving that God sent angels to comfort His people, and one can feel the touch of their wings. She gave Margaret a tentative smile. "You're the second person recently who has told me that God has plans for me."

Margaret squeezed her shoulders. "Then maybe you should listen. Do you have good memories of your husband and daughter?"

Lillian wiped her eyes. "Of course I do. Craig was the kindest man ever, and our little Susan was the sunshine in our lives. She had my curls, but Craig's brown eyes. Her sweet spirit could make anyone smile."

"Sounds like God gave you a gift with your husband and daughter."

Were they a gift? A lifetime ago, she believed in God's goodness, but not anymore. "Then why did He take them away? Why didn't He protect them?" Angry words gushed from her mouth, the confusion that she kept stuffed inside rolled out. "I know you can't answer that. No one can. But I still don't understand how you can find anything good about God allowing your daughter to die. He literally jerked her from your arms."

"Lillian, remember that God loves her too, and He knows what is best for her. Trust in it or not, God has a good life planned for you. You just need to listen to His voice."

Even if Lillian forgave God, how could she listen for His voice when the person responsible for killing her family remained unpunished? Anger overpowered everything else; it reduced to nothingness friendship, love, and even God Himself. In addition to the guilt that twisted her mind during the day and haunted her dreams at night, it was anger that kept her locked in her own emotional horror. She hated the system that chose to accuse her of setting the fire while the true culprit ran free.

The law was broken, and no one cared. And now, with no new leads, the case of Craig and Susan Hunter had been closed. Unsolved.

And anger remained locked in a heart that secretly sought revenge.

~*~

The light reflected off the wet pavement as Lillian

drove the short distance home. Why did the bed and breakfast feel like home with pregnant Trina and suspicious Bill?

A car passed, throwing water onto the windshield. As the wiper crossed the windshield, the film disappeared. What if life could be like that, with a single swipe, remove the parts that hurt, leaving the future clear for living?

Her thoughts landed on Paul. Tall and handsome. And funny. She smiled, remembering some of his jokes. And his way with little Jimmy—he would be a great father.

Her throat tightened. She could never have a life with Paul. Of all the people she had met in Darlington, Paul remained the most dangerous. As Roger said, Paul was a police officer first.

Pulling into the driveway, she flexed one aching hand then the other. When had her tension grown to monster proportions?

She needed to patch things up with Roger, but the man frustrated her. What had upset him tonight? He was a nice man, caring—just in a different way than Paul. After all, it was Roger she had turned to after discovering the gas cans.

So why did her mind keep shifting to Paul? She slammed the car door, teeth grinding. First, the Paul/Roger debate had sent her spinning, and then the Darlington fires. Where was the quiet life of scholarly dedication and seclusion she had counted on?

Thanksgiving was only a week away. She would to go back to Cleveland for the holiday. The change might be good for her, and Beth would be there.

Rain pelted against her body and rivulets of water streamed down her face as she ran toward the house.

Had her life really been that bad in Cleveland, or had she exaggerated the animosity? Had it only been six weeks since she had come south?

In five days, she would again pack everything she owned into her small car. The vision of her future lay blank before her.

15

Cleveland hadn't changed much in six weeks.

Lillian felt different, and had expected her environment to be different too.

The big city felt cold and rushed. Definitely more traffic than Darlington.

The tension that had driven her south in the first place remained. Both with her parents and when she sought out friends, the dance of pretense scraped against her nerves. She found herself cautious, as though some sense within her remained on high alert lest she do or say the wrong thing.

The kitchen smelled of roasting turkey. Every burner on the stove held a stainless steel pot, the moist heat reminding her of the homeless shelter. Her chest tightened with longing. But then memories of Roger's behavior erased the joy. She had been unable to see him before she had come home. The crack in their friendship caused her to be even more unsettled.

Sitting on a kitchen barstool, elbows propped on the white marble slab, she watched as her mother cut the apple and pumpkin pies bought from the Frazier Bakery. Their holiday pastries always came from Frazier's. Her mom declared them the best.

Lillian had agreed—until she ate Sandra's.

What were Trina and Ted, Bill and Sandra, and little Jimmy having for Thanksgiving dinner? She missed them, but tried to squeeze the thoughts of

Darlington from her mind. After all, she was home with her family, her real family. She belonged in Cleveland, not in Darlington.

"Lillian, are you listening to me?" Her mother's voice cut through her musings. "You don't seem yourself." Martha Goodson wiped her hands on a white towel with a large, colorful turkey appliquéd in the center. The Thanksgiving towel always came out the day before the holiday and was returned to storage the day after. Her mother folded the towel into exact thirds, and placed it, turkey facing out, in the center of the bar by the sink. "Are you sure living in the south is good for you?" Her lips puckered as she stared at Lillian, her gaze a challenge.

Lillian offered a wisp of a smile. How could she possibly describe the past six weeks when she couldn't wrap her mind around them herself? As an attorney, she had condensed the basest human actions into simple words, explainable to a jury. But now she couldn't define her own life for her mother. "I've made some good friends, and I love my job." No need to mention the fires, or the fact that her heart had awakened. Why spawn questions she was unwilling to answer?

Her mother's stare drilled into her face. "Well, your dad and I think you are being foolish. But then, you always have gone your own way."

The words stung as though she had been slapped. At the sound of rattling on the stove, her mom turned, lifted the lid off the front pot, stabbed at the potatoes with a fork, and then replaced the lid.

Simple actions completed through habit and routine. Should life be like that: a routine that one lived by, no matter what?

Nothing shook the stoic existence of her parents, and even though the predictability appealed to Lillian, the rigidity of their lives felt as false as hers had become lately.

In the letter of the law, her mother was right: she had gone her own way. Maybe it was time to grow up and come home. The time in Darlington had strengthened her, and she would miss Trina and the others immensely. Tears puddle in her eyes and she turned her back to her mother. Were the tears from her mother's hurtful words, or were they for a life that had never really belonged to her?

God held the answer, and she tried to trust, she really did, but her brain remained conflicted. Did God care about her anymore? Roger didn't seem to think so. She felt homeless as though the entire planet had cast her off, sending her spinning into the dark unknown.

"Lillian!" Her mother's sharp voice cut through her thoughts. "Am I so beneath you that you can't pay attention to me for even a few minutes?"

"Hey, Lilly!" Beth called from the next room. "Come help me set the table."

Her mom heaved a deep sigh. "Go," she said, brushing Lillian from the room with a swish of her hands.

Beth stood beside the table, a goofy grin spread across her face and one of the good china plates from the gold-rimmed set gripped in her hand. The white, linen, holiday tablecloth already covered the dark wood of the formal table.

Even though she was grateful to escape her mother's probing accusations, the dining room failed to offer the expected relief. Something felt wrong.

"Thought you might need an excuse to get away

from the hundred questions," Beth said, setting the plate on the table.

"Thanks." She hugged her younger sister, trying to ignore the uncomfortable itch.

Beth placed the second plate on the table.

"The table! That's the problem!" She pumped her fist into the air as a sense of release filled her. One itch solved. Maybe life was doable.

"What's wrong with the table?"

"You don't know?"

The dining room had been the source of numerous arguments between her parents. Her mother thought the room too small and wanted to move in order to have a larger formal space for guests. But her father disagreed, stressing the quality of the current home and their history there.

"You didn't put the table extensions in. Where is everyone going to sit?"

Beth stared with unblinking eyes. "They didn't tell you." She looked at the floor. "There'll only be the four of us."

Her parents entertaining skills shined during the holidays. Thanksgiving meant at least a dozen close friends sharing a feast.

She looked at the table again, diminished in size and importance, still draped in white, still adorned with the good china, but no longer filling the room with its imposing presence. "Just the four of us?"

"I guess they wanted you all to themselves." Beth placed another plate on the table.

There had only been two pies. She had assumed there were more in the pantry. Her mother's characteristic flutter had been replaced by jerking tension. She hadn't seen it until now. Her breath hung in her throat. "What aren't you telling me?"

Beth grasped her hands. Pools of pain filled her eyes. "I heard Mom and Dad talking." Her words were tight. "They weren't sure what you would be like when you came home."

"What do you mean, what I would be like?" She snatched her hands away.

As the look of misery on Beth's face grew deeper, Lillian thought of the two years when Beth had been her only friend, the only person willing to listen as she had poured out her pain over and over. "It's you and me, Beth. We're sisters. We've always been there for each other." Her voice softened. "You can tell me. What did they expect would happen when I moved to Darlington?"

A tear dribbled down Beth's cheek. "They thought you would fall apart, start doing strange things...or something. They thought when you came home you would be like you were after the fire."

Lillian clenched her teeth, remembering the inconsolability, the consuming grief. The blank spaces in her memory, days that she simply couldn't remember. She thought of her mother's stories; how she had to be stopped from getting out of the house in the middle of the night, convinced that Susan or Craig needed her. But most frightening was her mother's need to hide the matches after she tried to set fire to her bed.

At the time, Dr. Widder had reassured her parents, claiming these were normal reactions to trauma and not a permanent condition.

Over the months, her gaps from reality had become less, and now she felt as sane as she had ever been. In Darlington she had made friends. They trusted her. She had a good job. A life. Did her parents have such little faith in her strength?

Tightening her shoulders, she grabbed the stack of linen napkins off the sideboard and threw them on the left side of each plate, just as she had been taught as a child. But as a child, she had made sure the loose ends were toward the plate, the folded edge out. Now she didn't care. "Let's just get this meal over with."

Once her duty had been served, she escaped to her room and shut the door. She grabbed her Bible off the nightstand, hugged it to her chest, and flopped on the bed. She had turned to God's word less often over the course of the last six weeks. Guilt rose in her throat; she needed to be alone with God. He had not forgotten her, in spite of the fact that she had neglected Him. But He had been there. And He was here now. Tears spilled down her face.

God, what do You want me to do? She sat quietly and listened.

The murmured voices of her sister and mother swirled. The garage door rolled up and then down again. The furnace kicked on, sending the hated pine scent across the room.

But no words of comfort or instruction came from God. *God, if you don't want to tell me what to do, don't complain when I mess it up.* Frustrated, she threw her Bible onto the bedspread and strode back downstairs.

The next thirty minutes were busy with last-minute preparations. In spite of fewer mouths to feed, a dozen platters and bowls needed carried to the table: turkey, mashed potatoes, green beans, corn, dressing, cranberry sauce, salad.

Her mother lit the orange tapered candles at each end of the table, slid the matches into the pocket of her silk pants, and took her seat opposite her husband. One person graced each side of the table.

Lillian stared at the food—enough to feed the homeless men for a week, and most of it would be tossed out, uneaten.

Her father rubbed his hands together. "Looks good, dear. You've outdone yourself again." He reached for the turkey platter.

"Dad," Lillian said quietly, "I would like to thank God for our meal."

He stared at her.

"She wants to say grace, dear," her mother added.

"I know what she means." He narrowed his eyes. "This is why I didn't want you to leave home."

Lillian glanced at Beth, who sat primly in her place, both brown eyes crossed. Neither parent could see their younger daughter's face. She and Beth had created this secret signal back in their elementary school days. When one violated a family code of conduct, and the other was forbidden to speak in defense, she showed support by crossing her eyes. The message was clear. *This stinks; it will be over soon; I love you.* Lillian's burning anger tempered under Beth's silent sympathy. "Thanking God for our blessings is a good thing." She tried to keep her voice level. "Dad, if you remember, I've asked to say grace before."

"Not for the past couple of years." He crossed his arms over his chest, gold cufflinks sparkling in the candlelight sending incongruent vibes.

"Ralph, perhaps just this time…"

"This all started after she married that husband of hers." Her father glared, his eyes becoming dark holes in a pinched face. "You marry beneath you, and look what you get."

She refused to look at Beth, refused to allow sisterly support to compensate for her father's hateful words. Her self-control dissolved under the pressure of the anger releasing through her pores. "Craig was not beneath me," she said through clenched teeth. "He was a good man. He cared for me, and he showed me God's love, something you never did."

The single chime of the mantle clock announced the half hour. Its metallic tone sliced through the icy silence.

The muscles in her father's jaw tightened. "I am eating my dinner, which my wife has prepared for me. You do whatever you want." He grabbed the serving fork and plopped a large piece of turkey on his plate.

Lillian bowed her head. *Father, thank you for this food. I know that You are the source of all things that I have. Please help my family to —*

"Lillian!"

She jerked her head up to find her mother handing her the turkey platter.

Across the table Beth crossed her eyes.

"Mom and Dad, I love you, but I can hardly wait to go back to Darlington."

A mouthful of half-chewed turkey flew from Beth's side of the table.

The words had been unpremeditated, made in the tension of the moment. Had the decision come from God, or from Satan?

16

Late Saturday morning Lillian stumbled down the stairs, her fuzzy, oversized slippers slapping each step. Covering a yawn, she wandered into the kitchen.

Trina turned and smiled. "Hey, I heard you come in last night. Thanks for calling ahead; otherwise I would have sent poor Ted down the stairs with a baseball bat."

The image of Ted creeping around with a wooden bat played through Lillian's head. Peaceful, non-violent Ted. Now if Trina had sent Bill—that would have painted a different picture.

She glanced toward the dining room. "No guests today?"

"No, I think everyone wanted to stay home for the holidays. We only have one more booking through the end of the year. Do you want some coffee?" Trina reached for a mug on the open shelf. "I baked oatmeal muffins this morning in honor of your return."

Lillian sat at the table. "You're so sweet."

"I know they're your favorites." Trina handed the coffee to Lillian, and then reached for a round bowl covered with a red-and-white checkered dishcloth. She placed the bowl of muffins on the table and added a dish of fruit.

"Lillian closed her eyes as she chewed. "These are so good." She heard the scrape of the chair on the old floor and knew Trina had taken a seat across from her.

Her heart swelled until she had to swallow against the pain. When had she fallen in love with this family? She had never felt so unconditionally accepted, not even in Cleveland. But here, in this sunny kitchen, she, Lillian Hunter, college professor and friend, felt at home.

Trina's arms rested across her expanding abdomen, her attention fully on Lillian, "I really missed you."

"I missed you too." She took another bite of muffin. "I thought about not coming back."

"Why?" Trina's back straightened. "Are you unhappy here? Did we do something? Are things not working out at the college? You never talk about work much. Are you doing all right living here—"

She held up her hands. "Whoa, Trina. It's not you. I thought when I went back to Cleveland I would feel a longing to stay, but all I wanted was to come back here." She sipped her coffee. "Before I went home, I had hoped that the feeling of alienation would be gone. I actually only got to visit with one friend, and that didn't go too well." She sighed, pushing out bitter memories. "The tension at home, the expectations of perfection—don't put your glass in the sink, make your bed—all came rushing back to me. My mother's perfection and my father's controlling nature."

Trina sat silently, her eyes soft with compassion.

"You know, now that I've had time to think about it, I must have carried some of that rigidity to my own home with Craig and Susan. I must have driven them crazy at times with my need for order and control."

"Do you remember your first breakfast here?" Trina asked.

Lillian spooned chunks of fruit into her mouth.

"You were so nervous," Trina said. "Usually our

guests are on vacation, and in happy moods. But something about you bothered Dad. He said you had a burden of some kind."

"I remember the looks he gave me that morning, as if he expected me to pull out a gun and start shooting."

"Nothing that dramatic," Trina said, a gentle smile curving her lips. "But he was worried about you."

"I think he still is."

"Have another muffin." Trina pushed the bowl closer to Lillian.

"If you keep feeding me like this, I'll look like you, without the reward at the end."

Trina ran her hand across her abdomen. "I'm really sorry about your Susan…"

She pressed a finger against a crumb and transferred the morsel to her mouth, resting her fingertip on her lips just for a second. "Margaret told me something the last time I worked at the shelter. She said Craig and Susan were a gift from God." The hot coffee felt warm in her mouth as she sipped. "Margaret said that she rejoices in the memory of her daughter, knowing God provided those memories."

"I didn't know Margaret lost a child."

"From a genetic brain disease. She said that she still misses her daughter every day." Lillian paused. "At the time I wondered how she could still smile."

"Did you figure it out?"

Ted ambled in through the back door. "Good morning, Miss Lillian." He glanced at his watch and a smile spread across his face. "I guess it's still morning. Welcome back and hope you had a good Thanksgiving."

"Oh, it's 'Miss Lillian' now?" Lillian grinned at the

sparkle in Ted's eye.

"We're loaded up and ready to go."

Trina turned to Lillian. "Will you need me for anything?" She pushed herself off the chair and gathered dishes from the table. "Sandra has a limb on that old magnolia tree in her side yard that needs to come down. Ted and Dad are going to hack away at it—"

"We are going to do more than that, oh, ye of little faith. Your dad has a chain saw."

Trina's eyes sparkled. "Oooh. A mighty chain saw: the weapon of warriors. Why not come with us, Lillian? Sandra and I are set to supervise."

"And fix lunch, I hope," Ted added.

"And fix lunch," Trina said. "Come with us."

"I don't want to interfere in family time." She imagined the fun they would have together, so different from the constant tension at home.

"You're not a guest anymore. After two months at my house, you're my sister." Trina hugged Lillian's shoulders. "You eat in the kitchen, for goodness sake. Guests eat in the dining room."

Lillian looked at Trina. "Do you know how to cross your eyes?"

"What?"

"Just a sister joke. Let me get my shoes." She bounced up the stairs. Was it wrong to enjoy this family while being ostracized from her own? It seemed as if every time she allowed herself happiness, pain quickly followed. Would she bring misery to this family?

She pushed the image away as she tied on her shoes. What trouble could she possibly bring?

~*~

Lillian stared at the six-legged creatures marching up and down the length of the severed limb with the scent of freshly cut wood filling her nose.

Trina picked a stick off the ground and placed it in the path of the parade.

"Trina, let the bugs alone," Bill said, brushing sawdust off the top of his head.

"I just want to see how long it will take for some of the ants to crawl up my stick."

"Not very long, Aunt Trina," Jimmy said. "Look!"

Several ants climbed onto her hand. She dropped the stick and picked the ants off her arm.

"If you hang around Trina," Bill said to Lillian, "you need to know about her flaw."

"I know what you're about to tell her, Dad, and it's not a flaw. I can't help it. I just feel sorry for the creatures."

"It's a flaw," he replied. "Anyway, back to my story. When Trina was a kid she had a habit of catching the bugs that wandered into the house and taking them back outside. I tried to teach her how to do it right, to squish the little boogers, but even at that age she was stubborn and refused to listen."

"All God's creatures deserve to live, Dad."

Jimmy's eyes widened. "Do you really pick up things like spiders?"

Sandra held up her hands. "Enough! What am I to do about these ants?" She folded her arms in front of her.

Ted rubbed his chin. "I suppose we should call an exterminator."

"I bet those are termites!" Jimmy ran from one side

of the tree to the other, and then jumped over the sawed-off limb.

Longing tugged at Lillian's heart, but the ache failed to consume her as in the past. Did Trina hope for a child as wonderful as Jimmy? She thought of the story Trina had told her about Jimmy, how he had endured more in his short six years than any child should when he lost both parents, and more recently, had been at the mercy of a kidnapper for almost a month.

"How do you know they're termites, Jimmy?" Trina asked.

"I studied them in school." He assumed a rigid pose in front of Trina and counted off on his fingers. "Termites are a form of cockroach. They lived during the time of the dinosaurs. They live," he threw his arms wide, "in colonies of millions! And they eat dead wood." He looked at his grandma. "That's probably why they're in our tree." Jimmy ran and hurtled himself across the limb where he fell among the cast-off branches. "I'm OK," he said, laughing from the other side.

Sandra sighed. "Jimmy, you're getting in the way. Come and stand beside me." She grabbed his hand as he tried to dart past her.

Trina winked. "I'm with you on this one, Jimmy. How do all of you know they're not termites?" She bent over the crawling critters.

"*I* know," Bill said. "They're carpenter ants and we don't want them moving to the house now that their nest has been disturbed. We need to get this limb out of here."

"Grandma says you know things," Jimmy said. "You knew where to find me when I was kidnapped.

God tells you things."

Bill studied the exuberant boy.

"Jimmy, we can talk about that later," Sandra said. "And Ted, I doubt that I can reach an exterminator on Saturday, but I'll go make a few calls." She pulled the reluctant boy with her toward the house.

"Jimmy can stay with me if it's all right," Ted said. "He can help drag wood to the curb once we cut this limb into smaller pieces."

Sandra let go of Jimmy's hand and mouthed a "thank you."

The chain saw roared and Trina covered her ears. She turned to Lillian and shouted, "We might as well start lunch." The silence of the kitchen seemed tomblike after the ear-piercing noise outside. "Sandra has a nice house."

"I forgot you haven't been here before. Did you know her husband built it for her right after they were married?"

The yellow walls looked like sunshine, sort of like Trina's kitchen. White cabinets climbed all the way to the nine-foot ceilings while an old pendant light hung in the center of the room. A window looked over the side yard, framing the busy men. On the far wall, a round wood table stood surrounded by five chairs. White stove and refrigerator. Metal dishwasher. Black microwave. Unlike in her mother's kitchen, nothing matched, but it felt homey and lived-in.

"We'd better get the food cooking before the men start clamoring for sustenance," Trina said with a chuckle. "Will you cut the onion while I brown the meat?" She pulled ground beef from the refrigerator and reached for the skillet.

Lillian chopped the onion on an old, wooden

cutting board and scraped the pieces into the skillet with the meat. She inhaled deeply. "I love the smell of cooking onions. What else do you need me to do?"

"I think Sandra has some vegetables in the refrigerator. You can clean them and make a veggie tray to go with the sloppy joes."

The sound of knife against wood and the sizzle of meat represented domestic bliss to Lillian. She glanced at Trina and wondered again at the joy that radiated from her friend. Would she ever find that depth of contentment?

"What did Jimmy mean when he said that Bill knows things?" Lillian asked.

"Jimmy was kidnapped right after we moved here. The person was coming into our house and stealing things from a cellar we didn't even know existed, and Jimmy saw him. Then, about a month later, I happened to go downstairs for water and caught the man in the house. God led Dad to both of us and saved Jimmy's life. The doctor said he couldn't have survived another day."

"That must have been awful."

"It was pretty bad. Jimmy was more scared than I was, and he still has trouble sometimes leaving Sandra, or when he hears strange noises."

"So that's all there is to Bill's strange power?" Dare she hope?

"Actually, since then, Dad has opened up to God's leading, and God has given him a deeper understanding." She grabbed the ketchup from the refrigerator. "It's hard to explain, but it's like Dad senses trouble ahead of time so he can prevent it. It's mostly a sixth sense about people."

"What can he tell about people?" The green

pepper fell into clean strips on the cutting board. She wanted to appear only mildly curious. As she saw it, Bill remained her biggest risk. If he discovered her history from Cleveland, and then somehow he found out about the gas cans...

"Oh, he knows things like if people are telling the truth, stuff like that."

"That probably comes in handy with strangers coming in and out of your house. Has he ever said anything about me?" She broke open a bag of radishes.

"Actually, he has mentioned you a couple of times." Trina hesitated. "He said you have a burden that you aren't sharing. And he senses danger around you."

The knife made a loud smacking sound against the wood cutting board as it pushed through the bottom of a radish.

"You said you thought about not coming back," Trina continued. "I wonder if Dad was feeling your doubt over leaving Cleveland...or something else."

Suddenly wishing she had remained back at the inn, Lillian remained silent, eyes focused on her task. The rejection of her parents, fresh from her visit over Thanksgiving, confirmed her inability to be loved. Her attraction to Paul remained a pipe dream, while Roger...she sighed.

"Do you miss Cleveland?"

"No, I miss what I used to have in Cleveland."

"Your husband and daughter?"

"Yes."

Lillian looked out the window.

The side yard was private, even in the middle of town, shielded from the neighbor by overgrown dogwood trees and azalea bushes. A redbird clung to the edge of the empty birdbath, undisturbed by the motions of men and boy. Marigolds and mums filled the circular flower bed Bill had been working on for Sandra.

No, she didn't miss Cleveland, but her heart ached from loneliness. This is what she missed. Belonging.

"I have never known God to leave one of His children in misery," Trina murmured.

Trina peeked at her from across the room, and Lillian rewarded her with a scowl.

"So how's it coming with the men in your life?" Trina asked.

If Lillian had been capable of laughing, she would have bubbled with mirth over Trina's sudden change of topics. So like Trina, always keeping the peace. "I don't think I have much to offer right now." She pushed the blade of the knife through a tall stalk of celery.

Trina slid the skillet with sizzling meat to a cold burner. "Oh, I think they might disagree with you on that." Another hesitation. "Paul's been asking about you lately. He thinks you're avoiding him."

"I'm not avoiding him."

"You and Roger seem to have plans on some Fridays. We miss you at family night."

"Trina, I can—"

"No, it's all right. What you do in your free time is your own business. It's just that Paul and Roger have been coming over to the house every Friday night for months now, and then you became part of our group. Now, suddenly, or it seemed sudden, two of you stopped coming. I just wondered if something was up." She smiled and raised her eyebrows. "So what about Roger? Are you becoming an item?"

"No." She set down her knife and looked at Trina. "It's just...no."

Trina laughed. "It's OK, Lillian. You can like Roger if you want to. This is just girl talk, you know, sister-to-sister. I'm good at keeping secrets—ask my dad. I was trying to keep my pregnancy from him, but he noticed some of my symptoms, like morning sickness and always being tired, and he thought I was dying. It was quite a scene until we got it all straightened out."

A smile pushed its way onto Lillian's face. "Trina, you're a joy. Life would be so boring without you." She gazed long at the younger woman. "And, sister-to-sister, I find both guys appealing in different ways. This just isn't a good time for romance right now. Life is complicated."

Sandra walked into the kitchen, clutching a phone book, and kept walking. "Try to find anyone at work on a Saturday around here." The words floated into the room as the back door slammed behind her.

Trina giggled. "Poor Sandra. Life is complicated for her too."

Tromping footsteps. "Yes, I tried them, Bill. I tried every exterminator on the list."

"What are you supposed to do in an emergency? This wouldn't happen in Ohio."

"I don't suppose most folks consider ants an emergency," said Ted.

Jimmy ran across the kitchen and grabbed onto Sandra's hand. "Guess what Uncle Bill can do? He can lift a log the size of a tree all by himself."

Sandra raised her eyebrows and a sheepish grin spread across Bill's face. "The chain saw got jammed. It was either drag the branch to the curb or kill myself using the hatchet." He grabbed a paper towel and wiped sweat off his face.

"You made the right choice," Sandra mumbled.

"Hey guys, go get washed up," Trina said. "Lillian and I have lunch ready."

Bill gave Lillian another penetrating look before he left the room. What was he sensing now?

~*~

Trina stifled a yawn. Usually she was the first to go to bed, but tonight she needed to talk to her dad. She either had to wait until he left the parlor so she could follow him, or she had to stay awake until Lillian went to bed.

Her father's ongoing suspicions of Lillian, and Lillian's reticent behavior at Sandra's, had left her uneasy. Saturday night television held no interest for her, but she refused to leave for the comfort of her room and a half-read novel.

Thirty minutes passed and the program changed.

"Lillian, you going to church with us tomorrow?" Trina asked more as a hint to the fleeing time than curiosity.

"I thought I would, but I can drive myself if you have plans afterward." Lillian seemed mesmerized by the toothpaste commercial.

"No plans. Just thought I'd ask." Nestled against Ted on the couch, warm and comfortable, she let her eyes drift closed.

Ted's voice awakened her. "I can't believe you're still up, babe." He rubbed her shoulder. "Usually you hit the bed about nine, and here it is almost eleven."

"Oh, my, is it that late?" Lillian jumped up from

her chair. "I need to get to bed. Good night, all."

Trina stretched and rubbed the sleep from her eyes. She waited until she heard Lillian's bedroom door closing. "Dad, I have something to ask you."

Bill, halfway out of the recliner, turned. "I was headed to bed, honey. What is it?"

Trina glanced toward the doorway. The entry, grayed to shadows, stood empty. She lowered her voice. "When we were at Sandra's today, and you guys came in for lunch, you gave Lillian a funny look. Were you feeling something?"

Ted clicked off the television.

The silence felt alive, waiting as anxiously as she for her father's answer. She wanted to know, but she didn't. Lillian had become intertwined with her heart, but her dad kept insisting the woman was a danger. She tended to see good in everyone, but even so, she could not believe Lillian concealed maliciousness within her. There had to be another explanation for her dad's concern, and the first step to figuring it out was to have her dad share what he had noticed earlier that day. She had been with Lillian in the kitchen; she knew what they had been discussing, maybe that would help.

Ted shifted on the couch, remote control dangling from his hand. "Did God tell you something about her?"

Bill rubbed his jaw. "Every time I look at the woman, my stomach knots and I feel ready to fight someone...something...I don't know. It's confusing."

Ted stared at his father-in-law. "Do you think she'll hurt Trina?"

"I keep remembering her first day..." Bill said.

"But Dad, she explained that." Frustration

mounted. Why didn't he move on? And why was she the only one to defend Lillian? According to Ted, even Roger held suspicions. Maybe she should talk to Paul, but what good would it do? She had no real information to share with him other than feelings and speculations.

Bill shook his head. "I know she explained it. There's nothing specific I can lay a hand on, but the feeling's still there, and it's getting stronger."

The baby kicked, and Trina placed a hand on her stomach. In spite of her attachment to Lillian, the most important consideration had to be her unborn child. What if her dad was right? God had given him a special gift. She liked Lillian and believed her incapable of evil, but if she had to be careful around her, she would do it. A load of rock fell into her stomach. She felt as if she had just betrayed her best friend.

17

"She's here," Ted whispered to Lillian when she walked in the back door. A glimmer of conspiracy shone from his eyes.

"What's she like?" Lillian cast him a secretive smile as she walked toward the sink. Water overflowed her glass as they glanced down the hall.

"This is called a lady's staircase." Trina's voice carried to the kitchen. "When the house was built, women wore hoop skirts, and by having the stairs in the back of the house, male guests were prevented from seeing up the ladies dresses."

Bill, a large leather suitcase in each hand, followed his daughter and the newest guest up the stairs.

The new guest had become a familiar experience to Lillian. The twinges of jealousy that used to accompany the arrival of each new person had eased. Initially, expecting to be relegated to the dining room when other guests were present, she had been pleased when Trina made it known she was welcome, perhaps even expected, to eat with them. And now she had her own role in welcoming new guests. With each new arrival, the routine remained the same.

Trina acted the hostess and Bill carried the luggage.

Ted hugged the background with Lillian, acting as covert spies, until Lillian had to assume her role as "satisfied client."

"She seems nice. I guess I should be used to ladies traveling alone by now." Ted pursed his lips. "It's just that, she seems like the kind of lady who should have a husband at her side."

"How so?"

"She's short and plump, like an Italian mama. But she's dressed like a million bucks with the tailored slacks and shirt. Gray and silver." He chuckled. "Wonder how Trina knew to put her in the gray room?"

Lillian playfully punched him in the arm. "You sound chauvinistic to me. Can't wait to meet her. How did I end up with this entertain-the-new-guest assignment?"

Ted punched her back. "You're just good at it. Want to help me get the refreshments ready?"

They had just set the tray with iced tea and cookies in the fancy parlor when Trina escorted the guest into the room. "Oh, Lillian, I'm glad you're home. I want you to meet Mrs. Blackwell. Mrs. Blackwell, this is Lillian Hunter, one of our guests, who is more like family now. She's been with us since the middle of October."

Mrs. Blackwell extended a hand that displayed manicured nails and a large diamond ring. "Please, call me Nadine."

The woman's skin felt like fluff beneath Lillian's fingers. Nothing like Sandra's grip. She must never do any work.

Trina motioned them to sit and proceeded to serve refreshments as Lillian scanned the familiar room: tall windows, thick moldings, and fireplace already crackling with life. What would a worldly woman like Mrs. Blackwell think of the feminine environment?

"What brings you to this part of the country, Lillian?" Nadine asked before Lillian could begin her job of putting the new guest at ease.

"I accepted a teaching position at Francis Marion University. FMU's the four-year college for this part of the state."

"And what do you teach, may I ask?" She took a small sip of tea.

"Political science. I worked as an attorney in Cleveland before I moved here."

Trina hovered around the small table. "Would you like a cookie, Mrs. Blackwell?"

"Please, call me Nadine. I insist. And no thank you, dear, but the cookies do look delicious."

"Oatmeal raisin, Trina's specialty." She choked back a giggle and hoped Ted was listening from the hall.

Bill strode into the parlor and handed Nadine her car keys. "Anything else I can do for you before I leave?"

"You will find I have very few needs." She smoothed the folds of her tailored gray slacks. "When I travel, I usually stay at hotels, but I heard of your place from a mutual friend, and decided to stay here instead. I believe I made the right decision."

Bill's cell phone rang and he looked at the caller ID. "It's Sandra. The exterminator must be there. I'm headed over to her place, but Trina, if you need anything, give me a call." His footsteps echoed down the hall.

"Bugs?" Mrs. Blackwell moved her snakeskin expensive-shod feet under the chair.

"Sandra's a good family friend, and she has ants in a tree *at her place*," Trina explained. "Nothing to worry about."

Mrs. Blackwell seemed right at home as the center of attention.

Lillian stared at the woman, feeling she had seen her before but where? The woman wore a scent that seemed familiar also, and then she remembered. Granny used to wear the same fragrance. She couldn't remember the name of it, but it had clung to her grandma like a second skin, no matter the time of day, as though imbedded in her pores.

The memory sent a bubble of pleasure into her throat. Granny had been her father's mother, and, in spite of her father's insistence that she be called Grandmother, the moniker of Granny had stuck. Granny liked it; her eyes had always sparkled with mischief whenever her son corrected the girls. Granny had died of a heart attack when Lillian was ten, and she still missed her tremendously.

Nadine Blackwell had to be someone special if she still used that same old perfume loved by Granny, so why the unexpected tension that seemed to have draped across her neck since coming into the parlor?

"Nadine," Lillian asked. "Where in Pennsylvania are you from? I'm having a hard time placing your accent."

The wrinkles on Nadine's neck jiggled as she chuckled, just like Granny's had. "You know how it is in Pennsylvania. We are the melting pot of the melting pot." She fluttered her hand over her head, and the light caught her diamonds, creating rainbows across the wall. "You have the Midwestern folk, and the mountain folk, and the easterners, and then those who commute to D.C. I'm sure," she said with a wink, "we even have some Clevelanders living somewhere in the state. Over time all these dialects blended together until you get what I call the Pennsylvanian smoothie." Her smile felt warm and friendly, grandmotherly.

Lillian rotated her neck against the tightness.

"As I told you on the phone," Nadine said, turning to Trina, "I won't be around much. I have meetings to attend during the day, and then business dinners in the evenings." She turned to Lillian. "I'm a buyer for a large department store. They're starting a new line, highlighting products from different regions of the country. I'm here interviewing various local artists and businesses. Right now, much of what I do is hush-hush, you understand, so I won't share much of my work. And now if you will excuse me," she rose from her chair and handed Trina her glass, "I have my first meeting this evening and need to prepare."

Lillian carried the tray to the kitchen.

Ted stood by the sink pretending he had been there all along. "So, what's the official report?" he asked.

"Well," Lillian said. "She's different. Grandmotherly, but not like Sandra."

Ted made a snorting sound. "No doubt she can pay her bill."

"No doubt." The woman was just another in a long line of guests since Lillian had arrived. Nothing different from all the others. So why did she feel one moment as if the woman was her grandmother in another body, and then in the next breath a storm was just over the horizon? Maybe it had nothing to do with Nadine Blackwell at all, just the coincidence of timing. Again she sought a memory of why the woman looked familiar but nothing surfaced. She shook her head as she helped Ted wash the glasses.

18

Lillian rubbed the small of her back. "Joe was my last."

"I'm done, too," replied Margaret. "A lot of men with coughs tonight. It'll only get worse as the weather gets colder."

Someone cleared his throat from the doorway.

Lillian turned, expecting to see one of the homeless men. "Paul!" She hated the excited thrum of her heart.

He seemed to fill the opening, and now, dressed in jeans and a flannel shirt, he looked more handsome than she remembered. The reason she had avoided him for the past several weeks played in her mind. He was a cop. But it had been weeks since she had discovered the gas cans.

Apparently, whoever had planted them had moved on to other games.

"I got off duty an hour ago and stopped at the house. Trina said I could find you here." His southern drawl flowed over her like thick molasses. He thrust a hand into the pocket of his jeans. "I wondered if you would like to stop for a cup of coffee before you go home."

Her heart leaped. She wanted to say yes, but could she trust her emotions? Her attraction to him remained strong in spite of Roger's words. *He's a policeman first and foremost.*

"Paul, I really need to call it a night." The words tasted bitter and clung to the back of her mouth. "Tomorrow is a work day, and—"

Margaret cleared her throat. "Ah...why not go for coffee? We finished early. It's only a little after eight."

She sent Margaret a scowling look. How could she refuse now without looking like a real jerk? Alright, she would go for coffee, but she would weigh every word that came out of her mouth. A thought wiggled into her mind. What if his real interest was not in her, but in seeking information? Two could play that game. At the end of the night, she would know as much as the police about the fires.

"All right, a quick cup of coffee." She grabbed her purse and followed the smiling Paul to his truck, trying to convince herself her motivation was business, not pleasure. In spite of good intentions, contentment settled over her as she positioned herself in the seat of his vehicle. Being in his truck, being close beside him, felt like a comfortable pair of worn pajamas. Her dad always accused her of attracting the wrong crowd. She imagined his displeasure if he knew her companions included homeless men and a cop. A smile crept across her lips.

Paul drove around the square to C-Bones, one of the few local establishments that remained open after supper. She felt like a princess as he held the door open and led her to a table in the side room. Stucco walls and arched openings between the three dining areas lent the feel of the southwest, except it smelled slightly of fish.

"I've never been here before," she said, sliding her chair beneath the oilcloth-draped table.

He put an arm across the back of the adjacent

chair. "It's just a small place, but the food is good." He sought her eyes. "You should try it for supper sometime."

The waitress, a young girl with long hair with too much body approached. "Hey, Paul. What can I get you tonight?" The pretty blonde eyed Lillian. "Do you want something besides coffee? Desert or anything?" She flicked her mane.

"Coffee's fine."

"Two coffees." As she sauntered away, pad of paper in hand, she threw another look at Lillian over her shoulder.

The silence made Lillian squirm. Or maybe her discomfort related more to the man across the table. She caught a whiff of his cologne and inhaled deeply, pulling in his fragrance.

"You all right?" Paul's brows were drawn together.

Heat flushed her face as she exhaled. "Sorry, just relaxing after the night's work." She smiled, hoping her explanation covered her embarrassment. Trying to appear casual, she placed her hands on the table.

His hand started to creep across the space.

She slipped the temptation to her lap, all the while wondering how it would feel to have her hand cradled in his.

"So how are you liking Darlington?"

"It's a nice place. It feels like an old sweater."

Paul laughed. "I've heard Darlington described a lot of ways, but 'old sweater' is a first."

"You know what I mean." Avoiding his gaze, she looked toward the window but the reflection of his face bounced back at her. She might as well be staring at the man himself. His good looks tugged at her heart as she settled into the warm comfort of simply being with him. It felt so right. Excited shivers ran up and down her spine. She tried to push the emotion out of her mind, after all, she couldn't trust her feelings, but the giddiness remained. What was she doing here? He had the potential to destroy her life. Still, she basked under his soft gaze.

Two cups clanked on the table, the coffee sloshing into the heavy white saucers.

Paul took a long swallow. "I feel like I hardly get to see you anymore."

"You see me on Friday nights at Ted and Trina's."

"Not lately." His brows puckered. "Sometimes you and Roger don't show up."

Those eyes again. So blue. So caring...unless he was probing.

She had forgotten the real reason she had come for coffee with him in the first place. Her eyes narrowed. She had told Trina not only about the fire that destroyed her family, but also about her history with matches. What if Trina had shared this with Paul? What if he already knew about her past and this pleasant drop-by visit had a deeper hidden agenda than even she first imagined? The coffee soured in her stomach. Could Paul be this deceitful? The thrilling tingle turned to daggers of ice, and she gripped the coffee cup for its warmth.

"When are you headed back to Cleveland for the holidays?" His question interrupted her thoughts before she could develop an escape plan. One thing seemed certain. Paul Studler was trying to hook the fish.

"I'm not going home." The words scraped against her dry throat. "I was just there for Thanksgiving." No need to add frustration with her family on top of her other sins or paint her any darker than she believed he already had. "My parents are headed to the Bahamas, and my sister has to work over the holidays."

No one would be in Cleveland for her, and she had no desire to accompany her parents on vacation or sit alone in Beth's Chicago apartment. Looking across the table at Officer Studler, she wondered if Christmas in Darlington would be any better.

His face brightened. "So you'll be at Ted and Trina's?"

"If they'll let me stay." His eyes reminded her of those belonging to the neighbor's beagle puppy, all warm and mushy. "I really need to be looking for a different place to live."

He laughed. "They love you. There won't be any problem letting you stay. I think your bigger problem will be getting them to let you go."

The waitress returned with refills.

Conversation lagged.

"So how is the police investigation coming for the fires?" She lowered her eyes, watching the soft swirl of steam lift from her cup and float toward the door, which was where she should be headed if she had any sense.

Paul sighed. "We have a few clues."

In spite of the easy way he said the words, her jaw tightened. Would those clues involve her and her history of fire setting? Acid pushed its way up her throat. "So can we expect an arrest soon?"

"The law's complicated, Lillian. You know that from your work as an attorney. But the pieces of the puzzle are coming together."

She forced a smile.

"Lillian." His eyes remained soft, but his mouth hardened. "I know you've been spending time with Roger, but I want you to be careful when you're with him."

Her breath stuck in her throat. This was the last thing she had expected to hear. Was his motivation jealousy? "Careful around Roger? Why?"

He rubbed his shoulder. "Just be alert, OK. And if you ever need me, all you have to do is call."

Torn between anger over implying Roger was dangerous, and loving Paul for his concern, she sat with her mouth half open. Paul, the caretaker of women. Then the laugh erupted, nervous and harsh. "You're acting as if you're my dad when I was about to go on my first date. Do you know something about Roger that I don't?" Her heart thudded in her throat as he glanced at his half-empty cup. Had she gotten Roger in trouble for hiding the gas cans? He had never told her what he had done with them. What if someone saw him and reported it to the police?

Paul stared at her long before answering. "He just feels wrong to me."

She spit out a brittle laugh. "I promise, Dad, I'll be a good girl and never get myself into situations you wouldn't approve of."

Paul grimaced. "I'm sorry. I was out of line. How about supper tomorrow night to make it up to you?"

"I'm sorry Paul. I can't."

"A rain check then?"

She focused on the table, wishing Margaret were here to force her to say yes. "I'll think about it."

~*~

Bill leaned against the stainless steel sinks, dishcloth in his hand.

Sandra turned off the large overhead exhaust fans that helped to keep the heat and humidity tolerable in the confined space.

The swish of mops in the dining room soon stopped, replaced by the clang of metal handles on mop buckets. Half a dozen workers, mostly the older crew, lingered in the kitchen as the last of the men to be sheltered wandered toward the sleeping quarters.

Lillian had asked him once about the men. There were the faithful few, but new faces appeared every week. Some even came a second time before they disappeared. She had asked him where they went, and he had no answer for her. Recently, he felt as much adrift as the men he served. He grabbed a paper towel and wiped the sweat off his face. "Any more dishes lying around?"

"I think that's it," Sandra said. "Time to head home." She looked around at the volunteers. "A big thanks to y'all for helping out."

"Our pleasure." A man removed his white burlap apron. "It makes me appreciate what I have."

"I never knew there were so many homeless men in Darlington," replied a woman about mid-thirties. "I never see them on the streets."

"They're called the invisible population for a reason," Bill stated. "We don't notice them so we don't have to do anything about them, or more often because they blend in to the environment."

"Do you always have a sermon after the meal?" the woman asked.

"Almost always. The local pastors volunteer, and some of the local men take turns too. It isn't hard to find someone to share their faith." Bill grunted. "What's hard is coming up with something that's relevant. Words don't mean much to these men."

"That's why our presence is so important," Sandra added. "We're as much the gospel to them as the words from the pastor."

"More, I would say," Bill added.

"Well, I'll come back again, next time our church volunteers," the woman said.

Sandra gave her a hug. "We appreciate it."

As the volunteers headed out the back door to the parking lot, Bill switched off the kitchen lights. "Everyone done in the clinic?"

"I'll go check, and get the lights back there. Meet you in the parking lot." Sandra walked down the hall, her hips swaying slightly with each step.

Bill stared after her. He had delayed going back to Ohio at the end of the summer so he would be around to help when Trina delivered his soon-to-be grandchild. But there had been more to his decision.

Sandra tugged at his heart. Nancy had been dead over fifteen years now, but still the feeling of being unfaithful remained. He wanted a wife, had prayed for a mother for Trina, but he wondered if he could really love another woman as he had loved Nancy. And if he couldn't, cultivating a relationship when he doubted the strength of his love was wrong. And yet, he looked forward to being with Sandra. She had become entwined in his life, as had little Jimmy.

And now he couldn't leave if he wanted to.

So far Lillian seemed to be exactly what she said — a Midwestern woman with a tragic past.

But fear put him on alert when around her. Sometimes strong, other times not so much. He had tried to analyze the feelings of danger to determine a pattern, but there didn't seem to be any. Sometimes when she was gone, the sensation of imminent danger almost bent him over. Other times the feeling hit when she was present, like at the Friday night meals. Never when just the two of them were together. And the Ohio house created another complication. When had his simple life become so complex? He scratched his head as he walked toward the car.

Light escaped from the windows in the back of the building and created puddles in the dark parking lot.

Sandra exited the side door and checked to make sure it locked behind her.

A smile creased Bill's face. Sandra, always the cautious one. Who would want to break into a building of homeless men? He held the car door for her.

Companionable silence accompanied them as they drove the short distance to her house. That was one of the things he loved about her—no need to constantly chat about nothing.

"Want to come in for awhile?" she asked as he turned the car into her drive. "Jimmy's spending the night with Trina again. I hope he isn't too much for her right now. She doesn't have to keep him, you know."

"Trina loves it. The two of them have a special connection."

Sandra placed her hand in his as they walked toward the house. He wrapped his fingers around hers. Soft, but not too soft. Warm. And comforting. Too soon, they were in the kitchen, where she pulled her hand from his to flip on the light. Heading to the sink, she began filling the coffee pot.

"I just don't want caring for Jimmy to become too much for her. He can be a handful."

"She'll be fine." Bill settled in a chair at the kitchen table and thrummed his fingers on the wood. "The realtor called me again today."

She shut off the water and turned toward him. "Does he still want to cut the price on your house?"

He rubbed his jaw. "Yeah. Betsy says I have it priced too high, too. But it seems the place ought to be worth more." He watched as Sandra opened the plastic storage container and measured out the grounds. He always liked the smell of fresh coffee. Made any place feel home-like. Not like that sweet tea southerners liked.

"You should trust your sister's judgment, Bill."

"I know. I have to give it some thought." It was proving hard to sell the place. The house represented his last connection to Nancy, and it was where he had raised Trina. What if he decided to go back to Ohio? Had he really made up his mind to stay in the south forever?

The coffee finished and Sandra poured two mugs and sat across from him. He sipped and watched as Sandra poured just the right dab of milk into her cup, and added one level teaspoon of sugar. Very precise, very sure of what she wanted. A woman who knew her mind. He liked that about her.

"The exterminator came today. He killed most of the ants, but the tree is rotted and needs to come down. I'll call and check on the cost of having it taken out."

"Ted and I might be able to do it. There are ladders and ropes out in the garage. I might be able to scrounge up some extra help at work."

"Some of the guys at church might be willing to help."

"Let me check into it before you go and hire

someone. All we need is a bigger chain saw."

The wind swirled outside. Dry leaves, oak and magnolia, brushed against the house. This would be his first winter in the south. Trees didn't shed leaves in South Carolina like Ohio: maples, all done and over within a week or two. These southern leaves dribbled off a few at a time. It kept him busy raking here and Trina's. And the flowers he and Sandra had planted were still blooming. Who would have thought? Flowers in December?

Lillian had commented about that back in October.

"I saw Paul come in right before we closed." Sandra's voice was laced with question marks.

"Yeah, he wanted to take Lillian out for coffee. Asked me where she was." He sipped his coffee, enjoying the hot burn. "So what do you think she's up to?"

"Bill, you need to give this up."

He ran a hand across the top of his head. "I just can't. God keeps sending me these signals. I ignored them when Jimmy was missing. I won't ignore them again. Something is wrong."

"But remember, Bill, you misinterpreted God's message with Jimmy. Isn't it possible you're getting this wrong too?"

He drew his brows together. "I just don't know. Danger surrounds her. That much I'm sure of." Lillian meant danger, but right now, at this very second, he was where he wanted to be, and the comfort lulled him.

"Do you ever regret moving?" Sandra asked. Her expression looked dreamy. A soft smile, Madonna-like, shaped her lips.

"No, I don't regret being here. Trina needs me,

and I was fortunate enough to get the teaching job. I hate leaving Betsy alone in Ohio, but she has her friends and really doesn't need me." He stared at Sandra. She was so beautiful, just what he had always prayed for: a Christian wife who loved Trina as her own. But there was no way he could ever love another woman like he loved Nancy, not even Sandra, and the thought settled heavy in his heart. "I'd better get home. It's off to work tomorrow." He leaned over and kissed Sandra on the cheek before letting himself out the kitchen door.

The temperature had dropped, and he shivered in his cotton shirt. Clouds covered the stars that surely were shining overhead, just as they always did. His heart should have been filled with joy. He had a baby coming soon, his first grandchild. But he knew the reason for his despondency: Sandra deserved to know that there would never be more between them than friendship. She should be free to accept other relationships if she wanted. He needed to tell her, but the time never seemed right. The longer he put it off, the harder it became. But he needed to do it before Trina's baby came. Not only did he have to worry about breaking Sandra's heart, but he also had to figure out what was going on with Lillian. The feeling of danger was getting stronger as time went on. One challenge felt weighty enough, but his back bent with responsibilities.

Could he battle whatever loomed ahead?

19

Lillian woke and glanced at the clock radio. Six-fifteen. Almost time to get up. Her droopy eyes closed until the radio flipped onto the Christian music channel. She rolled to her side, her body still heavy with sleep. Dangling her legs over the edge of the bed, she looked around for her slippers.

Beside the far wall sat her walking shoes, covered with dirt and grass. She tried to focus her thoughts. There shouldn't be mud on her shoes. When had she worn them last? As she bent to pick one up, the room began to spin. Gripping her knees with her hands, she waited for the dizziness to subside before turning her attention back to the shoes. The mud felt damp and the grass fresh.

The floor waved and rolled. She tried to gauge where to place each foot. Was she getting sick? She couldn't remember ever being light-headed. Her muscles ached as if they had already done a day's work and deserved time off for good behavior. Feeling slightly nauseous, she headed to the bathroom.

A shower helped clear her head, but the fatigue remained. She dressed for work, her hands clumsy as she tried to fasten buttons. Maybe a cup of coffee would help. She went to the kitchen, each footstep an adventure.

"Hey Lillian!" Jimmy sat at the old oak table, a bowl of frosted cereal in front of him. His brown hair

227

had already been slicked down for the day, a futile activity since the wispy section on top would be standing up again before he made it into the school building.

"Good morning, sunshine." Lillian replied, surprised at feeling thick tongued. She poured a cup of coffee, gripping the cup tightly, and carefully sat in a chair at the table.

The sound of clinking china came from the dining room. Trina would be setting the table for their new guest who, usually, was a late sleeper. Apparently her supper meetings started earlier today.

"I only have ten more days until school is out for Christmas break." Jimmy spooned another bite to his mouth. "Then I get two weeks off."

"I thought you liked school," Lillian said, the caffeine already loosening her tongue.

"I do, but I like Christmas better."

She chuckled. "Well, I have you beat. I only have two more *days* until I'm off for Christmas, and I get three *weeks* off."

The two of them had made a game of being able to beat each other at anything that came along: who finished eating first, who got the car door open first, who colored the best picture.

"Wow, three weeks. I wish I went to your school."

"You will someday, or one like it." She sipped her black coffee, trying to focus on the boy across from her. "So what's happening in school today?"

"Art. I love art." He looked around mischievously. "Don't tell Gram, but I'm making her a present."

Lillian pretended to zip her lips closed.

Trina wobbled into the kitchen. "Hey, I thought I heard your voice. What can I get you for breakfast?"

"You know I get my own breakfast." She turned back to the boy across from her. "So, Jimmy, do you recommend that cereal?"

He pointed both thumbs into the air.

"That good, huh? I guess I'll have what he's having."

"I hate it that you don't let me help you," Trina said. "You're living in a bed and breakfast."

"And I slept in a bed and now I'm having breakfast. I wouldn't do it if I didn't want to." She poured cereal into her bowl and added milk.

"Ha, you spilled yours!" Jimmy said when some of cereal fell over the top of the bowl. "I didn't spill mine."

Lillian yawned. "Well, that's one for you. That makes us even so far today."

Trina sat down beside Jimmy. "I might as well rest while I can. Mrs. Blackwell shouldn't need anything else."

"You mean Nadine," Lillian said with a chuckle.

"I can't bring myself to call her by her first name."

"Me neither. She looks like a Mrs. Blackwell to me."

"May I be excused?" Jimmy asked, his spoon clattering to the table.

"Yes, you may," Trina replied. "Go brush your teeth. But remember to walk."

The boy ran out of the room and stomped up the stairs.

Trina grimaced. "So much for walking."

"You'll be a great mother, Trina."

"Hmm. I hope so." She grabbed a banana off the tray and pulled back the peel. "You look tired. Did you have trouble sleeping?"

Bill's footsteps sounded on the stairs. "Hey, you should have the news on," he said. "Another house burned down last night."

Suddenly she was awake, tracing a line of thought to a horrible conclusion. First, there had been the gas cans in her car. Now dirty shoes in her room. And fires that began *after* her arrival in Darlington. It was impossible, and yet, how did her shoes end up with *fresh* mud and grass on them? No one had access to the house, or to her room, except the family. She trusted them with her life. Her spoon fell to the table as she stared ahead, unseeing.

Dr. Widder had warned her about the potential of unexpected behavior, and she had exhibited some, but that had been months ago. Many months.

She was better now. Better than she had ever been in her life. Why would she suddenly start sleep-walking? Shaking, she took her half-empty cereal bowl to the sink and crawled up to her room. She had to clean her shoes, and destroy any potential evidence.

Should she seek mental help? Call her old psychiatrist, Dr. Widder? Tie her feet to the bed at night? Her hands trembled as she watched mud swirl down the drain of the sink and disappear, much like her disappearing life. Now she couldn't even trust herself.

~*~

Christmas had never held much interest for Roger except during the few years of his marriage. But he had to admit, when Ted and Trina trimmed for Christmas, they did it big. The old house stood transformed, like one of those old-time Christmas cards where the room was draped with ribbons and garland. All that remained was the tree, a hovering seven-foot pine that occupied the place of honor by the front window of the family parlor.

Trina had designated the foyer for snacks for the evening, and had covered the table with a red skirt. The antique crystal punchbowl graced the center. The punch, made from green powdered drink mix, lemon-lime soda pop and lime sherbet, looked festive against the red cloth.

Sandra had provided a tray of home-baked cookies and had included oatmeal raisin just for Trina. But it was the spiced cider that made the entire downstairs smell like cinnamon and cloves.

Too bad Paul had been called to work before he could enjoy the food.

Roger glanced toward Lillian as she placed a ball on the tree. The woman confused him. He could swear she suffered from multiple personalities. After her trip home at Thanksgiving, she had returned a different person—cheerful, more confident. And now, all of a sudden, the jumpy, nervous Lillian had resurfaced.

He walked toward her and placed a hand on her shoulder.

She jumped as though his touch were lightning, and walked away without explanation, stopping beside Trina at the punch bowl.

Shrugging, he turned back to the task at hand. Might as well finish and be done with this silly tree trimming nonsense.

He took one of the remaining ornaments out of the box and stared at the ball with its stripes of pink and white running up and down the frosted glass. "Where did you get all these things? Good thing you have them, though. There must be a tree in every room of the house."

"Nope," Bill said, plopping down onto the couch that had been moved to the opposite wall from the tree. "There's none in my room."

Sandra laughed and looked at Trina. "We tried, didn't we?"

"And I said if you put a tree in my room I would shove it out the window."

Sandra leaned over and gave him a hug. "You might act like a big bully, but we know better."

"There's one in my room and I love it." Lillian said.

Roger glanced at her. That was the most she had said all evening.

"I'm glad you like the tree in your room, Lillian," Bill said, "but my room will remain my domain."

"One point for you, Uncle Bill," Jimmy said, making a slash mark in the air with his finger.

"Give me five, buddy." Bill clapped palms with the young boy. "We can't let these women think they control us."

"Right." Jimmy puffed out his skinny chest.

"Come on, Dad, don't teach Jimmy bad things." Trina put a hand on each of Jimmy's shoulders and bent her head toward him. "Women don't control the men, and men don't control women. We work together, just as God intended."

Lillian didn't seem to notice the interaction, or the good-natured jesting that followed. She stood, staring at the tree, and then her gaze shifted to the wall, and then at nothing.

Roger's gut clenched. What was going on with her? They had established trust, at least he thought so.

What had happened that she wasn't telling him?

"Back to your question about the decorations, Roger," Ted said, "we found trunks full of them in the attic. Either each generation bought new ones, or this house has been decorated Trina-style sometime in the past."

"I guess it helps to own the house your ancestors have lived in since before the Civil War." Sandra fingered a glass bell. "We should get some of these ornaments appraised."

Trina gave a huff. "You would never sell them."

"You never know."

"Where's Nadine?" Lillian asked Trina.

"I invited her to help us, but she had a meeting to go to. She said she'd try to get here before we finished."

"She'd better hurry," Roger replied.

What was with Trina inviting house guests to family events lately?

"How about this one?" Jimmy took a delicate-looking glass Santa from the box.

Sandra lifted the decoration from his hand. "Honey, let Grandma give you the pieces you can put on the tree. Some of the ornaments are fragile and you don't want to break them."

"I won't break them, Gram."

"You won't mean to, but accidents happen." She pulled a wooden reindeer with a piece of holly held in its mouth from the box.

"We could go to the store and buy some more if these got all broken," Jimmy said as he attached the wooden ornament to a lower branch.

Trina grinned. "You would never be able to buy these at the store, honey." She gave the boy a hug and pulled him to the couch with her. "Do you know some of these decorations are over a hundred years old?"

Jimmy stared at the tree, his eyes wide. "That's older than Uncle Bill."

"All right, hotshot," Bill said. "Since I am so old, how about getting me a couple of cookies off that table over there—not the raisin ones, either."

"Can I have some too?"

Bill glanced at Sandra. "Grandma said yes."

"But only one," Sandra called as she bent to remove Jimmy's reindeer from the branch that already drooped from the weight of too many decorations. "You've already had more than enough."

"That's the last one. All the decorations are on," Ted said. "And now, stand back and wait for the great tree lighting! If you will assist me, Miss Sandra." As Ted reached for the end of the electric cord, Sandra switched off the lights in the entry and the living room.

They stood in darkness until a rainbow of color brightened the room. Awed silence filled the space.

"That's the most beautiful tree I have ever seen." Sandra clutched her hands to her chest.

Lillian stood in the back of the room, staring at the tree. But rather than showing pleasure, deep lines pulled at her face.

Roger slipped beside her. "Hey," he whispered, "you don't seem yourself." She flinched when he touched her arm. "Has something else happened since…" he glanced around but no one seemed to be paying them any attention, "since, you know…the gas can incident?"

She turned toward him. "It's worse than ever," she murmured, her eyes pools of pain. "I may know who's setting your fires."

He grabbed her arm. "How do you know?" What had happened in the past few days that she had not told him? He thought they were beyond secrets, that she shared everything with him. Isn't that what women did—talk? Every muscle in his body trembled as he tried to keep from shaking her.

She pulled away. "I'm not ready to talk about it. I need to pray about it first." She joined Trina at the snack table.

He stared after her in frustration. What good would prayer do? As he snatched his jacket off the corner of the chair and barged toward the door, the hair on the back of his neck stiffened. He rubbed his skin, trying to ease the sensation.

Bill continued to stare at him as he walked out the door.

~*~

Decorating over, Bill drove Sandra and Jimmy home. He enjoyed the times alone with Sandra, but there weren't many of them. Between Jimmy and Trina, the instances when it was just Sandra and him amounted to late-night visits, usually after working at the shelter. Jimmy would soon be going to bed, so tonight was a bonus.

He told himself his attraction to Sandra wasn't romantic, but more a need to share with someone his own age. Even at the high school, he was one of the older teachers. But selfishness nagged at him. Sooner or later, he had to be honest with her, but he hesitated to share his true feelings. She would surely reject his friendship once she knew he had nothing more to offer.

"Why don't you make coffee while I put Jimmy to bed," Sandra called over her shoulder as she shepherded the reluctant boy through the kitchen.

He reached into the cupboard for the coffee and filters.

Jimmy's arguments over bedtime drifted from across the house.

Bill smiled, remembering similar nights when Trina was Jimmy's age.

Sandra might be gone awhile.

With the coffee on, he sat at the table to wait. All evening he had expected the thrust of fear to grip him, the sensation of danger that accompanied Lillian to disturb the special night. But the feeling never came. Shifting in the hard chair, he mulled over the change. The sense of danger came less often, and sensation hit less intently as time went on.

Had he misinterpreted God's message again? There was no way he could have conjured up the pain and fear on his own. God had sent them, sure enough. So what did this change mean? Had Lillian grown to love his family, and given up her angry intent, whatever it had been?

He shook his head in frustration. A mark on the silverware drawer caught his attention. Needing something to distract him from his thoughts, he grabbed the dishcloth off the edge of the sink. Sandra liked a clean kitchen. As he hovered over the spot, he found the paint by the handle of the drawer had worn off. Strange he had never noticed that before. Looking around, all of the cupboards showed use. He chuckled, thinking most likely Sandra had scrubbed off the finish from her constant cleaning.

With the coffee only half done, he went back to the

table. What about the rest of the house? Sandra kept the two-bedroom 1,200 square feet spotless, but, as far as he could tell, nothing had been replaced since the house had been built around 1970. The bathroom fixtures were old. The tile dated. Did she even know about things like furnace maintenance?

Jimmy's irate voice reached him, followed a stern reprimand from Sandra. Too many cookies—partially his fault. The corner of a magazine jutting out from under a pile of mail caught his attention. Hoping for a distraction, he pulled to remove it and the envelopes lying on top scattered across the floor.

"What an oaf," he muttered to himself as bent to gather the papers off the floor. The contents had been removed from the envelopes, exposing overdue bills. Lots of them. The electric bill, the water bill, insurance. Surprise mingled with a tightening in his gut. Sandra wouldn't forget to pay her bills. His frown deepened as he piled the papers back onto the counter as near to how he found them as he could. When Sandra finally appeared in the kitchen, he was sitting at the table flipping through the magazine.

"He put up quite a fight tonight." She chuckled as she reached for the mugs off the shelf. "Most likely too many cookies." The cups were soon filled with coffee, and he watched as she added the measured amount of sugar and milk to hers before carrying them to the table.

He took a sip, hesitating to ask, but knowing he must. "Sandra, I know it's none of my business." Her innocent gaze made his throat tighten.

"But...?"

"I noticed the overdue bills on the cupboard."

Her eyes widened. "You went through my mail?"

She placed her cup on the table.

"I pulled out this magazine," he waved the offending copy of a home interior magazine, "and the mail fell on the floor. Honest, I wasn't snooping."

Sandra stared at the wall. Her silence lasted so long he wondered if he should leave. Finally she spoke. "I know. I need to get the bills caught up. I promise, tomorrow morning I will sit down and get them done." She sighed and stared at the wall again. "I've been really busy lately, with Christmas right around the corner." When she turned to him, her smile did not reach her eyes.

He remembered Roger's words about her financial situation. "If you need money..."

"Bill Iver, it will be a cold day before I accept money to keep a roof over my head." The ice of her voice was challenged by the fear in her eyes. She needed money.

How could he have not noticed before? She seldom went shopping, and when she did, it was for Jimmy. The house, although solid, needed repairs. He rubbed his chin, wondering how to approach her without being offensive. "Look, we're family. Let me help if you need it. There's no shame in that. Heaven knows, you've been kind enough to Trina and Ted."

Sandra's dark expression shouted that he had crossed one of those invisible lines that women seem to draw.

He held up his hands, "Sorry. I won't mention it again. Just promise me that if you ever need help, you'll let me know."

Even as she promised, he still wondered about the stack of unpaid bills. It wasn't like her to put things off. He tried to shrug off his concern; why did he care, anyway? He had enough problems of his own.

Sleep came slowly that night.

~*~

As soon as Lillian could slip away from the family festivities, she went to her room. Falling on the bed, she prayed. *God, I'm so confused and frightened. You sent me to Darlington. Why create a new life for me, and fill it with pain? Haven't I proved I love You? God, please tell me I did not start these fires.* Tears flowed. She pounded her pillow with tight fists, venting the frustration and anger she no longer could hold in. Emotionally drained, she waited for divine answers to float down in the darkness, like manna from heaven. Silence pervaded, and she remained as starved for answers as she had before.

The house settled into quietness; the night providing its blanket of sleep.

But no rest came her way. In fact, the more she waited alone in her room for the voice of God, the more claustrophobic she felt. Sighing, she pulled herself off the bed, tied the laces of the now-clean walking shoes and slipped on a navy jacket. It was almost midnight.

The downstairs lay in darkness, but the path from the stairs to the kitchen door was familiar. Outside, she inhaled deeply of the night air. A floral scent filled her, but she couldn't identify it. Sandra would know. All tender petals had long ago frozen in Cleveland. She set a power-walking pace, hoping both to burn some of the calories from the cookies she had eaten, and melt off some of the stress that had built up over the past few days.

There were few streetlights on Cashua Street, and the moon lay hidden behind a storm front that had been heading east for the past week. Silhouettes, darker than the night sky, darted overhead—bats out for their night feeding.

Once her muscles warmed, she thought about jogging, but feared she would end flat on the sidewalk from tripping over a crack in the cement. Many of the houses were adorned with Christmas lights, and the glow relaxed her. As she walked, Roger's face surfaced. He was kind. She had known that from the first day they had met. But sometimes, when he stared at her, his eyes took on a strange look, almost guarded and wary.

A low branch, reflecting the red and blue of the holiday lights, hung over the sidewalk. She pushed it to the side as she jogged past, and heard the swish as it returned to its rightful place.

She smiled, thinking of the times Roger had accompanied her to church. During prayer, she had looked behind shielded eyes and had been warmed by the devotion in his face. Lately he had started asking questions about her faith, and she shared as honestly as she could.

God had been good to her, and she wanted Roger to understand His divine love. There were secrets in his past; she could tell by the way he answered some of her questions. And the pained expressions he tried to hide. But he was a good man, so why was she hesitant to return his affection?

He was not Craig. Roger was a good man, but there would never be another Craig. If she ever married again, she would never experience the deep love that had been hers the first time.

Her expression turned wistful as she remembered Paul and her first reaction when he stopped her for speeding. She felt so safe around him, but there was no man less safe than Paul Studler. If only he weren't a policeman...

Educated to rely only on the truth, she knew that wishes were nothing more than puffs of air built without foundations. Her pace increased, feet thumping on the sidewalk, each step one length closer to pushing Paul Studler from her mind.

As her mind roamed to the fires, her breathing tightened. She stopped to rest, surprised to find herself already at the square. The center of town wasn't really square, but more a rectangle. The courthouse sat in the middle, with a huge decorated pine standing beside a fountain that, even in December, spurted water into a round splashing pool. Most of the businesses surrounding the outer edge of the square closed at five. She stood alone in the dark.

A silent figure rounded the corner of the courthouse.

She sucked in her breath as her heart raced. Standing in the open alone made her an easy target. She strained to see through the darkness, desperate for a place to hide, or a weapon. Just because Darlington was a small little town didn't mean she should turn stupid.

Sprinting away from the square, trying to stay against the brick building, she hoped her dark jacket would help conceal her. She chanced another glance over her shoulder and stopped. The stranger's shuffle seemed familiar. Her heart lurched upon recognition. He should not be in the square anymore than she at this hour of the night. Oblivious of the dark, she darted across the empty street and around the courthouse, trying to reach the man before he disappeared.

"Joe!" Her voice bounced off sleeping buildings. Panting, she reached the startled man. "Joe, what are you doing out here? Shouldn't you be at the shelter?" The short speech stole her remaining breath and she bent over, hands on her knees. "Can we sit down?"

"What are you doing out here?" She repeated once they had settled on the concrete bench. The coldness penetrated through her clothing and she pulled her jacket tighter.

Joe stared at her, his dark eyes blank. Finally he spoke. "Why are you not home?"

She smiled. Strange how her choice of friends had changed. "I needed to go for a walk to clear my head so I can sleep. But why aren't you at the shelter?"

"Sometimes I have a better place."

"A better place? Here in Darlington?" A laugh bubbled at the back of her throat. There wasn't another shelter in the city.

"Too noisy."

The noise she could understand. "I needed some time alone myself."

"I saw that man again."

Startled, she scanned the area for another late-night walker. As much as she cared about Joe, he would be no help in a fight.

A light breeze shifted the strings of lights on the tall pine across from them, sending splashes of color onto the black shadows. None of the shadows moved.

She looked longer, harder, daring the darkness to shift, to breathe, to reveal its hidden stalker.

The night remained still.

"Not here."

Confused, she turned toward him. Then she remembered. "Oh, you mean Roger." She signed in relief. "Why don't you like him?"

A car sped around the square, its headlights settling on them long enough to expose Joe's deep scowl. She had known him long enough to recognize his expressions. He was worried.

"Joe, did you try to rent a house from Roger?" He rarely sought her eyes, so when he locked his gaze on her, the intensity of his concern shook her.

"He is an angry man."

"Do you mean that night at the shelter?"

He removed his gaze from her. "Not just then."

A light breeze shifted the strands of lights on the tree, the shimmer reflecting off Joe's hand. She stared at it, intrigued. Strange she had never noticed it before. "Your ring, Joe. It has unusual marks on it."

"My wedding band."

The fact that Joe might have been married had never crossed her mind. In fact, she had never thought of him as having a life at all. Of course, he had not always lived on the streets.

"You're married?"

"Helen. She died." He shuffled his feet. "I moved the ring. It doesn't fit anymore."

"Joe, I'm sorry. I was married once too." She wanted to touch him, to share physical comfort by hugging his shoulders, but she knew he feared touch, as did many of the homeless men. Instead, she focused on the dark nothingness in front of her. "My husband's name was Craig. We had a little girl, Susan." She felt his eyes burn into the side of her face. "They died in a house fire."

"No, not your house. His house."

"Not here, Joe," she murmured quietly. "I lived in Cleveland then. That was two years ago."

"He burned his house."

His words pulled her from her memories. She turned toward him, the darkness and cold forgotten. "Roger burned down his own house? How do you know that?" Joe had to be delusional.

"I saw him. Then he ran away."

As an attorney, she had heard hundreds of sworn testimonies where actions had been misinterpreted. Like a dozen witnesses who give twelve different versions of what they watched happened. Roger couldn't have set his house on fire. He wouldn't.

Her mouth went dry as the weight of Joe's words settled over her. He had to be wrong, but even so, the fact that Joe suspected Roger of malice added to the divisiveness in her life. Suddenly she ached to be home in her bed. Her arms were shaking, and she wrapped them around her body. The openness that she had hungrily sought an hour ago now felt big and dark, hovering, with monsters hiding behind each shadow. She jumped from the bench. "Joe, will you be all right? I can go home and bring back my car…"

"I am fine."

As she turned to go, he grabbed her hand. He had never touched her before; she caught herself before she jerked away. His stare again held steady on her face. "He is not good."

Forgetting the heaved-up cracks in the cement, she ran home.

Joe's face stayed in front of her and his voice kept repeating his warning. "He is not good…he is not good."

20

Roger's head throbbed. He barely heard Chief Watson's explanation of the latest fire, something about this event being different. *Will these headaches never end?* When had they started? Maybe about the time he had made an agreement with his partner. No, before that. Shortly after his marriage, when his father-in-law—

"So do you have any idea who it could have been?" The chief's hard gaze was locked on Roger's face.

Roger ran his hand over his eyes and felt the wetness that had accumulated on his skin. "What was that again?"

"The body." The chief clenched his teeth. "The remains were badly burned. Who lived in the house last?"

Who had lived there? Throbbing pain attached itself behind his eyes. He opened the file Latoya had placed on his desk. "Janet Brown and her four kids. Single mom, but in-and-out boyfriends if you believe the gossip." Nausea gripped him and he swallowed hard.

Chief Watson scribbled the name on a piece of paper. "Current address?"

Roger gave him the new address for Janet and her brood and watched as the chief wrote it down and shoved the paper into his pocket.

"This last fire has changed everything," the chief said. "Arson was bad enough, but now it's murder."

The pain felt like someone was closing his coffin, one pounding nail in his head at a time. He had to get out of Darlington. Everything would be better then. So why the reluctance to finish his job with Lillian? As soon as she was dead, he could go anywhere he wanted.

"One more thing," the chief said. "The only identifiable item on the body was a ring. Sound like any of your clients?"

Did the man have any idea how many people came through his office? How was he supposed to remember details like that? "Most of the people I see wear rings all over their bodies. A ring is no big deal."

"So you have no idea who this person could be?"

"Sorry."

Chief Watson stared long at him before standing to leave. What was going through the man's mind? Acid rose from his gut and the pain in his throat mingled with the pounding in his head. He couldn't take any more of this. Tonight he would finish what she had started.

~*~

"Where's that husband of yours?" Bill asked as he walked through the kitchen door and helped himself to a cookie. A heavy stream of air pushed through his nose as he settled into the kitchen chair.

Trina set a platter of cookies on the table, poured herself a glass of milk, and sat across from her dad. "He's out in the workshop."

"He's been out there a lot lately. Can I expect a big

Christmas present?" He chuckled and grabbed another cookie, stuffing the round pastry into his mouth.

"Ha, you can wish. No, he's finishing a big job for a college in Columbia."

"Columbia, as in the capital of South Carolina, or Colombia, as in South America?"

"Oh, Dad, you're so funny." She took a sip of milk and peered intently at her father. "I'm glad you decided to stay. I know it was a big sacrifice, but I love having you here every day, being a part of my life again. And I'll love having you help raise the baby."

Trina was lovely as she blossomed with child. His heart ached with love for her, so why was he so torn between staying and going back to Ohio? Nothing waited there for him but his old life and his house. His daughter needed him, and he needed her. It should be simple, but it didn't feel that way. He got up and got himself a cup of coffee.

Trina's eyes grew round. "Quick, give me your hand. The baby's moving." She placed his palm on her abdomen and gave a big smile.

He held his hand still, waiting. Trina had let him feel the baby move a couple of times before, and the joy of sharing in new life was indescribable. Waiting patiently, he felt the light push against his palm. The shape of a foot under Trina's skin made him grin, but the tiny bump quickly pulled away from his touch. The miracle of life amazed him. How could anyone believe that humans just happened? And how could he possibly consider giving this up? And yet, how could he stay? The house in Ohio would never sell in today's market, and it would sit there and deteriorate. A home needed attention, someone in residence.

A sharp rap sounded at the back door, and Paul

strode in, his face pale, rigid with its lack of expression.

This was not a social call.

"I didn't see Lillian's car," Paul said. "Are you expecting her back soon?"

"She went to the office to clean out her files and get a head start on the next semester's work," Trina said. "She'll be back about four. Is something wrong?"

"It's almost four now if you want to wait." Bill's heart rate escalated as he returned to his place at the table. So this was about Lillian. There had been no premonitions of danger. Had she somehow gotten below his radar? She had been here weeks now, as the sense of danger waxed and waned, his concern had followed course. In spite of it all, he liked the young woman and had hoped he could prevent whatever she had planned.

Paul took three cookies and shoved one into his mouth.

"Want a cup of coffee to go with those cookies?" Trina asked, her eyes twinkling. Her attempt at humor was lost on the tense officer.

"No thanks." Paul slumped into the chair at the table that faced the door. He wiped his face with his hand.

"Bad day?" Bill asked.

"Too many bad days lately."

Bill slurped his coffee. "So what's with you and Lillian?"

"This is a business call."

"Good enough, but it seems to me you've been going out of your way to avoid her." Bill stared at the younger man. "Tell me if I'm wrong, but I kind of thought you might be sweet on her."

"She prefers Roger."

"Are you sure?"

"Look, I'm not happy to be here, and you aren't making my job any easier. Let it drop, will you?"

"Lillian's here." Trina pulled up from her chair. "I have things to do upstairs."

Bill watched his daughter leave the room before he turned to Paul. "You want to talk to her alone?"

"It's not confidential...but maybe...I really wanted Trina—"

"For goodness sake, man, spit it out. Do you want me to stay or leave?"

The door squeaked. "Hi, Paul. I saw your cruiser outside."

Paul stood as Lillian dumped her purse on the counter and grabbed a cookie. Dressed in jeans and a holiday sweater, she looked as carefree as her students probably felt.

"You might as well sit down," Bill said.

She raised her eyebrows.

"I have to ask you some questions about last night's fire," Paul said.

She took a few even breaths before sitting across the table from Paul. Fear flickered in her eyes.

As Bill began to stand, Lillian motioned him to sit.

"If you don't mind," she said.

Why would Paul need to interview Lillian about the fires? And why she would want him to stay? No longer hungry, he went to lay the cookie on the table. Crumbs fell from his fist.

Paul stared at Lillian, and to her credit, she returned his gaze. Neither showed any emotion. Two blank faces hiding a ton of secrets.

Finally, Paul pulled a small envelope out of his pocket and placed it in front of him. The contents of the envelope apparently held the reason for Paul's visit.

"That homeless man you're friends with..."

"Joseph Callahan?" Lillian's face furrowed. "He likes to be called Joe."

"What's this all about, Paul?" Bill had not expected questions about one of the shelter's frequent fliers. Surely, Paul wasn't here to question Lillian about the time she almost hit the man, not after all these weeks. Suddenly, what he had imagined to be nothing took on a larger shape. His jaw tightened as his mind ran in quick circles looking for answers.

Paul stared at Lillian. "There was another fire last night."

"You think Joe started the fire?" Lillian asked. "That's ridiculous. Joe wouldn't do that. He's a kind man, down on his luck maybe, but he's working on it." Her face reddened. "I really didn't expect you, Paul, of all people, to be judgmental. Just because he's homeless doesn't make him a villain. You need to look somewhere else..."

"The investigators found a body in the house."

Lillian's eyes widened as she clutched her throat.

"Do you have any idea where he goes when he's not at the shelter?" Paul asked.

Lillian looked at Bill before answering. "I...I don't know for sure. I asked him once, and he just said sometimes he needed to get away and be alone." She slumped in her chair. "You think the body is Joe's?"

Paul opened the envelope and slid the contents across the table: a blackened and tarnished ring.

Tears ran down her face. "That's Joe's ring. It was his wedding band. He had to wear it on his index finger because he lost so much weight." She looked at Paul, sorrow etched across her face. "He was a decent and kind man." Then anger flashed in her eyes. "Who could have done this?"

"I don't know." Paul returned the ring and envelope to his shirt pocket. "But I intend to find out."

Emotions battled for priority. Bill had expected to feel tension, but there was something more flowing through the room: fear.

And it didn't emanate from just Lillian, but from both of them.

Was there another reason for Paul to interview Lillian? What could he be looking for?

~*~

"I know you aren't in the mood for all of this," Roger said, "but maybe it will help distract you for awhile."

Lillian tucked a cold hand under his arm. Even with jackets, the night air held a frosty nip that promised frost by morning. "I just don't understand why he had to die."

He placed a finger on her lips. "For tonight, for now, just soak in the present."

He led her through the paths of Brookgreen Gardens, the nighttime darkness broken by hundreds of strings of holiday lights and the legendary thousand candles. The scent of pine, hot chocolate and spiced cider added to the festive feel.

They mingled among other visitors: families with children, couples slowly navigating the nighttime paths, and the volunteers in their red vests, maintaining posts throughout the garden, ready to answer questions or direct the guests to a sought-after attraction. Just another couple, nothing special. The kind one passed by and forgot.

Just what Roger counted on.

Winding paths among towering oaks and pines led to one hidden venue after another, unexpected pleasures such as ponds with floating candles, trees draped with lights, some rainbows of color, others white like holiday snow. Several provided laser shows. Christmas carols drifted from speakers hidden within the depths of the pines. Together the lights and music transformed the darkness to a place of magical wonder.

Roger glanced down at Lillian. "I'm glad I talked you into coming."

"I'm glad you did too." She looked at the fairyland around her. "Who does all this decorating?"

"Volunteers."

"And do they light the candles, too? A thousand candles...imagine."

"Actually it's more like five thousand five hundred, all lit nightly by stalwart retirees."

"It's so beautiful. We should come back again during the day. Fifty acres of landscaped heaven."

The revolver tucked in the back of his slacks caused shivers of excitement to creep along his spine. A smirk played on his face. Lillian thought the park was beautiful. She had no idea that beautiful to him meant power. She would soon find out.

It would be after midnight before he arrived back in Darlington. Alone. Or maybe he wouldn't go back at all. Why should he? He had his passport with him, and his cell phone. Make quick airline reservations. He would be beyond anyone's radar before Lillian was missed.

If only things could have worked out differently.

He pushed aside his feelings. Unless she turned up dead very soon, he would be in jail. His heart quickened as he kissed the top of her head. Passion, that maddening throb, would have to be denied. "Want to walk on the beach before we head home?" He breathed in her scent and trembled with anticipation. The act, a display of his skill and supremacy, always excited him.

"I hate to leave here. It's so peaceful, even with the crowds. And it's been such a horrible day."

Three children raced down the illuminated path, bumping into Lillian.

As she staggered, he pulled her closer. She nestled into his side and he murmured in her ear, "The beach is peaceful, and we won't have to work to be alone."

And they must be alone.

She looked into his face and smiled as he guided her toward the parking lot.

Excitement poured into his body, the ecstasy that always accompanied a successful mission. This time, he would not fail.

He drove the car across the highway, obeying all the rules, careful not to attract the attention of every off-duty police officer managing the traffic. Trying to hide his heightened excitement, he scanned the side of the road for the pull-off he had found earlier. Breaths came tight as he feared missing the obscure entry.

Beside him, Lillian relaxed against the back of the seat, blissfully unaware this would be her last moments.

His heart thundered in his chest. Heat radiated from his body. Breath hissed through flared nostrils as he spied the turn-off he had created. Obscured by the vines he had pulled over the opening, no one had penetrated his lair since he had left it.

"Are you sure this is the right place?" Lillian pulled herself upright.

He eased the car off the road between hanging limbs thick with Spanish moss and drove through the five-foot bramble. Roger smiled. "Give me a chance to show you."

Limbs scratched the frame of the car, emitting an eerie, ear-piercing cry. Drying grasses illuminated by the headlights looked like wizened limbs reaching toward them.

"It feels as if we're in the middle of a jungle." Her voice trembled as she leaned forward in her seat, staring at the tangle of trees and vines through the front window.

Entering the small clearing, just big enough for him to turn his car, he shut off the engine, removed his seatbelt, reached across and unlatched hers. His face brushed against her cheek, still warm with life. Her breath, like feathers, stroked his skin. Soon she would be burning heat against his hands as she struggled to push air from her compressed throat.

Pocketing the car keys and feeling for his gun, he helped Lillian out of the car. As a last thought, he reached into the storage compartment and pulled out a flashlight. "The beach is only a short walk ahead of us."

They pushed through withered ferns tangled among vines thick as ropes. Summer grasses grabbed at their legs in the total darkness created in part by the canopy of hovering overhead. She trembled as she clutched his arm.

"I want to go back, Roger."

He pulled on her arm, moving her forward; she

balked.

"Can't we at least have some light?"

Sounds of traffic filtered through the thick growth, but looking back, the headlights from the adjacent highway were concealed. Knowing they could not be seen, he switched on the flashlight and kept it pointed toward the ground.

Lillian shivered.

"Are you cold?"

"I don't like it here. It feels like the setting of a murder or something."

His laugh came from deep within, bubbling up from the dark chambers of his heart. "Do you want me to turn the light back off to better add to the mood?"

"No!" She squeezed his arm tighter.

His breath came in raspy streams as he pulled at towering vines and created a path through the overgrowth. A thick layer of pine needles softened their footsteps. Thick trunks of trees, many over a hundred years old, dictated their path. In the daylight, the spreading branches of the live oaks had seemed almost romantic in a southern way. Now the limbs seemed to reach toward them. "No one had been back there since summer, so nature has taken over. We should come to the creek soon, and that will take us to the beach."

Only they weren't going to the beach.

Except for the crack of dry twigs underfoot, this section of the Maritime Coastal Forest remained silent. Even the sound of cars no longer penetrated the wild growth. With the temperature just above freezing, crickets and chickadees and frogs were gone for the season. Even alligators, which could be seen most days in the summer crossing the paths from one marshy area to another, lay tucked safely in deep water most of the time. The beach remained too far to hear its roar. They had the coastal woods to themselves.

Estimating they had walked about halfway to the beach, he looked for the marker he had placed where the marshy water reached the path. She had to be in the water.

Illuminated by the flashlight, their legs appeared as gray beams supporting bodies of swaying black masses. Shadows just out of reach of the light thickened into grotesque shapes.

Lillian lifted her face toward him. "Do you think he suffered?" she asked.

Her voice was a nuisance, a distraction from the work ahead. The best victims were silent ones.

She tugged at his sleeve. "Roger, do you think Joe suffered before he died?"

Frustration hissed from his nose. "My guess is the smoke got him before the flames." He couldn't allow her to distract him. The ground was becoming increasingly marshy, and the scent of rotting vegetation intensified. The light cut swatches of clarity, and he panned the beam back and forth. The candy wrapper he had jabbed onto a tree limb earlier in the day had to be somewhere close.

Lillian sniffed and pulled a tissue from her coat pocket. "Life is so unfair. I have to keep reminding myself that God's in control. No matter what happens, it's because God allows it to happen. He has a purpose and a reason for good."

His jaw tightened. God did not have a hand in what he was about to do. It was impossible to imagine such faith, to actually believe in a God Who controlled all. Maybe if he had more time, he could have learned to believe.

She felt warm beside him as her form melted into his.

He allowed himself to believe they belonged together.

Tension tightened his gut. The gun poked into his back. The thoughts stopped, a bubble broken just in time. Fantasy had never been part of his life, and he could ill afford to allow his emotions to rule his heart. Killing her would be hard enough without weak sentimentality thrown in. His teeth ached beneath his rigid jaw. Where was that marker? The sound of their footsteps no longer crackled in the dry underbrush. When had the path turned to sand? His heart thumped as he recognized his mistake.

Lillian stopped. "I hear the surf!"

In his weakness, he had missed the marker. They had come too far. Fisted hands hung at his sides as Lillian tugged at the sleeve of his jacket. Flames of self-loathing hissed from his nose. Blackness descended on him, blackness with claws that tore at his mind and he groaned with fury.

With Lillian pulling him forward, the path turned, and the ocean came into view. Streams of silver moonbeams reached down to the water and showered the waves with glitter.

"I've never been to the beach at night." Her words sounded husky. "I think it's more beautiful now than during the day." She clutched his arm with both of her hands and turned her face toward him. He hated the sparkle in her eyes as she searched his face.

He had a job to do and the beach was empty.

The few summer rentals stood on dunes far to the north, their windows nothing more than black, sightless eyes.

Grabbing her arm, he pulled her to him.

~*~

Roger slammed the useless weapon on the desk beside his bed. The crack ricocheted around the silent room. Hands fisted, he pounded the wall, leaving gaping holes as evidence of his rage. Anger coursed through every nerve in his body; self-loathing gushed from his pores.

He sat on the side of the bed and lowered his head to his hands. He prided himself on being able to think on his feet, format and implement a new plan quicker than most people could blink. The skill had saved his life more than once. But when he needed it the most, it failed him.

Why hadn't he followed through and killed her? The plan was modifiable. No one had been around. He could have killed her on the beach and carried her body back to the swamp. Or they could have had a romantic walk before he finished the job on the way back to the car. Fingernails dug into his face, the frustration of failure so intense the pain failed to register.

Falling backward on the bed, he let out a hollow groan. Not since his childhood had he felt so worthless. Lillian possessed his mind. Could she really do that? He blinked hard, trying to rid himself of the ludicrous thought. Fear wound around his body just as her sensual presence wrapped around his will, paralyzing his actions.

He shivered as he lay staring at the shadows overhead. As he watched, the darkness congealed into thick bands, ribbons of emptiness, blacker than night. Groaning, barely able to breathe, he lay transfixed, watching, as the bands twisted together and created a body, then the outline of a face. Lillian's face.

Leaping from the bed, gasping for air that never reached his lungs, he groped for the light on the nightstand. As his fingertips found the ceramic base, the lamp flew into the darkness and shattered across the room.

Eyes wild with fear, he searched the darkness, looking for any break in the oppressive presence. Cold tendrils touched his face. Moaning, he slapped them away, only to have the strands of wetness return again, accompanied by icy fingers stroking his arms, his chest...

As he stumbled across the room, the blackness thickened around his throat. Pushing at the inky horror with one hand, he groped along the wall for the light switch. It should be there!

The smothering blackness encased his body in a chrysalis of death.

~*~

In spite of the warmth of the down blanket snuggled around her, Lillian lay awake. The past twenty four hours had been exhausting, yet her mind remained too full to allow sleep to enter.

There had been little time to comprehend Joe's death. But now, alone, visions of the blackened ring resting in the palm of Paul's hand burned behind her eyes. Tears slid down the sides of her face, wetting the pillow under her head. She let them fall, wondering if anyone else would grieve the man.

She reached across the bed and in the dark touched her Bible, still on the night stand where she kept it. How long had it been since she had actually picked it up and read words of wisdom and guidance? Not since Thanksgiving. Maybe tomorrow, tonight her mind rumbled with confusion.

Her mind latched onto the message from Paul that had been on her phone when she got back from the beach an hour ago. She had left her cell phone in her room on purpose, in no mood to talk after finding out about Joe, and then not having the strength to refuse Roger's offer.

Poor Paul. Concerned that he had upset her. Wanting to know if she would go to dinner. How many times had she refused him? Six? Seven? And each time her heart ached. That must be how Eve felt in the garden when confronted with the forbidden fruit, desiring what she couldn't have without appreciating the good right in front of her. Roger.

Was that the answer to the pain that clung to her heart? She really had not given Roger a chance as a romantic interest; she had been too busy fighting with herself over the fires. Too busy lusting after a man she couldn't have. A smile hovered on her lips as she thought of Paul as the "dangerous man" that women seemed to flock to. His slow demeanor and kind actions made him about as dangerous as a teddy bear, and yet, for her, it was not the man but his job that defined their relationship.

Drowsiness descended softly as the nighttime dew. She turned on her side and pulled the covers under her chin. What was Roger doing? All evening he had been distracted, putting his hand behind his back, and in his pocket. Her grandmother would have said he was fidgety. Almost as if he had planned to propose...

It was way too early in their relationship for that. But what if he had? What would she have said? As she contemplated her answer, sleep enveloped her.

21

Roger awoke on the floor by the bedroom door, curled in a ball, cold and stiff. Dawn seeped through the bottom of the curtains, gray and colorless. As awareness returned, he struggled to sit, the memory of the past night filling him with renewed dread. Running hands over his body, nothing seemed amiss. There were no visible signs of whatever had attacked him: no bruises or red marks. Nothing. Had he imagined the whole thing? Was it some major nightmare spawned by his failure to eliminate Lillian?

The shattered lamp lay against the closet. Thick bile coated the back of his throat; last night's spectacle had to be connected to the beast. He had begun referring to the darkness that lived in him as a beast years ago. It had made its presence known shortly after the first assignment. As the horror over his deed faded, giddy joy replaced it. The power he had wielded had felt good—more than good.

And then the waves of energy had rolled over him for the first time, like the accolades of the throngs of people. Lifting his arms in greeting, he had breathed in the essence that surrounded him, the fabric of invincibility. Never once did he question the source until now.

Something lived within him, something he could not control. He lay on the floor shaking.

The morning sun marched across the sky, leaving

in its wake shifting strips of light under the curtains. He thought about his plight. He thought about the darkness. Confidence built within him, slowly at first, like a man learning to walk after a stroke. New thoughts connected, links he had overlooked.

Lillian would awaken believing he loved her. Could he use that to his advantage? After all, he had fostered the caring relationship; he had wanted her to depend on him, to seek his friendship. And he had succeeded, fooling even himself.

He rose from the floor with a new plan, one that felt more appropriate than being sacrificed to nature. Lillian would die in this house.

~*~

Lillian had chosen the DVD, but to be honest Roger had no idea what was on the screen. With her snuggled close to his side on the couch, stocking feet touching on the coffee table, all his attention focused on her nearness. He had never killed someone he had grown close to. The others had been worthless bits of humanity shirking their obligations to his boss. Death was their due.

He should have killed her sooner. That was the plan. What had happened?

Her face reflected the drama on the screen. She, at least, was totally caught up in the fictional story, oblivious to the reality unfolding around her.

The scent of perfume rose over that of the popcorn. Breathing deeper, he closed his eyes and held the scent in his lungs as long as possible. She was not the heartless demon he and his partner had thought her to be; she had only been doing her job. Not that it mattered. Only her death would free him.

The credits rolled across the screen. She clicked the television off and stretched her arms over her head, a soft smile spread across her face. "I love happy endings," she said, settling back against his side.

He draped an arm over her shoulders; his heart aching over what he had to do.

"Life hasn't always been good for me," she murmured. The intensity of her eyes burned into his. "I lost my husband and daughter in a house fire."

For weeks, he had wanted to hear the story so he could wallow in her pain like a pig in mud. Now he wanted to close his ears and pretend it never happened.

"I should have been there."

He put a finger softly against her lips. "You don't need to talk about it."

She wrapped her hand around his and held it in her lap. "We had argued that morning." Her voice was little more than a whisper as she stared across the room, seeming to focus on the closed blinds. "I had just finished a huge case and the preparation had been exhausting. The trial went on for weeks, and ended in a conviction. The man had ruined hundreds of lives by using his business as a front for drugs. I had hardly seen my husband and daughter in two months."

Roger's mouth went dry. He didn't want to know this. "The past is over, Lillian. Let it be."

"You don't understand the pain of seeing all you love going up in flames."

Roger kissed the top of her head as his own pain surfaced. The words tumbled out. "I know better than you think. I lost my wife in a fire too." Her hair felt soft under his cheek, a source of comfort as he talked. "Our baby daughter was born with birth defects. I found out later that Carla, my wife, had been eating the flaking paint off the windows. The doctor said depression can cause pregnant women to eat strange things like paint, or even dirt. Our daughter lived less than a day." His voice choked. "Carla was never the same, and within a month she set fire to our house. She remained inside. The coroner said she was dead before the fire reached her."

Lillian searched his face, her misty eyes haunted and yet filled with tenderness.

"It is my personal vendetta to never allow this to happen to anyone else."

"The houses you control, do you know which ones have lead?"

He glanced at her, wondering at her question. She already knew the answer; she had to. "All our properties are inspected. If lead is found, the homeowners have it abated. Otherwise, I don't rent it to young families."

"You have a way to work out your grief," Lillian said.

"But there is always more grief to follow." His resolve fled under the warmth of her touch; she would live another day.

~*~

As Lillian pulled into the drive of the bed and breakfast, the light filtered from the guest parlor window. Ted must have forgotten to turn it off when he went to bed. The creases in her forehead deepened; Ted never forgot.

When she pulled to the back of the house, her confusion increased. Nadine Blackwell's car sat in its assigned spot. Even though it was after midnight, several nights Lillian had heard the woman walking down the hall toward her room at well after three AM. The long hours must have finally caught up with the quiet woman.

Yawning, she quietly closed the outside kitchen door. Nights with Roger seemed to drain her energy and left her confused. Especially tonight. He had never mentioned the death of his wife and child before. And then, after sharing his story, he had seemed distant, as though regretting he had told her. One minute the man was warm and loving, the next a stranger.

Slipping off her shoes, she headed toward the parlor to turn off the light. No need for Ted to get a chewing-out from Trina about wasting electricity.

As she entered the room, she sucked in a lung-full of air, then exhaled and chuckled. She had expected the room to be empty.

Nadine sat in one of the straight-backed chairs reading. Her dark green silk robe shimmered against the light; the air hinted of her grandmother's perfume.

"Sorry to disturb you. I thought Ted forgot to turn out the parlor light." She turned to leave.

"I would enjoy a few minutes of your company if you don't mind."

They had rarely seen each other during the two weeks Nadine had been a resident at the bed and breakfast.

Lillian ached to crawl into her cozy bed and be alone with her thoughts, but, forcing a smile, she settled into the companion chair, wiggling to find a comfortable spot. Why would anyone sit in this room when the other parlor was so much more comfortable?

"I find it curious that a young woman with your talent is living here in this small town." The woman waited, obviously expecting a response. Her hands remained folded in her lap, resting on top of her book.

Lillian wasn't sure what the woman wanted to know. "I came to teach political science at the local university."

Nadine waved a plump hand in the air. "I know all that. What are you *really* doing here?"

"I...um."

Nadine smiled. "Forgive my bluntness. I have been stuck in meetings for days and need some good old-fashioned girl time." She sighed. "The whole business process is wearying. But, this will be my last assignment. I have accomplished my goals and can retire with the satisfaction of a life well-lived."

"And what were your goals?" Lillian asked.

"To give the public what it demands." She paused. "So, if you don't want to talk about why you are here in Darlington, can you share *your* life goal?"

She had never really thought about it. At one time, it would have been becoming a partner in a successful law office. To raise her daughter to adulthood. To grow old with Craig. But all of that had changed. She returned Nadine's stare. "My goal is to live whatever life God gives me."

"And how will you do that?"

"God sends opportunities and —"

"Like moving to Darlington? Would that be an example of God's opportunities?" The woman curled her nose.

Lillian stiffened.

Nadine's rejection of God sounded too much like

her father.

"I feel as if God led me to Darlington for a purpose."

"And what else has God provided, or did He simply set you down in Darlington and expect you to deal on your own?" The woman smiled. "Oh, I see you squirm. Don't mind my questions. I love to study human nature, don't you? You must have done a lot of that as an attorney."

The woman had a different personality at night. She had never been this abrasive in the mornings and Lillian regretted staying to chat. As for what God had provided, well, the parlor they were sitting in had been dressed with love, and the other rooms, her comfortable bedroom, the welcoming kitchen, the den where so many happy memories had been created, all were gifts from God. "Trina and Ted are the kindest people I have ever met. God wisely brought me here."

"I see. And have you been able to make other friends?" Her penciled eyebrows rose slightly, giving her an owl-like appearance.

Lillian understood why the department store had sent Nadine to negotiate contracts. Her skill lay in getting information.

"You want to know if I have a boyfriend, and yes, I do." As soon as the words flew from her mouth she stiffened, and then smiled as the shock of what she had just said circled back to her ears. Was that her answer? Were the weeks of ambiguity and doubt over? Was she finally willing to open her heart to Roger?

Nadine smiled. "So tell me about your young man. Does he return your affections?"

Conflicted and confused, she needed time to process this revelation. Half her mind focused on

Nadine, the other half remained caught in the web of her confession. "Well, if you mean does he like me in return," she stammered, "yes, he does."

"So what type of man was able to win your heart?"

She tried to pull her focus back to Nadine. "He's hard-working, honest, caring and he treats me like a princess." She didn't share her other thoughts, the confusion over his behavior, his random acts of affection balanced by periods of distraction.

"Like a princess?" The woman pursed her lips. "I would have thought a liberated woman like you would prefer to be treated as an equal."

"Princess isn't the right word. He sacrifices what he wants to make me happy."

"I see." Nadine fingered the book in her lap. "I'm sure you must be tired. Run along to bed. I will see that the light is turned out when I retire." As easy as that, Nadine had dismissed her. The queen on her throne.

Lillian quietly went up the stairs, her mind pondering the strange Mrs. Blackwell. Would she someday be like her, alone and living off the lives of others? But now Roger…

Slipping under the cool covers, Lillian reached for her Bible. Yawning, she set it back down and turned off the light. Sleep came easily, but with it dreams of princes who turned to frogs when kissed. Dozens of frogs jumped around her, clinging to her long skirt and getting tangled in her hair as she scrambled to kiss each prince, hoping one would remain true.

22

The six paintings propped against the dining room wall looked like God's creation of the universe on canvas. Colors sprouted and grew, moved and flowed in ways that gave Bill pause. He ran his hand across the stubbly hair on top of his head as he stared at his favorite, *Gethsemane*. Green predominated with splashes of red and blue and an overtone of darkness. The scene evoked emotions both hopeful and deep. No matter how many times he looked at the painting, it always elicited a mood within him.

Footsteps sounded and soon Lillian stood beside him. "Looks like Ted is getting ready to crate up his latest work." She stared at the paintings, hands on her hips. "He has an amazing talent."

It had been awhile since he had been alone with Lillian. He searched his feelings, quieted his mind to allow God to send a message. No bells of impending danger jangled at his nerves. And yet Lillian stood beside him. As hard as he tried, he could not trust this woman. And he had tried. Everyone seemed to like her—no, they loved her. She had become a part of the family, yet there remained that doubt God had placed on his heart at her arrival.

"Where is Ted, anyway?" she asked.

"Out getting the things he needs to secure these canvases." He tried again to sense anything unusual. Normally the feeling of danger overwhelmed him; he didn't need to go searching for it. "So what are you up to today? Going out with Roger again?"

Now he felt it—not danger but confusion.

"He's coming to pick me up after lunch. We're going to do some shopping in Florence."

"Hey, Lillian."

"Hey, Ted. Just admiring your work." She gave him a smile. "I need to get my list ready for the shopping trip to the big city, unless you want me to stay and keep an eye on big mama while you're gone."

"Going all the way to Florence, are you?" Ted asked. "It's what? Seven miles?" His grin lit his face. "Trina would kill you if she heard you talk of needing to watch her. She thinks she's a pillar of strength."

"I know, but if you want me to stay…"

"I'll be here," Bill said. No way would he leave his daughter alone with Lillian. He watched as she left the room, as much at ease here as she would be in her own home. "Any idea how much longer she's going to stay?" The dreaded feeling of danger had not surfaced, but his nerves still jingled. He scratched his arms. Something was up.

Ted placed the stack of wooden packing frames, screws, a hammer and two screwdrivers on the floor, and turned to the row of canvases. "So what do you think?"

"I'll never understand your work, but I've grown to appreciate it." He ran his hand across the stubble topping his head. "Ted, what do you know about Lillian?"

Ted let out a deep sigh. "Are we back to that? Bill, you're the only one in the family who worries about her."

"I know, and a prophet is never heard in his own

home."

Ted lifted a painting off the floor and swaddled it in bubble wrap.

Bill held the wood strips as Ted lay the protected painting over them, placed supports on top, and inserted screws to hold the two layers of wood in place.

"Do you think Aunt Betsy will come for a visit once the baby's born?" Screws dangled from between Ted's lips.

"Are you kidding? Nothing short of the Second Coming will keep her away. She mothered Trina after Nancy died, and now she thinks she has a personal claim to my first grandchild."

"She may have to fight Sandra for baby time." Ted stared at him. "Any new developments between you and Sandra?"

"What do you mean?" He took a deep breath. If the air had felt thick before, it suddenly became concrete.

"For awhile I thought a romance was building, but lately you seem to be backing off. You know, not making excuses to go to her house. Not beating a path to her side every time she shows up here."

Bill slumped into a chair. "That woman confuses me."

Ted grinned. "I think that's their job." He wiggled fingers in the air. "God made the female species deep and mysterious."

"Seriously, Ted, I don't know what to do about her."

Ted stopped working; his expression serious. "What's going on?"

"It's crazy, but I can't shake the feeling of doing

something wrong when I think romantic thoughts about Sandra." He grappled to put his feelings into words, never having been good at expressing emotions. But he had learned to appreciate the strength of his faith-filled son-in-law, and knew he could share his thoughts with him, man to man. "I turned down another offer to sell the house."

"Hmm. Was it a fair offer?" The screwdriver twisted against the board beneath Ted's hand.

"Not really, but then, what's fair anymore? The house is paid off, and ten years ago it would have sold for twenty thousand more than today."

"It's a nice place, and you've kept it up. It'll sell."

"Not if I don't want it to." He turned from Ted's open stare. "The house is the last link to my old life."

"So do you plan to go back to Ohio?"

"I don't think so, not now anyway. But who knows in the future?"

Ted secured the frame around his painting. "Sounds like Sandra would tie you here."

His son-in-law seemed to read his hidden thoughts, and it annoyed him. A man needed his privacy. "Right now I have two lives. I can only live one."

"Do you love Sandra?"

"Love has nothing to do with it. I will always be there for her and Jimmy, but that doesn't mean I have to marry her."

"Marry...wow."

Bill pushed himself out of the chair. "Come on Ted, you know how I feel. I can't marry Sandra when I'm still emotionally tied to Ohio. If I marry again, what happens in heaven when I meet up with Nancy? How do I explain Sandra?"

Ted grinned. "Is that what's bothering you? God doesn't prohibit remarrying after the death of a spouse, so I'm sure He has the two-wife-thing worked out."

"Someone will love these," Bill said, taking the opportunity to change the subject. He had talked enough about his personal life. Anymore and his brain would blow up.

"They're all headed to International Christian College in Columbia, ordered for their new chapel. Administration wants to hang them before the community Christmas Eve service."

"Aren't you putting this off until the last minute? This is what, the middle of December?"

"I had to wait until the oil paint dried. I'm headed to Columbia after lunch. Want to ride along? There are a couple of gifts I need to pick up while I'm in the big city." He shared a big grin.

"Isn't it supposed to rain?" A few gray clouds drifted as though in no hurry to be displaced by angrier dark cousins.

"It is, but I need to get these delivered."

He glanced toward the hall. If he went with Ted, it would leave Trina alone with Lillian. In spite of everyone else's opinions, the woman still had danger clinging to her like stink to a skunk. Maybe Sandra would come over for awhile in his absence. No, Lillian said she and Roger were going to the mall. The crowds would be awful, so she would be gone for hours. "I can keep you company. You'll need some muscle to help you carry these into the church."

"Then let's grab a sandwich and hit the road. We can be back before supper."

With another glance out the window, he followed Ted into the kitchen, hoping he had made the right decision.

~*~

Lillian stretched and sighed. She loved lazy days like this, snuggled on the couch with a pillow, blanket, and a good book. The men had just left, and Roger would be here soon to take her to the mall. She needed to get ready.

The cell phone in her pocket jangled. "Hey, Roger. I was just thinking of you."

"Will you care very much if I have to postpone shopping until tomorrow?"

"Actually I'm lying on the couch with a good book, trying to motivate myself to get up and get ready. What's up?"

"Just a last minute glitch at work. Nothing to worry about. Maybe we can even go later, if you want."

Stifling a yawn, Lillian glanced out the window. "It's supposed to rain. Let's wait for another day, if that's all right with you."

"Good with me. Call you later."

She glanced across the room at Trina, propped in her father's old recliner. It was hard to see the woman's face over her protruding belly, and twinges of jealousy wedged their way into her conscious.

Trina groaned.

"Are you all right? Do you want the couch? I can sit in the recliner if you want to trade places." Those were the right words. Give up her comfy spot, even though she didn't want to. Her lips tightened. To say envy didn't eat at her would be wrong. Every morning she confronted the one thing she wanted most and didn't have—a loving husband and a child. How would Trina, the faithful "God is good" woman, react if her baby were taken from her?

Trina sent her a smile. "I have trouble being flat, so the recliner is better, but thanks."

Lillian grimaced against her negative thoughts. It had been weeks since she had considered Trina as anything but friend. Besides, she had been spending so much time with Roger, she seldom saw the woman except in the mornings. She tried to settle back into reading her book, but the story no longer held her interest.

Trina flipped the page of her book, closed it and tossed it to the floor. "I'm getting some juice. Do you want anything?" She struggled to sit up.

"I'll get it for you." Retribution for bad thoughts.

"Thanks, but I need the exercise." Trina managed to stand, hands supporting her back as she gained a tottery balance. "Listen to that wind."

Lillian parted the lacy curtains. "It's really gotten dark; looks as if we're in for another storm." Her hand slipped between the cushions of the couch. "Hey, look what I found." She held up a roll of green duct tape.

"Looks like Dad's missing tape has been found."

The room darkened. A clap of thunder shook the house. Lillian shivered and pulled the knit throw closer to her neck. The murky gloom felt unnatural, as though swirling vapors hid in the shadows. *Come on, first you turn on Trina, not you're seeing ghosts.*

Trina turned on the overhead light, banishing spectral bodies to the other rooms, and snatched the remote. "Maybe we should check the weather."

Both women focused on the screen. The announcer pointed to a line of severe storms currently situated over the Pee Dee region which included Darlington County: heavy rain and high winds expected for the next couple of hours.

"Swell," Trina said. "Rain and wind. I hope Ted has the sense to not drive home." Suddenly she bent over and clutched her abdomen. A low moan escaped her lips.

~*~

Thunder rattled the plates hanging on the yellow kitchen wall.

Jimmy's hand jerked, splattering cookie dough across the counter. Wide eyes met those of his grandma.

"It's all right, sweetheart." She wrapped her arms around his slight shoulders. "It's just thunder. We're safe inside." The sky broke loose with a volley of power, and Jimmy cowered against her. Her heart ached, remembering the horrors he had endured while restrained and alone in a black and airless shed.

Rain pelted the wood siding of the small house. The overhead light did little to erase the mid-day gloom; the shadows simply shifted from one corner to the other. Another flash of lightning, a crack of thunder.

Jimmy clamped his hands over his ears.

"Let's forget these cookies until the storm passes." She covered the bowl with a dishcloth and turned off the oven. Jimmy's hand felt like ice in hers. He was normally so brave. Lately he had been more agitated than usual. To be honest, her nerves were a bit thin too, and her skin burned with apprehension. And now, with the storm, they both needed a distraction.

"Let's play a game. How about something fun?"

Jimmy loved board games and, hopefully, the activity would burn off some of his tension. He responded with a weak smile.

She had dug the games from the attic when Jimmy came to live with her. They had belonged to Jimmy's father; some things were too precious to part with. Sorrow tugged at her heart as it always did when she thought of her son beside his wife in the cemetery on Worley Street. Just three years old when they died, Jimmy had few memories of his parents. The games connected them. Both father and son enjoyed the challenges and skills involved in playing them.

The sound of the wind wailed through the walls while rain bashed against the windows as if the hands of Satan were beating against them.

Sandra gathered Jimmy onto her lap and murmured a prayer for safety.

A soft whisper reached her ears. "And keep Trina safe too, and my new baby cousin that will be born soon. Amen."

"Amen."

Sandra settled Jimmy at the table, his back to the window. Sneaking another look outside, she took a deep breath before removing the lid to the game.

~*~

Lillian helped Trina back into the recliner and propped up the footrest. *Swell, now she decides to take on the sick role. Ted better get home to coddle her.* In a distant corner of her mind, Lillian wondered at the strange, negative thoughts. She'd slept well, but maybe the storm was making her restless. She could deal with a cheerful Trina, but not a whiny one. "You rest. I'll get your juice."

The windows rattled against the force of the wind. Bits of debris pounced on the glass as dampness filtered into the room.

"In Cleveland, it would be snowing," she mumbled.

Back from the kitchen, juice in hand, she found Trina struggling to get out of the chair. "I think my water just broke!"

Oh, dear God, please, no. Placing the glass on the table, she reached over to help Trina out of the chair.

The lights flickered, and then died. Cave-like blackness filled the room. Rain pounded against the walls, beating a cacophonic sound like a myriad of drummers lacking a conductor. The darkness and noise distorted her senses.

She clutched onto Trina, hoping they both wouldn't end up on the floor.

A streak of light blended with ear-piercing thunder, sending vibrations through the room. Cracking sounds split the air followed by a muffled thud.

Lillian turned huge to eyes Trina. "I think lightning hit that old oak. At least it missed the house."

"Oooooh." Trina's body stiffened. "The pains are getting worse."

Standing in utter darkness, gripping a moaning woman, Lillian felt out of control. The storm raged and she had no idea what to do. She glanced toward the window where floor–to-ceiling glass encompassed most of the front wall. The limb had missed the house, but what about next time? What if something airborne shot through the window? Panic consumed her like fire through kindling. "We need to get out of this room."

~*~

The popping of plastic pieces from the game helped drown out the sound of frantic rain and hurricane-like wind.

But with each streak of lightning, Jimmy jumped, his elfin face becoming more ashen.

Sandra thought of Bill, and wished he were there. He would protect them. Even if he seemed to be losing romantic interest in her, he was a good man and would still keep them safe. Something special between them had ignited, but lately he had pulled back, seeming distracted and nervous around her. *Now is not the time for romantic regrets.*

The lights died.

Guided by the edge of the table, she worked her way to her whimpering grandson and wrapped arms around his shaking body. *Why didn't I think to get out some candles?* "Come on Jimmy." She pulled the reluctant boy from the chair. "Walk with Grandma to the sink. There's a flashlight underneath."

"Can I hold it?"

"Of course you can."

As she grabbed the flashlight, lightning split the sky, the jagged spear temporarily illuminating the room. "We need to leave the kitchen," she said, her voice trembling.

She guided Jimmy to the living room and placed the quivering boy on the couch with the flashlight. As he cast a beam for her, she pulled the heavy drapes across the large picture window and mentally reviewed the house. Where could they go that would be safe?

With each volley of thunder, her panic rose until she felt as though waves were crashing over her. She couldn't remember a storm like this since Hurricane Hugo in the '80s, and back then she hadn't been responsible for her grandson.

They both jumped as something large smashed against the side of the house. Jimmy burrowed his head into her chest. What if the projectile had hit the window? Even the heavy curtains would be unable to provide an adequate barrier.

Another hard thump.

With her heart ready to explode from her chest, she pulled Jimmy toward her bedroom.

~*~

Trina cried out as Lillian steadied her. The seat of Trina's maternity jeans was wet. Liquid dripped onto the floor.

"We need to get somewhere safer." The hall was perfect—almost. She lowered Trina back into the recliner. "I'll be quick."

"Can you drive me to the hospital?" Trina gritted her teeth and her hands made deep indents as she pushed them into the padding of the chair. "The pains are really close together."

Anger tightened Lillian's jaw. "Trina, look out the window." *Sure, let's go out in the storm. You won't even stand up by yourself and you expect me to get you to the hospital?* Again, Lillian wondered at her thoughts. She brushed them aside for the current situation. She'd have to think on it later. "Maybe the squad can get here." She pulled her phone from her pocket and dialed 911, only to hear a busy signal.

"Aaaah! Lillian!" Trina's panting breaths were almost lost among the reverberations of the storm.

Grabbing in the darkness, Lillian pulled the cushions off the couch and dragged them to the hall, bumping into the recliner and smacking into the wall during the process. As she felt her way back to the den, rain and wind assaulted the windows; the old glass probably couldn't take much more. Tension tightened her throat. "Let's move, Trina."

"I can't!" A cold hand grabbed hers. "It hurts too much." Trina let out another moan. "Something must be wrong!" The woman's hysteria sapped heavily on Lillian's reserves. "My baby is going to die!" Trina jerked her hands from Lillian's. "Your baby died, and now mine is going to die!"

Wanting to slap her back to reality, but knowing the movie trick probably wouldn't work, she glared in Trina's direction, the lack of light preventing Trina from seeing her angry expression. "If you want to stand here by yourself, go ahead." She took a few steps before Trina's words stopped her.

"My dad is right. You are dangerous."

"What did you say?"

"Dad doesn't trust you. Says you're here for a reason, something bad." Trina groaned in the darkness. "He feels death all around you."

Rage pushed its vicious head into her heart. Hadn't she proven her trustworthiness? How dare Bill think terrible thoughts of her?

Across the black space, Trina emitted a low guttural scream. "I know why you're here! You're going to kill my baby. Oh, God, oh, God. That's why you won't take me to the hospital!"

Lillian stiffened, too many blows hitting her at once. First Bill, now Trina. How could Trina even think that? She stood frozen to the spot, mouth gaping and eyes filled with tears. *God, You got me into this. I didn't want to stay here, but You made me. And now this. I can't handle any more...*

Lightning ripped the black sky. She grabbed Trina's face between her hands. "Listen to me. Susan died in a fire. I should have been there, but I wasn't. But I *am* here with you." Arms dropped to her sides, anger drained. "I know you're afraid. I am, too."

"It hurts so much!"

"Trina, listen to me. Labor hurts, and it can last hours. When the storm is over, I'll get you to the hospital. Until then, I'll be with you." She half-dragged and half-carried the pregnant woman to the hall. "Lie down on these cushions." She braced Trina against her legs and lowered her to the floor. "I'll get some pillows and blankets."

Arms extended, patting her way between piercing bolts of lightning, she grabbed four pillows and the throw she had been using on the couch. Stumbling over something hard, she picked the duct tape off the floor and hung it over her wrist. Trying to think what she might need, she groped around in the dark until her hands landed on two more throws. She shuffled her way back to the hall.

Panting for breath, hoping she had enough time before projectiles pierced through the house, Lillian threw one of the throws over the top of each of the glass doors that divided the entry from the long hall. The doors groaned as she struggled to close them. Above the sound of the storm came a distinct crack as the wooden frame split. Bill could fix it later—served him right. Strips of duct tape held the fabric barriers in place.

She groped her way back to Trina and propped pillows under her head and knees.

The blackness felt alive, and she brushed her hands across her arms, wiping the illusion from her. "Where do you keep your candles?"

"I don't know." Trina rolled back and forth on the cushions.

Nostrils flaring, she gripped the younger woman's shoulders. "I can get us some light, or we can sit in the dark. Your choice." Another pain peaked, and Lillian waited until the moaning stopped. "Think, Trina. Are there any candles in the kitchen?"

"Under the sink. Ted put an emergency box there, too."

She found her way to the kitchen then the sink. Opening the lower cupboard, something soft landed on her fingers. Gasping, she jerked her hand back and shook it, trying to remove whatever had landed on her, most likely a spider. Hesitantly, she explored the opening. A box of dishwasher detergent fell over, gritty powder coating the shelf. Cleaning pads, bottles of something. Hard plastic tube—the flashlight!

Grateful to be released from the darkness, Lillian pressed the button, and an anemic beam greeted her. She continued to search the cupboard and spotted a green metal box pushed against the back wall, looking very military and utilitarian. Hoping it was Ted's emergency stash, Lillian laid the flashlight on the floor and pulled on the heavy container.

The flashlight went out.

Tears of frustration filled her eyes.

"Lillian! Where are you?"

Gritting her teeth, holding back the verbal lashing that pushed to be released, she turned. "Hold on. I found Ted's emergency box."

"Please hurry." Fear etched Trina's voice.

In the dark, Lillian ran her hands over the box and fingered two metal latches. No lock, thank goodness. She flipped up the lid and hesitantly lowered her hand into the invisible space. Hard, round shapes lay on top. D batteries!

Blindly she grabbed the flashlight, dumped the dead batteries on the floor, felt for the positive and negative ends of the new ones, and inserted them. The strong beam felt like air to her drowning spirit.

From inside the box she pulled out matches, four candles, a foil survival blanket, two bottles of water, and several envelopes of dehydrated soup. In the bottom lay a one hundred dollar bill. As she grabbed the candles and matches, she snickered.

Never had money been less relevant, unless she used it to start a fire...fire! The fact that she would even think of the hot flames when her mind needed to be on saving Trina made her muscles tighten. Always fire.

Was she becoming some sort of beast who focused on anger and self-righteousness when a woman labored across the shadowy space? When her labor had started, Craig had been at a ball game, his cell phone in his car. As her pain grew worse, contractions coming closer together, she had tried calling the emergency squad, but her hands had been shaking too hard to press the three numbers. By the time Craig got home, she had been a mass of tears, almost hysterical with fear.

Trina had proven her stiff backbone time and again.

What if this was Bill's prophesy? Flashes of recent behavior played out in her mind: her anger over Trina's dependency, her unwilling to show kindness, her jealousy of a God-given child. Tears wet her face as she struggled to her feet. It would be hours before the baby would come, and she would make those hours as comfortable for Trina as she could.

Entering the hall, the beam from the flashlight revealed a tinge of red seeping onto the cushions. This could not be good.

Droplets of sweat ringed Trina's face. "I'm so scared."

"I am too." She stroked Trina's cheek, trying to calm the nerves that controlled both of them as the storm blasted against the house. "What can I do for you?"

Trina turned her head toward the wall, then back to Lillian. Eyes round with pain, she looked into Lillian's face. "I'm so sorry about what I said...about my dad."

"Look Trina—"

Another pain gripped the woman. When it passed, she sank exhausted onto the cushions. "Trina, how long ago did your pains start?"

Damp hair clung to the pillow. "Sometime last night maybe...or this morning. I don't know."

Fear churned in Lillian's stomach. "Why didn't you say something?"

"Didn't want to bother anyone until I knew for sure."

Well, she had succeeded. But if Trina had gone into labor hours earlier than Lillian had expected, she could be ready to deliver before the storm passed! *God surely You don't mean for this baby to die, like my precious Susan. You have to save Trina's baby. Let this storm end so the squad can get here!*

Punching in 911 over and over, the phone continued to beep busy.

With the severity of the storm, the chances of the emergency squad reaching Trina before her baby came were slim.

Lillian ached to run to the door, to shout for help, but she knew no one would be there; instead her words would be shredded and tossed back. *God, I know I don't deserve Your help, but Trina does.* Prayer used to be a routine part of her life. Even after the fire had destroyed her family, she had not forgotten to seek God. So what had kept her from His throne in the past few weeks? She had been so busy with Roger. With a quaking heart, she looked at Trina. "Listen, I can't reach anyone by phone. But that's OK. We can do this, but we need to pray. Give me your hands."

As Trina's shaking arms reached toward her, she grabbed them. "Lord, Your precious child is coming into this world. Please help Trina to do her part, and guide me in mine. We really look forward to holding this blessing. In Jesus name, Amen." She opened her eyes, unsure if God would hear her prayer.

The walls shook as she lit the candles. Completing the job, she looked around. Too many quivering shadows. Chiding herself, she turned to the next task. "Trina, lift your hips if you can. I need to pull off your jeans."

Together they struggled to remove the sodden clothes.

She covered Trina with one of the throws.

The contractions seemed to come every minute. Trina's face held beads of sweat even as Lillian grappled with her own trauma, fearing Trina and the baby would die.

With her terrified mind only half working, Lillian tried to process what else she might need. *Something to wrap the baby in. Suction to remove gunk from the mouth. What else, what else?* Her brain refused to cooperate. *God, I have no idea what I need. Help me!* "I have to go to the baby's room. I'll hurry." Lillian reassured even as she stood.

Trina's eyes were closed, her mouth a tight line stretched across a ghostly white face.

The nursery, usually full of light and softness, now stood dark and foreboding. Jerking open drawers, Lillian found blankets and grabbed all of them. Then the nose sucker thing—she didn't know if it had a name—and a hairbrush and fingernail scissors. Thunder ricocheted. She needed to get back to Trina. She grabbed at random: a knit hat and a pair of white satin baby shoes.

~*~

As the storm pressed against the walls, the bedroom seemed less protective.

Sandra was grateful for the darkness; at least Jimmy could not see the panic on her face. "One more move, Jimmy," she murmured, stroking his soft hair.

The boy stared without blinking as she pulled him to the hall.

"We can sit here; there won't be as much noise." With a shaking hand, she latched the bedroom door in front of them and crouched against the long wall. "It will be all right." She pulled the frightened boy closer, pressing her mouth against the top of his head. "God will take care of us."

They rocked back and forth, bodies molded together.

The wind raged around the house, thrashing against shutters and siding. Lightning battled the darkness, the silvery shards slipping around the edges of the living room curtains, sending ghostly streaks across the hall.

Jimmy pushed his head harder into her chest.

Glass crashed in the living room. Wet cold followed.

Dear God, help us!

Terrified, Sandra grabbed Jimmy and headed to the last safe place she could think of.

~*~

After stumbling down the stairs, Lillian dumped the supplies on the floor. Now came the hard part, even harder than enduring the raging storm that beat for admittance. But if the baby was coming, she had to do it. Swallowing the embarrassment that colored her face, she knelt at Trina's feet.

She had never looked *down there* at another woman before, and guilt filled her with dread. She touched Trina's legs. "Honey, I need you to bend your knees up." She tucked the blanket over Trina's legs just like they did at the doctor's office, leaving her a view of the birth area. *Water and a wash cloth, why didn't I think of water?*

The flicker of candles reflected against Trina's pain-filled eyes. "I have to go to the bathroom."

All the bathrooms were upstairs. It would be impossible to get Trina that far. What to do? She tried to think of options, like a mason jar or a bowl. None of them would work in Trina's condition. "Honey, I don't know what to do. Just pee where you are. It's all right."

Trina thrashed on the cushions. "I don't have to pee!"

"Oh. *Oh*! That's good news," she said, hoping God would see the fear that clutched her heart. "That means the end is close." What had the nurses told her when she had been at this point in labor? "When your next contraction starts, you need to push, just like you're having one gigantic poo." Her own tense muscles squeezed until she felt like the top of her head should fly off. Was this the right advice? Maybe Trina shouldn't push yet. She glanced toward the front of the house, forgetting she had covered the glass doors. If only help would come.

Trina cried out and groaned. Her face reddened as she pushed. Tissue bulged.

"Trina, I just saw the top of the baby's head!"

With each push, more of the baby's crown emerged, wrinkled and looking more like brain than skull. Was it supposed to look like that? *Oh, God, don't let anything be wrong with this baby...*

"I'm so tired," Trina mumbled. "I can't do this anymore."

The flickering light against Trina's flushed and sweating face reminded Lillian of the birth of Jesus. Mary must have been just as frightened as Trina, and she may have had just as little help. She had no idea how long they had been in the hall. "You're doing great, honey. One more time when you feel the contraction."

A moan escaped Trina's lips. "One's coming."

"Push hard!"

The head came out!

Lillian grasped the slippery surface tenderly. Another contraction and another push, but the baby remained in place. Quaking with uncertainty, she wondered if she was supposed to pull on the head. Didn't babies just pop out? Frozen with panic, unsure what to do, she watched as the head turned from face-down to sideways, rolling smoothly in her hands.

Engulfed in the drama of birth, she no longer heard the storm. With a mighty whoosh, baby boy Hancock filled her hands. Trembling, she laid him on the cushion between Trina's legs, grabbed the suction gizmo, and gently pulled secretions from his mouth.

He lay silent and unmoving between his mother's bloodied legs.

~*~

Sandra struggled to rise from the floor. Her muscles refused to obey her unconscious thoughts, so tight from fear. The hall had suddenly become a wind tunnel complete with lashing rain. Giving little thought to anything but saving her grandson's life, she pulled him up from his crouched position against the hall wall. "Come on, Jimmy, we're going to the bathroom." Her voice sounded other-worldly as it became caught up in the maelstrom around them.

The boy looked pale and lethargic. "But Gram, I don't have to go."

Without responding, she pulled Jimmy into the bathroom and closed the door behind them.

Standing in the middle of the small space, he

looked up at his grandma. His trusting eyes pierced her heart.

Would she fail his trust?

Something smashed against the house and Jimmy began to whimper.

Sandra wrapped her arms around him but he remained stiff in her arms, no longer melting into her protection. Tears filled her eyes as her heart pounded against her ribs. If only Bill were here...

When another loud volley of thunder shook the floor beneath her feet, the need for security became overwhelming. Sandra picked up Jimmy and placed him in the tub, then crawled in on top of him, covering his slight body with hers.

Even facedown, her eyes hurt from the sudden glare. Pain burned from her nerve endings, as though she were on fire.

And then the bathroom wall collapsed.

~*~

The horror was worse than any she had ever experienced. She had failed when needed the most. This time her absence had not been the cause, but her presence made the outcome even more sickening. She had delivered a dead baby!

The blue, but perfectly formed baby lay silently on the cushions.

Guilt pressed against Lillian. Breath refused entry into her leaden lungs as she stared at her failure.

The small chest expanded and a faint, quivering sound passed between purple lips.

With wide eyes, Lillian gathered the baby in her arms. As she stared at him, he emitted a hearty wail.

Nothing had ever sounded more beautiful. Tears streamed down her face and then she jumped into motion, wrapping the crying infant in one of the dozen or so blankets she had brought downstairs. She placed him on Trina's chest. "Here is your baby boy," she murmured, her arms aching to hold the child, but knowing he belonged to another. But she had saved him! Never had she felt more pride. More love.

Trina stroked her son's cheek, her smile of love all the more powerful in the flickering candlelight.

Common sense told Lillian to hunt for towels and clean the new mom, but her arms and legs wobbled like bands of rubber. She slid down the wall beside mother and baby.

Thank You, God. Thank You.

Within a half hour, the storm abated. The squad arrived just before the car came squealing into the drive, Ted at the wheel. He dashed into the house, followed by Bill.

Mother and son sat peacefully on the cart, a paramedic on each side.

Ted stopped. His mouth spread in a silent circle. Arms hung at his sides.

"Come and see our son," Trina murmured.

He leaped to his wife's side and smothered her in his embrace. With shaking fingers, he stroked his son's cheek. Eyes round with wonder, he touched the hair that looked as if it would be blond once it was clean.

Ted turned. "Come and see your grandson."

A sob caught in Lillian's throat and tears dripped of her chin. This is what she had at one time. And yes, she wanted it again: the unity and bond that family provided. Her thoughts turned to Roger. Then her mind drifted to Paul. She allowed the daydream. A life with Paul could never happen. But Roger—she could have a life with Roger.

The paramedics rolled Trina out of the house, Ted close beside her.

Lillian knew she would never be the same again. God had guided her hands when she became incapable. On her first trip to Darlington, she had prayed to be allowed to make a difference, and she had. Around her lay the evidence: soiled cushions and piles of unused baby items. Feeling as though she could float, she began gathering the stained items that bore testimony to the miracle that had just taken place.

God had been there all along, even when she had turned her back on Him. And today, when she needed Him the most, He had been at her side, ever faithful.

But doubt crept into her thoughts. Had God been there for her or for Trina?

Trina's words had seared her heart. If Bill felt death surrounding her, it must mean she would, eventually, be a danger to someone close to him. She shook her head against the thought. She would never intentionally cause harm.

Her foot bumped against a candle, tipping it over. The flame flickered greedily on the wood floor and she stomped her foot on the hungry tongue. She stared at the blackened area that already made a mark that remained on the wood.

23

Almost as soon as the thunder emitted its last soft growl, Roger's cell phone rang. He looked at the caller ID and groaned. The "Cleveland Contact," as she wanted to be referred to. No names. It was always her way, and it always had been, ever since he had known her.

"What?" He didn't bother to mask his anger, hoping it would limit their conversation to essentials. If he could change one thing in his messed up life, it would be agreeing to help her.

"Update me on your plan." Her voice flowed smoothly, almost sensually. "You do have one don't you? Or have you forgotten why you're still in Darlington?"

Rage bubbled just beneath the surface of his skin. A little more heat and his resentment would break open, but the only one to wear the scars would be him. "We need to talk."

"Go ahead and talk." The sound of ice tinkling against glass filtered through the phone. She must be drinking again. Great. There was no reasoning with her when she was drunk, which seemed to be most of the time.

"Lillian isn't like what we thought."

Raucous laughter jarred his ear. Gone was the attempt to be coy. Now the real woman emerged: a drugged-out, drunken has-been holding all the cards.

A hungry barracuda anxious to feed. "You're going soft on me. You never did have any backbone."

"Listen, she doesn't deserve to die." He knew his words would mean nothing, but he had to say them. He had to tell her they were making a mistake.

Something pounded on a hard surface, either her glass or her fist. Her voice screamed through the phone. "She killed my husband. And she killed my daughter, *your wife*, in case you have forgotten her."

Blood ran hot through his fists. His hands quivered in rage. Good thing she was in Cleveland or he would choke her to death—just as her husband had taught him. "How dare you think I would forget my wife or my child? Where were you when I buried them, one at a time? You didn't even have the decency to show up even once." She didn't want anything to do with him then, but oh, now...now that she needed someone to do her dirty work, now she needed him. Her raspy breaths carried as though she were standing beside him. His skin prickled.

"So what will you do about the woman responsible for their deaths?"

"Lillian is not responsible." His heart hammered against his ribs. The ache of defeat tried to swallow him. No matter the outcome, he would lose.

"You can think what you want, but I still hold you to your promise. My fingers can send this file to the police anytime I want." She laughed. "Ah, the wonders of the digital world. Instant send."

He knew the contents of the file; it would land him in prison for life. Even get him a death sentence. Death didn't sound all that bad right now, but even his death would not save Lillian.

"You have three days." Her words hissed like a

cobra preparing to strike.

The line went dead.

The sickle of death swung toward his throat. Three days. He threw the phone against the far wall where it broke into pieces.

~*~

Bill stood beside Lillian, both of their shoulders sagging with exhaustion.

The blankets had been removed from the glass doors, the floor scrubbed, and the soiled towels and blankets put to wash. The couch cushions now lay outside, the only remaining testimony of what had taken place.

"I need to thank you for what you did." Bill knew words failed to portray what he wanted to express. For the past hour, he had tried to thank her. If she had wanted to cause harm, today had been the perfect opportunity. After all, what did she know about birthing babies? He scratched the top of his head. Kind and loving, a believer in God, yet gripped by the icy hand of death. *God, what are You trying to share with me?*

Lillian stared up at him, and for the first time she didn't avert her eyes.

He waited. If there was one thing Trina had taught him, it was not to push.

Tears dribbled down her face and she brushed them away with her hand. "Who are you, Bill Iver?" she murmured.

He had been asked that question before, by Sandra.

She continued to stare at him, her expression a mixture of pain and hope. "I'm not a danger to you or to your family." She turned from him. "It's just that...there is something I need to share with you, but not now."

He wanted to probe for more, but she would talk when ready.

Somewhere a chain saw sounded. That log that had fallen in the front yard would need to be cut up. Amazing it hadn't hit the house. A car drove by; pools of water arched from the tires. Soon natural darkness would replace the lingering gray from the storm.

"You haven't heard from Sandra, have you?" He wanted to tell her about the baby.

Lillian covered her mouth with a hand. "I forgot about Sandra!"

He pulled the cell phone from his pocket and dialed. Good, he could be the one to tell her. Intermittent buzzing, and then the phone rolled to voice mail. He disconnected and stared. Something had happened.

Tension ate the back of his neck. Maybe she had gone outside. No need to invent more trouble. "I'm heading over to Sandra's. Want to come along?" He wanted to drag the words back as soon as he said them. As regret soured in his mouth, he remembered the saying that it's better to have an enemy at your side. He stomped out the back door, Lillian following.

In the backyard, Bill growled. "Ted parked my car in." The space between his back bumper and Ted's front end couldn't be more than three inches. Streams of frustration hissed from his nose. Now they would have to walk. Urgency tugged. He needed to get to Sandra's.

"We can take my car." Lillian ran into the house and quickly returned, dangling car keys from her hand.

"I'll drive." He grabbed the keys from her hand.

24

The steering wheel jerked under Bill's hand as he tried to control Lillian's car on the water-filled streets. The closer he got to Sandra's the evidence of the storm became more apparent. Trees lay uprooted, debris covered the yards. He swerved to avoid a green city trash can. Shingles lay everywhere.

Lillian moaned as she clung to the edge of the door. "I had no idea all of this was happening."

In the dusk, the exact extent of the damage was hard to determine.

Finally, Sandra's street.

His muscles loosened. In spite of the destruction around it, her house seemed undamaged. Amazingly, the tree that he promised to remove a couple of weeks ago remained upright, tenaciously clinging to the soil with limbs reaching toward heaven, as though seeking mercy against the storm.

He knocked on the kitchen door and jiggled the knob. "Sandra!" With the dim light that penetrated through the window, he spied her cookie-mixing bowl on the counter, and the board game on the table. His heart warmed. No one tried harder than Sandra.

"Maybe she's in the back yard," Lillian said.

Bill grunted and headed around the house. A lake had formed in the center of the yard. Broken limbs stretched from the water. *Great place for snakes to collect. Cleaning this mess would be top priority in order to keep*

Jimmy from getting bitten. He had seen moccasins traversing the streams in Williamson Park. Sandra's neighbor had killed a nest of copperheads just last week back by his shed.

Lillian's shrill voice came from the side of house.

He ran toward her, then stopped, stunned. Where branches should be, the roots of the tall oak jutted upward. A jumble of limbs and branches were tightly packed in the narrow space between the twisted trunk and the house. As he examined the damage, breath caught in his throat. Even in the waning light, he could see that part of the house was missing. The tree had slammed down onto the roof, crushing its way through the side wall. One major branch still hung precariously from the trunk, held in place by the limbs beneath it.

Ominous silence pressed against him. The feeling of urgency grew. Sandra should have seen him, or heard him. His stomach clenched. "Sandra!" Not waiting for a response, he sped back to the kitchen door, and fumbled to fit the key she had given him into the lock.

She and Jimmy could have gotten out. They could have gone to the neighbor's.

Or they could be crushed under the branches, unable to breathe….

The key slid into the lock. Bill tensed, preparing himself for what he might find. Why had he never told Sandra that he loved her? Why had he not spent more time with Jimmy? Tears misted blurred his vision.

The kitchen smelled damp. The lemon scent that usually greeted him was missing, replaced by the smell of wet carpet and plaster. He pushed out her name through a thickened throat. "Sandra!"

"Bill!"

She was alive! His heart lurched as he raced toward the sound of her muffled voice. *God, let them be all right.*

The grayness of the kitchen melted to deep shadows as he entered the living room. He knew his way, and continued to speed toward the voice at the back of the house. Suddenly he found himself falling. Sharp points penetrated his clothing and outstretched hands and scraped against his face. For a few precious seconds he lay in the unwelcoming arms of the barrier. With a lurching heart, he pulled himself free. Tree branches! In the opening to the hall. He balled his shaking hands and tried to catch his breath.

"Uncle Bill!"

"Honey, where are you? Talk to me. Are you hurt?" He reached for the barrier and clawed at its thick form.

Laughter filtered through the space. "Who are you calling honey, Jimmy or me?"

Lillian's distant voice followed. "Maybe it's me!"

They were safe! He pulled blindly at the branches. They seemed to be wedged into place, glued together by sheer mass. Sweat ran down his face. "Stay put, Sandra!" He dashed back toward the kitchen and out the door.

Lillian stood on the trunk of the tree, one hand clinging to the side of the house for balance. "I can't see them, Bill."

"We're in the bathtub, and we can't get out."

He and Lillian exchanged looks. "You're in the bathtub?" he called back.

"Long story. I can tell you later if you want."

"Uncle Bill, I have to pee."

He laughed. Nothing had thrilled him more than

their voices since his grandson's cry. *His grandson!* "Sandra, we have a baby!"

"I delivered him!" Lillian exclaimed.

"We have our baby? Y'all have been busy since I've been stuck in here."

The deepening dusk limited his vision. He turned to Lillian. "I need some light."

She grinned and pulled a red plastic flashlight from the waist of her jeans. "I figured we'd need it so I ran back to my car while you were in the house." Her lips tightened. "I've been stuck in the dark once today; that's enough."

"Sandra, hang on. I'm trying to find a way to get you two out of there." He moved the beam back and forth across the damaged house, the gash full of tightly woven branches. "This is a mess," he mumbled. "I don't see any way to get them out."

Lillian stood beside him. "What if we work from the inside?"

"What good will that do?" He continued to pan the light across the damaged house.

"The limbs at the top of the tree are smaller."

The light stopped moving. He grabbed her and gave her a hug. "You're right!" He turned the beam back toward the gap in the house. "Sandra, listen up. We're going inside and will try to get you out that way."

Their feet squished on the wet ground as they raced to the other side of the house. Inside, the narrow beam revealed mangled limbs packing the hall, spilling out into the living room.

"This is worse than I thought." He rubbed the top of his head.

"That's the same thing you said outside."

"This looks more like a beaver's dam than a hall." Desperation choked his air. Sandra and Jimmy were inside. Putting the light on the floor, he grabbed a thick limb, braced his foot and pulled. The limb didn't move. He grabbed a second limb, and then a third with no results.

"What if we try taking out some of the thinner branches first?" Lillian asked, picking up the flashlight from the floor. "Maybe the small ones are holding the bigger ones in place."

Hating that he hadn't thought of it, but willing to try anything, he grabbed a fistful of twigs and tossed them toward the front door. After propping the flashlight, she joined him. Soon they had cleared a sizeable space, but the distance to the bathroom loomed large beyond them.

Sweat dripped off his face. "I'll have you out soon. Jimmy, you still with me in there?"

"It's too late, Uncle Bill." Jimmy's words came in hitches.

Bill stood stricken for several seconds. What had happened? She had been fine moments ago. And then he grinned. "That's OK, buddy. I may have just wet my pants, too."

"Bill!"

The sound of Sandra's voice—even if to reprimand—flowed like chocolate syrup over the ice cream of his heart.

Footsteps thumped in the dark. "You need some help in here?" A middle-aged man dressed in coveralls, with a ball cap pressed on his head, stood behind them. A green chain saw dangled from his right hand and a red container was gripped in the other. He had a large industrial flashlight tucked under his arm.

"Hey, Pat," a disembodied voice called. "Thanks for coming to my party."

"That you, Miss Sandra?" Pat peered into the dense branches.

"I'm in here, too!" Jimmy shouted.

"Hey there, James, my man. You should have seen those puppies during the storm. They sure were missing you."

"Can I hold one when I get out?"

"They'll be waiting."

Pat turned to Bill. "Noticed the tree came down, and saw the two of you running around. Thought you might need some help."

Grit caked the wide grin on Bill's face. "Looks like you brought the muscle we need." He nodded toward the chain saw.

Rubbing his whiskered chin, Pat examined the hole as Bill shined the light. "Let's get at it!" Pat pulled the starter cord and the motor roared to life.

As sawdust spit into the air, Bill and Lillian pulled out the cut limbs.

After about fifteen minutes, the chain saw sputtered and stopped. "Out of gas." Pat reached for the red container. The hole now extended halfway down the hall, close to where the tree had smashed through the house.

Three heads jerked up as a sharp crack split the air, and then a thud, followed by the sound of limbs cracking and splintering. Then silence.

Bill's heart felt as if it stopped beating. "Sandra and Jimmy, you all right?"

Sandra's voice came in tight gasps. "Something must have fallen. It put more pressure on us."

Lillian bent into the opening. "How is Jimmy?"

"He's tucked beside me. He's fine, but hurry."

"Give me that thing!" Bill shouted, grabbing at the chain saw.

Pat held firm. "Hang on a minute. We better go see what happened outside. We don't want to be pulling and pushing and cause the rest of that tree to fall on top of them." The man's face crinkled in concern.

As one, the three raced outside and across the front lawn to the side yard. Darkness now blanketed the damage, and with all electricity gone and no stars to lighten the night sky, they had to rely on the two flashlights to cut the inky blackness.

Bill shivered as the cool air penetrated his sweat-soaked shirt. He ran his hand across his eyes, remembering the sound of Sandra's panting breaths. They reminded him of Nancy as she breathed her last. Was he about to repeat history with Sandra?

At first glimpse, the side yard looked the same.

Bill slid the beam from Pat's light over section of the house, and then another.

Suddenly Lillian gasped. "Look!" She pointed away from the house, toward the thick limb that had been propped by fallen branches. The limb had slid and now one end lay directly over the bathroom, putting pressure on the intertwined limbs, while the other still remained attached to the trunk by a thin strip of bark and wood.

As they watched, the branch slipped a few more inches, the anchor holding it to the tree becoming thinner.

"If that limb falls, it'll crush Ms. Sandra and the boy." Pat's voice sounded flat as he stood staring.

"Help me," Bill yelled. "We've got to prop that limb up!" He gathered fallen limbs and shoved them under the branch. The effort was futile. The branch was too heavy and would crush right through the thin branches.

An engine rumbled and two beams of white light cut through the darkness. Lillian drove her car into the side yard. She motioned for them to move; a devious grin spanned her face. With a roar worthy of the Darlington Raceway, she crashed through limbs and wedged her car under the branch.

She turned off the engine and the door cracked open. Limbs pressed against the car holding her inside.

Pat headed toward the car, chain saw gripped in his hand.

The offending branch could bear its weight no longer, and, with a moaning crack, it separated from the tree. The thick wood fell across the car as intended, leaving a mass of mangled metal, shattered glass, and intertwined limbs. The car lay almost hidden beneath its shroud of limbs.

"Lillian!" Branches flew as he cleared a path to the car.

Pat worked beside him.

"Get the flashlight," he called to Pat over his shoulder. "Lillian!" The ominous silenced filled his stomach with dread.

Sandra's voice wafted across the clearing. "What happened?"

"A limb fell, Ms. Sandra. You and the boy all right?"

"Why is Bill calling for Lillian?" Fear chilled her voice.

"I want out of here!"

"Jimmy, stay still, sweetheart. Grandma can't hold these limbs off you if you move around."

The sound of Sandra's voice added to the tension that roared around in Bill's body.

Lillian had prevented the limb from crushing Sandra and Jimmy, but at what cost?

He turned his head toward the house. "Jimmy, just relax in there, big guy. Give us a few more minutes. Try counting to a hundred, can you do that?"

Pat ran toward him with the flashlight. He grabbed the light and shoving his weight through the thicket that still separated him from the car. Reaching the car, he focused the beam through the broken window. Breath escaped his body.

Lillian lay against the seat belt, her body skewed toward the passenger door. Blood dripped from a gash in her forehead. Red streaks stained the deflated airbag and smeared a path across her limp arm.

~*~

This had to be the best day of his life. Ted's smile stretched his face until he thought it would rip out his cheeks. And then he grinned even wider. *A son! I have a son!*

The doctor had come and gone, declaring their boy a perfect specimen, and praising Lillian for her cool head.

While Trina was examined, he had held his son, now clean and wrapped in a blue-and-pink striped hospital blanket. He could have stayed forever, just holding his child, but Trina had pushed him out, worrying about the house, the mess she must have created, and their houseguest.

Mrs. Blackman apparently had weathered out the storm somewhere else. The roads might be too impassable for her to get back to Darlington that night, but just in case, someone needed to be at the bed and breakfast to greet her and provide a light for her bedroom.

Lillian had already done enough, and most likely Bill would be at Sandra's.

Deciding to hike home from Wilson Hospital had been easy. He couldn't reach Bill and it was only a couple of miles. It was the darkness he hadn't considered. The hospital was functioning with a generator, but the rest of Darlington still lacked electricity. Windows from most of the houses winked kerosene lamps or candles, but the light didn't filter to the streets.

He stepped over dozens of branches before falling prey to one, landing hard on his hands and knees. His good pants ripped. Trina would be ticked. In spite of the pain in his knee, the smile returned as he lumbered up the hill and past the barking dogs that irritated him most nights. Finally, he reached his house.

No glow shimmered in any of the windows. He had expected Bill to have some type of light rigged up. Most likely, he had gone to Sandra's, but he had expected his father-in-law would provide light for Lillian. Limping up the front stairs, he let himself into the house. Groping around, he found candles on the kitchen counter, then his flashlight. No notes lay on the counter or table. Where was everyone?

He placed a candle on the kitchen table, in the parlor window, and kept the flashlight with him. His tasks done, loneliness settled over him. The old house was always full of sounds: talking, motors from the furnace or refrigerator, radio or television. But now only silence kept him company.

Deciding to examine the damage from the fall, he found his khakis had two small tears. Maybe Trina could turn them into shorts. His knee felt stiff, but was only scraped. Nothing to worry about.

Out the kitchen window, black shapes lay hunkered in the silence. Focusing the beam of the flashlight, he noticed that Lillian's car was missing. Most likely, she had gone to Roger's. Chuckling, he noticed that he had parked Bill in. His father-in-law had done some walking, too. No doubt, he gone to Sandra's to share the news about the baby.

There wasn't much for him to do. He would give Mrs. Blackwell the big flashlight, and he would manage with Trina's smaller one. There was another flashlight in the bedroom. He always kept a spare in his nightstand. And surely, Bill would have one or two either in his car or his room.

With the situation under control, he spread a thick layer of peanut butter on top of bread. No need to open the refrigerator. Filling a glass with water from the tap, he headed to the den to wait. What was his baby doing? He imagined him bundled in his blanket asleep either in the plastic crib or in Trina's arms.

The grin returned.

~*~

Bill's chest tightened. "Lillian!" He stretched his arm through the broken window and reached for her neck. "She's alive!"

"Pull those limbs away from the door after I cut them," Pat called. The chain saw roared to life and soon both men were covered with sawdust. The smell of oil and fumes quickly replaced that of damp sand.

Fear strengthened Bill's hands as he pulled free one thick branch after another and heaved it over his back. He glanced again at Lillian's still form, and guilt tightened his already heavy chest. Surely, this was not what God's message had meant. Yes, God revealed that Lillian was shrouded in danger, but he never once thought he was supposed to *protect her. God, You need to make these messages more clear, or take them away!* The faster he worked the tighter his jaws clenched his teeth. As soon as he pulled away the last thick branch that blocked the car, Bill grasped the handle and jerked. The door refused to open.

"Let me help you." Pat's hands felt hot on top of his.

"On three." With loud grating of metal against metal, the door let loose and hung awkwardly on one hinge.

Bill groped for the seat belt, released it, and pulled Lillian against his chest. As her head fell backward, she moaned. As his arms supporting her tightened, he felt the steady beat of her heart against his chest. "I'm so sorry," he whispered. "I'm so sorry."

~*~

Her head hurt. Bad. She tried to lift her arm toward the throb but it flopped back to her side.

"Steady girl," a voice murmured. "Just sit here a few minutes while we try to get you out of the car."

The voice had quivered. Was she hurt?

She took a breath and coughed against the pain in her chest. With the fuzziness clearing, she moved her arm again, and brushed against a strong, hairy one.

Turning her head, at first all she saw was darkness with streaks of harsh light. Then she saw Bill supporting her body, his face smeared with sweat and sawdust and tension. "The tree limb?" she asked.

"On top of your car."

She smiled. "Better than on top of Sandra and Jimmy."

"Can we get her out yet?" Pat asked.

"How about it?" Bill looked at her. "Can you move at all?"

Her legs were squeezed between the seat and the steering wheel. She couldn't feel her feet. "I don't think anything is broken." She waved a hand over her head, hitting the gash at her hairline. Fresh blood dribbled from the wound. "Ouch. How bad is the cut?"

"Not bad. Let's get you out of there."

Between Bill and Pat, they managed to compress the seat cushion and spread the metal enough to slip her from under the steering wheel. She dangled her legs out the door, letting the sensation return and the wooziness that gripped her stomach to settle.

"Bill! Pat! What's going on out there?" Sandra's voice filtered like ghostly ribbons across the space.

Bill looked from Lillian to the spot that confined Sandra, indecision etching his face.

"I'll hold on to the little lady. You go calm Ms. Sandra." Pat's bony ribs replaced Bill's soft chest. "Nasty gash on your noggin. Gonna need stitches most likely."

"Bill said it wasn't too bad."

"Yeah, well, on second thought, it's not all that bad."

"I think I can stand now." She shifted toward the edge of the seat.

As Pat steadied her, she stood on her feet and the queasiness returned. "Down."

Back on the seat, she rested her head on her legs. "OK, let's try this again."

Pat extended his arm and she reached for it. He pulled her up gently as she wobbled back and forth.

Taking a few breaths, she smiled. "I'm all right. Let's go see about Sandra." She walked slowly, still clutching to Pat's arm. Darkness forced her to lift each foot with exaggerated height as she waded through the mass of discarded limbs. Stopping to catch her breath, she glanced back and groaned. The flashlight, propped in the branches where the men had placed it, reflected light off the crumpled metal. "Look at my car."

"Yep, it's a goner."

Her stomach clenched. She was lucky to be alive. "Well, the car did what it was supposed to do."

Once she reached the side of house, Bill indicated the thick branch close to the opening and she sat. "Sandra, this is Lillian," she called.

"Hey, honey, how are you? Bill said you saved our lives." Sandra's voice hitched. "I want to hug you."

"I'll take that hug when we get you out."

"I think I can crawl through here," Bill examined the reconfigured hole into the house.

While she called encouragement to Sandra and Jimmy, Bill and Pat ran back to the demolished car for the flashlight and chain saw.

"Miss Sandra, you and Jimmy will need to keep your eyes closed," Pat said. "The chain saw makes a lot of dust."

Jimmy began to whimper.

"Are you doing all right, big guy?" Bill called into the dark cave.

"Bill, you need to hurry." Sandra's voice sounded thin. "I don't know how much more of this Jimmy can stand."

"Uncle Bill…I want out."

The two men glanced at each other. The chain saw sprang to life. Brambles flew as Bill tugged against each limb blocking his path to Sandra and Jimmy.

Bill held up a hand and Pat shut down the chain saw.

Jimmy's excited voice called out. "I see something!"

Lillian wiggled the beam of the flashlight back and forth. "Do you see that, Jimmy?"

"I see it!"

"It's my flashlight."

Pat scratched his belly. Wood chips fell off his arms and shirt. "You think one of us can fit through there yet?"

Bill took Lillian's flashlight and shoved his body into the opening. Left in darkness, cracking limbs shared his progress. Soon he backed out of the hole. "I can't get all the way in. We need to make the opening bigger."

Lillian bent over to stand. Her head pounded from the movement. "I'm smaller than you, Bill. I can make it."

"No way. You're hurt. We'll get it."

Snatching the flashlight, Lillian crawled into the opening. The light bounced off crushed limbs and stabbed her eyes. Squinting against the light and falling bits of dirt, she grabbed the limbs in front of her and used her feet to move forward. Progress came in inches, and soon sweat dripped in her eyes. At least it stung like sweat. Breaths came in pants, each one stabbing her chest. "I can see the edge of the tub!" she called.

"Are you coming to get me?"

"Jimmy, lay still."

Lillian laughed. "I'm coming. Can you stick a hand out of the tub, Jimmy?"

"No, Grandma's got me trapped."

"I can put a hand out," Sandra said. "Does it matter which one?"

"Either one is fine." Branches snapped in front of her, and soon the light illuminated the soft hand of her friend.

"Lillian, do you need help?" Bill's voice boomed through the darkness.

Directing the light, Lillian examined the maze around Sandra's hand and the branches that still covered the tub, one in particular that seemed to be responsible for most of the pressure on the tub. "I'll be right back," she called to Sandra. She ran a hand along the thick branch as she backed her way out.

Still gripping the offending branch, she allowed Bill to help her from the opening. Fresh air filled her lungs, and she shivered as the cold air met her damp skin. "This limb is holding the others in the tub. Once we cut it out, we should be able to get them out."

Pat wiggled his way into the tunnel. His voice echoed back. "Miss Sandra, cover your eyes. Let me know if I make things worse."

As the chain saw roared to life inside the tunnel, the branches outside shivered against the vibration. Soon the shape of the tunnel changed as the large branch compressed the wood beneath it.

The chain saw quieted. Pat backed out of the tunnel. With Bill in front and Pat behind, the men wrapped their hands around the log and pulled.

Unable to see their faces in the dim light, Lillian listened to the grunts as they applied pressure to the log.

Nothing happened. Then the sound of cracking wood filled the air.

When the sawed end of the log cleared the opening, Bill ran toward the hole. Within seconds he returned and grabbed her flashlight, a sheepish grin spread across his face.

Pat focused the second light on the newly enlarged hole. Lillian hugged her arms, both against the chill and in anticipation. She hardly noticed the throbbing head or painful ribs as she focused on the illuminated space.

Sandra's voice, then Jimmy's filtered from the dark.

More limbs cracked, and Bill released Jimmy to Pat.

"Hey, there you are." Pat smothered the boy in a hug. The man's voice had an unexpected husky overtone as he brushed twigs off Jimmy's hair.

Soon Sandra emerged, followed by Bill. She straightened her back and smiled. "Y'all can't begin to imagine how good this feels."

Feeling out of place in the intimate scene, Lillian stood to the side.

Sandra spotted her, ran and wrapped arms around her shoulders. Sandra's tears felt wet against her cheek. The older woman pulled away and dabbed her eyes. She scanned Lillian's face. "You got hurt."

"It's nothing. Bill said so himself."

"Bill," Sandra called over her shoulder, "the girl has a gash on her head. How can you say that's nothing?"

"It's not bleeding, is it?"

"Not right now."

"Well then, it's nothing. You can wash it later if you want."

Sandra sank to one of the logs. "I'd offer y'all iced tea, but I'm not sure what shape my kitchen's in."

Jimmy turned in a circle, examining the shadowy space. "Wow." Then he turned toward Sandra. "I could have some iced tea, Grammie."

Bill lifted the small boy, smelly and wet as he was, into his arms. And then he gathered Sandra with the other. "To the inn, and I will serve all of you. That includes you, Pat."

"How you planning on getting all of us to your place," Pat asked, "seeing as how your transportation is stuck under a tree?"

"Oh, yeah."

Slipping from Bill's grip, Sandra stepped over the tree limbs toward Lillian. "What about our baby? I need details!"

Lillian put an arm around Sandra and laughed. "As soon as you tell me how you and Jimmy ended up in the tub!"

~*~

Exhilarated, but exhausted from the day's events, Lillian thought it would take an earthquake to move her from her bed. Life had taken a turn for the good with Bill's thawing attitude. All that remained were the unexplained fires. But she had a plan. The idea occurred to her as she had wiggled her way to Sandra, and the branches kept hitting her in the face. If only she had brought that duct tape, so useless during Trina's delivery, but just what she needed to hold back the lashing limbs.

The only way to definitely know if she was setting the fires was to make sure she never left her room. She would tape herself to the bed. It seemed silly, but it might work. After preparing for bed, she pulled the duct tape and a pair of scissors out of the drawer.

Bible reading done and prayers said, she put on a pair of socks. The duct tape released from the roll harder than she had thought. Had she ever used duct tape before? It wasn't one of the things she kept around her house. She wound the strip around her ankle over the sock, and secured the other end to the bed frame and lay down.

The short length of her tether kept her from moving, and she knew she would never be able to sleep flat on her back all night. She pulled off a longer strip, and tried again. Three tries and she got it right, and then duplicated it for the other leg. Now she could roll from her back to her side, but could not get off the bed. Even if she cut the tape in her sleep, she would find the discarded sections in the morning. Not scientific, but at least she would know.

The only downside to her plan was the need to anchor herself to her bed until another house burned.

25

Roger arose from bed, groggy from lack of sleep. This was day three, and as much as he hoped otherwise, he knew his partner would remember as well. He had never felt so alone. There had always been a solution, some better than others, but an acceptable way out of all past situations. Until now. Only one scenario showed promise, and with it came the pain of losing a woman he had learned to love.

He turned toward the closet probably for last time. After opening the box and pulling out the thumb drive, he inserted it into the computer. New data needed to be entered. The familiarity of the task steadied him. Two families had vacated their homes in the past week. As he waited, the spread sheet appeared on the screen. Finding what he wanted, he scanned the information and then pulled open the desk drawer, empty except for the city map marked with dots. Glancing at the screen for confirmation, he put an X over another dot. Now more than half the dots had a black X over them.

The call had come at three in the morning. Another house had burned; the fire chief would be in to see him first thing. These meetings were getting harder.

How much longer could he conceal the truth? He pounded a fist into the desk. Why was he keeping this data? What did it matter? Nothing happened as planned. He gripped the sides of his head, the headache already beginning to creep up his shoulders. And it was only 6:00 AM.

Needing coffee, he headed toward the kitchen only to be disturbed by the ring of his cell phone. He looked at the caller ID and allowed the ring to continue to the point of rolling over to voice mail before he answered. "What do you want?"

A chipper voice responded. "Today is the day. It's day three, and I have a ticket to Jamaica in my hand."

Roger had never heard her sound this happy, or to be awake, for that matter, this early. Hatred for her sizzled under his skin but he held it in check before it gained control of him. Lillian had helped him realize he had to let go of his anger. But how could he forgive someone who was bent on destroying not only his life but Lillian's as well? "I can't do this." He lowered himself onto a kitchen chair.

"Of course you can. Soon it will all be over, and both of us can start our new lives. Just think, with the money Leo helped you hide in bank accounts, you can go anywhere you want, live like a king. You can leave that dreary little town behind."

He gritted his teeth. Monstrous thoughts pushed to be released, but none of them mattered. "Lillian doesn't deserve to die."

Silence.

He could imagine her face reddening, eyes narrowing until they became angry slits. When she spoke, her words dripped with venom. "I understood my husband well, and I knew what he planned to do as soon as the guilty sentence was read, not that I blame him. His eyes told me. The thought of spending the rest of his life in prison was worse than death."

"He had to pay for his crime."

"His crime? Leo took the fall for both of you."

He pulled the phone from his ear, her rage still banging against his eardrum. The past circled around him like a vicious lion, and he had no way to escape.

"He made sure you were squeaky-clean of the drug trafficking charges. Oh, he could have squealed on you, probably gotten himself less time, but he didn't. Let me ask you this, goody boy. Who put you through college?"

His arm shook as he tried to suppress the urge to disconnect the call. If he hung up, she would just call again and again, until she had her say. "We both know Leo paid for my education, and then I agreed to work for him."

"Two for one, I'd say. A free education, and then a guaranteed job. And you married our daughter."

Anger, no longer to be denied, exploded within him. "Carla was never part of the deal. I loved her. I loved her more than you ever did."

"Don't you tell me about love, you ungrateful snit. You dragged her from her home in Cleveland to live in a dump."

"It was all I could afford on what I could make here. We were happy—or we could have been."

"You have no idea how miserable she was. You drove her to suicide. She hanged herself because of you."

Angry lies, a low blow even for her. Carla had died of smoke inhalation. He had the autopsy report...

The woman's voice blurred. He closed his eyes. He hated his past deeds. He hated them more since listening to Lillian talk of God's love. But it was too late.

"Didn't you wonder why Leo was so willing to allow you to marry Carla? She was the light of his eye. His only child. He kept her innocent, out of the family business. But giving her to you would guarantee your cooperation."

"And I got her away from you as fast as I could."

"So you could let her die?" The angry words hissed. "Carla is gone, Leo is dead, and Lillian has to pay. Today. Or I go to the police."

There was no way out; Lillian had to die. But at least he could make it fast, and as painless as possible. His soul was already dammed. One more deed, good or bad, wouldn't make a difference. If he didn't kill Lillian, his partner would.

Lillian had promised to fix supper for him today while he was at work. He would pack whatever he intended to keep and stow it in the car. Looking around, nothing except his metal box warranted saving.

26

Lillian unlocked the door of Roger's house and dropped the grocery bags onto the cupboard: ground meat for meatballs, tomatoes, tomato paste, onions, and fresh herbs for the sauce. Linguine from the new Italian store in Florence. The hour trip had been well worth it; fresh linguine tasted better. Salad and garlic bread would round out the main meal. Then cheesecake for dessert.

She started a pot of coffee and put the perishables in the refrigerator. It felt awkward to be in Roger's home alone, but when she had offered to fix dinner for him, he had said yes, and had given her a key. She looked around with uninhibited eyes. He certainly wasn't one for decorating. No pictures broke the starkness of the walls. The living room looked as if it had come from one of those room-in-a-box stores. The impersonal space didn't come close to reflecting the personality of the man who alternately tugged at her heart and caused her fear. Even though their conversations lately had become more intimate and revealing, she still knew very little about Roger Jenkins. She smiled. That was about to change.

Reveling in the domesticity she never had time for in Cleveland, she put the meatballs in the oven and started on the sauce. After dipping the spoon into the simmering pan and lifting it to her lips, she added more oregano. And garlic. One could never have too much garlic.

The bouquet of fresh flowers she had bought for the table would add a romantic touch.

The euphoria had started first thing in the morning. The duct tape had worked! During the night, another house had burned while she had remained safely anchored to her bed. Legally her trick did nothing to clear her name, but that wasn't important right now. She knew the truth, and the relief felt enormous.

As for Roger, she had prayed for God to lead her to the man that was to be a part of her life. God would handle the details.

Looking through the kitchen cupboards for scissors and tape, plastic tape this time, and finding none, she wandered down the hall to the master bedroom. Roger had a desk in his room, and that was most likely where he kept the tape. While waiting for the meatballs to cook, she would wrap his Christmas gift.

Entering his bedroom, she sighed at his compulsive neatness. The bed was made, all his clothes put away. Walking into the master bathroom, she shook her head. The toilet seat was down and no toothpaste coated the sink. But he must have forgotten to open the drapes, leaving the room cold and dark. Humming to herself, she pulled the curtains and straightened them neatly.

The desk looked like one of the cheap fiberboard varieties sold at office supply stores. It had the expected long middle drawer with three drawers on each side. Pulling out the top right-hand drawer where she kept her tape, she found it empty. So was the next drawer, then the bottom one. All were empty. With each empty drawer, the unease creeping up her back intensified. Who had a desk and put nothing in it?

She opened the long middle drawer and gasped.

~*~

"I'm sorry you're leaving us," Sandra said.

Nadine Blackwell continued eating as her coffee cup was refilled. "My business is finished."

"It's always a blessing to be home for the holidays. Will you be with family?"

Mrs. Blackwell smiled. "Yes."

"I know Trina would like to say goodbye, but under the circumstances…"

The woman wiped her mouth, leaving red lipstick on the linen napkin. "I fully understand. I'm glad Lillian was there for her."

"Ted can bring down your luggage if you can wait a little bit. He's…busy at the moment." She stared toward the parlor.

Ted had been on his knees in prayer since before she had arrived.

"Bill would have carried them down for you before he left for school, but we didn't know…"

"Oh, it's quite all right. I am capable of carrying my bags."

Nadine Blackwell had to be the strangest woman she had ever met, but apparently, she could hold her own with business executives.

Sandra shook her head. The world held all kinds.

A half hour later, footsteps sounded on the stairs.

Sandra dried her hands on the dishtowel and walked to the kitchen door.

Nadine descended the stairs, her suitcases gripped

in her hands.

"Is there anything I can do to help you, Mrs. Blackwell?" Anxious to get to the hospital and see the baby, she hoped any needs Nadine might have would be small.

"You have done more than you know."

27

Lillian wasn't sure how long she stared at the paper in the open drawer. Her heart, which moments ago had leaped into her throat, now lay flaccid in her chest.

A map of Darlington. The streets clearly identified. Marked off with X's, the houses that had burned since her arrival.

She started to shake. Why did he have this list? Had he tracked her actions, trying to predict which house she would burn next? Did he still suspect her, even after she told him someone was trying to frame her? And now she had proof of her innocence.

The longer she stared at the map, the muddier her thoughts became. If he was tracking the houses that had burned, why had he circled ten additional addresses? Were those houses recently vacated?

With trembling hands, she reached into the drawer and hesitated, fingertips hovering just above the paper. She could close the drawer and pretend she had never seen the map. But could she really hide her emotions, or would Roger look into her face and see reflected the hidden X's?

The scent of tomatoes and basil reminded her of the sauce still simmering on the stove. Supper could burn for all she cared. She grabbed the map, hoping Roger would have an explanation. As she strode back to the kitchen, she stared at the paper. There must be some clue that she was missing, but what?

The kitchen door handle rattled. Her breath caught in her throat. Roger wasn't due for two hours yet. That meant whoever was trying to gain access was doing so for ill gain. The map in her hand burned like fire.

Roger stepped into the room.

She heaved a sigh of relief and planted a kiss on his cheek. "I thought you weren't going to be home until after five."

Roger's eyes narrowed as he noticed the paper in her hand. "Where did you get that?"

She glanced at the map, and then back at Roger, her nerves zipping against her skin.

"I trusted you," he said. "Why did you have to snoop?" His eyes softened. "I know what you have been doing, Lillian. Let me help you. I have a plan."

As he reached for her, she turned to run.

He grabbed her wrist. "Lillian, listen to me. We can work this out."

His touch burned her skin and she jerked her arm free. Emotions raging and close to tears, she needed space to sort her feelings. Was he friend or foe, and what had he meant by knowing what she had been doing? What had *he* been doing? The map was in his desk, not hers.

Suddenly the swirl of thoughts coalesced. She clutched her throat. Her eyes widened in horror. Her anger wasn't about the map, but about the consequences. A sour mixture of betrayal and rage ignited within her. "You killed Joe!"

That's what she had been trying to connect with the map, but her subconscious had refused to allow the connection until now. Tears filmed her eyes, sorrow for the loss of life, anger over how easily she had allowed him to manipulate her. Why had she not seen it before? Roger set the fires and she had been his patsy. That explained the map. It explained everything.

He stared at her, his eyes soft and pleading. "How could I kill Joe when you set the fire? Let me help you, Lillian" Again he reached for her.

She backed into the living room, not taking her eyes off him.

How could he blame her for the fires, his eyes so innocent? He had to be mad.

If she could just get to the front door and she would be free, but could she unlock it before he stopped her? Grabbing the closest object she could reach, a ceramic lamp, she threw it at him and ran.

His arms circled her waist, and she screamed.

He clamped a hand across her mouth and pulled her tight to his chest. "Listen to me." She struggled against his grip, fear roaring through her veins.

~*~

"Well if this isn't a pretty little scene."

At the sound of the voice Roger's hands dropped.

Lillian half ran, half stumbled toward Nadine Blackwell. Trying to control her panic, she grabbed the woman's arm. "Run!" She tugged at Nadine, but the woman remained fixed in place.

"Nadine, we have to go!" Fear threatened to steal her breath. There was no time to wonder why Nadine Blackwell stood in Roger's living room; they had to escape. She glanced over her shoulder toward Roger, expecting to see him moving toward them.

Instead he remained fixed in place, barely

breathing, his face contorted by a mixed expression of shock and confusion.

She looked back at Nadine, noticing for the first time the woman's cold eyes. Both Nadine and Roger seemed to have forgotten her.

Lillian bolted toward the kitchen. The retort of a gunshot stopped her. She was no expert, but Nadine's gun looked a lot like the gun her husband used to keep locked in a safe in the bedroom.

The woman's eyes glared cold and hard, almost as cold and hard as the pistol pointed in her direction. Nadine wagged the barrel of the gun. "Move back into the living room where I can keep an eye on you."

With legs barely supporting her, she shuffled around Nadine while trying to keep a safe distance from Roger. Nothing made sense. Nadine with a gun? Roger with a map of burned houses?

And why was he just standing there acting as if he had seen a ghost?

Nadine kept the barrel of the gun pointed toward her as she shifted her gaze and gave Roger a cold smile. "Surprise."

"What are you doing here?" His voice was thick, barely a whisper. "I just talked to you an hour ago, and you were in Cleveland."

Lillian's muscles shook, and she leaned against the wall, trying not to crumble onto the carpet. Nadine wasn't in Cleveland an hour ago, or a week ago. She lived in Pennsylvania, but she had been at Ted and Trina's for the past two weeks.

With her free hand, Nadine reached into her jacket pocket and retrieved her cell phone. "The advantage of modern technology. You can call from anywhere."

"Nadine, what's going on?" Lillian stood

motionless against the wall, sandwiched between the two.

Nadine must harbor a past hurt against Roger and had just found out he lived here. She couldn't be evil; she couldn't really want to hurt Lillian.

Having ignored her since Nadine's arrival, Roger finally turned to her. "You know her?" His attention did nothing to shovel away the mounds of confusion.

"I told you all about her. She's the lady staying at Ted and Trina's."

He sucked in air. "You've been here for two weeks?"

"I have actually been in the area much longer, but decided to play a little cat and mouse. I checked into your bed and breakfast to keep a better eye on our friend." She laughed, the sound twisted along Lillian's nerves like a cat on the prowl. "It has been quite fun avoiding you all this time."

Lillian stared. Nadine had been hiding out all this time? She knew all along where Roger lived? As she glanced from one to the other, she realized the issue between the two had to be bigger than what she had expected. Unable to trust either one, she had to escape.

Roger blocked the front door, and Nadine with her gun blocked access through the kitchen.

Air hissed in and out of Roger's nose, the sound loud in the quiet space. He shifted toward Nadine. "There's no need for the gun. Put it down."

"No need, you say? No need?" The shrill voice left Lillian trembling. "We had a deal, and you haven't met your part." Her eyes became black slits. "Have you forgotten your wife, my daughter?"

"I haven't forgotten."

"How can you be so beguiled with this woman?

She destroyed our family."

Nadine's words startled Lillian. She turned to the woman and swallowed the knot in her throat. "Nadine, it's me, Lillian. I didn't destroy your family or Roger's. I didn't even know you until you came to Ted and Trina's."

The woman's nostrils flared as she glared at Lillian. "He was just another notch in your belt. You didn't care what prison would do to him."

Lillian stared blankly. Nadine had to be crazy. But when she turned to Roger, his shoulders were slumped. The spark of energy that always clung to him was gone.

Nadine glared at her. "You don't even remember. Let me refresh your mind. Two years ago, you sent my husband to jail. A twenty year sentence. He wanted to cut a deal but you refused. You were out to make a name for yourself, the high and mighty Attorney Hunter. And the media loved you. Your picture was everywhere. He chose suicide rather than a life behind bars."

Leo Narducci. The case that had cost her the family she loved! Yes, she had been out to build her career one conviction at a time. That seemed like a lifetime ago when a big name meant something to her. That goal had been buried with her family.

"Now we will finish what *you* started," the angry woman said between tight lips.

"Are you going to shoot me?" Wanting to close her eyes, but afraid to lose sight of the deranged woman, she considered her options. There were none.

"Shooting you would be too easy. You got by me once, but you won't do it again."

"How did I…"

Nadine had started the fire that had killed her family.

Desperation gripped her. "Roger, help me. Look at me, Roger, please."

He locked eyes with her. His hopeless expression frightened her more than Nadine's gun.

All hope unraveled.

"So you haven't shared the truth about her family's death, how you set the fire? What were you talking about during those late nights? Or weren't you talking?" Nadine snickered.

Her heart lurched. What was this woman saying? How could she accuse Roger of setting fire to her house? She remembered the map still clenched in her hand. Fresh tears sprang to her eyes as she dropped the worthless paper to the floor. She no longer knew what was true. "Roger?"

"I'm so sorry."

This couldn't be happening. Roger had killed her family? She had trusted him, shared secrets with him. It no longer mattered if Nadine used the gun because the essence of her life, that bit of humanity she had been clinging to since the fire two years ago, fled, leaving behind an empty shell.

"You were supposed to be inside, asleep," Nadine continued. "Instead you let your family die without you."

The ramifications of Nadine's words finally penetrated the maze of her confused mind. With uncontrolled rage, she leaped at Roger. "You killed my family!" She pounded fists into his chest. She sought his face, lashing and hitting in blind rage.

Blood flowed from his lip and nose as he stood motionless.

She continued to pound.

A sharp crack made her stop. The muzzle of the gun still smoked as she looked toward Nadine.

"Now you know the truth." Nadine's voice sounded like a purr and it reminded Lillian of an evil villainess she'd seen on television. "We brought you here to finish what *you* started. Roger, get the rope and tie her up. Be quick about it. We don't have much time."

Lillian glanced from one to the other, fear raging within her. "Roger, please..." In spite of what Nadine had said, he loved her; she knew he did. She noticed her bloody hands and stared at him.

Already one eye had swollen closed, and his face was coated with his blood.

How could she have done that to him?

"Move Roger!" Nadine's voice boomed through the room. "This house will be in flames in about ten minutes."

Roger turned, his eyes heavy. "I love you, Lillian. Why didn't you trust me with your secret? I figured it out, you know. You found the map I used to track you. I tried to help you. I kept you away from Paul. I would have gotten you mental help."

He rubbed his face and looked at the blood-smeared hand. A spark flickered, giving life to his dead eyes. His jaw tightened as he moved toward her.

Her heart lurched. What was he going to do? He was as crazy as Nadine, talking about Paul, and helping her, and the map. She had just beaten him with all the strength in her body. His sticky blood still coated her hands. As he raised his arm, she tensed, ready for the punch that was coming. *Dear God, help me.*

28

Officer Paul Studler grabbed the paper as soon as the fax machine spit it out. Either his hunch was right, or he was out of options. He scanned the page and ran to the door, his heart racing. He had to be in time!

Ted and Trina's lay exactly two point six miles from the station. A red car pulled in front of him and he flicked on the siren. What happened to moving out of the way of the police? As he zipped around the slowing traffic, his hands tightened on the wheel. Why hadn't he figured it out sooner? Bill had been saying all along there was danger surrounding Lillian.

Gravel spun as he swerved into the drive of the McIverson Bed and Breakfast. Not bothering to pull to the back, he raced up the front steps and pushed open the door. "Where's Lillian?" His voice echoed down the hall.

Sandra exited the kitchen. "Hi to you too, Paul. Why all the excitement?"

"I need to find Lillian." He moved down the hall, urgency growing within him. "Lillian!"

Sandra stared with round eyes. "Is something wrong?"

"Something's very wrong." He scanned the dining room and kitchen.

"Paul, she's not here."

"Where is she?" He had to find her. His gut had never felt so right before. Time would mean life or death, and he wasn't ready to turn her over to the grim reaper.

"I don't know. She left shortly after lunch and said she wouldn't be back until late."

The back door banged. His heart leaped as he pushed past Sandra and ran to the kitchen. His face fell.

"Looking for someone prettier than me?" Bill placed his empty lunch sack on the counter.

"He's looking for Lillian," Sandra said.

"Something wrong?"

"I just need to find her. Now."

"Where's Ted?" Bill asked, glancing in the direction of the den.

"He went to the hospital to bring home Trina and the baby."

Bill ran a hand across the top of his head. "Strange, Lillian's been on my mind all day. I thought this sense of urgency had passed..."

The two men locked eyes. "Get in the cruiser," Paul yelled over his shoulder.

By the time Paul had started the engine, Bill sat buckled beside him. Paul had a good idea where Lillian had gone.

God, please let me be on time.

~*~

Lillian closed her eyes. She couldn't bear to see Roger's expression of hate as he hit her. She tensed for his blow, but felt an arm circle her waist. Her eyes flew open and she looked up at him. His returning gaze held her in its strength. As he pulled her snugly into his side, she nestled into his warmth.

"What we planned was wrong," Roger said.

Nadine's lips thinned as she stared at them with empty eyes. "I didn't want to do it this way, but you leave me no choice." She aimed the gun directly at Lillian's head.

The sound of the gunshot filled Lillian's ears. Pain flamed through her shoulder as she hit the floor. Rolling to the side, hoping to avoid the next bullet, she spied Roger slumped across the room, the stain on his shirt growing.

"Roger!" She scrambled toward him.

His eyes were open, and he smiled. "I love you, you know." A grimace distorted his face. "I didn't plan to love you." He reached up and she grabbed his hand.

"You always were a fool," Nadine said. "My daughter was just as big a fool to marry you. And then after the trial you carted her off to this god-forsaken place. All of my family, stolen from me by this woman." The words spat from her mouth as she wagged the barrel of the gun at Lillian.

She pressed her hand against the flow of blood.

Roger moaned.

"I've got to stop the bleeding, or you'll die," she murmured, her eyes pleading.

Gripping her wrist, he asked "Why did you start the fires?"

"I didn't start the fires, Roger. I found the map in your bedroom. I thought…"

"Oh, pity, pity." Nadine's voice grated like sandpaper against Lillian's nerves.

For a second she had forgotten the woman.

"I guess I might as well join in this sweet confession. You both are going to die anyway."

Lillian focused on Roger's wound as Nadine's

voice filled the silence. "I set those fires, just like I taught you, Roger, at Attorney Hunter's. It's simple when you know how to do it."

Her attention on Roger and with the swirl of information streaming in her head, she almost missed Nadine's words. She jerked her head up. Nadine started the fires? The mire of confusion continued to grow.

Roger struggled to sit. He groaned and slumped back onto the floor. "Why?"

Nadine's face tightened. Even the wobble on her throat seemed to turn to stone. "You moved my daughter to a house full of lead paint. My grandchild died because of it." Her black eyes radiated pure hate as she stared at Roger. "I drove down here when she refused to answer my calls, and I found her swinging from the light fixture in the living room."

"You're lying." Roger coughed. Bloody froth sprayed from his mouth.

"She must have just jumped. When I cut her down, she still had a pulse. I reached for my phone but stopped. If I saved her, she would just try again until she succeeded. I decided to allow her to die in dignity." She gave a snarling chuckle. "They never figured it out, did they?"

Lillian wanted to put her hands over her ears, to stop the horror of Nadine's confession. What kind of woman would let her own daughter die? No wonder she didn't hesitate to use a gun. Sitting beside Roger, his blood seeping through her fingers, she knew her own death was imminent.

"It wasn't hard to find someone to hack into your system. And that secretary of yours is so faithful about sending lead data to your email."

Her smile made Lillian want to retch.

"If you did one thing right, you saved others from my pain."

Lillian had to get herself and Roger out of the house, but that meant disabling Nadine. She scanned the well-known room.

Roger's breathing came in tight gasps. Blood dripped off his shirt onto the floor. His ashen face complemented the blue ring that circled his mouth. Even as she looked at him, her heart remained conflicted. This was the man who had killed her family, and yet he had shielded her from a bullet.

The blast shook the house.

Lillian fell backward, cracking her head on the coffee table. Stunned, she lay in a daze. An inner sense aroused her. She opened her eyes and the pain caused tears to pour from them.

Gray smoke billowed around her. She could barely see. Desperately, she twisted around hunting for Roger. She had to find him and get him to safety! Her heart pounded against her ribs as the smoke thickened. She had to avoid Nadine as she pulled Roger to safety. Straining for any signs of the woman's location, she heard nothing but the snap and pop of fire. She knew she was going to die. Flames shot around her. Heat intensified. She didn't have much time.

Heading toward what she thought was the front door, she fell onto the couch. Pulling her shirt over her nose and mouth, gasping for breath, she turned the opposite direction. She had to find Roger and a way out! As the roar of the fire filled her ears, she heard her name.

Nadine!

Urgency strengthened her resolve as she crawled

across the room, hopefully away from Nadine.

A hand grabbed her.

She let go of her shirt, and fought against the vice-like grip.

The roar of the fire consumed all other sounds.

She couldn't breathe. No air. Her last thoughts as her strength left her were of Craig and Susan.

~*~

Green leaves fluttered in an ash-filled sky. The snarling sound of fire, shouting voices, and the metallic slamming of vehicle doors. Feet running. Something covered her face and mouth. A paramedic peered down at her.

How had she gotten out of the house?

Sluggishly, Lillian reached for the oxygen mask and slid it off. She turned her head toward the roar. Orange and blue flames shoved their way out of the windows. Thick streams of water hit the fire and danced before being gobbled by the hungry heat. Terror filled her. Her family was in there! She had to get them out! She shoved the paramedic and staggered to her feet. Halfway to the house, someone grabbed her around the waist. She screamed and thrashed, knowing she had to save her family. Hot tongues of fire mocked her. "My husband! My daughter! They're still in there!"

"Lillian, this isn't Cleveland. You're in Darlington."

As she struggled, the house cracked and groaned, and finally collapsed. Sparks shot into the air.

Grief threatened to tear her apart, one memory at a time. The vision of her family inside coffins returned just before blackness took control.

~*~

Fresh air blew in her face. The overwhelming roar of the fire had faded to crackling and hissing.

She locked gazes with the same paramedic who had attended her before. Memories returned and with them a new danger. This was Darlington! Wide-eyed, her throat tight, she again struggled to sit up. "Did they get out?"

His face remained blank.

She knew that expression. She had seen it on the doctors at the hospital. "There were two others!" *Oh, please God!* She fell back onto the cart. How could she live through this nightmare again?

Someone touched her arm. "Lillian."

Paul Studler knelt down beside her, soot covered, and a bandage circled his left lower arm. His expression held hesitation, and warmth.

A million emotions filled her as she reached out her arms to a familiar face and found herself in his embrace. As she cried, he stroked her hair.

"How's she doing?"

Lillian pulled herself from Paul's chest and looked into the concerned face of Bill Iver. He squeezed her shoulder. "Are you ready to come home?"

Home. How good that sounded.

29

She focused on the mud caking the soles of her shoes, only this time she knew how it had gotten there.

Trina held her arm as the dozen or so people stood around the gash in the ground.

Wiping her feet on the grass, she tried to remove the dirt, but it wouldn't come off. Ironic in its own way.

The coroner had released all three bodies: Roger, Nadine, and Joe.

Nadine's ashes had been sent to Ohio to rest beside her husband.

Lillian had purchased the plot beside Carla for Roger. A handful attended his graveside service; Latoya was the only one besides Lillian to shed tears.

Lillian had asked her parents not to come, and had begged her sister to stay away. This was something she needed to do without them. They had never been a part of her Darlington life.

But this trip to the cemetery had been the hardest. She had paid for Joe's interment and purchased the urn to hold his remains. She had personally placed his wedding band inside with his ashes. The ring meant a great deal to him, and it was only right that he kept it through eternity.

The pastor might have had a touching message, but she heard little of it. As people milled back to waiting cars, dry winter grass crackling under their feet, Lillian threw one last rose in the gaping hole. A tear ran down her face. He didn't deserve to die. Not this way.

Everyone was gone.

Trina pulled gently on her arm. "We need to go home," she murmured.

Ted waited with the car doors open. They had all been there for her. Ted and Trina, Bill, Sandra, and Paul. Margaret Franks had stood beside her. Many of the homeless wandered by, standing on the fringe, but present. As their love finally reached her, the tears flowed.

At home, Sandra laid out the food brought by neighbors and friends.

"Lillian, may I fix you some lunch?" Jimmy stood in front of her, stiff and tall, most likely prompted by his grandma.

Her stomach resembled a churning sea, but the look of expectancy on the boy's face won over. "Just a little, Jimmy. I'm not real hungry." She watched as he spooned food onto a plate, hesitating at some dishes, while piling on others.

The finished plate had small heaps of many different items. She smiled and an ache tugged at her heart. All the servings *were* small. After pushing the food around with her fork for awhile, she set her plate in the sink and went to the parlor, but the holiday spirit clashed with her aching heart. Retrieving her jacket, she let herself out the front door and sat on the swing.

The familiarity of the squeak of the chain against the bolt soothed her. Bill had said a dozen times he would give the spot a squirt of oil, but he never had. Today the grinding reminded her that life goes on—

with or without those one cared about.

Paul exited the front door. "Want some company?" He sat beside her on the swing. "This must be tough on you."

What was she supposed to say? She felt empty, numb.

"I should have figured it out sooner. I could have prevented—"

"Paul, don't take the blame for this. Besides, you saved my life." She turned to him. "I don't think I've even thanked you."

"No need."

"You ran into a burning house, and I fought you like a crazy woman."

He rubbed his chin. "Yes you did."

"I thought you were Nadine."

There were no pedestrians on the sidewalk with the temperature a chilly fifty degrees, but the squirrels didn't seem to mind the cooler air as a pair darted across the brown grass and scampered up the tree. Small piles of sawdust stood testimony to Bill's removal of the fallen limb. A car passed. There were few sounds except the swing. Even the dogs were quiet.

"How did you know I was in danger?" The question had nagged at her since the fire.

"Something about Roger bothered me." He rested his arm on the back of the swing. "Not like Bill's intuition, but I kept thinking I had seen him somewhere before. I tried several searches, but came up blank.

"Then you showed up, and he started acting weird, almost as if he was two separate guys: some days nice, other times almost vicious. When you seemed to be attracted to him, I worried about your safety."

Lillian sat quietly beside him, her feet keeping pace with the rocking motion of the swing.

"That news segment about drugs being smuggled into the country, it made me remember. I had seen Roger's face in the news. It took awhile, but I finally found his picture, and connected him by marriage to a drug lord in Cleveland. But he denied ever living in Cleveland. And then I found out you were the prosecuting attorney.

"All this was going on and I had no idea? Why didn't you tell me?"

"It would look as if I wanted to break up your relationship with Roger. I had to wait until I was sure."

"And when were you sure?"

"The day of the fire at Roger's. I got a fax from the authorities in Cleveland about Roger. They felt he might be connected in some way to several murders there, but they could never find any evidence that would stand up in court. The fax had a picture of Mrs. Narducci and her daughter and Roger right after the conviction of Leo Narducci. Mrs. Narducci looked exactly like Nadine Blackwell."

"No wonder she wanted to avoid Roger. She was supposed to be in Cleveland."

"As soon as I realized who Mrs. Blackwell really was, and her connection to Roger, I knew you were in danger. I had to find you and tell you. Unfortunately, I was too late."

"No, you weren't. You were right on time."

He slid his arm around her shoulders and she stiffened, and then relaxed. She didn't need to fear him anymore, nor suppress her feelings for him. A smile flittered across her face.

30

"Any of those for me?" Jimmy asked as Lillian carried an armful of gifts to the tree.

"Oh, maybe one or two." The boy's excitement was infectious, and she grinned at him. "But you won't know until tomorrow."

Jimmy stared at the packages while she arranged them around the tree. "Can I shake mine?" he asked.

"No."

His lips formed a pout; then he brightened. "What about if I just hold it?"

"No." She stifled a giggle.

"Can I at least touch it?"

She extended the remaining box. "You can touch it with *one* finger."

With his face contorted in concentration, he stroked the blue paper decorated with snowmen. His index finger slid back and forth across the box, as gentle as his touches to baby David.

"Now it goes under the tree," she said.

Jimmy danced around the room. "I know what's in it!"

"You do not. You're just trying to trick me into telling you, and I'm not going to."

Sandra called and as Jimmy skittered away to the kitchen, Lillian sank into a chair. Her usual place. Each of them had a spot in the room. No one had assigned them; it had simply become routine. Kind of like at church, where one knew someone was missing by looking to where they always sat.

The tree held center stage in the parlor. Ornaments, heavily loaded toward the bottom thanks to Jimmy's help, reflected the light from the colored bulbs. Her chest tightened as she sought out one, then another of the decorations, remembering the night they had gathered to hang them on the tree.

Trina padded into the parlor. "Hey, there, you want company? I just finished feeding David, and he's fast asleep."

Dear, sweet David. Just thinking of him brought a smile to her face. "He's a good eater."

Trina lowered onto the sofa. "For sure. I think he wants to be as tall as his dad by tomorrow!"

"You ought to take this time and rest."

"I would rather talk to you. How are you doing?"

Her throat tightened. "I'm fine." She forced a smile.

"Come on, Lillian. I know you better than that. How are you really?"

Sighing, she met Trina's eyes. "I don't know how I am. Confused, I guess. I try to wrap my mind around the fact that Roger—"

"None of us knew. He fooled us all, Lillian."

Pulling a well-used tissue out of her pocket, Lillian dabbed at the tears that trickled down her cheeks. "I thought I was done crying."

If there was one constant in her life, it was Trina. God's blessing, and she had almost run away from it. "The funerals, they brought back so many memories."

"You amazed me, how you took responsibility for making sure the man and woman who had hurt you were given a proper burial. You could have turned your back on them. I would have."

"No you wouldn't, Trina." She wiped her nose. "It was the right thing to do. In his own way, I know Roger cared for me. I can't imagine being caught in the trap he found himself in." She studied the tree, seeing but not seeing. "He died for me, you know."

"Did you love him?"

"I have asked myself that a dozen times. I don't think I did. Oh, I wanted to badly enough, because of the fires and all, but I never had the deep commitment I should have felt."

"We're all going to the midnight Christmas Eve service at the church. Will you feel like coming? It will be David's first big trip out."

In reality, she wanted to bury herself in her bed and never come out again. But she knew she had to push to heal, just as she had done before. "Of course I'm coming."

Trina hugged her. "He'll be wearing the little outfit you gave him."

Lillian sagged against the upholstered chair, the scent of pine keeping her company as Trina headed upstairs.

Sandra and Jimmy's voices drifted down the hall, discussing the appropriate sprinkles for the latest batch of sugar cookies.

Ted and Bill were both out in the workshop: some secret last-minute project.

With nothing to do and no motivation pushing her, she simply sat. Her heart ached. Her mind felt numb. Was life really worth all of this pain?

~*~

A couple dozen red poinsettias graced the front of the church, their color bright against the pale blue and beige interior. Sitting on the end of the pew, with Bill next to her, then Sandra, with Jimmy beside Trina, and Ted on her other side, they filled the row.

The piano emitted soft music and candles flickered in the dim light. Voices murmured as people greeted each other and found a seat, waiting for the service to begin.

A hand tapped her shoulder. "Room for one more?"

Like dominoes, everyone slid closer, making room for Paul. They must have looked like a can of sardines, all squeezed together when there were plenty of empty seats available. But no one wanted to leave the closeness of the family for a little extra shoulder space.

Paul's leg pressed against hers. He turned and smiled. No words, just a smile. Aware of the warmth of his body, she relaxed for the first time since the fire at Roger's ten days ago.

The service started with familiar carols, followed by a mother-daughter duet. Sniffles sounded all around her.

David was shifted to Sandra, who sent him to Bill. The beaming grandfather cradled his grandson in his arms.

Pastor Steve shared the Christmas story, followed by another special.

David squirmed and gave a couple squeaks.

Lillian tried not to laugh at Bill's panicked expression as he passed the infant to her.

Trina leaned forward, and Lillian smiled.

That was what life was all about. Praising God

surrounded by family. Bad things happen, but family buffered the pain. She thought about her parents, now off skiing somewhere for the holidays. In their own way, they had tried to protect her. They had made decisions she would not have made, but still, the intent was for her good.

David opened his eyes, and she placed him on her shoulder, just as she used to do with Susan. Already he was losing that baby-curl, where his legs were always pulled toward his chest. Stretched out like this, he would soon outgrow the outfit she had bought him. Good thing there was a new one under the tree.

The service ended, and she passed David back down the row to Trina.

Warmth remained wrapped around her as they headed home.

31

Lillian rose from the table, her stomach too full for comfort. She could not remember a better Christmas day. All the gifts under the tree during her childhood could not compare to the sweet unity of this family who embraced her as one of their own.

"Here, Lillian, watch David for me." Trina nodded toward her son sleeping in the infant seat beside the table. "I'll help with the dishes."

Lillian loved how generous Trina was with her baby. There was nothing she liked more than holding David and burying her face in his soft blond hair, but she sighed and shook her head. "You've been up enough, little mama. Besides, you did most of the cooking; I'll help with the dishes."

"Sandra did most of the cooking," Trina murmured.

"I'll take care of David." Jimmy crouched down beside the sleeping infant.

"That's a good idea," Paul said, his hands stacked with plates. "Why don't you take Trina and David to the parlor and count those presents one more time while I help Aunt Lillian in the kitchen?"

She smiled, remembering the day Jimmy had found out she had been given "aunt" status to David. He had pronounced her his aunt, as well. Aunt Lillian...it sounded good. She glanced at Paul. Both warmth and shivers flowed over her whenever she was near him. Roger would always hold a place in her heart, having given his life for her. She hoped he had made peace with God before his death. But the affection she had for Paul felt different. And she had a feeling he shared her sentiments.

While Jimmy entertained Trina, and as baby David slept, the other adults tackled the dishes.

"Hurry up, you guys!" Jimmy shouted from the parlor.

"What's the rush?" Ted yelled back. "I thought I'd take a nap."

Jimmy bolted through the kitchen door. "We have to open presents!" He tugged at Ted's arm. "Come on!"

"OK, OK!" Ted's eyes twinkled. "Just let me put this last plate away."

Soon the family gathered in the parlor. The scent of pine suffused the air and mingled with the leftover aroma of ham. Even though late afternoon sun lit the room, the tree lights were on, adding color and cheer. A couple of the bulbs had burned out and would need replaced before next year. The tree skirt, calico blocks sewn long ago by an unknown ancestor, was hidden by packages.

Bill sat in the leather recliner while Sandra took one of the wingback chairs beside him.

Ted and Trina had the couch, with baby David on the floor in front of them.

Lillian sat on the other wingback chair, and smiled when Paul stationed himself at her feet. She placed her hands on his shoulders, enjoying the feel of his strength under her touch.

Jimmy bounced from one person to the other and eventually settled in front of his grandma.

"The tree is perfect." Trina gazed at the tall pine in

front of the window.

"It should be," Bill said. "Ted and I had to go to six places before we could find one that suited you. Thank goodness for cell phones with cameras or we would still be hunting."

Trina giggled. "Next year when my tummy isn't so full of baby, I'll go with you."

Ted picked up his Bible from the stand beside the couch. "During my childhood, we always read the Christmas story before we opened gifts. I would like to continue the tradition in my home." He smiled at Trina, and then leaned over and stroked the top of his sleeping son's head.

Lillian's throat filled with emotion.

Ted looked at each person in the room, one at a time, and it seemed that he gave a piece of love to each of them. "I want to read from Luke chapter two verses one through nineteen."

The silence in the room was disturbed only by the swish of soft pages being turned and the gentle hum of the furnace as it clicked on.

Ted read, occasionally glancing at David or Jimmy.

She had never heard the Christmas story presented with more power or meaning.

And Joseph also went up from Galilee, out of the city of Nazareth, into Judea, unto the city of David, which is called Bethlehem; because he was of the house and lineage of David to be taxed with Mary his espoused wife, being great with child. And so it was, that, while they were there, the days were accomplished that she should be delivered. And she brought forth her firstborn son, and wrapped him in swaddling clothes, and laid him in a manger; because there was no room for them in the inn.

And there were in the same country shepherds abiding in the field, keeping watch over their flock by night. And, lo, the angel of the Lord came upon them, and the glory of the Lord shone round about them: and they were sore afraid. And the angel said unto them, Fear not: for, behold, I bring you good tidings of great joy, which shall be to all people.

For unto you is born this day in the city of David a Savior, which is Christ the Lord.

And this shall be a sign unto you; Ye shall find the babe wrapped in swaddling clothes, lying in a manger. And suddenly there was with the angel a multitude of the heavenly host praising God, and saying, Glory to God in the highest, and on earth peace, good will toward men.

And it came to pass, as the angels were gone away from them into heaven, the shepherds said one to another, Let us now go even unto Bethlehem, and see this thing which is come to pass, which the Lord hath made known unto us. And they came with haste, and found Mary, and Joseph, and the babe lying in a manger. And when they had seen it, they made known abroad the saying which was told them concerning this child. And all they that heard it wondered at those things which were told them by the shepherds. But Mary kept all these things, and pondered them in her heart.

Sandra wiped tears from her eyes. "Thank you Ted."

"Is it time for presents now?" Jimmy asked.

Bill hefted himself from his recliner. "I suppose we've waited long enough." He winked at Jimmy. "How about you help me pass them out?"

"Yahoo!" Jimmy stood ready as Bill reached for a gift.

He handed the package to Jimmy. "This one goes to Aunt Lillian and it's from David."

Jimmy frowned as he took at the package. "David went shopping already?"

"He had some help. Now give Aunt Lillian her present and come back for the next one."

Lillian glanced at a smiling Trina, who bounced in her seat.

The square box, wrapped in green and gold striped paper, was heavier than she had expected. The contents shifted slightly as she lowered the gift to her lap. She glanced at Paul, and his beaming face spread sunshine into her soul. It also gave away the fact that he knew exactly what was in the box.

She lifted each piece of tape, wanting to take her time with this gift from the baby she had delivered. Between David's birth and the honest advice of Margaret Franks, her pain over seeing children had eased. She still ached when she thought of her precious Susan, and she probably always would, but now when memories of their times together filtered into her mind, they brought joy rather than pain. As she lifted the lid off the box, her eyes filled with tears.

Trina sprang from the couch and knelt beside her.

"It doesn't make you sad, does it?" Trina rubbed Lillian's arm with her warm hands. "I wanted you to have something special from David."

Tears flowed unchecked. She wanted to tell Trina how perfect the gift was, but words seemed too inadequate. She grabbed her friend and pulled her close.

"I haven't seen it since Ted finished it," Sandra said.

Lillian lifted a framed picture. The top left-hand corner held a pencil drawing of baby David's sleeping face. On the lower right were two footprints stamped neatly together. The center contained a poem penned in calligraphy. She opened her mouth to read the message, but only gentle sobs emerged. She handed the gift to Trina.

Your hands pulled me
into this stormy earth,
and as your courage and love
welcomed my first breath,
your fears rose into the clouds.
I will love you forever, Aunt Lillian.

"Ted did the drawing, and Dad and I managed the footprints," Trina said quietly. "I wrote the poem too, but Sandra did the calligraphy. And Jimmy helped me wrap it."

Paul lifted up a handkerchief and Lillian wiped her wet face.

"This is perfect." Her voice shook with emotion. She walked to where David slept in his seat, picked him up, and held him tight in her arms. He opened his eyes and stared into her face.

"Look, he smiled at you!" Jimmy said.

She gazed at the newborn, the baby she had brought into the world. The medical profession would probably try to tell her the smile was nothing more than a gas bubble, but she refused to believe it. She had been given an extra gift.

~*~

Soon Bill had handed Jimmy the last present except the one he had hidden under the folds of the tree skirt. His heart beat double time as he pulled out the tissue box he had rescued from the trash to hold his gift.

With family surrounding him, his heart swelled with thankfulness. And they were his family—each of them—and he held them in his protective arms.

Jimmy jiggled pieces of wrapping paper in front of David, and laughed as the newborn's eyes crossed.

Ted, the son-in-law he had resented before God taught him about unselfish love, had his arm draped around Trina.

Trina. His only daughter and his life. It wasn't easy raising a girl without a mother, but they had forged a relationship built on trust and respect. Now she had given him a grandson, who had been delivered by Lillian, the newest addition to his family.

He would always be there for Lillian, as long as she allowed. His eyes shifted to the man seated on the floor in front of her and he smiled. The spark that flew between Paul and Lillian would soon ignite into a love of their own.

He cleared his throat. "Look, there's one more present." He handed the box to Sandra.

"Who's it from, Bill? I've already unwrapped a present from everyone."

"Just open it," he murmured.

She pulled apart the blue snowman paper, exposed the tissue box, and chuckled. "I think I threw this box into the trash, Bill Iver." As she removed the tissue her eyes softened.

Bill knelt beside her as she lifted out the small square box nested inside. He gently took the box from her hands and opened the lid, exposing the diamond ring he had chosen just for her. "Sandra, I am not good with words, you know that by now. But I love you with all of my heart. Will you marry me?"

The room's silence was broken only by the gentle sob from Trina and a cooing gurgle from David.

Jimmy looked from Bill to Sandra and back again.

"Bill Iver, I have loved you from the moment I first met you."

Bill ran his thumb around his shirt collar. "So does that mean yes?"

Trina bounced on the couch. "Yes!"

"Yes!" Tears ran down Sandra's cheeks as Bill placed the ring on her left hand.

Jimmy pulled his eyebrows together and looked at Bill. "So are you still going to be my uncle?" he asked, "or are you going to be my grandpa, like David's?"

Bill pulled the boy to his side. "And what would you prefer me to be?"

"My grandpa. I have a grandma, but I never had a grandpa before."

"Then grandpa, it is," Bill stated, ruffling the boy's hair.

Trina grabbed Sandra. "I love you so much, and now you're *really* going to be my mom." The women beamed at each other's tear-stained faces.

Ted clapped Bill on the shoulder. "About time, old man."

With wrapping paper scattered over the floor in colorful heaps, he watched as the girls took turns admiring Sandra's newly adorned hand. His grandson and soon-to-be grandson added the childlike dimension of Christmas that felt so special. He knew that if houses had feelings the old homestead would be beaming with joy. A family reunited. A new generation living within its walls. Fresh starts.

Amid all the excitement and joy, he sensed heaviness. It belonged to Lillian. As she bounced the fussing David on her shoulder, with Paul at her feet and a smile brightening her face, her eyes spoke of a hidden sadness.

"Stop, stop!" Sandra held up her arms. "Listen...I think I hear a phone ringing."

As the chaos quieted, Lillian's face paled. "That's my phone." She shifted the baby to Paul's hesitant arms.

Bill was certain that after she checked the caller ID, she hesitated to answer the phone.

~*~

Lillian glanced at the caller ID and her heart sank. Her father's cell phone number. He had refused to return her calls since she had moved in October. Even her mother's calls were short, claiming the time as inconvenient. Only her sister had remained on friendly terms, but could offer no advice on how to fix the fracture that existed with her family. Lillian didn't know where to begin when her parents rejected everything she believed in. As she pushed to answer the call, she walked toward the kitchen. "Hello."

"Merry Christmas, Lillibelle."

She squeezed her eyes closed as the tears formed. She had ached to hear her dad call her by her pet name, but why now? He no longer held the same affection for his oldest daughter that he had before she became a Christian and married a man he considered beneath her.

"Merry Christmas, Dad." She waited for him to share why he had really called.

"Lillian...I'm sorry how things ended between us at Thanksgiving."

360

She leaned against the sink.

Was he really sorry, or was this another ploy to get his way, get her back home where he could use his power to revert her life back to what he felt it should be? He had manipulated her so many times before.

Her muscles tensed. She stiffened her resolve, and, at the same time, hated defending herself from her father.

"I have something to tell you that may surprise you," he said.

She gripped the phone even tighter. "Dad, if you are going to argue with me again, I don't want to hear it. I love you, but I have to live my own life, and I'm doing a good job of it."

"Lillian, I—"

"No, Dad, not this time. You'll have to hear me out." She took a deep breath. "I am a Christian, a follower of Jesus. I don't judge the value of an individual by his job or education, but by his heart. Craig had a loving and giving heart, and so did my precious Susan. I lost them both because of my selfishness. But my decision to come here was the right one. My job is satisfying. I'm making a difference in young lives. And I have wonderful, supportive friends. They are good people, all of them. And there's a baby..." A sob escaped from her throat, the first of many emotions building within her.

"Your mom and I have been going to church."

Was this some cruel joke? She sank into a kitchen chair.

"Did you hear me, honey?"

"You're going to church?" This was the last thing she expected to hear on Christmas day, or any other day for that matter.

"Pastor Cooper stopped by the Saturday after Thanksgiving. You remember him, don't you?"

"Of course I remember Pastor Cooper." He had baptized her and buried Craig and Susan.

"Pastor Cooper said your mom and I had been on his mind since you moved south, and he felt led to give us a visit." She could hear her father's breathing. "You know, honey, I got to thinking about what you said when you were home. None of our friends called us during the holiday. Not one. But this man who had only met us once felt compassion and stopped by. He invited us to church the next day, and we decided to go. His sermon was different. The music was different. The people—they seemed actually happy to be there. In church. Imagine."

Lillian heard him chuckle as her own mouth hung open.

"Your mom and I were overdressed, but we felt welcome."

He paused and she knew she should say something, but her mind whirled. Nothing could have surprised her more even if he had told her little green men were walking all over his yard. She took a deep breath. "I'm glad you went, Dad. Pastor Cooper is a godly man."

"We went back the next Sunday, and the next. We haven't missed a Sunday since Thanksgiving. And we're attending a Bible study on Wednesday nights at one of the church member's homes."

"I don't know what to say." She had been praying so long for them.

"You don't need to say anything, just accept my apology for being narrow-minded and short-tempered. I am truly working to change, Lillibelle. It won't happen overnight, but if this Jesus is Who I think He is, then your mom and I are in it through the home stretch."

"Lillian, honey, this is Mom. I miss you."

"Mom…" Her voice caught in her throat.

"What your dad said is true, sweetheart. Most of our friends don't understand, but we are making some great new friends."

"Mom. Dad. I'm so happy. I'm just overwhelmed right now."

"I bet this is the last thing you expected on Christmas day," her dad said. "We're planning a visit. We want to meet these friends of yours. Can we stay at your bed and breakfast?"

"You're taking time off work?"

"Amazing, isn't it? I think I need to use some of those weeks of vacation I've been stock-piling for the last twenty years."

Her face stretched into a smile so broad that her cheeks hurt.

Her parents were going to church! They wanted to come to see her instead of taking her dad's rare time off to go to Europe or some other exotic vacation spot.

"There's plenty of room here. Just give me the dates and I'll reserve you a place." She wanted to jump up and down right there in the kitchen.

"How about tonight?"

"Tonight?"

"We're sitting out in the driveway—"

She dropped the phone and ran to the front entry. She flung the door open. Her dad and mom stood on the porch. Sobbing, she wrapped her arms around her parents and pulled them close.

"Lillian?" Trina stood in the doorway. "Is

everything all right?"

Trina and Ted, with David now in Sandra's arms, stood in the door of the parlor.

Jimmy peeked around the doorframe.

Paul and Bill had moved close behind Trina and Ted.

All her friends. She beamed, showering her joy on them. "Everyone, these are my parents. Mom and Dad, these are the best friends anyone could ever have."

"Hey, don't stand out there in the cold. Come on in," Trina said. "Have you had anything to eat?"

Ted reached for David as Trina and Sandra headed toward the kitchen.

Lillian grabbed Paul's hand. "Mom and Dad, I want you to meet a special friend of mine, Paul Studler." She waited for the expression on her parents' faces and wasn't disappointed. "Yes, that really is his last name, and I wouldn't change it for anything." She turned and gave the red-faced man a long look.

"You two have any luggage you need to bring in?" Bill asked. "I'm Trina's dad, and serve as the bellhop around here."

As Bill and her dad headed back outside, Lillian reached for the baby.

Ted lowered his sleeping son into her arms. She gazed at his peaceful face, his mouth pursed in a soft circle, eyes twitching beneath pale eyelids. "And this is David," she murmured, not removing her gaze from his face. "I delivered him." She looked at her mother and smiled. "I'm officially his auntie."

"May I?" her mother asked.

Ted nodded in approval.

Mrs. Goodson slipped out of her jacket and handed it to her husband. She cradled the child to her chest. "There is nothing like a baby. Somehow they make everything right." A tear trickled down her perfectly made-up face. "I miss Susan."

A knot rose in Lillian's throat. During Susan's short life, her mom had hardly acknowledged the child as her granddaughter. But love had a way of growing.

"Your father is not the only one who has a lot to be forgiven for. If only we could start over."

"We can't start over, Mom, but we can start again."

Trina's footsteps moved toward them. "I have food on the table. Come and eat!"

Still holding the baby, Martha Goodson followed the others to the dining room.

The men returned from outside, laughing and patting each other on the shoulders.

Jimmy grabbed Bill's hand and walked with them.

Only Lillian and Paul remained in the foyer. "I hope you meant it when you called me your special friend." His eyes softened as he stared into hers. "I would like to be more than friends, when you're ready."

Reaching up, she took hold of the back of his neck. She met his lips with hers. Arms wrapped around bodies as the kiss lengthened. She sighed as they parted. "I plan on that being the first of many."

Hand-in-hand, they walked into the dining room amid a jumble of laughter and talk.

She looked at her parents and the people she had learned to love. Six weeks ago, she had promised retribution for her sins. God had taken those sins and made something good come from them, just as He had promised.

David gave a couple of good grunts and the air in

the room turned foul.

"Give him to me," Lillian said, reaching for the baby. "I'll do diaper duty this time." Lillian smiled down at her little bundle. Life would not be without challenges, but God remained in control.

Thank you...

for purchasing this Harbourlight title. For other inspirational stories, please visit our on-line bookstore at www.pelicanbookgroup.com.

For questions or more information, contact us at customer@pelicanbookgroup.com.

Harbourlight Books
The Beacon in Christian Fiction™
an imprint of Pelican Ventures Book Group
www.pelicanbookgroup.com

Connect with Us
www.facebook.com/Pelicanbookgroup
www.twitter.com/pelicanbookgrp

To receive news and specials, subscribe to our bulletin
http://pelink.us/bulletin

May God's glory shine through
this inspirational work of fiction.

AMDG

Free Book Offer

We're looking for booklovers like you to partner with us! Join our team of influencers today and receive at least one free eBook per month. Maybe more!

For more information
Visit http://pelicanbookgroup.com/booklovers
or e-mail
booklovers@pelicanbookgroup.com